MW01128592

Blood Ties

A Modern Tale of Na Fianna

Book One

By Hazel B. West

Hazel B. West

*This one is for my grandma, finally a book with Faeries, as
promised!*
~H.W.

Blood Ties

"But we in it shall be remember'd;
We few, we happy few, we band of brothers;
For he to-day that sheds his blood with me
Shall be my brother."

~Henry V — Shakespeare

"The true soldier fights not because he hates what is in front of him,
but because he loves what is behind him."

~G. K. Chesterton

Author's Note

I've always loved urban fantasy, it's actually one of my favorite genres, so of course I had to attempt writing one. *The Modern Tales of Na Fianna* is a little different, however. Not only is it a fantasy based in the modern world but that modern world is not necessarily like the one we live in. It's a mix of modern and ancient, kind of taking the best parts of both and throwing them together to create a weird, pseudo-neo-medieval society. I want to state first off that this is not historical fiction even though some actual historical events are mentioned, this alternate reality was created by myself for the sake of my story and doesn't exactly follow all the rules you're used to, but I hope you like it anyway!

If you flip to the back of the book, there is a bunch of goodies to explore, explaining the world and the base of folklore and other such things as pronunciation guides for the names and translations of the Irish words and phrases you'll find in the book. Plus: recipes! Because books are always better when you can eat what the characters do.

I hope you all enjoy *Blood Ties* the first book in this new series. I certainly had a good time writing it!

~Hazel

Prologue

He was hauled through the underground fortress, barely able to keep his feet under him in his weakened state, but he forced himself to stay upright even though he was mostly being supported by the two Goblins who held him from either side.

He was brought to the throne room where the Goblin King sat in a dilapidated yet regal throne, torches blazing against the stone walls of the mountain dwelling. The whole place was wickedly, crumblingly beautiful; a relic of a bygone age that was still frozen in the past despite its living occupants. Aeden admired its horrible beauty even as it sent chills up his spine.

The guards threw him to his knees and he hauled his upper body straight so he could look up into the cold, calculating eyes of the tall Goblin who sat on the throne. The creature rose languidly, his lean frame straight, his hands held behind his back, holding his tattooed head high. A long black coat swung around his legs and his glossy boots tapped out a leveled pace that echoed through the domed hall.

"Aeden Mac Cool," he said. "A pleasure, as always. Have you had a thought as to what you will discuss with me this time? I trust you found your stay in the rat hole comfortable."

"Comfortable enough," the Finar replied, watching as the Goblin's clubbed ash blond hair swung back and forth down his back as he paced. "But I shall not talk to you now, or ever."

"Shame; you seemed so eager to talk before; so eager to take the place of the princeling, that I suspected you must have something of import to tell me." The Goblin sighed in a long-suffering manner, turning around with a bored expression on his face. "Very well, we shall have it your way then. I begin to wonder whether you enjoy pain so much, Mac Cool."

The Finar was hauled to his feet and chained to a rack on one side of the room. The Goblin drew a thin blade from his boot and walked over to him. "I honestly don't even find this amusing anymore, I've done it for so long," he said, grabbing the Finar's face in one hand, his long nails digging into the young man's cheeks. "But if you wish the pain to continue, by all means, keep defying me. But tell me what I want to know, and I will let you go back to your family. You know I am not unnecessarily cruel."

"And what of the others?" Aeden spat contemptuously. "Would you send them back as well?"

"If they give me what I want, I might consider it. But one thing at a time."

The Finar only smiled and the Goblin began his knife work with a businesslike manner, slowly flaying a strip of skin from the Irishman's hip up his left side. Aeden Mac Cool gritted his teeth and breathed out slowly between them.

"No?" the Goblin asked.

Aeden didn't say anything. The Goblin shrugged. "Very well then." He ripped the strip of skin off and the Irishman couldn't help the scream of shock that ripped from his throat. Blood ran down his side, soaking the top of his worn leather trousers.

"You see, you have only tasted a bit of the pain I am capable of causing you," the Goblin said, coming behind Aeden, leaning close. His breath wafted against the back of the Irishman's neck and sent a shiver of disgust up his spine. "If you do not wish to sample any more, let me know, and this can all end here with only a few answers to my questions."

"No," the Irishman forced out.

"Very well then," the Goblin said again and motioned to his guards. "Bring all my instruments to me. I shall have him talking by the end of the day." He shot a hand forward, gripping Aeden's neck and wrenching his head back, his lips nearly pressed against the Irishman's ear. "And if you don't talk, I will start on the princeling, and we'll see how you do when you're forced to watch your king's brother suffer."

Aeden Mac Cool swallowed hard, and closed his eyes, willing his mind away by thinking of his family; his parents, brothers and sister who likely all thought he was dead. He would not give in, for their sake. He could not give in for the sake of Erin herself. But that did not stop the mountains from echoing with his screams.

Part One

The Company

Chapter One
Tracking

The mists rolled off the green hills, still damp from the morning dew, and the will o' the wisps curled around my legs as I loped easily through the heather, leaping from rock to rock as I focused my attention between the ground beneath my feet and the track ahead, forging the way not by signs, nor by memory this time, but by carefully deducted paths recreated from collected visions and common sense. The wet air, still smelling of dawn, refreshed me, brought all my senses into focus, so that I could concentrate on my task. This was my favorite time of day to track, and I would have felt an unnamable joy in that morning's duty had it not been for the subject of my tracking.

I climbed onto a big rock, bracing myself halfway up and looking back down into the valley where I could see Tierney still picking up the tent as I made my last scout. It was foolish, I knew, Aeden had been gone for nearly six months, but this had been where he was patrolling when he disappeared, and I felt there had to be *something* that would tell me where he might be. That he was still alive.

I took in the landscape, picturing Aeden standing in my exact position, scouting the way ahead. If he had been chased, where would he make a stand? I knew already before the question had barely passed through my mind and was off, sprinting soundlessly over the dewy ground to the valley on the other side of this hill.

My memory had not failed me, I saw with satisfaction as I crested the rise and trotted down into the valley. There was the circle of standing stones, so old that no one knew whom they belonged to now, or what their purpose had been. Several had fallen like ancient stone warriors lost in battle, but most were still standing in their original circle. For want of a better location, it would have been the only spot that a few men could have stood to defend themselves, and the stones were said to offer protection to warriors who were true to Erin. I felt in my bones that this was the place my brother had made his stand and surely it was the place Daegal had dreamed about. I took the picture he had drawn for me and held it up in comparison. It was identical.

I entered the circle slowly. I always felt there should be some ritual to entering a stone circle, but if there ever had been, the knowledge had been lost in centuries long past. I did bow my head in respect though, for the sake of whatever spirits or Fae that might guard it still. The stones seemed to create an energy of their own, not really tangible, but some-thing that allowed my mind to work more clearly, take in more. Na Fianna were known for their connection with the land, being an old race, and such ancient landmarks as these seemed to give us strength. I looked around the circle, taking the scene in and again trying to picture the events that had happened here in the past.

I was drawn to one stone, one of the fallen ones, and crouched to inspect it, finding an old rust-colored stain in a crack of one of the swirling designs carved into it. I had seen enough blood to know it for what it was, and being red, it was hardly Goblin blood. There was no telling how much blood there had been to begin with, for whatever had been there surely would have washed away long ago, but it was enough to tell me my suspicions were correct, and my stomach knotted in instinctive uncertainty of my brother's survival.

I braced a hand on the wet ground as I contemplated this confirmation. By rights, I shouldn't even have been out there looking, knowing my father would berate me for having false hope, but I hadn't been home for three months, and I had missed Aeden more than I could say, and when Daegal and I had spoken on the phone in my absence, he always had new dreams of his to report, telling me about this place and how he thought it was connected in some way with the patrol's disappearance. I knew I wouldn't be able to rest before I at least checked, and Tierney and I had a few days before we had to report back to the court of High King Eamon O'Brian so we had camped in the area below, spending that time tracking and trying to map the path Aeden and his patrol had taken before they met with an unfortunate Goblin attack that had nearly sent our people back into another long and bloody war.

I sighed as I thought again how hopeless this venture was. I was about to head back to Tierney when my fingers found something at the base of the stone, hiding in the grass. I dug down and pulled it out, feeling engraved metal hanging from a leather strap. My fingers knew what it was before I recognized it by sight, opening my hand to look at it; my fingers knew the shape well. It was a pendant identical to the one I wore about my own neck, a simple bronze medallion about an inch in diameter with the Mac Cool crest emblazoned on it, depicting Fintan the Salmon of Wisdom from the ancient story. Daegal hadn't been wrong. Aeden had been here sure enough. Now the question was whether he was still alive or if he had perished here.

Two years ago now, there had been an uprising of Goblins and Na Fianna and all the other warriors and kings of Ireland were called upon to do battle with them. It had been a feud going on for as long as there had been Ireland and though the enemy might not have always been the same, the struggle was, and there was always a new enemy to take the place of the one who was finally defeated. First it had been my ancestor, the great Fionn Mac Cool who had fought the Viking invaders, being the reason why the Fianna had been feared in the first place. But there were more than just Norsemen my ancestors had to deal with, for there were always enemies of a more fantastical nature.

The first Goblin War had happened while the rest of the world was fighting WWII; another had arisen in the '80s, which was quelled after two bloody years only to come to a head again, just three years past. This was the quickest and bloodiest of the three, naming it, in grim humor, the War of the Red Hills for all the blood that had been spilled—mostly ours. After only a year of fighting, the Kings of Ireland had formed a tenuous peace with the Goblin King, paying him heavy tithes to seal the pact, but it had not lasted for more than a year, for there was a sudden, nasty uprising in the north and due to certain events, which no one knew the origin of, Goblins attacked a city on the Borderland and decimated the people, nearly wiping them all out. Our High King gathered his warriors and went out to do battle, knowing that the time had come to wipe the Goblins out all together. And he nearly succeeded, but at heavy cost, for though he did kill the Goblin King, he left his son, Lorcan, alive, and lost his own life as well as that of over half his men in the process. They say that Erin wept blood for her lost children that day.

And then only months ago after an unstable peace of nearly a year while we picked up the pieces of the last battle, the Goblin prince, Lorcan, turned king after the death of his father, began to make small attacks despite the agreement. One day a patrol of Fianna warriors went out to scout Goblin trails, and never came back. One of them was my older brother, another was the younger brother of High King Eamon—Oran, the crown prince. Many more had lost loved ones too that day, but like my father, didn't want to risk the hope that they might still be alive for it seemed that six months was enough time to give up hope of recovery. I, on the other hand, didn't share those sentiments, and there were others who felt the same.

I turned away from the stone and something else caught my eye. A glint of silver caught in a crack of one of the other stones. I knelt to inspect it and saw it was a hair bead like all warriors wore to show their status, but this one was especially fine, and engraved with the pattern of the High Seat of Tara. It was also still attached to a braid of jet-black hair, cut off at about three inches. I pictured the owner frantically chopping it off himself, finding he was caught in the stone after being thrust back against it. I held it in a clenched fist for a moment before I tucked it into the script at the side of my belt.

I cast about a little more, but everything that was to be found there had been found, and it was enough proof to prove my and Daegal's theory of where the patrol had disappeared. It was no proof of life, but it was a start.

I looked at Aeden's medallion again and then pulled it around my neck, tucking it in under my leather breastplate while my own stayed resting on the outside. I had called Eamon yesterday when we had still been in town and capable of mobile service, and told him that Tierney and I would be back at the Hall by noon. We would have to hurry if we hoped to keep that appointment. And he would be eager to hear of our side trip, especially now that I had something to show for it. Finally.

Tierney had finished packing up the tent and sleeping bags by the time I got back to the camp and was just loading them into the back of my Vanquish when I came trotting down the hill. He looked up expectantly.

"Well?"

I silently showed him what I had found and he nodded, hands on hips, neither of us knowing what to say. We had been right, but that wasn't enough. I knew he had hoped I might find something from his father, but he knew there had been no guarantee that we would find anything at all and the knowledge that our trip had not been fruitless was enough for the moment. Still, I felt his pain and disappointment keenly in the fresh air and punched him lightly in the shoulder.

"Come on. We need to get back. I'll let you drive." I tossed him the keys and he smiled, even though I suspected he knew I was just trying to cheer him up, as he slid into the driver's seat with an eager air. I pulled off the sword I wore over my shoulder and tossed it behind my seat before I climbed in as well. And then we were off and on the road as Tierney eagerly gunned the car into motion, laughing.

"If you do anything to this car, I swear I will hurt you," I told him but was grinning as well.

"Don't worry, I won't hurt your sweetheart," Tierney said mockingly, stroking the dash with a wink, and only went faster. "I'll let you drive the Noble next time."

With his driving, we were back in Tara before ten o'clock and stopped at a pub in town for a quick breakfast before heading to Tara Hall on the hill overlooking the town; giving the otherwise modern day setting of the village of Tara a medieval flair, the Hall had hardly changed since the days of my ancestor Fionn Mac Cool. My mobile rang as we headed to the car again and I answered it as I sat down in the driver's seat, digging my keys out of my pocket.

"Hello?"

"Where are you?" It was Killian O'Hara's voice on the other end, *Captaen* of Eamon's guards and a good friend, if not somewhat self-important.

"At Lannagan's, we're on our way in one minute if you hang up."

"Insolence, insolence," Killian chided but I could hear the smirk on his lips. "See you then."

I slapped the phone shut and started the car once Tierney was in and we were off on the road to Tara Hall.

Chapter Two
Tara Hall

Once upon a time, the High Seat at Tara had been in the possession of the Mac Art family back in the day of the original Fianna. Cormac Mac Art had been a friend of Fionn Mac Cool himself and Fionn served him faithfully, climbing to position second only to the High King himself, more influential than even the lesser kings. The High Kingship had changed hands several hundred years later to the O'Brians—descended from Brian Boru—but my family continued to be influential to the royal house, and often acted as advisors (as my cousin Ceannt did now) and were always the first warriors to call when needed.

Tara Hall was a magnificent castle in the old style. It seemed to have been added to over every century and carried hints of the ancient warrior's hall that had stood during the times of Fionn Mac Cool, as well as that of later dates, such as medieval, and even some later gothic architecture that could be seen in the vaulted throne room, giving it an odd mixture of a cathedral and warlord's hall all at once.

I pulled up in the roundabout at the front of the Hall, and grabbed my leather coat and sword from the back of the car, pulling on the coat and settling the sword properly over my shoulder to look presentable in front of the king. Tierney did the same and we nodded to the guards who opened the wide double doors carved with intricate knot work that led into the foyer.

Killian, the *Captaen na Gurda* — captain of the guard — was already there waiting for us, as I assumed he would be, sitting on a bench and taking the time to sharpen his sword which hardly needed any more grinding. He gave us a withering glance as we came in, sheathing his sword with a hiss of well-oiled metal as he stood up and made a show of checking the time.

"Five minutes late. Whatever will I do with you?" He shook his head then smirked and motioned for us to follow. It was all pomp and ceremony, for we had known each other all our lives and Killian had always had something of an overbearing personality.

His heavy boots clumped down the marble halls and echoed around the corridors, even though he was light on his feet. Tierney and I, though we wore heavy fighting boots, made little sound at all, for Na Fianna were notoriously light on their feet and could walk silently over a forest of twigs and never snap a single one — thanks in part to our mixed Fae blood.

We reached the throne room and Killian grasped the door handle, opening the door and motioning a hand inside with a flourish.

"Ciran Mac Cool and Tierney Mac Morna, *Airdrígh*."

Tierney and I bowed respectfully to Eamon who was standing in the middle of the room, holding a conversion with a girl about our age who looked vaguely familiar though I couldn't place her. They both looked up as we came in and Eamon strode toward us immediately.

"Ciran, Tierney, it's good to see you again; how did your training go in Dublin?"

"Very well," I replied. "I think we learned well enough, though I don't think the lads down there have anything on ours. We defeated them all too easily. We'll also be glad to get back home to our mothers' cooking." Tierney gave a comical shudder.

Eamon laughed merrily, his black eyes twinkling. Everything about Eamon was dark and joyful, his hair jet black and tightly curled, almost covering the intricate silver circlet he wore and from his usual manner, one might misjudge him as cavalier and unworthy of his station—and many have made that mistake. He had come to the throne early, having lost his father in the last Goblin war I spoke of earlier, and he was only six years older than I. But he had a head on his shoulders, and he often surprised his councilors and the other kings with his intelligence, not to mention the fact that he always had a cool head in crisis. He had almost been replaced with a regent after his father had been killed, but it had been my own father who insisted he keep the position as rightful heir, for Eamon had been the one to lead the men to victory after his father fell, a young prince, who charged the Goblin ranks with only his young sword-brother Killian at his shield arm. His courage and bravery won the hearts of all the warriors that day and it did not take much persuading to give him his rightful place, though there were still some kings who resented the fact that he had gained the seat so young and tried to peg him as inexperienced whenever they found the chance. But Eamon was out to prove them wrong, and I knew that he would succeed in the end.

Today he was wearing none of his kingly garb but the circlet. His usual cape had been replaced by a canvas jacket, accompanied by a plain leather breastplate and a worn pair of jeans and boots. He watched me with scrutiny for a few moments; I had often wondered how much he took in when he did that, and figured it was probably a lot more than I expected.

"What of the other thing?" he asked quietly.

I sobered, motioning to the large windows that looked out on the training grounds that resided on one side of the Hall gardens. We retired there away from the others, and Eamon leaned his shoulder against the window frame, crossing his arms as he looked at me expectantly.

"Did you find what you went seeking?" he asked.

I nodded and I could see him swallow in anticipation, shifting slightly. "Daegal was right. It was at the Faery stones out by Mullingar. Tierney and I tracked the planned rout of the patrol for two days and that's where it ended up. They made their last stand there."

"You're sure?"

I met his eyes meaningfully as I reached under my collar and pulled out the second medallion that I had found that morning.

"Aeden's," he said, standing up straight, interest and a little fear on his face. It was not a question; he knew as well as I what this meant.

"Yes."

His eyes had turned thoughtful and sad and I reached into my script to retrieve my other find. I pulled it free in my closed fist and held it out to him. "I also found this."

He held his hand out to receive what I had and I let the braid and bead fall into his palm. He only looked at it a second before he turned quickly to the window and closed his eyes, inhaling deeply to gather himself, but I could tell from his trembling shoulders that he was about to fall apart. I knew exactly how he felt. I waited patiently for him to recover and he held the small, pitiful memento close to his chest.

"Was—" he started then stopped before continuing. "Signs of struggle? There—there must have..."

"Yes," I said quietly. "I think Oran cut that off himself. I found it caught in the crack of a rock."

"It doesn't mean anything," Eamon said, more to himself than to me. "It doesn't mean they're still alive, but..."

"We do know for certain now that they didn't die in the fight. We will not give up hope," I said earnestly, clasping a hand on his shoulder.

"No, we will not," he shook his head and closed his eyes again. *"Mo deartháir leanbh."* He finally turned to me again, tucking the braid into his breastplate, pulling himself together again. "Have you told your father?"

"I've told him nothing yet," I admitted somewhat shamefully. "He doesn't know I've been looking. If I had not had your blessing..."

"You would have done it anyway," Eamon said with a smile, some of the light returning to his eyes and I shrugged in agreement. "I know you well enough, and I know I'd do the same if I was in your place. I wish I was— I can hardly stand sitting here in my bloody great palace while my little brother could be dead or languishing in some filthy hole in the hills. By the saints, he was only sixteen." He shook his head. "No, I need you and Tierney to do this for me, Ciran, so if your father gets angry at you for doing so, send him to me."

"He will not be angry," I said with surety. "He won't

like it, but I don't think he'll be angry. And I plan to tell him when I get home."

"Ah, and about that..." Eamon said, all business again, indicating that we rejoin the others. "I'm afraid I can't send you two home *quite* yet, more's the pity. There've been some reports of Goblin activity up north a ways around Cavan area, and I need someone to go and check it out. All my other Fianna are otherwise engaged at the moment and I can't spare any of my guards because there's a meeting and inspection going on this afternoon — annoying business. Besides, it's really a Fianna task, after all."

"We'll do it," I said, casting an inquiring glance at Tierney who nodded in acceptance.

"Three person job, though, at least for safety's sake," Killian put in. "I'd go with you myself, but we have that bloody council meeting this afternoon and His Majesty needs me to make sure he stays awake." He smirked and winced simultaneously as Eamon kicked him in the shin. "I suppose we can call in Deaglan. He's likely hanging around his favorite coffee shop picking up the ladies."

I winced. Not that I bore any real ill feelings toward Deaglan but our families had had a long feud that went back to our founding ancestors Fionn and Dairmuid. I certainly wasn't looking forward to trekking with him.

"I can go."

Tierney and I both looked up in surprise at the girl who was still standing next to Killian's shoulder. I had forgotten her with all the talk of business, but I took her in now, wondering who she was. The blond captain put his arm around her shoulders and drew her forward.

"Lads, I don't know if you remember my baby sister, Caitlin? She's been training with the ladies down south for five years but you should have seen her at some point when you were younger."

I did know who she was, though I'll admit I had never really talked to her in the past besides when we were really little. I was thirteen when she left and lads and lasses rarely cared for each other at that age and at the time I had just been starting on my official warrior training. I nodded politely to her, but was unsure of what to respond. I took her in as I thought. She seemed to be the exact opposite of Killian, dark-haired, where he was blond, but they had the same bearing and stance. She was dressed sensibly in a knitted tunic that went down to mid-thigh, flat-soled boots and leather pants and jacket. A short sword hung against her left hip and the hilt of a dagger peeked from the top of her right boot. Her hair was done up in the style of female warriors, formed into several plates held with metal beads that fell down past her shoulders. I liked the looks of her in any case, but I wasn't sure how I felt about her joining us; it's hard to have someone thrown into a patrol who you have never fought with before. I turned to Tierney and he shrugged one shoulder slightly, but I caught the approving look and couldn't help a smirk at him that made him roll his eyes.

"If it's no trouble, I suppose," I told her.

"None at all," she said with a smile. "I've been here for a week and am already sick of my brother and *this one* who is no better," she said, indicating Eamon who scrunched up his face comically. "I'd like to see a little bit of scenery, and getting rid of some Goblins along the way isn't a bad prospect either."

"You'll have to leave immediately, I'm afraid," Killian informed us, then amended, "Though you may stay for lunch, I suppose."

After we had been fed a quick meal in Eamon's private study where he practically lived when not on duty, Tierney and I left with our new companion. Killian saw us out of the hall, leaning up against the wall while playing with the hilt of his sword.

"You two scalawags take good care of my sister," he said. "Mainly because if you disrespect her she'll happily maim you, and I wouldn't wish that on any man."

"I daren't ask the nature of the maiming," Tierney said, half laughing, but knowing enough of Irish women, having grown up with three sisters, to be wary and respectful. I grinned and shook my head.

"Don't worry, Killian, it's not like you're sending her out with Deaglan."

He scrunched up his nose but smiled. "You know as well as I that Deaglan is not all that bad. There's just bad blood between you, that's all. I suppose it is in the Celtic tradition to forget *nothing* no matter how many centuries have passed." He looked up as Caitlin rejoined us from gathering her things, a burlap bag slung over her shoulder.

"Ready?" she asked.

"If you are," I replied.

She kissed her brother on the cheek and he sighed as he looked at his watch. "Do be good, *deirfiúr leanbh*. Make sure the boys behave. I must go and prepare for that bloody meeting and make sure His Royal Fashion Nightmare is in his kingly garb so he doesn't shock the council members. And I have a date tonight too."

"A date?" I inquired.

He smirked. "Maeve," he said.

"Then you had better take your own advice, Captaen," I cautioned, but was secretly pleased my sister had found such a match.

Killian guffawed. "Oh, don't I know it? Get on then, the Goblins aren't going to wait for you to catch them. Now be off!" He sauntered off in a ridiculous swagger that sent his cape swinging gloriously and caused Caitlin to roll her eyes; but I could not help but notice the small smile in the corner of her mouth. It was obvious that she loved her brother, despite his shortcomings.

"Best go if we plan to get back before dark," I said and we left the hall. Caitlin crawled into the cramped back seat of the Vanquish and settled in as I started it up and sped out of the lot, saluting the gate guards who shook their heads at us in fond admonishment. Na Fianna were the only people who were allowed to speed without marks on our license, for not only did our occupation call for fast action on the drop of a pin (the reason we all drove ridiculously fast cars) but we also had the heightened precisian reflexes of a warrior race with part Fae blood and could handle a car like no normal human could. Whatever they like to say about ninjas none could beat a Fianna warrior — it's been proven.

We drove for a while in silence, and it felt a little awkward at first, for about this time Tierney and I would start joking or listening to music but we both seemed a little shy in the presence of one of the fairer gender. Tierney, of course, had three sisters, and I had one, but neither of us was home much and ever since our training started we mostly spent our time with the other lads. We had both craved and dreaded female interaction in the past month. I was incredibly grateful when Caitlin started up the conversation herself, seeming to carry some of the tact her brother had — when he wasn't being cocky and sarcastic.

"I heard you two are trying to find out what happened

to the missing patrol," she said.

Tierney and I exchanged glances and I gripped the wheel tighter, not sure whether we should admit to it or not. She laughed, sounding amused.

"Stop conversing telepathically, lads, don't think I don't know what you're doing—I do have two brothers." We grinned sheepishly.

"We are," I replied to her question. "Eamon asked us to look into it whenever we get the chance."

"And now you've found something." It was not a question; she must have known I had found something that morning even if she didn't know all the details.

"Yes," I replied with a small sigh. "But it doesn't mean that they are alive."

"I miss my brother too," she said and suddenly I felt like an idiot. I had forgotten that the loss of Killian's brother would, of course, have meant the same to her. It had just been so long since I had associated the Captaen with having a sister that I knew it would take me a while to think of her in association with him. I had known Flagan better, for he had been one of Aeden's good friend's and I had grown up with him around.

"We'll find out what happened to them," I assured her. "And if they are alive, we will get them back. When we settle the problems with the Goblins up here, I'm going to ask Eamon to let us go out and track some more. My younger brother might have had another vision by then."

"Your brother has the Sight?" she asked and I could hear the interest in her voice. "Is that Daegal, or Finbar?"

"Daegal." I nodded. "Yes, he inherited that side of the family. He helped me find the connection of the patrol to the place I searched this morning. Unfortunately, the trail goes dead there—it was the place of their last stand. If I can find another clue from that location, however, we might have a good chance of recovering more information."

"Or we could just drag a Goblin in for questioning if we take any today," Tierney said. "Throw him in your boot for a couple of days and he'll talk."

I chuckled at the thought of trying to stuff more than a small suitcase into the boot of my Vanquish, but a part of me didn't think it was a terrible idea to get information. "We'll see if we can find any first."

Once we got to the destination or thereabouts, I parked my car in a pull off and we got out to continue the journey on foot. Caitlin handed us our swords from the back seat. I popped open the boot and Tierney and I pulled out our leather breastplates, strapping each other up before I slid my jacket back on and slung my sword over my shoulder. Caitlin already wore hers and she watched us as we suited up with an approving glance. Tierney grinned at her and I closed the boot, locking the car and motioning them forward.

"Let's go. Hope you can keep up with Fianna, Caitlin."

She smiled and did a few running stretches. "I think I can manage."

We took off over the hills at a lope, springing lightly through the heather. There was a chill spring wind, and it blew through my light brown hair that hung long and ragged over my ears. I pointed several spots out to my companions that looked like places Goblins might have stood, and then stopped to inspect one where I knew they had been.

"There's holes where someone stuck several arrows into the ground," I said. Goblins are fantastic archers. With the 80-pound longbow that was their weapon of choice, they could hit a moving target from three hundred yards easy and they rarely missed. They were good with swords and spears too, but the bow was their specialty, whereas it wasn't ours. The Irish have forever been famous scrappers and we don't like to stand back from a fight. If our swords don't taste blood they get grumpy. There were a few girls I knew who used a bow, but only one Finar, and that was Deaglan—maybe another mark against him, though I had to admit he was bloody good.

"How long ago?" Caitlin asked.

"Hour at the most," Tierney said, on his knees, sniffing the ground. "No, thirty minutes, if that. I don't think they're far away. I wonder if they were waiting for one of our patrols."

I felt he was right. There would be no other reason for the Goblins to have stayed here this long, and the hills seemed crowded like there were more presences around than just us. There was an outcropping up the hill to our left where the rocks formed a little alcove that would be a perfect place to spy out the surrounding countryside. I nodded upward to it. "Let's head up there. They probably would have used it as a lookout, and might return—if they're not still there now. In any case, it will give us a good vantage point to keep watch. We'll stay an hour and if we see nothing, we'll scout a little more on the other side before we head back."

We trooped up the hill and ducked down into the alcove. I cast about a moment, but the smell of Goblin was all over the place: earthy, but oddly clean smelling, like mossy rocks and mud. Probably because they lived in the ground under the mountains in huge stone fortresses that were the places of legend. No man or warrior had ever come alive out of a Goblin fortress, at least not in recent history.

"They were here all right," Tierney said for Caitlin's benefit for she did not possess the heightened senses Na Fianna warriors did.

We settled down to watch, keeping a lookout in three directions. Caitlin took a chocolate bar out of her pocket and passed some squares around.

"How long since you graduated from the Academy?" I asked her, noticing the Academy torc she wore around her neck. Warrior women went to the Academy of Maeve which had been started in the 1800s so that women could learn to take up arms in the old Irish tradition and fight for the home front while many of the men were off fighting Napoleon. I knew from Tierney's older sister, Meghan, that they went through training nearly as rigorous as we did to enter the ranks of Na Fianna, if not more so. With Na Fianna, you had to be of the bloodline of Fionn's original warriors, and if you were, it was a given you would get in unless you chose not to, but you still had to pass the training which consisted of several tests of agility and strength that were nigh impossible to the average human—Fianna warriors carry Fae blood in our veins: extra strong, extra fast, and have the ability to heal quicker than normal men, but were by no means immortal.

"Only this January," she said.

"You came back about the time we left for our last couple months of training," Tierney said. We had both started our last semester of training at sixteen like all the normal Fianna who trained for two years after the initial schooling before becoming full Fianna warriors. But because my father had been crippled in the last Goblin War, and my eldest brother and Tierney's father had been taken on that fateful patrol, we had advanced a year early as the heads of our household and Eamon needed us. There were a lot of young Fianna now after the war, some might say inexperienced, but Eamon was notorious for holding us up in front of the other kings and well he should know, for he was only twenty-three and held power over them all even though they resented him for it. Na Fianna traditionally served the High King directly, and that was still the case. So while we could go and help the other kings, which we did, and each kingdom held it's garrison of Fianna, our orders were exclusively from the *Airdrigh*, and no one else could override that. Though the council tried their best when they came across something they didn't care for.

Though we had been promoted to full-fledged warriors early, we still had to serve some necessary training whenever we got the chance, but we had just finished the last of it and had received our brotherhood tattoo on our left shoulder as a sign of our official graduation just the week before, at age eighteen. There was even graduates younger than us, testifying as to how many we had lost in the war.

"I met your sister Meaghan at the Academy, Tierney," Caitlin said as she passed around another square of chocolate. "She'll be home when you get back. She always talked about you, and I can admit truthfully, it was always with pride." She winked and turned to me. "As for you, Ciran, I'm afraid I know more about your sister than about you, and she didn't even go to the Academy." I laughed as she rolled her eyes in mock exasperation. "Apart from that, I just vaguely remember playing in the woods and making mud pies with you and Tierney as a kid."

"How come I'm the last to know about Killian dating Maeve?" I asked with a laugh. "I was only gone for three months, and he never mentioned anything, nor did she."

"I think he was afraid of what you'd do to him," Caitlin said, laughing along. "I'd be careful though, Killian fancies himself a match maker. He wanted me to scope out an eligible candidate for Eamon while I was at the Academy, as if I didn't already have enough to think about. How about your sister, Tierney? She's a sweet girl with a good head on her shoulders."

"No," Tierney said. "Not to slight our *Airðrígh* of course, but still. Why not you?" he added with a wicked smirk.

"Me and Eamon?" she laughed in surprise. "He's like my brother since Killian and Flagan and I grew up in Tara Hall and we played with Eamon and Oran all through our childhood. I still remember some of the things Eamon and Killian got up to—stealing food from the kitchens and hiding in cupboards among other things. They went through five cooks in a month before they realized that Eamon and Killian had been playing jokes and terrifying the poor things out of their wits." She smiled fondly. "If it wasn't for their positions, I doubt they'd be any better now. Thick as thieves. I love Eamon, true, but as a brother. I assume you know we were fostered by Eamon and Oran's parents when ours were killed in the Goblin Wars."

"Well, we'll have to find him someone as levelheaded as my sister then," I said with a laugh. "Don't worry, Maeve will definitely keep Killian in line."

"Hush," Tierney said suddenly, grabbing my sleeve. I was instantly alert, and I could see Caitlin's hand going to her sword hilt. "I thought I saw something over there."

We glanced through the rocks and scanned the hills below us. There were plenty of places for hiding down there and Goblins had as much talent for stealth as we

Fianna did. They wouldn't be seen if they didn't want to be. Perhaps they were coming back to their hide, and if that were the case, I didn't think we would escaped their notice.

"There," Caitlin said, nodding over to one side. There was nothing there when I looked but she added, "I thought I saw a movement—someone slipping from rock to rock."

"We might not be exposed up here, but if they close in on us, we're not going to have a way out," I advised. "Let's go now and slip back around that way. We'll try and cut them off." I waved out the general path as we scooted back and slid silently down the backside of the hill.

That was when I too, caught sight of something, only out of the corner of my eye, but it was there and I felt a strange jolt of adrenaline and fear course through me, pounding in my veins and my palm twitched for the feeling of my sword hilt. I wondered if this was what Aeden had felt before his patrol had been overtaken, and I had a sudden thought that the same would happen to us, but I urged the others on to a faster clip, skirting the next hill and being careful not to skyline ourselves at the top. We crouched down for a moment as we scanned the countryside again. I shook my head. "Do you see anything now?"

"Nothing," Tierney said.

"There was something out there," I insisted. "I can feel it. And if it's Goblins, I don't know what they think they're doing."

"Looking for another patrol," Caitlin stated grimly.

"Let's go, we have the information we came for," I said.

Just as we stood to leave, there was a whizz and Tierney dropped beside me with a short cry. I was on my knees beside him in an instant as Caitlin's sword leapt from its sheath into her hand, deflecting another arrow away from us like she was playing tennis.

"Tir, you all right?" I winced, seeing the arrow in his side, easily piercing the hard leather. He tried a smile but grimaced.

"I'm good, just help me up." He tried sitting, but fell back onto his elbows with a gasp.

"No time, get him up, we need to get out of here," Caitlin said and I looked over the rise to see three Goblins charging at us with spears in their hands, their pale, slightly greenish, skin gleaming in the sunlight, a contrast to the black leather clothing they wore. I grabbed the arrow shaft sticking out of Tierney and broke it off as close to his body as I could. He cried out, but I had no time to apologize, pulling one of his arms around my neck as I hauled him from the ground, looking around frantically.

"I'll hold them off, now go; I'll be right behind you, just get him back to the car!" Caitlin shouted.

There was no time to argue, the first Goblin was nearly upon us and she ran forward to meet him, grabbing the spear haft to block the blow he aimed at her and driving her sword below the creature's ribs.

"Run little Fianna," another Goblin said mockingly before Caitlin ran at him with a wild shout, giving him a crippling blow to the back of the leg before delivering a roundhouse kick to the face and started after us. I could see more Goblins coming and knew we had to hurry.

Tierney grabbed my coat frantically. "Ciran, leave me and help her fight them. I can get back by myself."

"You wouldn't leave *me* you eejit," I told him. We were almost to the car. I felt his hand fumbling in my jacket pocket and he produced the keys for me with a light laugh that soon turned into a grimace.

"Figured I'd help since you seem to have your arms full," he said.

"Thank you, *mo chara*," I said as he pressed the unlock button and I managed to get the door open, tossing him unceremoniously into the tight backseat. He gasped, but I had no time to apologize. I was already in the driver's seat, shamefully forgetting my seatbelt as I revved the engine into life and did a tire-squealing J-turn before I slammed down the gas and tore back up the road to where Caitlin was holding off the goblins. She was a wonderful fighter but I had no time to admire her form — her fighting form, I mean — for she needed rescuing.

She saw me coming, and seemed to somehow anticipate my intentions for she took out the Goblin she was fighting with her sword pommel to his jaw, and ran up the side of the hill as I sped off the road, scattering the startled Goblins, and spun the car full circle in the wet grass, leaning over to open the door. Caitlin needed no second bidding and leapt in. The Goblins were running, and I knew we were likely to have a chase on our hands soon. I should probably mention that while we Fianna loved our fast cars, Goblins had a certain fondness for motorcycles.

I didn't give her a chance to settle before I was off again just as she barely had the door closed and Tierney groaned from the backseat where he had propped himself up enough to look out the back window.

"Ciran, they're coming!"

I glanced in the rearview mirror and saw five motorcycles with Goblins tearing around a bend in the road, and coming after us. They must have had them hidden somewhere out of sight.

"Don't fail me, darling," I said to my car, gripping the wheel tighter.

The Goblins came up faster than I had expected, but I shifted gears and gave the car more power, putting a little more distance between us.

"How are you doing, Tir?" I asked.

"Hard to say," he replied weakly, and I felt a sense of worry clench in my stomach. I had never heard him sound so bad before, and suddenly recalled the anatomy of a Goblin arrowhead and how they were designed to do as much damage as possible. I hadn't had time to try and stop the bleeding, and knew that something would have to be done or Tierney might not survive long enough to get back into town.

I glanced at Caitlin who was watching the Goblins in the door mirror. "What do you know about first aid?"

She looked at me apologetically. "Not enough to trust myself with an arrow wound while you're driving over a hundred miles an hour."

"Then how are you with driving?" I asked.

She smiled. "I did have Killian as my driving instructor, so if you're wondering whether I can drive fast…"

I couldn't help a small smile. "I'll help Tierney; my mother is a healer. I want you to put your feet on the pedals—we can't risk stopping for a second—and when I give you the signal, we'll trade places, got it?"

She nodded and climbed over the gearshift until she was almost in my lap, and slid her feet next to mine on the pedals. I heard Tierney curse softly behind me. I slid my feet from under hers.

"Ready?" I asked, putting one arm around her waist as she took the wheel.

"Ready."

I shoved her into the seat as I slid underneath her and the car only swerved slightly as she got the feel of it and then put it back up to full velocity. I quickly rummaged through the glove box for the first aid kit and then lay the passenger seat back as far as it would go, lying half on it and half in the backseat with Tierney. He was deathly pale, and his eyes were half closed, but he still grinned.

"She's a keeper, Cir," he whispered and gasped as I started unbuckling his breastplate on the side he had taken the arrow, pulling the front piece up until it was free of the arrow shaft. Blood stuck his shirt to his skin around the wound, but there was not as much as I had feared; of course, that didn't speak for the damage he had suffered on the inside.

"Tierney, I swear if you bleed on the upholstery this arrow will be the least of your problems," I told him to make him laugh but he could barely manage a lopsided grin. I gripped the back of his neck with one hand, raising his head slightly. "Hey, it's going to be all right." His hand wrapped around my wrist, squeezing in a weak grip that scared me more than his appearance. I gave a fond yank on his warrior braid and turned my attention back to the arrow. If I took it out he would certainly bleed to death and it was definitely not an operation I planned to perform in the back of my Vanquish while we were currently in the throes of a high-speed chase.

I ripped open his shirt around the arrow shaft and pressed bandages around it to stop the bleeding as well as I could with the shaft still in him. Tierney cried out, cursing at me.

"I'm sorry, but it has to be done. And watch your tongue, we have ladies present," I told him, fumbling in the first aid bag and drawing out a flask. I unscrewed it and raised his head to press it to his lips. "Here, this is for the pain." He took a long swallow of the liquor and lay back with his eyes closed. I shifted my position into the back seat so I could see out and rested Tierney's head against my shoulder as I kept one hand pressed to the wound as best I could with the arrow still sticking from him, and hoping I wasn't just doing more damage. I glanced back and saw with a triumphant grin that the Goblins had fallen far behind and had finally stopped and turned back. They would not come any farther now that we were so close to the city. I nudged Caitlin's leg with my foot.

"So, how did you like your first patrol with Na Fianna?" I asked her.

She laughed and slowed to a more reasonable speed, but not too reasonable, I noticed with approval. "It was quite a bit more eventful than I expected it to be, I must admit. I'll definitely have something to tell Killian about when we get back."

I winced. "Yes, but first, we need to get Tierney back to my house. My mother will see to him. Are you good?"

She nodded and I leaned back against the seat while Tierney slept or fell into unconsciousness, I wasn't sure which. This wasn't exactly the homecoming I'd had in mind that morning, but in any case, I would be glad to see my family again, and there was much I needed to discuss with my father. My hand went unconsciously to the medallion that rested on my chest and my thoughts to the identical one hidden beneath my breastplate that could quite possibly result in a great family upheaval that very night. Yeah, maybe we should have stayed at school after all.

Chapter Three
Returning

Calling my family estate a house was an understatement. It was a castle—literally, late 1500s—and kept in beautiful condition by my mother who was a restorer, a healer, and a weaver among other things too numerous to mention. The land held a stable, a rookery, dog kennels—we bred hunting hounds directly from the lineage of Fionn's own favorites, Bran and Skolawn, and when I say hunting hounds, I don't mean pheasant, we bred them for war—and lastly my da's forge. He forged all the swords and weaponry for the royal family, and Na Fianna, and his workmanship was beautiful still, though he needed my brother's hand to help steady the tongs. The estate was rivaled only by Tara Hall, showing full well that we still remembered our high ancestry with pride.

I did not admire it as I usually did coming home after long absence, for I had only Tierney to think of now and he was worsening by the minute. Caitlin leapt out of the car as soon as she drove into the front drive and yanked the seat back with a viciousness that made me wince to help me get him out. She took his legs and helped me lift him so I could slide out and take him fully up again.

"Run ahead," I said, but there was no need for it, because my mother had likely heard the Vanquish tearing up the cobbles and had run out with my sister, Maeve, to greet us.

"Ciran," she called, seeing my friend's limp form as I hurried to the house. "What happened?"

"Goblin arrow; we were attacked on patrol."

"Take him to the guest room by my herbarium," she told me and I did as I was told. She hurried ahead and tore the quilt off, throwing a sheet over the bed before I laid him down. He groaned and I was glad to hear from him, even if it wasn't entirely coherent. I gripped his hand tightly.

"It's all right now, *mo chara*," I told him. "I've got you back to my place."

"You'll be all right soon enough, Tierney," my mother said, already divesting him of his breastplate and shirt and doing so far more gently than I had. "My kit, Maeve."

My sister handed her a rolled leather pouch and a bowl of herb-scented water that she washed her hands in before opening the roll and producing a thin knife. "Hold him, Ciran."

Caitlin and I both went to grip Tierney's shoulders as my mother made a small cut around the arrow shaft and pulled it out carefully. I felt Tierney tense beneath me, his breath catching, and I gripped his shoulder tighter but it was over in an instant and my mother pressed a cloth to the wound to stop the bleeding and tossed the arrowhead onto a tray on the bedside table.

"Those things are horrid, but I have to say also rather impressive," Maeve said as she picked it up and cleaned it off, revealing the deadly, yet elegant design of the arrowhead, made almost like a leaf with a curved bit on the points.

"Maeve, go make some coffee for them in the kitchen, I'll finish with Tierney and join you shortly."

I was reluctant to leave my friend, but knew he was in capable hands and also that my mother worked better alone.

"I need to call Killian and make the report," I said.

"I'll do it," Caitlin offered, reaching into her pocket. "Blast, I left my mobile back at Tara."

"Use mine," I said, fishing the device from my pocket and handing it to her, before I teasingly drew it back. "Ah, and I'll be wanting my keys back."

She smiled mischievously but dropped them into my outstretched hand before she snagged the phone. "Hopefully this won't take long. They might still be in the council meeting, but I don't think Killian will cry too much for having a reason to escape."

We made our way to the kitchen, and I helped Maeve with the coffee as Caitlin explained about our mission.

"So," I asked my sister, with a grin. "You and Killian?"

She hit me in the shoulder and turned away, but I could tell she was smiling. "I couldn't do much worse, could I?"

"I don't know, there's always Deaglan."

She laughed. "As if Da would let him on the property, even if I *wanted* to date him." She poured me a cup of steaming coffee and I spooned honey into it thickly before she took the jar away.

"Killian's a good guy," I told her. "And a good friend. I'd like to see him with someone sensible like you. You might be one of the few who could keep him on the ground and half way sane."

"Thanks." She smiled genuinely.

Caitlin finished with her call just as my mother walked in.

"How is he?" I asked.

"He'll be fine; he's sleeping right now. There wasn't too much damage and thankfully he didn't lose more blood," she took the coffee Maeve gave her then took me in her arms as I went to greet her properly, kissing her on the cheek. "You three were lucky to get away with just one arrow wound between you." I knew what she left unspoken: *You could have all been taken, like your brother.*

"Mum," I said as I pulled back, wanting to change the subject. "This is Caitlin O'Hara, Killian's sister, I don't know if you remember her, she came with us as an extra hand today."

"Of course I remember you, dear, I was your mother's midwife." I watched them hug with a fond smile, secretly glad Caitlin seemed to win my mother's approval so easily. I had to admit I had been extremely impressed by Caitlin's performance both with the fighting and the driving. But then again, she *was* Killian's sister and I didn't think he'd allow her to be any less than that.

"It's good to have you home again, Ciran, it seems you've been gone so long," my mother said, running her fingers through my dirty hair with a frown as I sat at the counter, grabbing a muffin from a bowl sitting there, and savoring it with a contented sigh. My mother had always made muffins and I had missed the perpetual bowl of them while I had been away in Dublin where the best you could get was something wrapped in cellophane.

"It has been a long time, but the training's over now,

and we hopefully won't have to leave for so long again."

"Ciran!"

I turned around to see my three younger brothers all come trooping into the house with their two favorite wolfhounds, Brian and Oisin. Daegal had his arms around me first while little Sean wrapped his arms around my knees and Finbar, always the quiet one, clasped my forearm in the Warrior's way, his hands strong and calloused from working in the forge. The dogs greeted me with just as much affection, before I shoved them back down with a laugh.

"Did you finish your training?" Daegal asked. "What was it like?"

"Did you bring me something?" asked Sean, eyes wide and a smile on his lips as he jumped up and down in excitement.

"Let me see your tattoo," Daegal added, pulling the jacket from my shoulders before he stopped, looking at a streak of red on his fingers with shock.

"Are you hurt?" he asked, looking at me with scared eyes.

"No, it's not mine," I said, realizing I had gotten some of Tierney's blood on me and I took my jacket from Daegal to wipe it off the worn leather. "Tierney was hurt, but he'll be okay; he's resting in the downstairs guest room right now."

Daegal looked little appeased by that. I showed him my tattoo to cheer him up. "See? A knot of brotherhood. You'll get one of these too when you become a Fianna warrior."

He smiled but I could tell something was bothering him and I had to stop myself from reaching to the medallion around my throat. Daegal had always been able to know when something wasn't quite right. He might dream the actual future at night, but during the day, he still carried that sixth sense that made him so perceptive — strange for an eleven-year-old boy. I stood up and turned to my mother. "I need to see Da, where is he?"

"In the forge," she said, giving me a perceptive look. She too could tell there was something I wasn't telling her, but we both knew I had to speak to Da about it first and I wanted to get it over with as soon as possible.

"I'll be back soon, why don't you show Caitlin around the place, lads?" I told them, motioning to our guest.

The three of them took her eagerly into their care, Sean making sure he was the one who had the honor of holding her hand and I smiled as she was hustled off with the escort of the younger Mac Cools and two wolfhounds. I headed out the kitchen door and crossed to the back of the property where the forge resided.

My father had always loved his forge, but now he spent almost all his time there, ever since my brother had disappeared. He took his grief out on the metal — grief for my lost brother, and grief also for the loss of his right hand in the last battle. He had lost less than others who had not returned from the field that day at all, but yet, in a way, he had lost so much more. Though he still held his life, he had lost his livelihood for he could no longer go to battle with only one hand, more for the danger it would cause his comrades who depended on him than to himself, and even smithing proved difficult without the hands of ever patient Finbar.

When I found him, he was carving the wooden hilt of a knife; painstakingly doing with his left hand, what he once did so deftly with his right. An ache always formed in the center of my chest when I watched him work and I admired Finbar every day for being able to do so. But I never let this show, for any sympathy would not be taken well. I tried to push the pain away and stepped into the forge, feeling the warmth of the fire cut out all of the cool spring wind outside.

"Da?"

He turned and stood. "Ciran, you returned." He did not smile a greeting, but I didn't take offense of that. He hadn't smiled since Aeden had disappeared. I held out my left hand but he stepped forward to pull me into his arms instead. I wrapped mine around his broad shoulders. My father was tall and broad like the hero kings of old, and with his auburn hair—which only Sean and Aeden shared—that fell in plaits and beads down his back in the style of the old warrior lords, he looked to belong to a different century. It still hurt to feel only one large hand on my back, but I tried not to let it bother me.

"How did your training go?" he asked as he pulled back.

"Well, but that isn't what I came to tell you." I quickly detailed the events of our patrol first to get that out of the way. Maybe I was stalling, but I felt I should tell him this before anything else.

He listened quietly, but I could tell that it bothered him that we had been attacked and so close to home. It wasn't like we had been days up in the mountains, it was only an hour's drive north. Well, an hour my driving, but still.

"There's something else I need to tell you," I said after I had finished and assured him Tierney was all right—he and Tierney's father had been sword brothers as all men of our families were. Tierney's family had descended from Goll Mac Morna, one of Fionn's original warriors.

Originally, our two families had been feuding, but Goll proved himself time and again to be a fierce warrior and a loyal comrade. The ties between our families had come down the ages as firmly as those of animosity between us and the sons of Dairmuid. "I know I should have told you before, but it was so uncertain, I didn't want to let anyone know. But now that I do have something to show you for it, I felt I must let you know what I have been doing in my spare time."

"Ciran," he said warningly, but I shook my head, pleading with him to let me continue.

"Before Tierney and I left for Dublin, Eamon asked us to look into a few...things. Just some tracking—off the books. And at first we didn't find anything, but this morning, on our way back, we had a new lead, and we checked it out."

He had turned back to his bench and was gripping the edge tightly, his knuckles white, shaking his head, but I pushed on, unable to stop now that the damage had already been done.

"We went to the stone circle in Westmeath. They made their last stand there."

"Ciran." His voice was strangled with rage and grief.

"I found this." I yanked the medallion out from under my breastplate and put it on the table in front of him, more and more anxious to finish and win him over to my side on this matter for once.

He stood there for a minute, shaking with emotion; of what exactly, I couldn't be sure, but then he took the medallion that he had crafted himself and after a moment's hesitation, threw it across the room, overturning the bench with a violent shove and a thundering crash. "It's not my son, is it?!" he shouted.

I stepped back, more grieved than frightened. He swung around on me. "Why did you disobey me? This is exactly what I was afraid of. Finding something that would give us all false hope and for what? To find his corpse rotting on a spike someday in the north, or worse? You will not go back, Ciran, do you hear me? You will just forget this whole thing."

"I can hardly disobey the High King, *Athair*," I said, trying to keep my own emotions under wraps, fluctuating from indignant anger to fear and grief. "And what if he *is* still alive? What if we have left him and the others to die alone in pain, waiting for help that will never come? It's not just Aeden, it is Eamon's brother, our own crown prince, and as loyal country-men, subjects, and Fianna, we cannot give up so easily! It is our duty to push on!"

His good hand wrapped around one shoulder as the leather-bound stump crashed into the other, jerking me forward. "You will forget him, Ciran, and by Lugh, I swear, if you bring this up in front of your brothers..."

"Daegal already knows, and how can he not? His dreams were what guided me to the standing stones in the first place. Would he dream so often of these things if there was not some need to find them?" I asked.

"Ciran," he shouted, then softened and hung his head, his jaw tight. "Ciran, *mo fuaime*, please forget him. There is nothing you can do for your brother now. He is gone, and you had best start believing that. We had all best start believing that."

"Da?"

We both turned to see Daegal standing in the doorway, his large, dark eyes taking in the scene with intensity, and I knew he had heard the whole thing. I pulled away from my father's grip and went to wrap an arm around my brother's shoulders, pulling him against my side and forcing a smile as I drew him outside the forge.

"Mum said that supper was ready," he said. "And Killian called Maeve to say he and Eamon were coming."

"Double date?" I inquired.

He shrugged. "Don't know, there they are now, though."

I looked up as we rounded the west side of the castle to the front and caught sight of Eamon's Morgan rolling into the drive. He got out, looking even less like a High King than he had earlier, dressed only in his jeans and a leather jacket under which I could see a shirt with the Irish rock band, Swords & Shamrocks logo on it. Killian leapt out of the other side and made a scramble for the keys Eamon was about to pocket before he held them away from the shorter blond man, grinning.

"Not yet," he said as Daegal and I rounded the corner and Killian took advantage of Eamon's distraction to grab the keys, only to have them snatched back with a none-too-gentle punch to the ribs. "You know we can't let anyone see you stealing your High King's keys," he said to his friend who said something to him that no one should say to their High King, which only made Eamon laugh harder.

"Ciran," he said. "How is Tierney?"

"He'll be fine," I replied as Eamon clasped Daegal's forearm like a warrior, making my little brother grin hugely. "To what do I owe this pleasure?"

Eamon shrugged but I could tell he was immensely pleased about something. "It seems that after much discussion and persuading, the council has decided that your findings this morning were enough evidence to form a modest search party for the missing patrol."

"He got right furious about it," Killian whispered

loudly. "They were afraid to refuse." Eamon glared at him before he turned back to me.

"So I was thinking you might like to lead it, since you know more than anyone about the situation. Besides, you're the man I'd trust most with the job, and you're technically acting commander of Na Fianna in Aeden's place."

"What is a modest party?" I asked.

Eamon sighed. "They won't allow me to spare many, not with Goblins so far south. It's a volunteer mission, for those with reason."

"So those who lost family," I said.

Eamon nodded. "Yes. It will take a few days for me to get them together, and that will give Tierney time to heal, as I'm sure he won't let you leave without him. Will you do it?"

I hesitated and he seemed to understand. "Your father?" I nodded. "I'll talk to him. He can hardly refuse with the council's endorsement."

"It will only make it worse, I'm afraid," I said grimly. "But I will do it in any case. I wouldn't miss the chance. And I will take any man willing to stand with me."

Eamon nodded with a sad smile. "I only wish I could go with you. But I have my duties here, more's the pity."

The front door opened and Maeve came out, smiling at Killian.

"Are we ready?"

He took her hand and bowed over it. "At your service, my lady. Let's go," he hissed at Eamon before he handed her into the back of the car and climbed in.

"Will you stay for supper?" I asked Eamon.

"I'm afraid I have to crash Killian's date for a little bit longer for him to drop me off back at the Hall—his

McLaren is in the shop. I only came to deliver the news, and we should go before he can accuse me of ruining his entire night. I still don't know whether it was wise to let him borrow the Morgan, but only time will tell." He winked and I bowed respectfully as he climbed in and finally handed Killian the keys.

I turned back to Daegal as they drove off, and motioned him inside. "Let's have supper and then I'll tell you all about Dublin."

Chapter Four
Dreams

We ate supper, during which I discussed my training in Dublin but made sure to keep off any subject remotely relating to what I had found that morning, or my coming mission. My father said nothing all through dinner and left soon after, leaving me with a slightly empty feeling in my stomach though I had eaten well. I decided to go see how Tierney was doing and brought him a bowl of stew my mother pushed into my hands.

"If he's awake, let him eat, but if not, don't disturb him," she told me.

I walked down the hallway, gazing fondly at the tapestries that told the history of old Ireland and that of Fionn Mac Cool. My mother had woven them herself, painstakingly stitching in her fine hand, and I was comforted seeing them now after my absence, a reminder of my childhood and easier times.

The room Tierney had been put in was a cozy place off the back of the house, adjacent to a veranda where my mother grew her herbs. A fire burned in the hearth, and the light, calming, scent of the herbarium wafted in from next door. Tierney was covered in a comfortable patchwork quilt and I instantly regretted disturbing him, for he woke as soon as I opened the door.

"Sorry to wake you, Tir," I said apologetically, holding up the bowl. "But if you want to eat...?"

He smiled. "Your mother's stew, yes."

"It sure beats the canned junk and microwave macaroni and cheese we ate in Dublin," I replied with a grin.

"That is a certainty."

I perched on the edge of his bed, helping him sit up against several pillows as he ate the stew slowly.

"Eamon stopped by earlier," I told him, lowering my voice in case anyone was nearby. "He's gotten permission from the council to send out a formal search party for the missing patrol."

"From what you found this morning? That's great news, Ciran," Tierney said, and I could see the hope and longing in his eyes as great as my own. "When do we leave?"

"A week, if you're recovered by then," I replied. "Eamon says he's getting the lads together. It's only going to be a small patrol because they can't spare too many. But all those who lost someone are welcome to go."

Tierney nodded slowly then turned to look me seriously in the eye. "Ciran, how much chance do you really think we will have of finding them—all of them—alive?"

"From what I know of Lorcan he takes after his father in being a calculating enemy who takes everything into consideration. *I* think, and I think Eamon does too otherwise he wouldn't endorse the mission, that if Lorcan wanted them dead to prove a point he would have made sure we found out. He would have left them for us to see in plain sight. And on top of that, Oran is the crown prince until Eamon marries and produces an heir. He's a valuable hostage, and Lorcan won't get rid of him that easily, not to mention the fact that our men would hold information he would find valuable."

"They wouldn't talk," Tierney said quietly.

"No," I said just as quietly. "And that's why I think that if we are going to find them, we need to do so as soon as possible now that we have a lead. It's already been six months of waiting. It's not going to be pretty, and I think it will certainly be a miracle if they are all still there." I didn't want to think of that possibility. It was one thing doing a mission like this with a group of warriors who were not emotionally attached to the prisoners except in the normal way of comrades in arms, but it was another thinking that one or more members of the company could walk away without their loved one. Perhaps it would be me, or perhaps Tierney. Either would be equally hard, for his father had been like an uncle to me. And what if it were Oran? I was afraid that if Eamon lost his little brother like this, the last member of his family, the guilt would eat at him for the rest of his life. I reached out to grip Tierney's shoulder as an assurance against that possibility. "But as I said, I do think he would make sure we knew about any dead."

"Unless he wanted to keep it a secret so we wouldn't go looking for the prisoners before he has gotten the information he wants out of them," Tierney commented grimly. "Everyone breaks eventually, even Fianna warriors, and if they threatened Oran…"

"Hey," I gripped his other shoulder and shook him

slightly. "We are going to find your da, and Aeden and Prince Oran and all the others, and whether they are alive or dead, we will know what fate they met and we will bring them home and put Lorcan down once and for all. The Goblin reign will end, and we will bring Erin back to the beauty she had before."

He smiled slightly and knocked his fist against my shoulder. *"Beart de réir ár mbriathar,"* he said, quoting one of the mottos of Na Fianna: *action to match our speech.*

"That's right," I told him and took away the empty bowl he still held. "I don't know about you, but I'm exhausted. I think I'll turn in early tonight."

He nodded, settling back down into the soft bed. "Likewise, though I have little choice, I suppose."

"I'll have Finbar bring you some books in case you need something to keep you occupied in the middle of the night," I told him, knowing how horrible it was to stay sleepless from your thoughts with no distraction. "If you're really desperate tomorrow, I'll let you borrow my laptop to watch hours of TV shows and catch up on all we missed in Dublin."

He laughed. "Thanks, *deartháir.*"

I left him to rest and headed toward the stairs where I was accosted on the landing by my mother.

"Ciran," she said, putting a hand on my chest to stop me. "What did you say to your *athair*?"

"The usual disagreement," I told her, which didn't satisfy her one bit. She leaned against the stairwell, her arms folded, and I knew she wasn't going to let me go until I explained.

"You and Daegal know something the rest of us don't about Aeden, don't you?" she asked. "While you were gone, he was always taking the phone to his room to call you and using Finbar's computer when he wasn't around."

"You'll all know soon enough," I assured her. "I just didn't want to say anything about it before I was certain."

"And I suppose Eamon just wanted to tag along on Killian and Maeve's date, yes?" She raised a knowing eyebrow. I sighed. There was no getting out of it now.

"All right, Mum," I said. "Yes, Tierney and I found evidence of where Aeden's patrol made their last stand this morning. That's what I told Da when I got back. But he doesn't know this part, and I don't want him to know quite yet—no one is supposed to know yet anyway. The council has finally endorsed a rescue party. Eamon wants me to lead it."

She was silent, looking down at her feet and I stood awkwardly, waiting for her reaction. Finally she looked back up at me, biting her lip.

"Is there hope, Ciran?"

"There's always hope, *Máthair*," I told her gently, taking her hands into mine.

"Then you have *my* blessing, Ciran. And I dare say that when the time comes, you'll have your father's too."

Footsteps sounded in the hallway, and we looked up to see Caitlin, who had paused upon seeing us, but my mother smiled and she relaxed.

"I just wanted to tell you that Killian is back with Maeve and he's going to take me back to Tara Hall with him," she said and stepped forward to hug my mother, kissing her on the cheek. "Thank you so much for your hospitality, Lady Aoife."

"I hope you'll visit often now that you're back home, Caitlin," my mother said as Caitlin turned to me.

"Ciran," she said. "It was good hunting. I hope we might do it again sometime."

I wondered if I should give her a hug as well, but she held her hand out and we clasped forearms like warriors instead, an action that caused my mother to look like she was hiding a smile.

"I hope so too," I told her sincerely.

She thanked Mum again and went away. Free of my mother's interrogation, I hurried upstairs and took a hot shower, finally cleaning off three days' worth of grime, before heading to my room.

I breathed a sigh of contentment as I saw it. In Dublin, Tierney and I'd had to share a dorm room at the training hall and though I loved him like a brother, he was not a particularly tidy roommate. Although, I probably wasn't a model one myself, for they worked us so hard we usually fell into the tiny, hard cots at night, sometimes without even undressing, and our room sadly suffered for it—as did our personal hygiene. I had always thought that returning to one's own bed was the best part of coming home after a long absence.

My room was a mixture of modern and ancient like the rest of the castle, the walls were stone and I had one of my mother's tapestries of the Battle of Gavra hanging over my bed with my extra shield and the ceremonial sword my father had presented to me on my sixteenth birthday that I wore on special occasions. My ceremonial armor—a copper breastplate and green cloak—was worn by a headless mannequin in another corner of the room with the crossed flags of Erin and Na Fianna behind it. The first, a harp on a green background, and the second, the green arrow knot on white that was the same as our tattoos. The other corner held my desk and bookshelves above which was a wall of photos of my friends and family, and random bumper stickers I didn't want to put on the Vanquish but that caught my fancy. The picture that currently held place of honor in the frame on my desk was one of Aeden, Daegal and I from two years ago, crouched in the field out behind the forge and grinning as if we had just been up to the most glorious mischief.

It had always been Aeden, Daegal and I, just like it had always been Maeve, Finbar and Sean. It's not that we loved any of the others less, nor was it that way with the other three, it was just that the three of us had been cut from the same cloth. We were ones who, as Da liked to say, would carry on the blood of Fionn and become true Fianna warriors whereas Maeve and Finbar were quiet and calm like Mum. Maeve was already planning on taking up the healing craft, and Finbar would become the next smith in the family and act the levelheaded councilor to Eamon like our cousin Ceannt, for while Da still advised Eamon on occasion when he asked, he had left his position on the council when he had lost his hand. It was too early for Sean, who was only five, to decide what he was going to do, but he did have an almost unhealthy fondness for blades and he was best mates with Tierney's younger brother of the same age, Seamus, the two of them getting into all kinds of trouble together.

But it was indisputable that the three of us held a certain connection, stronger than we did with the others, and though Daegal was the only one who possessed the Second Sight, we all had a certain sixth sense when it came to one another — something that didn't quite work with Fin and Maeve — and it was that feeling that made me certain in my heart that I would know if Aeden was dead. I think I would feel a horrible emptiness as if I had lost something vital; something like what I had seen in my Da's face after he had lost his sword hand. No, I knew my big brother was still alive out there somewhere, and I was determined to bring him back home.

It turned out that I wasn't as tired as I had felt earlier. And I carefully polished my sword and hung it on its pegs next to my other on the wall and oiled my breastplate before setting it on the second dummy where it belonged. As soon as I nerved myself enough to get into bed, however, I groaned contentedly, and was much more kind toward the thought of sleeping. It felt like a cloud after the hard dorm beds I had been subjected to for the past three months when I hadn't been sleeping on a groundsheet or in a tent. I flicked my lamp off and buried my head in a pillow, falling asleep almost instantly.

I was woken sometime during the night when my warrior senses warned me there was another person in the room. My hand found the knife under my pillow instinctively, before I even opened my eyes but when I finally looked to the foot of my bed, I saw that it was only Daegal, illuminated in the moonlight coming through the window. I released the knife and sat up.

"What are you doing up?" I asked, though I knew well enough.

"I had a bad dream again," the lad said, shifting from one foot to the other on the cold floor. "And Sean is snoring."

I smiled and watched as Daegal didn't even ask my leave, but crawled under the bottom of my quilt, sliding up until he was under my left arm, a stuffed dragon he'd had for years between us. A cold nose poked me in the armpit, and I shifted to wrap an arm around the thin shoulders.

"What did you dream this time?" I asked.

He hugged the dragon tighter. "I've been dreaming of

Aeden the last few nights. He's chained in a dark place...hurt. It's almost as if my dreams have been leading me on a path to where he is. Now that you found the place they were taken, this seems to be what they show me."

"Was there anything else?" I asked him eagerly. "Anything that indicates where he might be?"

He shook his head. "Not yet. Hopefully, there might be something before you have to leave. I just know he's alive somewhere, Ciran, but Da doesn't want to believe that." He was silent a moment then looked up at me and asked suddenly, "Why doesn't he want him back?"

I combed my fingers soothingly through the tangled hair as I saw the hurt and misunderstanding in his eyes. "It's not that Da doesn't want him back, Dae, he's just afraid of false hope. He's lost so much already. And he does understand; he lost his own brother in the wars. He misses Aeden as much as we do, maybe even more, and that's why he doesn't want to believe that he might still be alive, because if he were wrong, it would be like losing him all over again." I thought of my father's face as I showed him the second pendant and a new wave of grief swept through me.

"It's almost been half a year now," Daegal said, and I could hear the breaking of his voice that told me he was trying not to cry. "I just miss him so much."

"It will be all right," I told him, leaning to kiss the messy hair. "I will not give him up, and I will not stop looking. If he is to be found, I will find him and bring him back safe."

A small arm wrapped around my waist as Daegal pressed his face into my neck. "I don't want you to go again," he pleaded. I held him tighter.

"Eamon is doing all he can to find the lost patrol and

he counts on me to help him do that since he can't leave his Hall. It's my duty as a Fianna warrior, and you will know that same duty one of these days. Besides that, it is also my duty as a brother to try and bring Aeden back if I can."

"I want to see him again," Daegal said. "I want it so much it hurts, but what if something happens to you on the mission and neither of you come back? I can't lose both of you, Ciran. No one else understands me like you two, not even Mum or Da though they try. I never really told them about any of my dreams because when I tried, Da just got angry. I wouldn't know what to do without you, Ciran." Tears slid down onto my shirt and I turned onto my side and gathered him against my chest, trying to soothe him as best I could.

"I won't ever leave you, Daegal. And no one, not even the Goblin King, can make me break that promise. We're brothers, and that means I will always, *always*, be there for you, no matter what." I was quoting something Aeden had told me when I was younger than Daegal and it made an ache start in my heart again. "Just like I know you'll do the same for me. But there are others who have lost brothers, and fathers and sons, and I have to help get them back too, because brothers in arms follow the same rules and we have to stick together and help each other."

He nodded against my chest, his hands clenched in my shirt. I rested my chin on the top of his head, realizing how much I had missed his presence when he sought me out in the middle of the night, and felt somewhat guilty for the fact that he had been without anyone to talk to when his dreams plagued him for the past several months, for I knew he wouldn't have confided in Maeve or Finbar. I pushed him back slightly and looked down at him.

"I'm hungry, how about you? Why don't we raid the

kitchen and watch a movie?"

He smiled, wiping his eyes on his dragon. "Okay."

We snuck downstairs and grabbed our provisions—ice cream, cola, and cheese balls—and returned to my room to sit on my bed and watch a movie on my laptop. As I had predicted, Daegal fell asleep against my side, holding the bag of cheese balls and I set them aside before tucking him into bed, and joined him soon after, being rather exhausted myself.

Chapter Five
Thoughts and Plans

I woke up next morning to sunlight streaming onto my face. It took me a moment to remember where I was, but then I realized I had finally made it home and smiled as I sat up and stretched, shaking my unruly hair out of my eyes. Daegal was still sleeping soundly, curled up in a nest of pillows and blankets, and I left him undisturbed as I dug into my closet and found an old pair of jeans and a t-shirt to wear before I left to go see Tierney and grab some breakfast.

I smelled coffee and something with cinnamon as I walked down the stairs and was planning on getting something for Tierney as well when I was stopped by the sight of the High King standing in the kitchen with a cup of coffee in his hands and my father standing in front of him with his arms crossed over his broad chest, glowering, though whether at Eamon or something he had said, I wasn't sure.

"*Do Maórgacht*," I said respectfully, bowing my head, for even if Eamon didn't particularly care for propriety, I knew my father did.

Eamon turned to me with a look that said *there is hardly a need for* that *when I'm standing in your kitchen holding a flowered coffee mug* — at least that's what I thought he would likely say in that situation had my father not been present. I was hard-pressed to keep the grin off my face.

"Ciran, good of you to join us," Eamon said, setting his mug on the counter. "I was just telling your father the news."

"Ah," I said, not sure what else to say, and indeed, a bit quelled by my father's glower which he had now turned upon me. I busied myself getting a cup of coffee and an apple muffin fresh from the oven.

"Ciran," my father said. "You didn't tell me this last night."

"I told him not to say anything, Niall," Eamon cut in to my defense. "I wasn't quite sure of all the details, but now I have worked it all up and have sent out the word to all applicable parties. It looks like you'll be leaving within a week or so, Ciran. Tierney should be well enough to travel by then, and Riordan and Keevan Crimnal, who will be joining you on behalf of their brother, are currently finishing a scout mission to the south where there was a bit of a mess with some hobgoblins. I've told them all to meet here when they can, if that is all right with you, Niall?"

"It seems I have little choice in the matter, *Airdrígh*," my father said, a bitter note in his voice.

Eamon looked at him with an expression that was apologetic. "I mean you no disrespect by this, Niall. You were a good friend to my father and have been both that and mentor to me. I feel I endorse this mission in the best interests of the country. The capture of the patrol was a huge blow to our people, and we cannot let Lorcan think he has beaten us. We must show him that such actions are not to be tolerated, and that we will not stand for their taking our family without giving them a fight. If we allow him this victory, he will think we are incapable of holding our own." He sighed deeply and then lowered his voice into a serious, weary undertone. "I want my brother back, and I will not rest until I know whether he can or cannot be recovered. I know you wish the same of your son."

If it had been me, my father would have likely flown into another tirade like last night, and even then I could see him trying to gain control of his temper, but he forced it aside and nodded. "You know that's true; but false hope is oftimes a very dangerous thing. I shouldn't need to tell you that there will be much pain if they return empty-handed."

"I know," Eamon said softly and I could see the pain in his eyes as he pulled a leather pouch from under his breastplate and pulled out Oran's braid that I had given him the day before. "Ciran found this yesterday, did you know? It is not proof of life, but it is proof enough not to give up. Oran is only sixteen; that was his first real patrol and he was so proud that morning, and I was so proud of him and never once did we think it might be the last we would ever see of each other. There is nothing in the world I wouldn't give to see him again. I would give my kingdom gladly if I were allowed."

"That is fool's speak, Eamon," my father said sharply, making me wince. "You said you value me as an advisor and mentor, so please listen to me this time: This is folly, and it will come to nothing. And I will not risk my next eldest son to a forlorn hope."

"*Athair*," I protested, my anger flaring up. "This is my decision, and I have already given Eamon my word that I would lead the company in his name."

"Ciran, we will speak of this later, but you already know my thoughts on the matter," my father growled.

"Ciran must go, Da." We turned to see Daegal standing in the doorway, still in his pajamas. "Aeden is alive. I know it. I saw him in my dream…"

"Daegal, this is not a conversation for you, go help your *máthair*," my father snapped.

"I know you don't believe me, *Athair*," Daegal said meekly. "Or don't want to, but we can't leave Aeden to his d-death if there is still a chance of saving him."

Da looked at him with cold eyes for a long moment, and all the while Daegal held his own, respectful, but not backing down. Finally my father sighed and turned back to me. "Fine, Ciran, you will go anyway, whatever I say, but I may as well give you my blessing. You are a man now, after all, and a full fledged Fianna warrior." The way he said it sounded more like he was cursing me, which he probably was mentally. He turned to Eamon. "And, yes, they may meet here. Now if you'll excuse me, I have work to do." He bowed before he turned around and left the room.

Eamon sighed and looked at me with a tired smile. "And I thought the council was hard to win over."

"If my father was still on the council, he would approve of the mission just to spite them," I said with a small smile as Daegal came to hover at my side. I turned to Eamon. "Have you told Lady Brenna about Tierney?"

Eamon grinned as if I had said something funny. "Your mother beat me to it, she called early this morning and the Lady Mac Morna and family are all crammed into Tierney's room as we speak, fussing over him. You should go rescue your poor sword brother before they coddle him to death." He looked at his watch with a sigh. "I really need to get back to the Hall. Training today and garrison inspection which we ended up not having time for yesterday what with the council taking forever. Killian will be eating nails if I don't show up in time. He's been working since dawn to shine the troops." We clasped forearms. "You should be bloody glad the Mac Cools are not of the royal line, Ciran. I would much rather be a warrior and only have to deal with hunting Goblins than making inspections on the guard and trying to pay attention during council meetings. It's even worse when Killian is texting me under the table, commentating sarcastically on all the members and discussions. It's like being back in school half the time."

I laughed, imagining it as I finished eating my muffin. "Well, I suppose it would be entertaining at least. I should go rescue Tir, though. Daegal, why don't you go and get your armor on and I'll train with you today?" He grinned and sped off with his half-eaten muffin in one hand. Eamon caught me by the shoulder before I could leave, lowering his voice.

"He said he dreamed of Aeden, did he dream of any others?"

"His dreams are more a suggestion of events, rather than actual visions of the future," I told him quietly. "Sometimes they're entirely symbolic. He hasn't seen anyone else, but that doesn't mean there are no other survivors, Eamon. Aeden is who is on his mind most, not to mention the blood tie, so it would only make sense."

"Of course," Eamon said dismissively. "But he was alive?"

"I would know if he were dead, Eamon," I told him earnestly. "I would know. And Daegal would know, and I believe my father would too, but he fears what will happen if he is wrong. I don't think he can allow himself to lose Aeden again, and that is why he closes him off."

Eamon nodded. "I understand his pain. I swore to my father that I would protect Oran."

"Losing Aeden was hard enough," I said. "I can't imagine if it had been Daegal."

Eamon shook his head and forced a smile back on his lips. "Well, we shouldn't speak more of it. The others should be arriving within a few days and as I said, I need to go. Thank your mother for the coffee. I'm going to steal another muffin to eat during inspection." He winked.

I laughed. "I think you just enjoy trying to see how much of a rebel you can be."

"I couldn't claim to be Irish if I didn't," Eamon replied with a grin and strode out after gulping the last of the coffee.

I went down the hall to where I could hear the gathered female voices. I pushed the door open all the way and leaned back against the doorjamb to watch the scene, unable to help a smile.

Tierney was propped up on the bed looking none-too-happy about the invasion. Three girls, one nineteen, one twelve and the other seven, crowded around him, squeezing his hand and stroking his hair, while his mother was trying to feed him something from a bowl that looked like oatmeal with too much sugar on it — I knew Tierney liked his best with just butter, but then, we had lived off instant oatmeal and microwaved toaster tarts for three months as far as breakfast went, and vowed never to touch either again. His little brother, Seamus, was jumping on the end of the bed with Sean, and my mother kept trying to haul them down only to have them spring up again. The funniest part of it was that in any other circumstance, this would have made a pretty scene—despite the rambunctious lads—and Tierney likely wouldn't have protested the care of three pretty young ladies—if they hadn't been his sisters.

He happened to look up through the forest of females and caught sight of me. "Ciran!" he practically shouted and held out a hand to me as if grasping for a lifeline while drowning in a sea of harpies.

I strode over casually, catching Seamus who leapt off the bed into my arms with a laugh as Sean tackled me from behind. I clasped forearms with Tierney and bent over the bed, Seamus tucked firmly against my hip as Sean strangled me from behind.

"Morning *mo chara*, how are you feeling?" I asked cheerily, bouncing a giggling Seamus in my lap.

"Oh, much better," he said just as cheerily before yanking me down to hiss in my ear, "*Help me!*"

"Ladies," I said to the sisters. "Why don't you visit the rookeries and the stables and leave your dear brother to the care of his mother for a while. And you two rascals," I added to the boys who still clung to me as they shrieked in excited terror at my mock seriousness. "You're coming to the training field with Daegal and me. We'll see what you can stand."

My mother and Tierney both cast me a *thank you* glance at the same time, nearly causing me to break into a snort of laughter as I ushered the boys and the two youngest girls Aednet and Cara—Meaghan was favored enough to stay—outside where Daegal met me with his training sword, dressed in his leather breastplate.

"Take the boys to get some swords, Daegal, you girls can go to the stables and if you want, you can pick your brother some flowers from the garden out back."

"Thank you, Ciran!" they cried as they hurried off.

"I'll be right back," I said to Daegal.

I ran to get my leather breastplate and training sword, but on my way down the stairs I nearly barreled into Finbar who scattered a stack of books he was carrying.

"I'm sorry, Fin, let me help," I told him, crouching to gather up his books. "I thought you'd be out working with Da."

He furrowed his brow. "I was but he sent me away. What did you tell Da last night that got him so angry he won't even let me help him in the forge today?" Finbar said in an accusatory voice as he stacked his books again and cradled them in his arms. "This isn't about Aeden, is it?"

I felt a stab of anger flare up inside me. "And if it is, you have no right to accuse me of anything. I know you want Aeden back as much as the rest of us."

"Of course!" Finbar said angrily. "But every time you mention it, Da gets so angry. We won't forget Aeden, Cir, but isn't it time to let him go? It's been almost six months since the patrol disappeared, and there's so little chance of him still being alive. Can't you just let us remember him as we should? You wouldn't even allow us a wake; that was never your call, Ciran, but you were so adamant, you and Daegal, that Mum and Da had to comply."

"He wasn't dead then, and nor is he now," I told him, my voice wavering with suppressed anger. "And I know Da doesn't think so either. I don't want to hurt him, Fin, but I can't lie to him either."

"It might be fine for you when you leave for months on end, but the rest of us have to stay here, and live with the ghosts every day. And while no one mentions it, I work with Da day in, day out, and I see it in his eyes, and in the loss of his hand, and I can't help but miss who he was before all this. And every time you come home, you somehow manage to bring it up and open the wounds all over again and then you leave before you can help pick up the pieces."

I stared at him in shock. I had never heard my normally quiet little brother speak to anyone like that before. "Fin, I never meant anything by it. Would you have me lie to Da?"

"Is lying so bad when the truth hurts so much?" There were tears in the corners of his eyes. "If you really want to help, let it go, Ciran. Let him go."

"It's too late for that now," I said, trying not to let my temper show through, but not managing it.

"Then don't labor under the delusion that everything is going to turn out for the better because of it!" Finbar said, snatching the last book from me and turning to run up the stairs, choking on a sob.

"Fin!" I cried, but he had already reached the top landing and his door slammed. I sighed, running a hand through my already messy hair. I'd have to reconcile it later when he had calmed down. As I went on my way back outside, I felt ashamed that I had never really thought about how much it had affected Finbar. He was always so quiet and kept to himself and I had been more worried about Da and trying to help Daegal figure out the meaning of his dreams and tracking the patrol and where they might have ended up if still alive. It hurt me to think that Finbar thought that about me as if I just wanted to make people hurt. I didn't, I just wanted my brother back, and I wanted people to believe that he was still alive as I did. I knew forgetting would never repair what we had lost; only Aeden could do that, or at least closure as to what had happened to him. And now I was more determined than ever to get him back home safely, or at least find some end to the matter — I just hoped it wouldn't be a grim one.

That night after supper, I went to the library that resided on the quiet end of the house across Mum's herbarium and the guest room Tierney was staying in. It was dark in a cozy way, and warmer due to the tapestries and the two fireplaces set in the room, accompanied by the comforting scent of old books and leather. My father always retired to that quiet sanctuary in the evening, and I knew I would be able to find him there.

I really didn't want to bring up the topic of Aeden again with him, but I felt I needed to talk to him about it as he was so obviously adamant about me not going and I didn't quite understand why. I needed to know; otherwise I wouldn't be able to fully immerse myself into the mission.

I opened the large door and breathed deeply the smell of old books, slightly tinted with wood smoke from the fires. It was a beautiful library, with a high ceiling and two stories of bookshelves, with a spiral staircase in one corner, leading up to the upper story. There was a reading corner with several sinfully comfortable leather chairs and a sheepskin rug and another place with a desk for studying. My father sat in one chair pulled up to the fire, his feet stretched out toward the flames, slumped in deep thought, the glow making his hair look even more fiery than usual.

"Da?" I asked as I closed the door behind me and strode over to him.

He turned as he heard me and stood up. "Ciran, did you need something?"

"I just wanted to talk, Da," I said hesitantly, not really sure where to start. "I can't do my duty with good conscience until you tell me why you don't want us to pursue this quest."

My father sighed deeply, closing his eyes. "Ciran…"

"Please hear me out," I pleaded, stepping closer to him. "Da, I understand that you might not want to raise false hope, but if we never know what really happened to them, no matter if they are alive or dead, will you ever forgive yourself that?"

"I do not want to have this conversation right now," he growled and turned around to lean against the mantle, looking into the flames. I carried on doggedly.

"Then when are we going to have it? Because no matter what, I am leaving with the others when the time comes. I'm, by rights, acting Commander of Na Fianna now. And it's *my duty* to lead the company. I would simply prefer to leave with an answer to my questions so I can have a clean conscience."

"I wish you would not, Ciran," my father said quietly, shaking his head. "Let's please have an end of this. I wish you would just stay here."

"No, *Athair*," I said firmly, seeing his shoulders stiffen. "I will not stay here. I will do my duty, and I will get your eldest son back."

He spun around suddenly, his hair seeming to be on fire with his anger. "I will not allow you to throw your life away to a forlorn hope!" he growled, his voice low, dangerous, an indication that he was really angry.

I stood my ground firmly, my fists clenching and unclenching in contained rage. "A year ago, you might have been able to stop me, but I am a Fianna warrior now, no longer a trainee, and I serve my king and must obey him even before you, *Athair*."

"If I believed that was all that drove you, I would not be so angry, Ciran." He shook his head. "You would go after your brother if the whole world was against you, Eamon included, so don't give me that bloody nonsense about king and country."

"And is that such a bad thing?" I cried, throwing caution to the winds. "Since when is loving your family a crime? Tell me your problem, Da, because I honestly don't know why you are so adamant about us not going after the patrol. I used to think it was your fear of false hope, but this must go beyond that. Daegal thinks you don't want Aeden back at all; do you want him to continue with those thoughts? I'm almost starting to think it myself now."

"You can't understand," Da said quietly.

"You should know how I feel, you lost a brother too."

He stiffened and I instantly saw the pain write itself over his face anew and began to feel horrible for bringing up the subject of my uncle, whose loss I knew affected my father greatly. "You will not understand until you have children of your own," was all Da said, inciting my anger even more, erasing any regret I had felt before.

"Oh, so having children makes you want to leave them to a painful death by torture?" I cried.

"Ciran Mac Cool, I am your father and you will show me respect." I thought for a moment that he would strike me, but he had never done so before, and it seemed he would not start now—although I knew if I was still a lad he would have had his belt to my backside for my insolence.

"I'm sorry, *Athair*," I said coldly. "Forgive me if I don't understand."

"Just go," he said tiredly, turning around to lean against the mantle again. "Let us speak no more of this." I turned and left, trying to cool my anger. I passed Tierney on my way up to my room and he looked at me inquiringly.

"Cir? Are you all right?"

I held up a hand to stop him. "Just…I want to be alone right now."

He let me go.

I lay in bed a long time that night, unable to sleep and pained at both the disrespect I had shown my father and his refusal to tell me what was wrong. I didn't know what to do, but I was certain that no matter what, I would be out looking for Aeden by the end of the week.

I tried to keep all topics off Aeden for the next few days but for when I spoke with Daegal or Tierney. The problem was that while we all seemed to pretend it wasn't a topic for discussion, everyone knew about the mission I would be going on at the end of the week and everyone was thinking about it. Da and I spoke hardly at all after the fight, and I grieved over that uncertainty still, though I would have done so even more if I had not been so caught up in everything else that was going on.

I was busy planning for the mission, wondering who exactly would join us, and also trying to get Tierney on his feet again. Na Fianna are very quick healers, thanks to our Fae blood, and by the third day he was out of bed, and by the fourth we were out doing 'gentle' exercises with our swords while Sean and Seamus—who had come with Tierney's mother to visit—were also practicing in our side yard.

Tierney and I finished a bout in a draw and laughed, performing a chest bump, which made him wince slightly but laugh even harder.

The two little boys decided to try it too, and gave a wild yell as they went for the chest bump, but only succeeded in knocking their heads together before landing flat on their backs.

Tierney and I laughed even harder as we went to help them up while they rubbed their foreheads, but Tierney turned at the sound of a car revving up the driveway, announcing an arrival that could only belong to a member of Na Fianna.

"Looks like one of the others is here early, Cir."

I turned to look as the red F-type Jaguar cabriolet spun into the driveway in fine style. "Looks like trouble," I said as I braced myself to meet our first companion.

Chapter Six
The Company

Tierney and I strode over to the new arrival, who swung out of his car with feline grace, and pulled a compact recurve bow and a quiver of gold-fletched arrows with him. He turned around, shutting the car door with his foot and delivering his most charming grin as he swept away his hatefully ruggedly-stylish hair from his eyes.

"Morning, brothers," he said cheerily.

"Deaglan," I said, offering my hand and clasping his forearm tighter than was probably courteous. For some reason it had slipped my mind that his father had been taken on the patrol too and it only made sense that he would wish to go with us on our mission. I couldn't begrudge him that, but we had never been friends, mostly because he was several years older so he hadn't trained with us, but also, shamefully, I will admit, for no other reason than the enmity between our ancestors. The thought of him staying in my house for three days wasn't entirely appealing.

"Can we help you with your things?" Tierney asked,

also overly polite. Since *his* family had always been loyal to mine, they might have hated the sons of Dairmuid even more than the Mac Cools did.

"I could use some help if it's no trouble," he said, looking cautiously between us, though he tried to keep the smile on his face. I felt a little bit sorry for him and knew we were being mean, but couldn't seem to help it. I vowed to try to be nice, however, because, after all, he was pretty much walking into enemy territory, and entering my house, especially with my father in the mood he was in, was quite possibly more dangerous than our mission would prove to be.

We grabbed two duffle bags from the trunk of his car and headed toward the front door. I almost smirked as I saw my father standing there, arms crossed, glowering at our guest. Deaglan tensed visibly, but then strode forward and knelt in front of my father, placing his bow on the ground in subjection. *"Mo thighearna Mac Cool, iarraim cead isteach i do theach. Thiocfaidh mé cosúil le cara agus leithscéal a ghabháil ar mhaithe le mo shinsir agus na héagóracha a dhéantar san am atá caite."*

His humble attitude surprised me and I shared a glance with Tierney before I turned back to see my father's reaction. He actually looked impressed, though only showed it mildly, and motioned for Deaglan to stand up.

"I grant you admittance to my home *i cairdeas*, Mac Dairmuid," my father said, sounding like a king himself.

Deaglan stood and bowed slightly before making his way in. My father's hand caught in the lapel of his jacket. "But if you look at my daughter…"

"I wouldn't dare, my lord," Deaglan said with not a hint of humor in his voice. "I'd have both you and Killian on me then. With all respect, I don't want that kind of trouble."

My father seemed satisfied with that, and let him go, casting me a slightly withering glance as Tierney and I followed with his things.

"Deaglan Mac Dairmuid," my mother greeted him kindly as she came out of her weaving room, her hair sticking to her brow from the steam and her hands purple from some new wool she was dying. She was always kind to everyone, even our family enemies, but then she was only married into the Mac Cool family and felt no lasting resentment through blood.

"Lady Aoife," Deaglan said and kissed her hand like a knight of old; I found myself rolling my eyes, glad Da wasn't there. "It's good to see you again."

"You too, dear," she said. "I'll show you to your room and then you can come and have some coffee and muffins."

Tierney and I followed with the bags, feeling like servants, but I did notice my mother put him in the drafty room on the corner that used to be Maeve's before she complained too much about the cold. Deaglan thanked her and us for carrying the bags and leaned his bow against the footboard of the bed and hung his quiver on the post before taking off his jacket, revealing a far too classy collared shirt and waistcoat beneath. He caught my scrutiny and smiled with a somewhat remorseful expression.

"I'm not here to make enemies with you, Ciran. I promise. In fact, I would really like to be friends. I think feuds are silly. We're both on the same side, we both serve Eamon, and we're going to be spending who knows how many weeks out in the hills together. I've lost my father, and you've lost your brother, and everyone else has lost someone as well, and we're all in it together, so let's kiss and make up and not have any bad blood between us, eh?"

"Forgo the kissing, and I'll accept," I said, unable to keep a smirk from my lips as I held out my hand. I appreciated his getting to the point if nothing else.

"Alright then!" Deaglan laughed heartily and grasped my wrist with a simultaneous back slap. I knew it would take me a while to really warm up to him, but I also felt it could be done, and was somewhat ashamed for not being the bigger man and suggesting the truce first.

"I'm still keeping an eye on you," Tierney said firmly. "But it would be cruel to begrudge you Lady Mac Cool's apple muff-ins, so you had best get some before the boys come back in and eat them all."

"I would like that," Deaglan said. "Then perhaps we can all go out and train a bit?"

"Challenge accepted," I said, interested to see what our comrade was capable of.

We spent a good part of the afternoon training and I had to admit that I was rather impressed with Deaglan's prowess with a bow, and began to think of how useful it might be to have a sufficient archer in our company. I guessed that he could probably shoot as well if not better, than most of the best Goblin archers, and he also had twin dirks that were balanced for throwing but could also be used in close combat. He demonstrated how he could fight against a sword with them, and blocked even the most brutal blows we hammered onto him—and we weren't being nice—by crossing the blades, and still managed to tap our breastplates on occasion, slipping past our guard.

"So what's the deal?" Tierney asked. "Are archers truthfully what's in with the ladies right now? Are swords too old fashioned?"

"I think it's more the way you use the weapon you

have," he said with a wink, sticking the toe of his boot under the blade of one of his knives on the ground and flicking it up into his hand.

"Well, if you think style is everything," I said, unimpressed.

Supper that night was interesting, for Deaglan was trying to keep up a cheery conversation with everyone, all under the foreboding glare of my father sitting at the head of the table. My mother, with her usual tact, kept the conversation going and somehow managed to calm the entire family and eventually we all joined in and worked a little more toward making Deaglan feel welcome. Within reason, anyway, for I had a feeling he wouldn't think much of our hospitality after spending a night in the drafty room. He should be thankful it wasn't the middle of winter when no amount of heating could possibly make the castle warmer.

The next afternoon, we met the rest of the planned company. We were out training again, and Tierney and I were boxing while Deaglan was showing Daegal how to shoot a bow, when a loud mechanical thrum was heard coming up the road and I looked over, barely catching Tierney's fist on my forearm, to see first Eamon's Morgan coming up the drive, and behind that a copper colored racing bike followed by an incredibly old and square Volvo in an unattractive green color.

We left off our sparring to go meet the new arrivals and I caught Eamon just as he was getting out of his car. Killian, as well as Caitlin, I saw with surprise and a little pleasure, were with him.

"Ciran, I brought the rest of your company," Eamon said, motioning to the two others.

I watched as the one swung off his motorcycle and

took off his helmet, revealing messily spiked red hair that must have had enough gel to stay in its carefully crafted unkemptness even under the helmet. He cast a mocking glance back at the Volvo that was still pulling into the drive, and grabbed a battle axe and round shield from the back of his bike, striding over to us.

"Ciran Mac Cool," he said in greeting, clasping forearms with a smack of leather bracers. This was Keevan Crimnal. I knew him in passing from Dublin, for he had been at the training academy at the same time as Tierney and I, but was a couple years younger than us, even though he was already a full-fledged Finar. We had never really hung out, as he wasn't exactly the type of person I usually spent time with, being something of a troublemaker and rebel; but I didn't think he was a particularly bad sort either. There's nothing wrong with always being up for a good lark, after all.

He turned now as the Volvo came to a stop and the door opened. "Riordan, park the bloody granny car already and come and greet our hosts!"

The second man was the exact opposite of Keevan. He was older, twenty-three or so, broad and tall, while Keevan was shorter and formed lithe and sharp like a blade. Riordan sported rusty brown hair and a short beard, while Keevan was bright red, and the younger's black leather ensemble rivaled Riordan's tired jeans and fisherman's jumper. I had never met Riordan, but we all knew about him. He was the only known Irishman at the time to be officially a berserker, in fact, he had gone to Norway right after his training in Na Fianna to learn the art from the berserkers there and he had to carry a license and everything. I was somewhat nervous with the thought of being around him as I didn't know a whole lot about what might set him off, but I figured he knew well enough how to handle himself.

Riordan smiled at me as he offered his hand. "It's good to meet you, Ciran. I'd like to thank you for your diligence in looking for the patrol. Without you, Eamon might never have let us go on this mission."

"Not true," Killian cut in. "The *council* never would have let you go on the mission." He walked over to me and drew me to one side. "Which brings me to another thing, Ciran. Everyone on the mission is representing a lost family member, apart from Eamon who can't go, though you have also promised to represent him as your position as acting commander dictates. *I* cannot go for my brother's sake, as I've got to keep this lummox in line, so I have one question for you: Will it throw you off to have a woman in your company?"

I instantly cast my eyes back at Caitlin who was talking with Keevan and Riordan while Deaglan watched her approvingly. I turned back to Killian who nodded in confirmation at my questioning glance.

"No, I wouldn't mind at all," I replied and watched him give me a glance that I knew all too well as a protective brother look, so hurried on, not wanting him to get the wrong idea. "I found her extremely capable and level-headed under pressure on the mission the other day, and I would be glad to have her."

"You give me your word that you will keep an eye on her and not let anything untoward happen?" Killian asked firmly. "I think I can trust you, and I might be able to trust Tierney, but Deaglan might be a problem. The sons of Dairmuid can't seem to help themselves."

"Oh don't worry, Killie, I know how to handle *those* types." We turned to see Caitlin standing to one side, grinning. She was dressed in a green tunic dress and leggings tonight and I noticed for the first time that her eyes were a bright emerald color. She turned to me. "Well, Ciran Mac Cool, will you have me in your company?"

"I think Flagan should have someone to greet him when we rescue them," I told her, holding out a hand. "I will gladly take you into my company." We clasped arms and I went back over to the others to invite them inside.

"Grab your things, lads; my mother will get you all settled, and I assume you'll all be staying for supper. Eamon?"

"Tonight, yes," he replied with a grin. "I will not miss my warriors' going away feast."

We trooped inside and my mother was there to greet the new arrivals almost instantly, greeting Eamon respectfully first before she turned to Keevan and Riordan.

"It's been a long time since I've seen any of you boys," she said with a smile. "Your mother and I were good friends—we learned the healing art together. You were just wee lads the last time I saw you, and Keevan no more than a bairn. You must let me know if there's anything you need. Ciran, help them bring their things up to their rooms."

"Well, I am perfectly happy with whatever accommodations you offer, even the couch," Keevan said as he punched Riordan in the shoulder. "But my brother on the other hand, is very particular about his schedule. He must have his herbal tea at no later than six a.m. after which he does his ridiculous yoga routine and then drinks more tea with breakfast—won't touch coffee, not even decaf—and he'll also need some quiet corner where he can imbibe in his knitting habit."

"Despite what my brother wants you to think, I assure

you, I'm not that difficult, Lady Mac Cool," Riordan said with a jab at his brother's side, which only caused Keevan to yank his braid. I flinched, wondering if that was the kind of thing one should do to a berserker, but realized they seemed very practiced in their teasing.

My mother was trying not to laugh. "Well, there's plenty of herbal tea in the kitchen that you may have any time you want, Riordan, and you may levy upon the yarn in my weaving room before you leave if you wish. Tierney's family owns sheep and they keep us supplied in more wool than we can use."

"Thank you," Riordan said with a smile as we made it upstairs and put them into the two rooms across from my own. Keevan dumped his things unceremoniously onto the sheepskin rug and pulled off his jacket, which joined the rest. He turned to me with a grin.

"If you hear me shout in the middle of the night, get out as if the banshee were chasing you, because it means the beast has awakened."

"Don't listen to him, Ciran," Riordan said with a sigh, as he came into the room and grabbed Keevan in a headlock as his younger brother tried to escape past me, and ground his knuckles into the spiked red hair, making Keevan shout in protest, trying to wriggle loose. "My brother likes to talk big, but very little of what he says is the truth."

"Easy for you to say, Granny Riordan," Keevan grunted and kicked his brother's backside as he released him. They headed back downstairs and I realized Tierney was standing at my shoulder, scrutinizing the scene.

"Well, this is certainly going to be an interesting trip," he said. "A berserker, a troublemaker, a warrior maid, and a chronic flirter and then the two of us who might possibly be halfway normal. I'll honestly be surprised if we actually manage to find the Goblin palace before we end up doing each other in."

"Well, I figure that if we survive supper tonight, then we should be off to a good start by morning," I said, clapping him on the shoulder reassuringly. "Now, how about that feast?"

Chapter Seven
A Common Goal

The feast was nothing less than a banquet of medieval proportions. My mother and Maeve had outdone themselves in a way I will admit I wasn't entirely sure was possible until I saw all the food set out on the long table in the formal dining hall where we held special dinners with guests. Eamon declined my father's position at the head of the table and instead settled at his right hand. I sat next to him across from Killian and found Tierney on my other side and Caitlin across from him. I smiled at her as we sat down, but soon turned my attention to my father who had rapped the table sharply to get everyone's attention. We all quieted, even Keevan who had been chattering non-stop since he got there and had already managed to stuff half a roll into his face before his backside had even met the chair.

My father stood and we all watched in respectful silence as he cast his eyes over the company at the table.

"*Laochra,*" he said in the simple, ancient respectful address, and I suddenly felt a swell of pride that my peers and I could be addressed as such. "Tonight is a feast not of celebration but of beginnings. This night will mark the beginning of your quest. May your journey be easy, may the light of the sun and the moon guide you. May the land shelter you and the rain wet your lips. May your road be easy to find, may you never lose your way. May the loyalty and the trust of your comrades keep you strong so you do not fear the dangers on the road ahead. May you go peacefully knowing you do your best for king, for Erin and for the blood ties that bind us all." He raised his cup and drank deeply and we all did the same, solemnly, reverently, the old warriors' blessing echoing in my mind and filling my heart with ache and gladness at the same time.

My father drained his cup and sat slowly, not making eye contact with anyone. "*Airdrígh*, would you like to say a word?"

"I would," Eamon said, and stood at the same moment I saw Keevan pull his hand back from a platter again, empty, as he waited for Eamon to finish his own words so he could eat.

"Lord Mac Cool has already given you the journey's blessing," Eamon said. "But I would like to speak to you a bit myself on the matter at hand. It is hard to form a company of a group of people who have not known each other very well. Normally, I would think this a hindrance, but you all share a common goal, and it is one that I know you will not compromise by letting personal feelings get in the way." I refrained from casting a glance at Deaglan when he said that, but only just and felt guilty because of it. "It is a brave thing you do. We all know what happened to our loved ones when they were caught in the wrong place at the wrong time. It could happen to any of us, and by going on this mission, you show enormous courage. I am a great believer in courage, and you all know I will not demean you because you are young. I believe you will succeed, and I know that if our loved ones are there to find, you will bring them back to us. Ciran."

I looked up as he spoke my name and he looked down at me, putting a hand on my shoulder. "This is your leader, my friends. And a braver young man I would be hard pressed to find. Do you all trust him to get you through this quest alive?"

I felt a swell of elation and embarrassed pride at the resounding "ayes" that were given around the table without hesitation. Eamon smiled at me and nodded to the others.

"Very well then. If there are no concerns, I think it is time we eat!"

That brought even more hearty cheers, and as soon as Eamon sat back down everyone launched forward to fill their plates from the copious platters on the table. There were three kinds of meat — beef, ham and mutton — and potatoes of all kinds, cabbage, vegetables, five kinds of bread, and countless cheeses. It was simple fair, but delicious as usual, and everyone ate with gusto. There was wine in the cups to begin with but afterward we only drank ginger beer for we could not afford to be groggy the next morning. I took a moment to assess my company as I ate, and they did not notice I was doing so. Caitlin, I knew I could trust to do what had to be done and follow orders. She had won my instant approval the day we had been attacked by that Goblin patrol. I wasn't quite so sure what to think about Keevan, Riordan and even Deaglan, however. My main concern with Deaglan was that I would have to fight my initial bias of him, but I knew that when I got past that, I would be able to trust him a lot better, and might possibly even be able to consider him a real friend. I certainly didn't underestimate his skills as a fighter, in any case.

Riordan honestly made me nervous. I didn't know how to act around berserkers, and I didn't want to come off as too cautious and polite, because, well, that never seemed to go over well and might just tick him off enough to go berserk. But I also didn't know what actually *would* set him off, so being at least a little cautious seemed to be perfectly reasonable. He was also older than me by some five years, so even if I was the leader of the company, I knew I would have to trust his judgment and self control. Keevan on the other hand worried me the most. He was a bit younger than Tierney and I at sixteen, and I wasn't usually one to judge on age, but he seemed rash, and somewhat flighty and I didn't know him well enough to look past that. I couldn't really hazard a true analysis until I had known him for longer than a few hours. You can only really find out about what makes people tick when you have been camping with them in the freezing rain for weeks. That was when you really got to know people on a very personal level and find out things about their character you probably never wanted to.

I was brought out of my thoughts as Maeve laughed loudly at something Killian had said and I smiled across the table at them before I heard Eamon speak on my left.

"Well, what do you think?" he asked quietly, so only I would hear him. "Is it a good company?"

I smiled. "It's too early to tell how we'll work together, but as you said; a common goal can do a lot to instigate camaraderie."

"You might have a few rocky spots to start off," Eamon said. "Everyone does, after all, and you're all very different and only you and Tierney and then Keevan and Riordan know each other really well. But I believe if anyone can get this rag tag group together it's you. You may not realize it, Ciran, but you have your father's presence, and ability to lead. I think he must have been a lot like you when he was your age."

I smiled at that, but found it hard to think of my father young and…well, like me at all. "I think you could persuade them if you had to."

Eamon chuckled. "Perhaps. But not without my esteemed *Captaen an Garda.*"

Killian looked up with his face stuffed as he heard himself mentioned and narrowed his eyes at Eamon before shaking his head and swallowing. "Well, it's good to know I'm still needed sometimes. I begin to wonder when you keep running off and making plans behind my back and all."

"It's not my fault you're so sensitive," Eamon quipped and Killian sighed, shaking his head as he appealed to Maeve who was smiling at the two.

"See what I have to put up with all the time? Bloody thankless job, if you ask me."

Supper went on merrily, with much laughter, though my father was still silent and I again promised myself that I would talk to him that night after the festivities and make my peace. He had given the company his blessing as was his place, but that was not enough for me. I wanted his personal blessing, father to son, and I knew I could not go on the quest with any real conviction without it.

Once everyone had eaten their fill, we retired to the large sitting room, which had been a solar in the old days for the ladies to visit and do their embroidering in. Now it was set with comfy sofas and a lit fireplace and everyone piled onto the sofas or the sheepskin rugs among the wolfhounds who sprawled around on the floor. I lounged against the side of one of the couches Daegal propped against me, and Oisin laying across my lap, the dog's tail swishing lazily across the floor as I fondled his ears.

It would not have been any kind of feast or party at all without music, so Maeve took up the large floor harp in the corner of the room and sang "Carrickfergus" and "The Meeting of the Waters" and "The Minstrel Boy" and all those other sad ballads. I saw Killian watching, rapt, and then was somewhat surprised when Deaglan came into the room with a guitar case and Keevan took up a bodhran from our musical collection and together they played and sang a rousing version of "Rocky Road to Dublin" in fine voice that had Eamon and Killian performing brilliant step dancing that Deaglan soon joined in on while Keevan pounded out a deft beat on the bodhran. Then Killian led us all in a raucous rendition of "The Wild Rover"—a song no set could be without—and after the final refrain, we had sung ourselves hoarse and the ladies, Caitlin included, left to fetch coffee, tea and dessert.

Daegal was leaning against my side with his head on my shoulder and I had thought he was asleep, but then he spoke to me among the happy laughter of the others, so quietly I barely heard him.

"I wish you didn't have to go tomorrow," he said. "I wish I could come with you."

I wrapped my arm around him and gave him a comforting squeeze. "I know you do, and I look forward every day to the time you are old enough to join me and fight with Na Fianna. I have no doubt that you will make a wonderful warrior, Daegal. But this time, you're going to have to stay here with Mum and Da. Stay here and dream and keep me up to date on what those dreams tell you. I will call you whenever I can and keep you up to date on my end."

He nodded and perked up a bit when my mother, Maeve and Caitlin returned, bringing in thick slices of apple pie with cream and steaming cups of coffee for everyone but Riordan who of course didn't drink it; and Keevan and Daegal who had hot chocolate. Keevan protested, but Riordan refused to let him drink coffee that late at night.

I savored the apple pie, done perfectly with a flaky crust, and well-baked apples, knowing I wouldn't get real food for a while if we were going to be in the hills. After that, Daegal really did fall asleep and Sean had already been put to bed. I decided to take the initiative, seeing it was nearly midnight, and stood up, gently laying Daegal down against Oisin's furry back.

"I hate to cut the celebration short, my friends, but I think it is best we turn in. I want to leave by dawn tomorrow, and we'll have some last minute things to see to before that." Killian and Eamon were loaning us two Range Rovers from the Hall that the guards used to get around when they needed to, so we wouldn't have to each take our own cars. We had packed provisions (my mother had seen to that personally) but our personal bags would still have to be loaded the next morning.

Eamon nodded in agreement and stood up. "I'll second him. It will be a long day of driving tomorrow and you'll want your rest. Lady Aoife, I wish to thank you for feeding my warriors tonight. And myself as well, of course."

"Any time, Eamon," she said as he kissed her on the cheek in parting, having no qualms about propriety for he had known my mother all his life since she had acted as his mother's midwife.

Killian bade farewell to my sister and left with Eamon while the others trooped off to their rooms. My mother looked fondly down at Daegal sleeping with the dogs, and I bent to gather him into my arms.

"I'll take him to his bed," I told her and kissed her goodnight. "I'll see you in the morning, Mum."

I carried Daegal upstairs and tucked him in before slipping quietly back down the stairs to go to the library. I knew my father was there before even seeing the light was on because I knew it was very unlikely he would be sleeping that night. I didn't knock, but I cleared my throat quietly as I came into the room, and my father turned around from his place by the fire and looked at me with an expression I couldn't quite read.

"Ciran, did you need something?" he asked quietly.

"I've come to make my peace, *Athair*," I told him respectfully, coming further into the room. "I didn't want to leave on such terms as we parted with the last time we spoke."

He nodded slowly, standing up to speak with me. I stood a bit awkwardly for a moment, unsure of what to say, then I took a deep breath and decided I couldn't do any more damage then had already been done.

"I never meant to cause anyone pain when I said that we needed to find Aeden," I said quietly. "I never...well, I never really considered that anyone would feel that way, but Fin explained it to me and now I see why you were upset, and I had no right to accuse you of not caring. That was cruel, I know. I just didn't really understand before, but I do now, and I want you to know that I'm sorry."

Da's face softened, though there was still a far away

pain in his eyes. "I think we were both in the wrong. I should not have tried to force you to give up hope. I know what it is like to lose a brother. As you well know, I lost Nollaig in that last battle and that loss is a hole that cannot be repaired. I am truthfully glad that you have such hope, Ciran. If you had not, then I don't think anyone would. I only pray so earnestly that your hope will not prove false. I would not wish that pain on anyone."

"It won't, *Athair,* I know it won't," I told him firmly. "I would...I would know if Aeden was dead. I know I would. Because I do not feel that ache, that hole that cannot be repaired."

"I think I would know as well," my father said quietly and I felt my heart soar even more. "And I know Daegal would."

"So you are at peace with me going?"

He looked at me with pain in every feature. "I am not, nor will I ever be at peace with it. But I will let you go."

"I would feel better if you were at peace, *Athair,*" I said in a small voice, sounding childish to my own ears.

"Come here," he said, and I hesitated, not sure what to expect. "Come here, Ciran," he said again, somewhat impatient.

I moved closer to him and was suddenly pulled into a tight embrace. I stiffened at first, not having anticipated that reaction, but then relaxed against his broad chest as his hand reached up to the back of my head to hold me there.

"You wanted to know the truth of why I am against you going, Ciran, and it's because I can't stand the thought of losing you too," he said quietly into my ear. "You are my heir now that Aeden is gone, but it's not only that which makes me fear, but for the simple fact that you are my son and I love you."

"Da," I tried, but my voice was choked and I had to fight against the tears that threatened to fall. "Da, you have to let me do this. For my sake, for yours, and Mum's and everyone else's. I don't do this just for me; I do this for Tierney and his da, and Eamon and Oran and the others I have been given as my companions for this quest. We will do this together, and we will not give up until we have brought back our missing family."

"You must take care and bring yourselves back as well," my father whispered. "That is a very important thing to remember. I can assure you that there is not one who would trade those who were lost already for the ones who went after them."

"I'll come back," I choked out, my chest heaving compulsively with a sob I fought to keep inside, feeling very unlike a warrior and very much like a boy. "I'll come back, Da. I promise." He held me tighter and let me have a little cry into his shoulder for a moment as I fought to gather myself. When he saw I was nearly done, he smoothed my hair and pressed his lips against my temple before he let me go and I scrubbed my eyes, ashamed. He squeezed my shoulder lightly.

"Go get some rest. You must have your wits about you tomorrow. You are a leader now and you must find the strength inside you to carry on as such so that you will make it to the end."

"Thank you, Da," I said sincerely. "Good night."

I made my way to my room and fell into bed, realizing I was more exhausted than I expected. I fell asleep quickly and was only vaguely aware later when Daegal curled up against my back. He had not come to me since my first night back home and I worried he might have seen something in his dreams that boded ill for the journey. I tiredly turned over and poked him in the back.

"Hey, are you okay?" I asked him.

He turned around and snuggled up against my side again. "It was hard to tell," he said sleepily. "But I saw a stone palace and I think it was underground because it was all lit with torches. That's all there was."

"It's a start," I said, already closing my eyes again. "Now try and sleep."

He nodded, but was already drifting off again and I hugged my little brother tightly, wondering when I would get to see him again, and worrying even more so about whether I would be forced to let him down.

Part Two

The Journey

Chapter Eight
The Beginning of the Road

I woke before my alarm the next morning, turning my head to look out the window and see that there was only a hint of grey dawn upon the horizon. Daegal was curled up in a wad of blanket and I didn't have the heart to wake him. I slipped out of the covers onto the cold floor and quickly pulled on my traveling gear. Na Fianna wore heavy, durable clothing, usually consisting of leather or canvas trousers and if we would be traveling and fighting, we wore a sort of sleeveless tabard that fitted to our upper body and was slightly padded so we could wear our hard leather breastplates over top of it and not have it rub or chafe — I wish I could say the same for the trousers.

I took my breastplate from its stand and was about to put it over my head when I heard the bed creak and I turned to see Daegal coming over with a sleepy but determined expression on his face. He took the breastplate from me.

"I'll act as your armor bearer this morning as it should be," he said proudly as I allowed him to put the formed leather over my head. "That's what I would have been in the days of old Ireland."

"You would have," I said with a smile as he buckled it at the sides. "And made a fine one too, *deartháir beag.*" He finished with my breastplate and went to grab my jacket, helping me into that as well. I zipped it up as he turned to take my sword from the wall and I stood still while he raised himself onto tiptoe to buckle the belt across my shoulder. He looked up at me proudly once he had finished and I put my hands on his shoulders and lowered my forehead to press against his.

"It won't be long before I'm back, Daegal. You'll see. I know it's hard to be the one waiting at home, but you must be here to keep everyone strong because I know that you can do that if no one else can. And keep dreaming. And remember, if anything you see in your dreams truly concerns you, don't hesitate to tell Eamon. He'll listen to you. Though I do believe that Da will as well. Don't be afraid to talk to him or Mum."

Daegal nodded and then threw his arms around me. I held him for a long time, but I had to pack so I finally had to let him go. "Go and get dressed in something warmer, then go see if you can help Mum in the kitchen—I can smell the coffee already. I'll be down soon with the others."

He hurried out of the room, tiptoeing on the cold floor, and I set about packing. Only two extra pairs of clothing, minimal toiletries—as in, a toothbrush—and small clothes and socks. I packed a few warmer things for cold nights on watch, but that was it. I would have to carry it on my back for the most part and I was not looking forward to any more weight than that.

I was just zipping up my bag when there was a tap on my door. I looked up. "Come in."

I was surprised to see Finbar slide into the room, seeming to be a bit uncomfortable, looking like he didn't really know why he had come and was regretting it.

"Hi, Fin, are you all right?" I looked up from my position crouched on the floor.

He hesitated and then seemed to steel himself, coming closer as I stood up to meet him.

"I'm sorry for what I said to you the other day, Ciran," he blurted. "I didn't really mean it. I was angry."

"No, no, you were right, Fin," I told him, gripping his shoulder tightly, seeing the anxiety in his face and wishing to repair whatever damage he had thought was done. "And I really must thank you for pointing that out. I regret that I don't always think of what other people might feel on matters *I* feel strongly about. I just miss Aeden so much that I can't consider *not* looking for him. I didn't realize the thought of that would give other people grief. I didn't really understand why it would. But I do now. I know you just want what's best for everyone else. So do I."

"I do want Aeden back," Finbar said. "You know I never wanted anything different."

"I know," I told him gently. "But I also understand how you feel being the oldest son now when I'm gone. And it is right of you to protect the family, to keep them together. And Finbar, I admire you so much for what you do for Da, you could never imagine. In many ways you are so much stronger than me. I can't stand to see him like that in so much pain, but you have to deal with that every day and you somehow manage to stay sane. I wish I could do that. So you have every right to get angry at me if I do anything to grieve him. In fact, I hope you continue to do so."

He smiled slightly and looked up at me. "I wish you

the best of luck, Ciran. I want you to bring Aeden back. I want us to be a complete family again. I don't think everything is broken beyond repair, but I do believe you are the only one who can fix it. And Da trusts you to do it. He told me so himself."

That made a well of emotion flow through me that I fought to keep down because I was determined not to start this journey as a leader with tears. I nodded, unable to say anything but feeling so proud. I knew that whatever happened in the near future I would only have to think back on this moment to find the strength to go on.

"Thank you, Fin," I said quietly and he was about to leave when he turned back and grasped me in a quick hug, surprising me thoroughly. Finbar had not hugged me since he was Daegal's age, not being as demonstrative as the rest of us, but I hugged him back before he pulled away, a sheepish smile on his face.

"I'll see you down stairs," he said and left the room.

I finished packing and then slung my bag over my shoulder and headed out the door as soon as I had gotten my boots on. I stopped by Tierney's room, nudging the partially open door wide with my foot as I ducked in.

"Ready?" I asked as he was just yanking the zipper of his pack closed.

He looked up with a determined grin. "Aye!"

We went into the kitchen to find my mother and Riordan drinking tea and chatting together. I was surprised to see the man so...well, as bad as it sounds, so calm. What made it even weirder was that he still wore his cabled jumper even though it was now underneath his leather breastplate; even in the armor, he was the very face of serenity. He looked up with a smile as Tierney and I came in and my mother moved to pour us cups of coffee.

"Morning," the berserker said congenially. "Have you seen my lazy brother yet or am I going to have to drag him out of bed?"

"I'm here, you great lump," Keevan yawned as he came into the room, dragging his pack and leaving it unceremoniously on the floor before Riordan gave him a stern look and he picked it up and set it more appropriately against the wall. He jabbed his brother in the side as he sat down next to him and accepted a cup of coffee from my mother and poured a heap of honey and cream into it.

"Easy Keevan," Riordan scolded but Keevan ignored him. I was rather impressed with the disaster that was his hair. I began to wonder whether he wore anything in it after all, for its natural state seemed to be trying its best to reach the heavens.

"Good morning, comrades!" came a cheery voice from the doorway and in strode Deaglan, looking fresh and clean and smelling of a manly cologne — of course he would never suffer from bed head like Keevan. I refrained from turning up a lip at him, but was thankfully distracted by Caitlin's appearance a second later, dressed in a rather — well — becoming outfit consisting of leather trousers, tunic and fitted breastplate.

Tierney nudged me with an elbow. "Staring," he hissed in my ear and I quickly turned back to my coffee, trying not to blush.

"Looks like everyone's here," my mother said with a small smile, setting out several different kinds of muffins and trays of fruit and a steaming rack of toast and then bacon which was gone in only a matter of minutes. The coffee was being drunk rather rapidly and the flurry of excitement was catching as the caffeine set in, almost making me forget the gravity of our quest. I knew it was nerves, and I fought hard to keep mine at bay otherwise I feared how they would manifest themselves, having been as emotional as a lass the last few days, much to my shame.

"Eat up, lads," Tierney said as he grabbed another muffin. "This is the last homely meal we will have for quite a while."

"I've packed you all a lunch as well," my mother said, indicating a huge cooler set beside the kitchen door. "I thought I might as well give you one more good meal."

"Thank you, Mum," I told her with a fond smile as I finished my coffee and glanced out the window to see the sun rising further. "Everyone finish up, we need to be going."

The doorbell rang and my mother left to go answer it, though I had a suspicion that it was Eamon and Killian. Those suspicions were confirmed when my mother came back in with the High King himself dressed in his traditional garb—embossed copper breastplate and gold embroidered green cloak and all, the silver circlet barely visible among his riotous black hair. We all bowed our heads in respect and he nodded back to us.

"I came to see you off," he said. "And I've brought some others with me. If you're ready, would you come outside to let them do so?"

I looked to my company and they all nodded, Keevan stuffing one last bite of toast into his mouth before he leapt to his feet and grabbed his bag. Riordan turned to my mother and clasped her hand with a smile.

"Thank you so much, Lady Aoife, for putting us up. Even my annoying little brother."

My mother laughed heartily. "Any time, dear. You are always welcome, and take this with you as well." She handed him a bag full of yarn skeins of all colors. "I imagine you might need something to help you relax on the journey."

He smiled graciously and tucked the yarn into his pack. Keevan knocked his shoulder into Riordan. "Granny got some new yarn to make jumpers with, or maybe it will be a sword cozy this time? That would be cute."

Tierney and I were the last ones to leave, sharing a glance that needed no words. This was it; this was what we had both wanted for a long time, but the enormity of the fact that it was now a possibility was a little overwhelming. I clapped a hand down on his shoulder tightly and he did the same in turn.

"Ready?" I asked more seriously than I had earlier.

He nodded once. "Ready."

We went outside with the others, my mother following behind and I smiled when we stepped out the door, seeing that the rest of my family, including my father, were waiting out there along with Killian, Tierney's mother and sisters, and another woman I didn't know, who was dark haired and standing next to a young girl of about ten or eleven—Daegal's age. It was Deaglan who dropped his pack and went to them and held the woman tightly before he bent to hug the girl just as tightly, brushing away the tears that ran down her face with a fond smile. I guessed it must have been his mother and sister and realized I had never given much thought to any kin of his, apart from his missing father.

I watched Tierney take leave of his mother and sisters and Seamus who fretted over him fondly and he had to pull out his own handkerchief to give to his mother who I knew was trying hard not to cry for she was not the type to do so, being of tough Irish stock.

"I'll bring Da back, Mum," Tierney told her gently

and I could tell he was struggling with his own emotions. "I promise."

A hand descended on my shoulder and I turned to see my father standing behind me. He still did not smile, but his eyes were softer and he stared at me fondly.

"*Mo fuaime,*" he said gently before he reached into his shirt and pulled out a medallion and held it in front of me until I reached out to take it. It settled into the palm of my hand, warm from resting against his chest.

"It's Aeden's," he said unnecessarily. "Give it to him when you find him."

There was nothing more that needed to be said. There was no *if* in that sentence, and there was no *if* in my father's voice this time. If I'd had any more doubts about going on this quest, they had all been blown away. I threw my arms around Da and held him tightly for a moment then let go before I lost hold of my emotions. I was then bombarded by Maeve, Finbar, Daegal and Sean who all enfolded me in a huge hug at the same time and I laughed, bidding them all farewell before I turned to my mother who pulled me close and kissed me gently on the cheek.

"Just come back, Ciran," she whispered and I felt a single tear fall onto my neck before she let me go.

I had to turn my back so I would not lose it. I made my way to Eamon and knelt in front of him.

"*Mo rí,*" I said formally. "May my sword and my heart never fail and may they always fight true for king and for Ireland."

"May they so," he replied traditionally. "Now go, *Laoch na hÉireann.* May the road lie easy before you." I rose and he took my arm, speaking quietly to me. "Bring them home, Ciran."

"I swear I will do all in my power and past that to

bring them back," I told him.

Eamon nodded and turned to the others, bidding them farewell as we all took leave of our families. Killian came and I clasped forearms with him.

"Best of luck, Ciran, and congratulations on your first quest," he said.

"Thank you," I told him with a smile. "Be good to my sister while I'm gone. And keep Eamon in line too."

He rolled his eyes comically. "One of those is going to be quite a bit more difficult than the other." He poked me in the chest. "You be good to my sister too."

"I have a feeling she can handle herself," I said with a grin. "You are her big brother after all." He grinned at that with a shrug of agreement and slapped me on the back as he went to talk to Tierney.

I grabbed my pack up again. The sun was almost fully up now, and there was no reason to delay any longer. The more we did, the harder it was going to be to leave.

"Come, my comrades!" I called to them and they reluctantly bid a last farewell to their families. I felt bad that Keevan and Riordan's mother couldn't make it for she was down south, but my mother had seemed to adopt them well enough. I supposed that if she could do so, I could come to think of them as brothers too once I got to know them better.

The two Range Rovers were waiting for us and we split up into two groups of three. I would drive one with Tierney and Keevan, and Deaglan would drive the other with Caitlin and Riordan. I had decided it was best to split the brothers up and figured that it would give me time to figure Keevan out a little better. I turned back before I climbed into the car, just as Eamon called out to us.

"Farewell and good journey. May the road rise up to

meet you!"

"Thank you!" I called and closed the door, revving the vehicle into life and getting onto the road before I hesitated another minute. We were all silent for a few minutes, but once there was only the road in front of us, Tierney sighed deeply and turned to me.

"Well, that's it then. There's no going back now."

"No," I agreed, my hands involuntarily tightening on the steering wheel. "That's why we need to make sure this goes well."

Chapter Nine
The Safe House

"We'll head to the safe house first," I told them. We had already planned to do so, but I felt better talking out loud. It made the situation seem real. I was still trying to get myself to believe it.

"I've never been to one of the safe houses before," Keevan said from behind me. "Never been on a trip long enough to need one."

"You'll like this one," I assured him. "It's pretty awesome."

"How many missions have you been on?" Keevan asked and I heard him rustling around in his pack, followed by the sound of crunching. I had at least figured out that he had a ridiculously high metabolism, even for a Finar.

"Not too many," I assured him. "Tierney and I go on small errands for Eamon a lot, but we've only been on a few potentially dangerous missions. We stayed at the safe house on a training mission when we were still at school in Dublin."

Keevan sighed. "Yeah, my group didn't get to go on that. I guess they thought we weren't quite ready, but I still graduated, so I don't know what the deal was."

I shrugged, but had remembered something about a group of boys who had put soap in all the toilets that week and flooded the bathroom with bubbles. Whether Keevan was actually part of the "Bubble Pot Plot" as it was later called in infamy, I wasn't certain, but his roommate was a known instigator so he got punished as well. In any case, it could have been a lot worse; the bathrooms were certainly cleaner afterward than they had ever been.

It was almost a four-hour drive (normal driving) to the safe house. It was a ways into the middle of nowhere which is exactly what it needed to be. There were safe houses stashed all over the country for Na Fianna and any other warriors who might be caught off guard in the wilds and need an emergency place to hide or re supply. Some of them were just huts with cashes of non-perishables, first aid kits, and extra weaponry with maybe a cot to sleep on if you were lucky; then there were three actual safe houses. One in the south, one in the far north that was in a bit of neutral land, and the one we would be going to which was in the middle of the country, right in the middle of a lake. How was that inconspicuous? Well, let's just say the architecture had something to do with it.

Tierney had put in one of my cds, a mix of Irish folk rock, and we were all singing along, Keevan very enthusiastically, as well as drumming on my headrest, when the safe house first came into sight. Keevan stopped singing and gave a shout of wonder.

"No way! It really is built into a rock!"

I grinned despite myself. The lake where the safe house was hidden had a large rock pillar in the middle of it, not so much an island as a standing isolated rock. One would never know unless you were looking for it, but on top of the cliff there was a small fortress built to look like the rock face, even painted and textured to keep the impression. If you looked hard enough, you could see several windows and the hidden staircase, but unless you had prior knowledge of its existence, you would never know it was there.

I parked the Range Rover on one side of the lake so that it was concealed from the road by trees and other foliage. The others were only a few seconds behind us and Deaglan parked behind me as Keevan leapt out of the vehicle to stare at the safe house with a huge grin on his face.

"Look at that!" he called to his brother as Riordan got out of the other vehicle. "Isn't that the most awesome thing you've ever seen?"

Riordan smiled and ruffled Keevan's hair fondly to his protests. "He doesn't get out much," he said apologetically and everyone laughed.

"Whatever, Rearend," Keevan snorted and kicked his brother in the backside before he went back to our Range Rover and grabbed his pack out of the backseat along with one of the picnic baskets. "Now how do we get to it? I want to eat whatever delicious food Lady Mac Cool packed for us."

"You've probably been eating the whole trip, I know you packed snacks in your bag," Riordan said accusingly.

"He has," Tierney replied blandly.

I grabbed my own pack and sword and headed to a small cove off to one side. "Come on, we'll get the boats."

Everyone followed me and I found myself walking next to Caitlin. I turned to her with a smile. "So, has the most coveted man in Ireland asked you out on a date yet?"

She laughed and winked. "No, he's being very professional, Ciran, don't worry. You don't have anything you need to report to my brother."

"Have *you* asked *him*?" I couldn't help but ask with a smirk.

"Shut up," she said, hitting me and not in a very girlish way as my smarting arm could attest. "You know why I'm here, and it's not to play every one of you against each other with my womanly attributes like some half-wit heroine from modern fiction. Besides, he's not my type. I could never date a man who takes more time on his hair than I do."

I nodded with a laugh, having a whole new respect for her and feeling the burn of every half-wit heroine out there. I gave her a slightly rueful smile. "I know. I think you are very brave."

She smiled teasingly. "You aren't saying that just because I'm a woman are you?"

I winked. "Not for potentially facing Goblins to rescue your brother—for coming along with a bunch of lads as crazy as us."

She laughed and I couldn't help but grin. She would never know quite how much I admired her for that.

"Here are the boats," I said, motioning to two rowboats that were hidden among the undergrowth, and threw my pack into one of them. "Luggage in the back. Tierney and I will row this one; Caitlin, sit in the front; Keevan, up front in the other. The entrance is on the far side and there will be a hidden docking there where we'll keep the boats. You won't see it until we're right in front of it."

I handed Caitlin into the bow after the luggage was

stowed and Tierney and I pushed the boat out before we got in and sat shoulder to shoulder on the middle bench and began to row out to the huge rock formation towering up in the middle of the lake.

The entrance was a carefully placed formation that opened wide enough on one side for the boats to slide into so that they would be hidden from prying eyes. We tossed the oars and Caitlin knelt in the bow and caught the post that we could tie the boat to. She took the rope from its coil on the floor and secured it to the post as Tierney and I stowed the oars in the bottom of the boat and began gathering up our luggage.

"This way," I said as the others finished the same tasks. There was a cleft in the rock face that held a staircase in it and I started on my way up, the others following close behind.

"It's kind of dark," Keevan stated.

I had reached the door at the top landing and called a halt below as I took the bar from across it and set it to one side. The door stuck so I set my shoulder against it and pushed it open, letting some light in. It opened into a cozy living room and I set my packs down on the floor as I turned to my companions with a grin, sweeping my arm dramatically around the room.

"Welcome to the safe house!" I said with a laugh.

"This is awesome!" Keevan shouted, throwing his things unceremoniously onto the floor and flinging himself down onto the couch. Deaglan turned several lights on and I called a halt to the exploring for a moment.

"Hold on, lads, and lady," I said. "Just because we're up here alone doesn't mean we can go wild. First, let's put our things into the bunk room and then we'll wash up and see what my mother packed for lunch."

Keevan groaned and Tierney made a face at me. "Such a killjoy, Ciran," he said with a laugh as I stuck my tongue out at him.

The bunkroom held four bunk beds, two on either side of the room, and had a small bathroom at the end of it with a shower. I put my own kit down on the bottom bunk of the bed closest to the door and motioned for the others to do the same.

"Pick a bunk, everyone, and no changes!"

Keevan immediately leapt onto a top bunk as Riordan settled onto the bottom one. The redhead hung down and grinned at his brother. "I'm going to stare at you like this all night, Riordan. Give you nightmares."

"I'll just kick your bunk then," the big man replied.

I turned to Caitlin with a sympathetic look. "If you don't want to sleep in here, you can have the couch."

She shook her head with a smile, taking the bunk next to mine. "Nope, this is fine. I'll have to get used to it sometime if we're going to be camping out in the open together. But if anyone snores, I will personally kick the culprit out to the living room."

"It'll be much better out in the open," Tierney said with a grin. "Then our manly stench will not be enclosed in tight spaces."

"Speak for yourself!" Deaglan laughed, tossing his hair out of his eyes in an annoyingly heroic fashion.

"Hey, man, you don't see any of us wearing cologne on a *mission*," Riordan said. "There's a reason for that."

"Yes," I agreed, sobering. "No more cologne, Deaglan, and use the soap that's in the shower tonight when you wash, it's scentless. The Goblins' sense of smell is already higher even than ours, and we don't want to risk them finding us early for some stupid amateur mistake."

Deaglan ducked his head over his bag, not replying, and I turned my back as I sat on my own cot, feeling slightly like the bad guy, but really. It was common training, just like don't camp with food around areas with large wild animals, or smoke when you're trying to lay low. I had a feeling Deaglan knew well enough, but was just letting his vanity get in the way. We'd have to see how suave he felt after three days in the cold probably rainy weather without a hot shower or a soft place to sleep. I was rather interested to see how his hair held up after several days of no conditioner.

Once everyone had got the kit settled we left to view the rest of the house. It consisted of the bunkroom, the living room and a fully stocked kitchen and dinning room.

"It's so clean," Deaglan said admiringly. "Not even any dust."

"House brownies," I said, and thinking of it, I looked into my mother's picnic basket and took out a jug of milk, finding a bowl and pouring some into it before I put it in the corner of the room. "They keep the place clean while no one's here. Best leave a few scraps for them in thanks."

Everyone nodded. We all knew Faery protocol, and I had grown up with a mother who was adamant in teaching her children how to respect the Good Folk. I never complained, for the consequences of forgetting the Little People were rarely enjoyable. You could wake up with every left sock missing or your hair tied in knots. But with a simple saucer of cream or honey, the brownies would keep a house clean.

"All right then!" I said, starting to unpack the baskets with Caitlin's help. "Let's have lunch, and then we can begin to think of our plan of action."

Chapter Ten
Planning

We devoured the sandwiches and the dessert my mother packed us and then when I finally had their attention when their stomachs were pleasantly full, I laid out my plans of action as I had mostly thought them up last night in the shower and then later when I was trying to fall asleep. I wasn't going to let on that that was the case, but it was the truth.

"I think we are all familiar with the object of this mission," I said and the solemn nods that were given to me made me feel a little better about continuing. Everyone seemed to have settled down for the moment at least, even Keevan. "And on that subject, I want to stress the importance of the fact that while this is very much a personal mission, it is also a mission sanctioned by High King Eamon, and he expects it to succeed. It's also of the utmost importance that we do not let our emotions get the better of us. We have all lost someone very dear to us who we are going on a mission to reclaim, but we have to work like professionals. We can't let our emotions show until we have Lorcan defeated or the prisoners back or both. Only then can we allow ourselves that luxury. Does anyone have any problems with that?"

There was a chorus of no's and shaking of heads. I took up a map I had put on the table and rolled it out, tracing a finger around our position. "We're here, right on the border of the Faelands. How many of you have been there before besides Tierney and I?"

Everyone cast glances around but Deaglan was the only one who raised his hand with a sheepish expression.

"I was there. Once. It wasn't on a mission, though, it was kind of a dare. My friend and I went and camped out one night to show how macho we were. It wasn't as bad as I thought."

I refrained from rolling my eyes. "Well, now we're going to have Goblin patrols all over the hills as well as whatever other races of the Good Folk decide they want to come and see what we're up to. It's not going to be an easy journey, especially because we don't have any formal idea of where we're going. The first part of our mission is finding the Goblin palace. The only thing we know for sure is that it's somewhere on the Northern Border and that it's underground, so we're going to have to cross all the way through the Faelands to get there and it won't be visible when we do."

"This will be interesting," Keevan muttered but Riordan nudged him with an elbow.

"Once we do find the palace and have a chance to scout it out, we'll work on coming up with a plan of rescue. Until then, we have nothing to go on, so we're not going to be able to come up with anything conclusive. We're planning on leaving first thing in the morning. Do you have any questions?"

Keevan raised his hand. "What's for dinner?"

"Seriously, Keev," Riordan groaned, shoving his brother as he stood up. "Take something seriously for once in your life."

"You need to loosen up," Keevan retorted.

"I don't think anyone else would appreciate my way of loosening up," Riordan said blandly.

"All right, guys, come on," I said, hoping to stop this before Riordan went berserk in the small safe house. "Let's just settle down and relax for the afternoon. Play some games and stuff, and get ready for tomorrow. We don't know how long we're going to be out there, we don't even really know the exact location of the Goblin palace so it could take us even longer than expected. And whatever rows you're going to have, let's have it out now, today, please. That way they don't interfere with the mission. I know you all want your family members back and I know you don't want to do anything stupid that will jeopardize that chance. Okay?"

There were nods and confirmation and then everyone went into the living room to talk and do whatever took their fancy. I was tempted to lie down in the bunkroom myself, having slept little the night before, but decided that probably wasn't the most professional way to start off the mission as commander. Instead I sat on the couch next to Tierney and we turned on a hurling game on the small television in the corner. Caitlin curled up to read in the corner of the couch, and Deaglan looked over his arrows and fletched new ones. Keevan wouldn't sit down, though and kept poking around, practicing fighting moves and alternated with that and pestering his brother who was knitting with a stoic face in a chair. The redhead finally settled a bit, by lounging over the top of the chair with his chin and folded hands on Riordan's head. The berserker seemed not to pay him any notice even when Keevan took the end of his braid and wiggled it into his ear and under his nose. I began to feel a little more relaxed with the prospect of having a berserker in the company. If he could last through his little brother's well-practiced torments, then I didn't think he would be very quick to fly off the handle at anything less than catastrophic.

I looked over at Caitlin who noticed I was staring and smiled at me.

"What are you reading?" I asked her.

"The new Donnal O'Toole mystery, have you read them?"

"Not as many as I would like to," I replied. "Don't have a lot of time for reading anymore. For some reason I didn't really picture you as a bookworm. Probably pre-conceived notions from Killian."

She laughed. "Killie's not much of a reader, but Flagan was—is," she corrected quickly with a wince. I pretended not to notice.

"Oh yeah?" I asked. "I never knew that either. Though he is quieter than Killian."

She nodded, smiling again. "Flagan is a bit different than Killian and I. Some people think he's shy, but that's not true; he's just quiet. While he is a brilliant warrior and can easily beat Killie and I together, he's much more of a scholar." A somewhat bittersweet look came over her face. "He always used to read to me before bed when I was little. All the wonderful adventure stories and sometimes the histories of Ireland, but the way he told them made them seem like the most brilliant tales ever, even when he was only a kid." She paused a minute, taking a deep breath before she continued more quietly. "I have a shelf back home and every time I read a book I know Flagan would like, I put it there and I keep them for him when he comes back. It's—it's how I've kept going. I felt that if I had something for him, it would be easier to think of seeing him again. Maybe it's silly, but it does help."

I didn't know what to say, only that I understood completely what she meant. "It's not silly. I'm sure he'll appreciate it a lot."

She smiled again and then suddenly reached out and clasped a hand around my wrist. I glance down at it quickly before I looked up again to meet her eyes. "Thank you," she said.

"For what?" I asked, confused.

"For letting me come. I was a bit afraid you wouldn't want a girl—and a fully human one at that—to interfere with the mission. Afraid you'd think of me as a liability."

I shook my head with a grin. "You've already proven yourself to me, Caitlin. There was no reason I shouldn't have brought you. And you're not a liability. You keep your head well in tight places and that's just the kind of man I need on this mission. Well, woman, anyway." I grinned and she laughed again while Tierney kicked me.

"Shh! I don't want to miss the end of the game!" he gestured toward the TV and I turned back to it, leaving Caitlin once again to her book.

Supper was not as good as lunch, but Caitlin and I made it work and I found that Caitlin wasn't a bad cook even when all she had to work with was canned food and other non-perishables. And she also made hot chocolate afterward for dessert, which was even better.

I made everyone take an early night and, though there were some teasing complaints, everyone, myself included fell asleep quickly.

I woke early and decided I would make coffee to get everyone else out of bed. I dressed quickly and headed out to find Riordan sitting in the middle of the living room, cross-legged, his eyes closed and a cup of steaming tea sitting beside him. He opened his eyes and smiled when I came in.

"Good morning, just doing some stretches," he said as he straightened his legs and bent over them to touch his toes.

"Morning," I replied with a nod and went to the kitchen. I started up the coffee pot, as Riordan came into the room, his mug of tea held in one hand. I turned around and leaned back against the counter to face him. He looked incredibly relaxed, wearing a green t-shirt and work out pants. I noticed for the first time that apart from the family medallion he wore like all Fianna, he also had a Thor's Hammer pendant to show his berserker status.

"Are you ready?" I asked.

He nodded. "I think so."

"And Keevan?" I raised an eyebrow.

He smiled a bit sadly and looked down at the steam rising from his cup. "I hope you'll forgive my brother. He'll be fine once we get out on the trail. He's not good at waiting. Losing Pat affected him pretty bad. We were both close to Pat, but never exactly close to each other, not in the same way. Things have changed a bit since he was taken, but still, it was hard on Keevan, being promoted so young." He sighed. "Sometimes I wonder whether it was a good idea for me to bring him along. But I don't think he would have sat at home. That would have killed him — or forced him to kill someone else. He needed to get out of the house and away from the memories."

I nodded in understanding. "Don't worry, we won't

let anything happen to him. As long as you trust him to do what needs to be done, I'm sure he'll be fine."

"Oh, it's not his bravery or his capability that I worry about," Riordan said with a dry chuckle. "It's the fact that he has far too much of it."

I smiled, turning to the cupboard to see what we could make for breakfast and found a lucky box of pancake mix. "I can see that. I was just afraid he might be the kind who falter when they actually see action."

"Not Keevan," Riordan said with a note of admiration. "He's far too proud for that."

I set about mixing the pancakes and heard Riordan set his cup down on the table and cough quietly.

"I hope you don't mind having a...berserker in your company," he said after a moment.

I turned around, shrugging. "I honestly have never known one before. I'm not prejudiced, and I don't think that you're all mindless monsters, if that's what you mean. As long as you feel you can control yourself properly and offer no danger to your comrades, I have no problem."

Riordan smiled. "That's good enough for me. And I promise I will be no danger to anyone but the enemy. The first thing a berserker is taught is how to control the rage and bury it." He grinned then. "As you can see I have had lots of time to practice patience."

I laughed. "I can imagine."

I heated up the pan, to start the cakes and by the time the coffee had finished everyone was out of bed and I put hot pancakes onto plates for them. Once everyone was done, I sent them all off to pack up their things.

"Leave the plates, the brownie will do them," I said, putting butter and honey onto the final pancake and leaving it on the table for said brownie. "It's already an hour past dawn and we need to be going."

I had decided we would drive partway up north to a place I knew of where we could stash the vehicles. That way we would have them a bit closer if we needed them for a quick retreat. We would camp there that night and then head forward on foot the next day.

We packed up everything in the boats again and rowed back to shore and took our things to the Rovers that were waiting for us. Everyone was charged, but yet oddly silent and I thought that, like myself, this was all finally becoming real to them. We were actually doing this. And the enormity and possibility of danger was beginning to sink in. I just hoped that wouldn't prove too much for anyone. Even Keevan seemed to be quieter than he had been all morning.

"Well, comrades, this is it," I told them before we climbed into the vehicles. "*D'Éirinn. Le haghaidh ár deartháireacha.*"

"For Ireland. For our brothers," everyone repeated and we climbed into the Range Rovers.

I started up the engine and looked over at Tierney.

"Well, this is it, brother. Whatever happens now, I just hope we don't come back empty handed."

"You and me both, Cir," Tierney said quietly and I began to drive, not even looking back. Because I was afraid that if I did, I might lose what little nerve I had left.

Chapter Eleven
An Unwelcome Invitation

We found the camp that afternoon easily enough and set up our bedrolls and a place to light a fire. We cooked a stew that night, but only with items we brought. It was never a good idea to hunt anything in the Faelands. You never knew if you were shooting a Faery in disguise or an actual rabbit and the consequences for either could be catastrophic. It was, in fact, best not to show anything any sort of disrespect whatsoever and never disregard a living thing whether it be animal or plant for nothing was really what it seemed there.

We had a pleasant night and joked happily, and I took first watch, setting up Tierney and then Riordan to go after me. As I settled down that night into my bedroll, after Tierney had relieved me, I almost could think I was just camping out with him again like we did during training or whenever we got the chance to go look out in the countryside for clues to the missing patrol. I thought with some trepidation that the last time we had camped had been the night before I went to the standing stones. It seemed like so long ago now, but it had only been a little over a week. So much in my life had changed in such a short time that I refused to think of it anymore, knowing it would only keep me up. I turned over and pulled my blanket tighter around my shoulders as I drifted off.

The next morning, Riordan was making porridge with Caitlin when I woke up and I greeted the still sleeping members of my company with kicks to the backside to get them up. Keevan protested the most and mumbled something incoherent as he stuffed his face into his pack that he was using as a pillow.

"I'll handle this, Ciran," Riordan said with a grin, getting up from the fire and leaning over his brother, grabbing him in one arm and slinging him over his shoulder while the redhead kicked at him with a groan.

"There's a fine stream over the hill that will make a good place to bathe. Cold and refreshing!" Riordan said casually, and Keevan shrieked and squirmed out of his grip to retreat to the fire.

"All right, all right, I'm up!" he growled and hit his brother before reaching for a cup of coffee that Caitlin gave him. I grinned and turned to Tierney who was yawning as he pulled his breastplate on over his undershirt again.

"I might dunk myself. I didn't sleep too well last night. Never do on missions."

"I slept fine," Deaglan said with a luxurious stretch, looking annoyingly fresh for having slept on the ground all night. I wondered if there was ever a moment he looked like anything less than an elven prince.

I buckled on my own armor as I went over to the fire to sit beside Caitlin who handed me my coffee and a bowl of porridge with a smile.

"So, how are you holding up so far as the only lady among us scoundrels?" I asked her with a wink.

She laughed as she dished out the rest of the bowls. "Actually, it's rather refreshing. I've never been a fan of hanging around with other girls, they just never seemed to understand me. To be honest, the Academy was practically my own particular hell. Being around girls twenty-four seven with all women instructors and rooming with them? If I didn't have Tierney's sister as my roommate at least the first year, I think I would have gone insane! I never played with girls when I was little because I just had Killian, Flagan, and then Eamon and Oran to play with really. I was just barely surviving the estragon pool that was the Academy."

I laughed as I drank my coffee, seeing her shudder playfully. "I can't really see you fitting in with them. I don't know a lot of shield-maidens but most of what I know of them is that they can occasionally be hard to deal with."

"Oh, there are the good ones," Caitlin amended. "The ones like me who want to learn to fight for the sake of defending our people, but there are certainly the horrid ones who think they're better than anyone else just because they're a girl with a sword." She snorted. "In any case, I'm glad to be finished."

We finished our breakfast and broke camp, packing everything up and making sure the vehicles were locked.

"We'll leave these here," I said. "We can't carry on with them; the terrain won't allow us to keep a good pace and we need to be more unassuming than that. Is everyone ready?"

With nods in the affirmative, we started out at a good pace over the hill on the first real stretch of our journey. At the moment, we were just scouting, but we were heading in a mostly northerly direction, for while I wasn't sure exactly where we might find the Goblin's dwelling, I did know it would be somewhere in the north, and thanks to Deaglan's dream, I knew we were looking for something built into a mountain and the ranges and cliffs on the northern coast came to mind.

We took a break at a stream around midday and had a bite of lunch. I looked warily up at the sky and saw ominous clouds gathering in the distance. I didn't think it would rain that day but it likely wouldn't continue to hold out through the night. That meant we would have to find a decent camp that was sheltered enough to keep us out of the rain.

Unfortunately, later, it was already nearing twilight and there was still no real shelter to be found. There was a forest running along to our left, but I didn't want to go in there. There was a chance we may never come out of it again, and certainly sleeping in such a place in the Faelands was never a good idea. If you happen to be unfortunate enough to fall asleep against a willow tree you might find yourself a permanent resident of the Otherworld.

"Why can't we camp in there?" Keevan asked, sounding tired.

"These are the Faelands," I told him. "There are tribes of the Good Folk that live in those woods and they might not take kindly to intruders. Either that, or they'll think it funny to play tricks on us; turn us around, take our gear, that sort of thing."

Keevan sighed. "All right, but I don't see anywhere else to camp."

I looked around again as I climbed up onto a hill and looked out at the surroundings. Tierney was beside me.

"What about the hollow?" he asked, pointing down into a valley. "That might be the best place we can find."

"Can't tell how sheltered it is up here, but I think you're right," I said, looking again up at the sky. The clouds were still holding off, but I knew it was only a matter of time before they opened up. I turned back down to the others to tell them it was time to go, but I saw Deaglan disappearing into the woods.

"Deaglan, what are you doing?" I called angrily. "Didn't you hear what I said before?"

He turned. "Call of nature, Ciran."

I cursed under my breath. "What a girl," Tierney muttered next to me.

"Fine," I said. "Don't go far."

He ran into the woods and a couple minutes later came out with an odd smile on his face. "Hey everyone, I heard music in there. Let's go see what it is."

"I hear it too," Keevan said suddenly with a slightly dreamy look on his face.

"No, come here," I commanded, getting a bad feeling in my stomach at the same time I too heard the airy melody drifting on the wind and felt compelled to follow it.

"It's beautiful," Caitlin said, stepping toward the forest and I reached out, rather reluctantly, to draw her back.

"No, we have to go," I said again, but felt less convinced of it this time. My words were forced as if in a dream. Did we really have to go? But even then I knew the answer was yes and started herding the others away from the woods.

"Don't go, not yet!"

We turned to see a beautiful young woman, standing beside a tree, smiling prettily. She was wearing a flowing green dress and her hair was adorned with flowers that covered the tops of her pointed ears. Deaglan grinned as he saw her and bowed low.

"Well, if such a beautiful lady as you is present, how can we say no?"

"Easily," I growled, grabbing his shoulder and hauling him back. "That's one of the Fair Folk, Deaglan."

"Oh, please let your friend come!" the Faery girl said, stepping out from the trees and dancing lightly through the grass in time with the distant music. "It's only a dance!"

"Come on, Ciran!" Keevan pleaded and leapt forward, but I hauled him back roughly, throwing him onto the ground even as I had to clear my own head.

"No! We're leaving now!"

I almost dragged Deaglan away before another Faery appeared, this one a male and all red hair and freckles and green eyes, grinning cheekily at Caitlin.

"Why, what a lovely human lass!" he exclaimed, bounding out of the woods with his hand outstretched to Caitlin. "Come and dance. Just one dance, please!"

Caitlin smiled, obviously flattered, and obviously under some enchantment, and reached out to take his hand, but I was suddenly in front of her, snarling at the Faery.

"We won't be dancing tonight. I'm sorry," I said and shoved Caitlin behind me even as she protested. The music seemed to be louder but I fought against it. The Faery's face darkened and he reached out to me but then stopped, seeing a ring on my finger and snatching his hand back. I stepped backwards, pulling Caitlin with me and called to Tierney to grab Keevan. Riordan seemed confused but wasn't running off into the forest to join the dance. I wondered if his berserker training had given him some sort of ability to resist such temptations.

Once I had them all going up the hill again, I did a quick head count and realized with a start that Deaglan wasn't with us. I turned around and saw him stepping toward the pretty Faery girl, holding out his hand. Her fingers nearly brushed him, but I flung myself at him and brought him down with a grunt. I tugged the ring from my finger and shoved it onto his. The Faery shrunk back with a slight gasp, and Deaglan's eyes cleared and he scrambled to his feet as I stood up, my own desire to join the dance fully apparent without the ring, but I fought through it and ran as fast as I could back to the others with Deaglan dragging behind me.

"Go!" I shouted as we joined them and we rushed down the hill and through the valley, not stopping until we reached the place Tierney and I had scouted for the campsite. We all stopped there, breathing heavily, not saying anything for the moment. Finally I turned to my company as I threw my pack down on the ground.

"And that's exactly what I was talking about," I said blandly. "If we had been pulled into that Faery dance we might not have gotten out of that forest for twenty years or more, if we ever did. No one would ever see us again and we would have forfeited the entire mission."

Everyone hung their heads, slipping off their own packs.

"I'm sorry, Ciran, I don't know what came over me," Caitlin said, disgust clear in her voice. "It just…seemed like such fun."

"I know," I said more gently. "That's why they do it. They really mean no harm, they just like to have company, but they like it too much, and they'd never let us go."

Deaglan sat down and started to pull off the ring but I stopped him. "No, keep that, you probably need it more than me."

He hesitated but left it where it was. "Iron?" he asked.

I nodded. "Yes. My mother doesn't approve of us carrying iron knives to keep the Fair Folk from bothering us unless necessary, so she gave us all iron rings instead. It's just a ward of sorts. Tierney has one too. The rest of you can either wear something inside out or carry a rowan twig. There might be something you can use. I should have warned you before, but I like to try and go as peacefully as possible. After this, though, I see we need as much protection as we can get." I nodded to Keevan and Riordan. "Make a fire with the peat we brought so we can have something hot for dinner. Don't worry, if we're cautious and think smart, nothing should trouble us or interfere with our mission."

I wasn't sure they were convinced, I myself wasn't entirely for I knew the Faeries to be a tricksy race at best, but I didn't think we'd run into any who actually meant us lasting harm either. After all, we were Fianna and in part, their kin, even if it was centuries ago we had been anything near like them. They might be more inclined to bother us if we were completely human, but I would have to have good faith that we could cross the Faelands mostly unmolested.

We were a lot quieter this night than we were the last, and everyone retired to their respective bedrolls early. I set Deaglan up on first watch and told him firmly to wake me even if he just thought he saw something, and proceeded to sleep fitfully, worried that the ring might not be entirely helpful to him. Yes, iron would ward Faeries, but it still took training and knowledge to outsmart them and avoid their little games.

Caitlin woke me for my shift, the dogwatch, and I stood and stretched as I watched her slip into her bedroll to get a few more hours of sleep before we would have to leave. I tugged on my jacket against the chill early morning air — I had slept in my breastplate for fear of having to move quickly during the night — and went to settle myself a little ways up the hill so I could look out over the camp and at the land beyond.

It really was beautiful up here in the north, especially in the springtime. The south was beautiful as well — all Ireland was so green at this time of year, doing its job in boosting the tourism levels — but up here, one could really see the Fae influence in the land. It appeared untouched, brilliant in color, the emerald green of the grass mixing with the bursts of color from the flowers. And the forests were dense and cool with bright green moss. I couldn't see much of the color in the dark, of course, but the moonlight shining down on the hills gave the land an eerie and ancient look as if one might hear the howl of a banshee at any moment. I utterly hoped not, but there was something, even among all this beauty and natural perfection, that filled the air with a certain anticipation. Maybe it was just my nerves.

When I saw the sun rising in the distance among the clouds that still gathered ominously, I once again looked down at my companions. Riordan was stirring and I walked over to him as he sat up and stretched.

"Would you watch the camp while I scout?" I asked him quietly.

"Sure," he replied, standing up. I went over to Tierney and nudged him awake.

He grumbled slightly but sat up, opening his eyes. "What?"

"I need a scouting partner. Come." He groaned and scrambled up, grabbing his sword as he tugged his jacket on and followed me at a trot.

We cast around for a bit, looking both for the path ahead and also for sign of anyone who might have passed that way already. We finally ended up in another valley adjacent to the one we had camped in and found the remains of a campfire. I knelt and rubbed the ashes between my fingers. Damp.

"The night before last, I think," I said and stood, looking around to see if there were any more clues.

"Goblins?" Tierney asked, although we both knew the answer to that.

I nodded. "Most likely. How many would you say?"

Tierney looked around the site. "No less than ten, no more than fourteen."

"They would outnumber us at least two to one." I bent to pick up a black feather that was cut on one side, telling me it had come from an arrow. "Fortunately, it looks like they're heading south. We might get lucky and not meet up with them."

"Until they make their way home," Tierney added grimly.

"That is a possibility. Long way away for a scouting party, though. They might just be stationed at the border."

I nodded and we looked around for a few more minutes but found nothing of interest so we jogged back to our own camp as a light rain began to fall. I cursed silently. I knew this was only the start of what was to come that day and I didn't look forward to slogging through wet grass and mud while trying to make sure we didn't have a patrol of Goblins on our tail. I would have liked to think the Goblins would pass us by, but unfortunately, I expected our luck to mirror Tierney's theory. I had a feeling we just wouldn't be lucky enough to escape them.

Chapter Twelve
Burden of a Leader

We had a quick breakfast and gulped our coffee even though it was too hot and we all added a hooded sweatshirt under our leather jackets to help protect our heads a little bit from the rain. I sighed and slung my sword over my shoulder as I hefted my bag. "Alright everyone, it's not going to get any better so we had best be moving."

There were a few half-hearted grumbles, mostly from Keevan, but nothing could be done, so he stopped after a few mild complaints, and a stern look from his brother.

I should have known that day was going to only get worse when the rain really broke around midday and drenched us. Our leather clothing protected us some, and we stayed dry for the most part, but warmth was another thing, for leather just wasn't warm and when it was wet, it was even less so. We found a small outcropping where we rested and took a bite to eat, knowing we had to keep our metabolism up in the cold weather. I wished we could make coffee, but we wouldn't have been able to light a fire.

"I wish we could have brought the small electric

stove," Tierney said as he gnawed regrettably on the beef jerky we were passing around.

"You could have carried it if you wanted it so bad," I told him and grinned. "Bet you wouldn't say no to those microwave dinners now."

He scrunched up his face. "Actually…"

Riordan clamped a hand over Tierney's mouth suddenly and he stopped talking, as did the rest of us.

"What?" I whispered.

"I caught a scent through the rain," the berserker said. "Almost smelled like Goblin."

"Are you sure it wasn't just the wet ground?" Deaglan asked, stomping his boot heel into it. "It does smell rather earthy around here."

Riordan glared at him. "I know the different between rain-wet earth and Goblin, Mac Dairmuid. Where were you during that portion of tracking class? Oh, I forgot, probably off larking with some colleen in the janitor's closet."

"Riordan!" I hissed as I saw Deaglan readying an argument that would only draw attention of an unwanted variety. "Focus!"

The berserker nodded, an apologetic look on his face as he turned back around and went to the edge of the outcropping to scout. He was only watching for a few seconds before he spun back around.

"There's a patrol of Goblins out there," he said. "Coming this way."

"That's our lads sure enough," Tierney said grimly.

"Come, we'll head out the back," I said, already moving. "We might be able to give them the slip."

We all gathered our packs quickly and rushed out of the place and around the backside of the hill. I caught sight of the Goblins disappearing in the direction we had just been and breathed a short sigh of relief as I urged my companions on.

"Come on, over the next hill before they come out."

But there was a shout behind us and suddenly an arrow whizzed past my cheek and another buried itself into Riordan's pack before he turned around.

"Run!" I shouted and we all broke into a sprint, slipping up the side of a hill and then practically sliding down the other on our backsides where we came out, unfortunately onto even ground. But there were still scattered rocks, and we made good use of them as the Goblins occasionally fired arrows at us, though I didn't think they wanted us dead, otherwise, they would be trying a lot harder to hit us. Either that or they weren't much good, which was a story I wasn't quite willing to bet my life on at that moment. I got the feeling they were just trying to keep us down so they could launch a proper attack. Take us alive.

"Over here!" Tierney cried, waving us over to one side. There was a slight drop off and a ravine down below with places we could hide. I looked back quickly to see the Goblins still a good distance behind us, and nodded. "Come on!" We leapt over the side, and only then did I realize how rocky it was, but it was too late to change course after that. I caught Caitlin just as she slipped and almost fell into the rocks myself, somehow managing to keep my feet even as I was running recklessly down the hill so that we could get out of sight before the Goblins reached the top. Keevan rolled several feet before he was rescued by his brother, but Deaglan wasn't so lucky. Riordan tried to grab him too, but the Finar's slick wet coat slid out of his grasp and he tumbled down the hill over several rocks and lay in a heap at the bottom.

"Deaglan!" I hissed, not daring to shout for fear of an echo. I skidded the last few feet and stopped beside him as Tierney nearly knocked me off my feet when he slid into my back.

Deaglan pulled himself upright from the rocks, looking pale and bashed around a bit, but seeming to be all right as far as I could see.

"Are you good?" I asked him gruffly.

"I'm good," he said, surreptitiously pressing his right arm against his chest, but I didn't notice because I was too busy turning to look up and make sure the Goblins hadn't made an appearance yet. "Come on, we need to go now!" I knew it was only a matter of time before they caught up to us and I wanted to at least have found a place to make a stand before that.

"Head to the left," I told them and we went farther into the ravine, slipping down another crack just as I heard the Goblins at the top. I led the company further until the ravine evened out and then we doubled back, having to press ourselves flat and hope the rain masked our scent as the Goblins passed not ten yards from us. After that we ran for a while longer before we could breathe a sigh of relief. We stopped for a moment and I listened but couldn't hear or sense any sign of Goblins anymore.

"I think we lost them for the moment," I told the others. "Come on, let's see if we can find somewhere to hole up for the night."

We set off again but kept a sharp eye out for any sign of goblins. I had no idea whether they would split up to find us or not. Goblins weren't quite as good at tracking as Na Fianna, but they weren't bad either, and I knew that if they were determined enough, they could find us even in this deluge.

The rain pounded down and the ground was slippery. Once I caught Deaglan by the arm as he slipped and he flinched away from me with a hiss. I glared at him.

"Are you sure you're all right?" I asked, putting a steadying hand on his back, having forgotten his fall in the commotion that followed.

He jerked away from me. "I'm fine, just banged up a bit." He hurried on and I glared at his retreating figure. The least he could do was be gracious about it. I was only trying to be nice. I shook my head at my dark thoughts. I was tired, cold, and worried and I just wanted to find a place we could all rest safely for the night and start again in the morning.

The Goblins did not show themselves again as we carried on and I hoped we had seen the last of them. I thought it likely they might go back to their palace and report our arrival and hoped that was true. They might bring more Goblins with them, but I figured we had a good chance of surprising them in their own home before that happened.

Riordan found us a small shallow cave that would give us at least some shelter from the rain. We sat huddled in the lee, wet and uncomfortable and shared a light supper of beef jerky and some granola bars. What I really wanted was a hot cup of coffee or soup, something to warm my icy hands on, but the Goblins were too close as it was, and there was no chance of setting a fire in this rain anyway. I was beginning to feel jealous of the fingerless gloves Riordan and Keevan were sporting—probably made by the berserker—and wished I hadn't forgotten to pack mine. We didn't even bother setting our bedrolls out that night, for they would only get soaked, and just huddled together, trying to share what little warmth we had, rotating who got the middle spaces every once in a while.

None of us slept well, and I didn't bother setting an actual watch, I just let anyone who couldn't sleep stay up and then wake someone else if they started to doze off. We were all freezing, and unfortunately, it numbed our senses as well as our bodies. I was supposed to be on watch; I really did try my best to keep an eye on everything, but just at the moment I was going to wake Tierney to take over, something caught my eye and I lazily looked over to see a flash of paleness in the dark. And that was all the warning I got.

The Goblins were on us before I even realized it. I grabbed my sword and shouted out for the others to rouse themselves. Tierney was at my side instantly, and Riordan was a strong presence at my back that, albeit, made me a little bit nervous.

"Deaglan, try and pick them off!" I shouted as the first Goblin charged and I leapt forward to meet him head on with my sword. We traded several blows before I cut him across the ribs and he fell with a scream of pain, staggering backward behind his comrades again. I turned to the next one, seeing Caitlin run past me to engage the others.

"Deaglan!" I called again, seeing him fumbling with the bow in an uncharacteristically clumsy fashion, likely due to his cold fingers. "A little more speed will do!"

He growled something impolite at me and raised his bow with a groan. I frowned but then caught sight of a movement out of the corner of my eye, and saw a Goblin raising his own bow and aiming straight for Caitlin who was engaging one of his comrades fiercely.

"Deaglan, shoot him!" I shouted angrily, just as the

other Finar began to draw his bow only to collapse with a shocked scream of pain, the arrow twanging off the string. I had no time to see to the fool, I threw myself forward and slammed into Caitlin, bringing her to the ground just as the Goblin released his arrow. He cursed and drew his sword instead, advancing on Keevan who was screaming and swinging his axe in a business-like manner. Caitlin wheezed as I rolled off her and hauled her to her feet.

"Sorry about that," I told her.

"No need to be sorry," she replied with a breathless laugh as she turned around to await the next enemy as I ran forward to engage another Goblin, trading several blows before I sliced him deeply across the thigh and he staggered back, barely able to keep his leg under him.

Another Goblin screamed and he staggered away from Keevan, grabbing the side of his face where it looked like he was missing an ear from a close encounter with the redheaded Finar's axe.

"Goblins retreat!" came a cry, and one Goblin grabbed the one facing Keevan and hauled him backward as they hurried away. I watched as they limped off, helping their wounded. I did a quick count and saw there were twelve. About eight now since some of them had been wounded pretty badly.

I stood panting, making sure they were gone, before I angrily wiped my blade off in the wet grass and spun around to face Deaglan. I strode up to him and gripped him by the front of his jacket, hauling him to his feet as he fought to keep from gasping in pain.

"Take it off," I commanded and before he could react, I had yanked down the zipper of his jacket and tore it unkindly from his right shoulder. He groaned involuntarily and I saw instantly that the shoulder was swollen around the socket. Instead of having pity, I flew into a rage red enough to rival a berserker.

"You bloody idiot!" I shouted in Deaglan's face, startling him. "I suppose you think it was brave that you kept your pain from us, but that was the wrong thing to do."

"So you want me to go crying about every little bruise?" he snarled, shoving me back, I shoved him harder and he fell onto his backside in the mud, wincing as the fall jarred his shoulder.

"You don't understand, do you?" I asked. "That dislocated shoulder disables you from using your bow, from being any use to us. You almost got Caitlin killed! It's not about personal pride, Deaglan; it's about what's best for the entire company! For your brothers! If a wound puts not only you but your comrades in danger, then you had bloody well let us know about it. Don't play the idiot hero—oh so strapping and courageous! There's no air-headed lasses out here to impress!"

"Ciran—" Tierney tried to intervene but I held up a hand to stop him, too angry and frightened by the gravity of the situation to listen to anyone right then.

"Riordan, hold him down," I said and before Deaglan could protest, the big Finar wrapped his arms around Deaglan's chest, pinning his sound arm to his side. I set my boot against Deaglan's sternum unceremoniously. I was in no mood for pity; I didn't even give him something to bite. I just grabbed his right arm and yanked the joint back into place with a vicious tug.

Deaglan yelled once, but then clamped his teeth shut, glowering at me, but too out of breath and pale from the pain to say anything. I reached into my pack and drew out a bandage, forming a sling out of it before I stood up, tossing him a flask.

"Next time, don't play the hero."

"Fine," he gritted out taking a deep swig from the flask. "Maybe you can lay off being a jerk too."

I lunged at him with a growl, some very scathing reply on my lips, but Tierney and Riordan had grabbed me by the arms and drew me back.

"Hey, Ciran!" Tierney admonished, shoving me backwards and standing between me and the injured Finar. "Calm down! Fighting isn't going to get us anywhere. It's over now, everyone's all right. He's learned his lesson."

I wasn't quite certain of that but I was in no position to argue at the moment either. Besides, I was the leader and it was unseemly to get into such arguments. Especially when we had the enemy around. I shrugged out of my companions' grasp and picked up my pack again.

"All right everyone, let's move. We can't stay here now. They'll likely be heading back to where they came from, if we can track them at all, we need to try."

No one argued, obviously sensing my bad mood. I didn't have the heart to change it just yet. I was still so angry at Deaglan. First he had nearly gotten us lost at a Faery dance while taking a pee in the woods, and now he had neglected to tell me of a debilitating injury that had nearly gotten Caitlin killed. He'd have to answer for his stupidity, but I knew better than to talk to him now. I was too angry and I'd likely say something I would later regret, and he was sore too, so I knew it was best to wait.

There was one good thing about that day however, for around mid afternoon the rain stopped and the sun even came out, warming us up and helping to dry our clothes. It put us all into a better mood and we were nearly content by the time we made camp that night, not having seen any sign of Goblins the entire day. We still didn't build a fire, not knowing how far away they were, but we were able to set out groundsheets to put our bedrolls on and were relatively warm. It almost made up for the cold supper.

I took first watch, as was my custom and in between scanning the landscape, I watched as everyone settled down to rest. I had been amused the first night out to witness their different sleeping habits. Tierney, of course, I knew well enough having camped with him countless times and been his roommate on more than one occasion. He always either sprawled on his back or front—hopefully on his front, otherwise, he would snore and rarely moved once deeply asleep. Caitlin brought a smile to my lips, for she slept curled up with her sleeping bag almost covering her entire head and I think she kept her sword inside with her for I never saw it anywhere nearby. Deaglan usually slept on his back with a relaxed look, and one hand behind his head that was not far from his bow; but tonight he was huddled on one side with his injured shoulder up. Riordan and Keevan usually slept next to each other, and it made me laugh, because they would start the night a couple feet apart and then Keevan would somehow move in his sleep so that he always ended up curled against his older brother's back like a dog. Riordan always slept on his side, unmoving, with one hand resting on the hilt of one of his twin swords. I marveled how they all looked so unguarded when they slept, so peaceful even though I knew they were all primed for action. I wondered with mild amusement what I looked like when I was asleep and hoped I looked half as restful.

But that night I had more troubling thoughts in my head than worrying about my sleeping habits. The attack that morning had been a surprise and we had not been ready for it. *I* had not been ready for it. It had happened quicker than I expected it to, and I didn't like those odds. It seemed more Goblins were coming down out of the northern Faelands, and I knew we only had a matter of weeks at the least to solve our problem. It could not be safe to leave it any longer. I was nearly positive that King Lorcan was planning something.

And then there was the new problem with Deaglan, something I had been afraid would happen when I took him into the company; although, I didn't necessarily believe he would *actually* cause a problem. But I guess my initial fears had been realized after all. I did not doubt his courage or his ability—no, on the contrary, I thought he had all too much. Something was going on within him, some warring faction that needed to be sorted out quick before the rest of us suffered for it. I only hoped that it had nothing to do with Caitlin. If he compromised this mission out of jealousy of winning our single female companion, I would personally kick his backside back south and deem him unfit to serve in our ranks ever again. Granted, I had acted like a bit of a jerk too, but I was frightened, and an icy hand still grabbed my spine when I thought of Caitlin almost getting shot because Deaglan had been stupid and not told anyone he couldn't shoot his bow. She might have been okay and forgiving, but I wasn't sure I could be the same. I didn't doubt Caitlin's ability one bit on the battlefield, not at all, nor any of the others, but they were my responsibility, and Killian had specifically asked me to look after his sister and I would do so as if she were my own. And if she were indeed my sister, I would not let Deaglan put her in harm's way just because he wanted to be a hotshot and shoot with a dislocated shoulder.

I was sitting on a rock slightly off to one side from the camp so that I could better keep my senses tuned to the surrounding landscape. I had seen several pixies dancing nearby in the moonlight but they would not harm us. Not Fianna, and the worst they would do to human travelers was make them lose their way for a while until they got bored with their games.

I suddenly felt a presence behind me, but even before I turned around, I knew it to be one of my comrades. I was just surprised to see which one it was. Deaglan.

He smiled slightly, but I did not return it.

"What are you doing up?" I asked sternly. "It's not your watch. You should rest that shoulder because I will not be going easy on you tomorrow when you still have two good legs."

He sighed, still smiling, and sat down next to me. "I don't want special treatment, Ciran."

I snorted despite myself. "Yeah, I gathered that when you wouldn't even admit you were hurt. I think that's taking the 'I don't want special treatment' thing a little too far, don't you?"

He was silent for a moment, picking at the sling I had tied his arm in earlier so it would stay still while he slept. "I'm sorry."

I wasn't expecting that, or at least not the unadulterated humbleness behind it, and I just stared at him, unable to think of what to say. He must have thought I was still too angry to accept his apology, because he continued. "Back home…I'm, well, I'm really only known as a lady's man. Sure, I get the girls, and the other lads get jealous of that fact, but…what I always really wanted was to be a great warrior. An honorable man. Like my father." He flashed another small smile, but this time it was sad.

"The other lads, sure, they'll go out for drinks with me, we'll be each other's wingmen, and we train and go on scouting missions together, but no one ever looks at me and says anything about my abilities as a warrior. I'm one of the only Fianna who use a bow, and, well, if you don't mind my saying so, I think I do it pretty well." I had to smile at that, feeling more comfortable with his normal cocky attitude than his apologetic one. "But no one ever looks at me and instantly thinks of me as a great archer. They always see me as the playboy, as a friend, but not a brother, not like you and Tierney are. I never had a friendship like that, nor did I have a brother to take that place either." He shrugged. "I didn't used to mind it; I was a bit rebellious as a teen, but when I got out of school and finished my training, I didn't really work on changing. My father, well, he thought I was wasting my abilities. He was not very proud of me. Ever." He took a deep breath. "We had a row right before he left on the patrol. He—he called me a wastrel, and I said some things I shouldn't have. And then he was gone." He stopped and looked down and I saw his shoulder heave once as he took a deep breath to steady his emotions. I stayed silent, allowing him to continue when he was ready. "I felt so terrible, and knew I had to change, not only for him, but for me. Because I realized for the first time that it did matter, and that I was not the man I wanted to be." He smiled up at me again, his eyes wet. "In school, I always admired your brother, Ciran. He was older, smarter, a bloody good warrior, and just a good lad all around. He was never mean, and never looked down on anyone, but he would tell you how it was, and he was always there when someone needed help. I always kind of hoped that I could be like him, but at the end of the day it was just easier to be like me." He shrugged ruefully and winced. "So I decided to start now, and I hope it's not too late."

"It's never too late," I told him kindly. I felt bad for thinking so much ill of him. I hadn't known half of what he told me, and I was certainly guilty of thinking of him as simply a lady's man without any real skills but in the wooing department. I was actually kind of glad to get to know him for who he was now. He might have been rash and a bit foolish at times but weren't we all? Overall I was beginning to realize he was a rather decent fellow. Even if his cocky manner and roguish good looks got a little tiring after a while.

"I didn't mean to be such an eejit about my shoulder today," he said with embarrassment. "I guess I was just trying to prove something. But whatever it was, it was pretty stupid, wasn't it?"

"I didn't have the right to yell at you like that either, stupid or not," I told him admittedly, smiling wryly. "That wasn't very befitting a leader."

"You had every right!" he insisted. "And I thank you for it! It brought me 'round and made me realize how stupid I was acting." He laughed lightly then turned serious again. "You're our leader, Ciran, and I don't think Eamon could have chosen someone better. You have a natural ability like your brother to take charge, and I want you to know right now that you are justified in whatever you say or do to us. If we're being stupid, let us know."

I laughed slightly at that and reached out to lay a hand lightly on his shoulder. "Well, I'd thank you all to do the same in regards to myself. Make sure you tell me if I'm being an arse."

He smiled then rubbed his shoulder absently, a grimace on his face. I took pity, and stood.

"Keep watch for me for a second and I'll get something to put on that shoulder," I told him, and stopped him sternly before he could even open his mouth to protest. "And don't say no, because I will smack you round the head. What did we just learn?"

He grinned sheepishly. "All right, it does hurt a bit."

"Good," I replied with a satisfied smile. "That will teach you your lesson."

I rose to get the salve and when I returned, I rubbed some onto his shoulder and sent him back to his bedroll. He went willingly this time, and as I stayed on my watch before I would wake Tierney at three, I smiled slightly, feeling that I at least seemed to be getting a feel for my comrades. I only hoped that knowledge would turn to trust and would come out when we needed it most.

Chapter Thirteen
Turned Around

We started early the next morning after having consulted the map to see exactly where we were. We had gotten somewhat turned around running from the Goblins and needed to get our bearings back. Thankfully, we weren't as far off course as I had feared and were actually farther north than we had been, if a little more to the west than I had originally planned. I packed the map into my bag and slung it over my shoulder as we broke camp. I turned to Deaglan who had taken his arm from the sling and was testing it.

"How are you doing?" I asked him.

He flexed it slightly with a wince and shrugged with his good shoulder. "Not so bad, I guess."

"It always hurts worse the next day," Riordan said knowingly. "You'll be fine day after tomorrow though."

Deaglan smiled wryly. "Yeah, I just wish I could be more useful. If we get into a fight I won't be able to shoot."

"You can still throw knives," I told him, clapping him on his good shoulder as he looked at me, seeming somewhat surprised by the comradely gesture. "You'll be fine."

"Just stay in the middle with the women and the children," Keevan told him with a smirk and Riordan pinched the back of his neck, making him scream in protest and scrunch up as his older brother laughed.

"Alright, come on, everyone," I said, secretly smiling at the antics of my company and feeling glad they were still able to joke.

We marched off, and the sun rose above us, finally giving us something that resembled an actual spring day. I knew the farther north we got, it was still cold enough to snow in the right conditions, but that day was pleasant, and I wondered if maybe the Faeries really did bring spring quicker like the old stories always said. I knew that in the realms that held the Faery Courts, winter never touched at all. I could certainly see the difference in the others due to the sunshine and the good night's sleep we had gotten on dry ground. I thought that overall, the prospects of our mission were looking up.

That was when Caitlin made note of a standing stone we had passed around midday. The problem was that it was now midafternoon.

"Ciran," she called, pointing to the single stone, a monument to some moment in the past and carved with ancient swirling designs. "Didn't we pass that earlier?"

I looked at the stone with a frown, going over to examine it more closely. "It does look familiar."

"And here's crumbs from those really hard granola bars we ate for lunch!" Keevan said, pointing to a trail of granola that he had left earlier, eating on the march.

"How could we have gone around in circles?" Deaglan asked, looking up at the sky as if that would give him the answer he needed. "We were heading straight... north..." He pointed to the sun in confusion, turning around as he realized it wasn't where it was supposed to be. I nodded with a wry snort.

"Yeah, we were. Which means we have been traveling in the wrong direction for the past hour."

"How did we manage that?" Deaglan asked, and I snorted again, wondering whether he had learned anything at all about the Faelands.

"I told you the Little Folk might try and trick us. This is one of their favorite games. To watch as confused travelers walk around in circles."

"But shouldn't the iron prevent that?" Deaglan asked, motioning to the ring I had given him.

I shook my head. "It will only keep Faeries at a distance, not protect you from their tricks." I took my jacket off and started to turn it inside out. "This will have to do, everyone turn your jackets inside out."

They all followed my lead and the instant we put them back on, there seemed to be a more normal feel to the air that I hadn't realized was even missing before. I felt more oriented and gave a small sigh of relief that it had worked.

"That should do well enough. Now, there's a river over there, let's follow it and see if we can find a place to make camp for the night." I was shocked to see that it was almost an hour away from dusk, the sun sinking lower in the sky than it had appeared to be before. I knew that getting lost on account of Fae magic could cause one to wander for hours without realizing the passing time, and we were lucky we had realized it soon enough to correct our track before we were completely turned around.

We made our way down the river and found that it dropped off a cliff several hundred yards in front of us. As we got closer, I could hear the rushing roar of the falls. I looked over and saw a moderate incline going into a valley. I pointed to it.

"We should be able to find a place to camp down there tonight and have plenty of water if anyone wants a wash." I turned back to Deaglan and Riordan. "How's your shoulder?" I asked the former.

"Fine," he said, flexing it to prove his point. "A little stiff, but most of the pain is gone."

"Good. I want you and Riordan to scout ahead for tomorrow. Get our bearings, and we'll compare them to the map when you get back. Try to get back before dark, but we won't call you missing unless you don't show up before midnight."

"Okay," Riordan said with a nod.

"Keep an eye out for Goblin patrols," I warned. "I don't know where they are. I hope they went back home, but they might have stayed around somewhere for the sake of their wounded."

"We'll watch out for them," the berserker said with a nod. "See you later." He tried to hug his brother, but Keevan wriggled from his grasp like an eel.

"So lovey, Rearend," he complained, but I saw a smirk on his face.

"I forgot your kiss, little brother, come here!" Riordan laughed as he grabbed Keevan around the neck and kissed the back of his head teasingly, grinning. "Be good, you imp."

"I will!" Keevan cried, wriggling away from him again. "Dang it, Granny, stop embarrassing me!" He slumped off with a red face as the rest of us snorted laughs and Riordan waved to me before he and Deaglan went off. I watched them for a moment before I motioned to the others.

"Come on, let's go make camp."

We started down the river again and were just about to head down the hill when I heard something in the distance, echoing off the rocks. I stopped, holding up my hand for the others to do the same.

"What is it?" Caitlin asked. "I can't hear anything over the waterfall."

I shushed her and noticed Tierney listening too, closing his eyes, trying to figure out where the sound was originating. Keevan watched us and then looked past my shoulder to the hill below. He seemed to be scanning the landscape and then his eyes widened and I lost my concentration as I watched him point.

"Goblin patrol!"

I spun around, sliding my sword from over my shoulder and hearing the answering rasps of my companions' weapons. Keevan had his shield up and was already in a crouch as I watched the Goblins racing up the hill toward us. I did a quick count. There were six. They were missing half their men and a couple of the Goblins in this group I recognized from the fight before, having fought them myself, so they couldn't have just left their wounded. I had a bad feeling the others had gone to intercept Riordan and Deaglan. Maybe they had been watching us the whole time. I could have smacked myself for my incompetence, but there was no time for that.

"Shoulder to shoulder," I told them. "There's only two more than us, we can take them."

But the terrain was uneven and wet from the waterfall spray, and as I planted my feet I did not feel the reassuring firmness I liked best in a fight. The Goblins charged at us, and thankfully we had the high ground. Keevan took out the first one, just by smashing a shield into his chest and sending him skidding down the damp hillside. Another Goblin who had been at the first's shoulder growled and charged the young Finar with his sword raised above his head. Keevan blocked the blow and staggered back and that was all I saw of that fight, before I was occupied with one of my own.

A Goblin charged me and I recognized him as the one who had tried to shoot Caitlin before. However, this time his bow was slung across his back and he was using a kind of long, deadly looking dagger and carried a small shield. I blocked his first blow with my sword but had to reverse my left arm and take the next on the back of my bracer, feeling a bruise already forming from the force of the blow. I kicked out at him and caught him in the chest, forcing him back several paces as I too leapt backwards, trying to distance myself from the Goblin. The movement only caused him to charge me again with even more ferocity and smash his shield into my shoulder, rolling me several paces as I fell with a grunt.

I nearly lost my sword, but gripped it tighter, and flung myself back onto my feet as he raced toward me again, his blade held ready to stab me.

I hadn't realized until then how close I was to the waterfall but only had a moment to let the potential danger of my position register before I was once again engaged in a life or death struggle.

"Nowhere left to run, half blood!" the Goblin said with a chuckle, jerking his chin toward the drop off behind me. I grinned and tossed my hair out of my eyes.

"If I fall, I'm taking you with me," I told him, swinging my sword in a figure-eight before pointing it at him and motioning him forward with a casual flick of my fingers.

"Come on then. What are you waiting for?"

He smiled tolerantly before he clashed his sword against his shield and leapt off a rock, flying at me through the air and bringing me down. I let his momentum carry him over my head with the help of my boot in his gut but he just rolled when he fell and was on his feet in an instant, even though he was winded, and lunged at me with a growl.

I grabbed his wrist to keep his blade from my throat and he grabbed my sword arm as well and was pushing me back, closer to the drop—how far down it really was I'd had no time to find out.

There was a moment when I couldn't quite believe the fact I was grappling on the brink of a waterfall just like in an overblown action movie, but yet there I was and Keevan wasn't far behind, still facing off with the same Goblin he had been before, who was pressing him hard. I couldn't see where Tierney and Caitlin were because I was a bit too busy for that at the moment, but hoped they were not in as precarious a position as I was or worse.

There was a sudden yell and, forgoing all training I had ever had, I looked over with concern to see Keevan slipping off his rock and falling down with the rushing water, the Goblin he had been fighting going with him.

I would have screamed for him, even knowing it wouldn't have done anything, but I was suddenly slammed in the face by the hilt of my opponent's sword. I teetered back on the precipice but gained my balance just before I received another strike that knocked the sword out of my wet hand. I kicked out at the Goblin, but he caught my leg and I knew then, with horror, that this was it. He grinned, knowing as well, and I flailed my arms as he pressed me back. The only thing I could do now was take him with me, but I didn't even get that chance.

"Have a nice swim, Finar," the Goblin said with a jeer, before he let me go and I fell backwards.

It wouldn't have been terrible, but for the fact that halfway down I slammed into the side of the cliff, smashing up my side, and by the time I hit the freezing water, well, I hardly remembered the impact enough to tell about it.

Chapter Fourteen
On the Brink

I awoke feeling like I had been thrown down a hill of rocks and snow and somehow survived the fall. Everything hurt, I was strangely chilled, and I found that my arms were pinned to my sides for some reason. I began to wonder whether I had been captured, and tried to recall what had happened before I had blacked out. I struggled weakly in my bindings, but only managed to make my right side twinge uncomfortably.

Well, if I was bound then I wanted to at least know who my captors were, so I decided instead to work on opening my eyes—something I strangely hadn't thought of doing beforehand. It took several blinks to clear them, but I eventually saw that I was staring up at a rocky overhang and there was some daylight shining in under it, looking to be mid-morning. Where was I? And what had happened? I remembered Goblins, fighting—yes, there had definitely been a fight. My head pounded as I fought to recall the details.

As I became more attuned to my surroundings, I had

the strange realization that someone was breathing against my neck. I instantly thought *Daegal* because he was usually the only person who ever shared a bed with me apart from occasional overly-affectionate wolfhound puppy, but I knew he was back home, so who? I turned my head with a wince and was surprised and, I'll admit, somewhat apprehensive to see Caitlin pressed up against my side, her head on my shoulder and one hand resting on my arm. I turned to my other side and saw Tierney with his back pressed up against me, breathing easily in his sleep.

I lay there for a few minutes, trying to puzzle my position out and then suddenly it all came to me. There was a waterfall and I had stupidly allowed myself to get pushed to the edge of it and had been thrown over by my opponent. The water would have been freezing too, likely the reason for all the blankets. I must have been near frozen when they dragged me out of the river, and I had hit my head on the way down. I felt better, at least mentally, since I had remembered what happened, and began to wriggle some more to get them to wake up. I managed to loosen one leg and nudged Tierney with my knee.

"Wake up," I croaked.

Tierney jerked slightly and turned slowly around, bleary, before he realized I was awake and sat up, looking down at me as he put a hand to my throat as if to check my pulse.

"Ciran, you're awake! I thought I'd lost you for a moment, brother."

I wriggled some more, slapping his hand away, wincing slightly as my ribs twinged. "Not so lucky, it seems. Can you please get me out of here, I can barely breathe."

Caitlin woke up then, slowly opening her eyes and

then sitting up rather quickly when she realized I was awake. She smiled brightly, putting a hand on my shoulder.

"Ciran, how are you feeling?"

"Like a haggis," I told her, starting to get irritated.

They laughed and began unwrapping me. They got about half way before I realized that the blanket was actually the only thing I was wearing, so once I got my arms free, I adjusted it around myself so that it was less constricting but still warm, not to mention covering me.

"Um, can I have my clothes please?" I asked, feeling rather awkward about the entire situation.

"I'll get you a new pair," Caitlin said, standing up. "Your others probably aren't dry yet." She hurried off and returned soon with my second change of clothes and a sweatshirt. "I'll go make some coffee," she said quickly and left. "It should be safe enough to start the fire now."

"Help me up," I said to Tierney who helped me dress before I sank gratefully back down onto the bedroll, my right side aching. "What happened anyway? I feel like I drowned."

"You did," Tierney said, supporting me with an arm around my shoulders as I zipped up my sweatshirt. "You hit your head when you fell. We had to drag you out down river. You got quite a ways before we could get to you, thankfully you ended up against a rock, but you had been forced underwater. You weren't breathing when we pulled you out." He motioned to Caitlin kneeling with her back to us by the fire pit, stirring some coffee. "Cait had to resuscitate you." He grinned and winked. "It seems she does know a little first aid after all."

I looked over to her, a new respect forming over top of what was already there. "She knows how to step up when things need to be done," I said admiringly.

"Lucky for you," Tierney told me with a grin, punching me in the arm. "I love you, brother, but I am *not* going to put my mouth on yours."

I laughed, punching him back. "Oh, so if she hadn't been there, you would have let me die? Some comrade you make."

"Not so," Tierney said, pretending offence. "I would have found a beautiful Faery to do it. But seriously, Cir," he added, sobering. "I am glad you're all right. You were so cold when we brought you back here and with that knock to the head? We were afraid we would never get you warm again."

"Well, I am still a little chilled," I said, truthfully. "But I'll be fine after some coffee, I think."

"Why don't you go sit by the fire?" Tierney said. "We would have set one last night, but we didn't want to attract attention. I hoped that Caitlin and I would provide enough warmth to keep life in you."

He helped me up, and I was happy with the fact that I could walk by myself for the most part, though Tierney kept a guiding hand on my shoulder just in case. Caitlin smiled as I sat down.

"Coffee's almost ready," she said.

"Thank you," I replied and pulled up my shirt to inspect my side, prodding the bruises gently, but finding that, amazingly, there were no broken ribs underneath them.

"We didn't think anything was broken," Caitlin said as she handed me my coffee and I wrapped my hands around it gratefully. "You have quite a knock on your head though. Just as a warning before you look in a mirror."

I gingerly reached up to touch it and winced as I felt

the lump and dried blood. I took a sip of the coffee and sighed in contentment as it slid down my throat, warming me from the inside out and working to help the headache.

"Where are the others?" I asked offhand, before a sudden thought struck me that nearly had me spitting out the next sip of coffee. "Keevan! Where is Keevan? He fell too!"

Tierney and Caitlin shared a look, their faces pale. I glared at them.

"Where is Keevan?" I asked them as if they were simpletons.

"We couldn't find him, Cir," Tierney said quietly. "We looked after we fished you out, but...he wasn't anywhere nearby and we had to get you warmed up or you would have died."

I was on my feet, pain shooting through my head, but I hardly noticed. "You left the youngest member of our company in danger to take care of me? Why would you do that? You must have known how I would feel about it!"

"Ciran," Tierney said firmly, taking my shoulder and trying to push me back down. "We *had* you, and so you were our first priority. We would not have left Keevan if we had known where he was, but we didn't know where to start and we didn't know how long it would take to actually find him, and in that time, you were dying. If it had been Keevan we found first, we would have done the same thing, but you were the one, so you were our priority. We plan to look for him now as soon as we get you settled."

I sat down, anger and grief washing over me. Part of me wanted to berate them, punish them for this, but the other more sensible part of me knew that they had done the right thing, and though I felt terrible taking precedence over Keevan's safety, it was one of the laws of survival. You always took care of the man you had with you first, then went after the others. I might have hated to admit it, but they had done the right thing.

"Where are Riordan and Deaglan?" I asked, rubbing my head tiredly, horror and guilt at the thought of Riordan's reaction to his brother's disappearance making me sick. "Are they out looking?"

"They haven't gotten back from the scouting mission you sent them on before we were attacked yesterday," Caitlin explained. "We were afraid they might have run into trouble."

I groaned. Could this have gone any worse? "What happened after I fell?"

"We wounded two Goblins pretty badly," Tierney said. "And the rest dissipated, calling it off. They whisked their wounded off and ran back north. We didn't really get a chance to see where because we were already running down to find you and Keevan."

"There weren't as many Goblins as the other night," Caitlin mused as if to herself. "Do you think the others might have been tracking Riordan and Deaglan?"

"I can only assume so," I replied tiredly, drinking my coffee and feeling the comfortable warmth flood through me. "I just hope nothing happened to them. Once we find Keevan we should go and search them out."

As if on cue, there was a shout of announcement and we looked over the hill to see Deaglan and Riordan coming back into the camp. They were both grinning and I felt instantly worse for the news I would have to relay.

"How fairs our noble leader?" Deaglan asked, clapping me on the shoulder and making me wince. He frowned as he saw my head. "What happened? Were you attacked? We routed a group of Goblins, which is why it took us so long to get back. I kept their heads down with my arrows and eventually they gave up, thinking there were more of us than there actually were and hurried off back north. We thought you would send out a rescue party when we didn't return, but when you failed to do so, we feared you might have been attacked as well."

Before I could answer, Riordan was frowning, looking around the campsite. "Where's Keevan?"

Caitlin opened her mouth to explain, but I stopped her, standing to face Riordan myself. It was my duty after all. "Riordan, Keevan fell off the waterfall when we were fighting. I'm afraid we don't know what's become of him, but we're going to go out looking right away."

There was a blank shock on his face first, then it slowly turned to rage. "What happened?" he whispered.

Caitlin related the story, and all the time, Riordan was slowly clenching and unclenching his fists, making me nervous. I could see him trying to keep the berserk at bay, but I wondered how long he would be able to do so.

"Riordan, we'll find him," I said, putting a hand on his shoulder, but he shrugged me off, striding toward the stream at a fast pace. I turned to the others.

"Let's go, we've wasted enough time already. Caitlin, you stay here and ready blankets and make more coffee and boil water. Get the first aid kit out and ready too, just in case."

"Ciran, you should stay, you nearly drowned and froze last night," she protested.

"I'm fine, really," I told her, and she frowned, but I gripped her arms and forced her to look at me. "My mother is a healer; trust me, if I was not feeling well enough to do this, I wouldn't. This isn't some foolish way to prove myself. You know Na Fianna heal faster than normal people."

She sighed, not really satisfied. "Fine, but if you feel bad, come back."

I smiled. "Yes, mum."

She gave me a longsuffering look then suddenly reached down and took up my sword, handing it to me.

"We did manage to find this. Luckily it had lodged into a bunch of debris when it fell."

I smiled genuinely. "Thank you," I said, slinging it over my shoulder and then jogging off after the others at a somewhat slower pace than normal.

At least we knew that we would have to look downstream, even if we weren't sure how far. I just hoped that Keevan was still alive. I hated the thought that my fall might have delayed us getting to him in time. Leader my foot, I knew Eamon himself would have felt the same as I did now, and if we couldn't find Keevan I would never forgive myself. Well, if we didn't find him, I might not have to worry about that after Riordan got a hold of me.

We spread out, Riordan and Deaglan running ahead; myself and Tierney, spending more time casting about for clues. We had been jogging for a long time down river and we began getting to the places in the bends where things gathered. I caught sight of something glinting in the sunlight and called over to Tierney who was on the other side where the object was.

"What is that down there in those branches?" I asked.

He slid down the rocky bank, digging his sword into the ground to anchor himself as he reached down to retrieve the item. I felt a sickness tighten in my stomach as he brought it out, revealing it to be a battle-axe. I knew it had to be Keevan's even before Tierney confirmed my suspicions, because Goblins wouldn't use one and there was no one else who would have left it.

"Keevan!" I began to shout, hoping by some miracle that he would be able to hear me—if he was there at all. I started jogging along the bank again, looking for sign. Riordan and Deaglan had started casting farther out to see if maybe he had managed to climb out of the river and holed up somewhere. I also vaguely wondered what had happened to the Goblin who fell with him. Had he been killed, and if so why had we not found the body? And if he had lived, was it possible he had taken Keevan captive and we were looking in the totally wrong place?

"Keevan!" I shouted again as I continued to cast about. It was hard for even Fianna to track in the water. We had heightened sight, hearing, and sense of smell to a degree, probably five times that of a good woodsman, but we could do little with the water. Tierney was running along the other side of the stream, calling out as well. He finally found a place where he could cross and hoped back over to me.

"I don't know, Ciran," he said grimly. "Maybe we're looking in the wrong place. If that Goblin was still alive, he might have drug him out of the river and taken him back to their own camp. That might have been why we found his axe there."

"We can't give up until we know for certain," I said. "On the other hand, if there is a Goblin camp close by they might come looking for us if they have a captive, and we left Caitlin all alone at camp." That sudden realization scared me. I didn't want to think of Caitlin at the mercy of the Goblins any more than I did Keevan.

"What are we going to do then?" Tierney asked.

I hesitated. "Keep looking until Riordan and Deaglan

get back to us and then two of us will go back to camp just in case."

I was interrupted by a weak, "Help!" that came from a little ways down stream.

"Tir," I hissed.

"I heard it," he replied and we headed off.

"Riordan!" I shouted. "Riordan! I think we found him!"

I looked around frantically, trying to see where Keevan was. "Keevan, call out if you can, I can't place you." Finally I caught the sound of a moan and then a weak, "Help, I'm over here."

I tracked his voice over the water and spotted a red head caught amongst the debris that gathered in a bend in the river that acted as a catchall. It seemed it had also caught Keevan for he was there too, only his head above the water, trapped in a tangle of rocks and vegetation.

"Are you stuck?" Tierney asked as we all got up there.

Keevan nodded. He looked blue and half frozen, not to mention half drowned. "My arm, but that's not all either. I couldn't move because I had to keep *this* from running away."

I noticed for the first time the pale head that rested on a rock next to him, glowering at us now and snarling with Keevan's blue tinted hand firmly clamped around the collar of his jacket. It appeared Keevan had caught the Goblin who had pushed him over.

"How is your arm stuck?" I asked, kneeling on the bank to see what I could do.

"This rock," Keevan said, weakly. "It happened when I tried to struggle out; I somehow got it caught underneath."

"Get a lever to move that rock, Tierney," I instructed,

but at that moment Riordan and Deaglan were running back to the stream and I saw Keevan perk up at the sight of his brother.

"Riordan!" he called out.

"Keevan!" Riordan shouted, flying past me and was already wading into the river, the water nearly going over the tops of his boots, before I could explain the situation. "Come here, Keevan, give me your arm."

"I'm—I'm stuck," he whimpered. "And you've got to get this worm out first because he'll run if I let him go."

Riordan quickly hauled the Goblin out by the front of his jacket and tossed him unceremoniously onto the bank where Deaglan and Tierney grabbed him before he could run, though he looked compliant enough and half frozen to death himself. Then Riordan grabbed the rock that had trapped his brother and rolled it away as if it were a pebble. Keevan moaned weakly as he did so and reached up with his other hand. Riordan ignored it and grabbed him under the arms, hauling him up out of the freezing river with a protesting cry of pain. Keevan's teeth were chattering and he collapsed onto the bank, shivering and unable to talk or move. I made to kneel by him, but Riordan had a dangerous, protective look in his eye and I decided it was probably best not to touch his brother just then no matter how good my intentions were. He had shrugged his jacket off and was wrapping it around Keevan's shoulders to offer a little warmth.

"Let's get him back to camp," I suggested. "You two make sure that *creature* doesn't escape."

The Goblin snarled at me half-heartedly, but seemed just as frozen as Keevan and didn't look like he would put up too much of a fight, wracked with shivers as he was and having lost his weapon somewhere in the river.

Riordan picked his younger brother up in his arms, and to my surprise, Keevan didn't protest, but only huddled closer to him for warmth, still shivering uncontrollably, and pounding weakly on Riordan's breastplate, cursing it for blocking his body heat.

"We'll get you warm in a minute," Riordan assured him. "Just hang on."

We came back into camp and Caitlin looked up with relief as she saw Keevan in Riordan's arms then frowned in-credulously at our prisoner. Tierney and Deaglan found some rope and tied the Goblin up tightly, staking a lead attached to him to the ground in the little alcove away from camp that they had kept me warm in the night before, away from prying eyes.

"Make some coffee for Keevan," I told her, but she was already boiling water on the fire and she poured it into the percolator. I sat with a wince, my body still aching, and turned back as I heard a moan to see Riordan helping Keevan into dry clothes, and wrapping him in a blanket and his sleeping bag. He looked so unlike the Keevan I was used to seeing with his hair slicked back on his head and wearing a dark green jumper and sweat pants and a look of pain and utter exhaustion on his face. I was worried, and felt bad for leaving him so long in the cold even if we had really had no choice. Riordan was briskly rubbing his arms and legs and thumping his chest to help circulate the blood and I watched Keevan wincing and whimpering, until he finally lashed out at his brother angrily.

"Stop, just stop!"

"What's wrong?" Riordan asked, worried and a bit angry himself.

"I fell off a bloody waterfall, you idiot! I was too cold to feel the pain before, but now that you've kindly managed to remind me of it with your pummeling, I wish you would stop."

I fished out the first aid kit and went to kneel by them, still not sure it was safe, but deciding I had no other choice. "Where are you hurt?"

"I don't know!" Keevan replied, an exasperated sob in his voice. "Everything hurts!" Riordan gathered him to his chest gently and wrapped the blankets tighter around him. Keevan really must have been in a bad way for he made no protest, only burying his face in his brother's jumper and shivering against him. Riordan looked at me with a worried expression. I gripped the back of Keevan's neck in a comradely gesture, worried at the cold clammy feel of his skin.

"Hey, it's all right, Keev. I'll let you warm up a little before we look over your injuries." I glanced over at Caitlin and saw she was pouring coffee into a cup, which she then brought over to us. Riordan took it and helped Keevan to drink it. I left them alone for a few moments, motioning Caitlin to come with me and we went over to where Tierney and Deaglan had the Goblin staked to the ground.

"Little worm says he won't talk," Deaglan said, nudging the Goblin none-too-gently in the backside.

"Oh, he won't?" I asked, crouching down to look the Goblin in the eye. "Well, guess what? That man over there is a berserker, and you managed to hurt his brother: congratulations. Life isn't going to be very nice for you from now on. So if you don't want me to loose him on you, you had best tell me everything I want to know so that we might possibly be able to keep this conversation agreeable. If not, I want you to know now that we have no scruples when it comes to your kind."

The Goblin sneered. "You really think I'm going to talk to you? I've watched my king work prisoners over. You can't scare me with any of your paltry little tortures."

I shrugged, standing up. "Fine. Have it your way. But don't come crying to me when Riordan breaks every bone in your body. I figure you have an hour at most. Once his brother is seen to, and he makes sure he's safe, he's going to come straight for you."

I walked back over to the fire and poured myself another cup of coffee. My head was still aching, and I still had a bit of a chill from my own fall into the river though I hadn't been there nearly as long as Keevan. If he hadn't been Fianna, he likely wouldn't have survived. I hoped even now that he didn't have hypothermia. I caught the tail end of the two brothers' conversation and felt an ache for Aeden as I listened to it.

"You were really brave, Keevan," Riordan was telling him as he helped his brother drink the coffee, his hands still shaking too much to hold the cup on his own, their heads bent close. "Da would have been proud."

"I thought he was our only chance of finding out where Pat and the others are," Keevan said through his chattering teeth. "I might have let him go, I was so cold. But I couldn't because I knew he would kill me if I did. I just had to wait until you came and found me. Took you long enough!" He sniffed.

"I'm sorry *mo deartháir*," Riordan whispered. "But you know I will always come for you. I promised you that before we left, remember? You *and* mum. *Nothing* will ever keep me from you and Pat."

My eyes smarted as I looked into my coffee mug, whishing I had some honey to put into it. I remembered Aeden telling me that once when I was eight and had gotten caught in a tree I thought I could climb, but realized too late I couldn't. I had stayed there for hours until it was suppertime and the others finally realized I was missing and started to look for me. Aeden was the only one who knew where to look and I had never been so glad at the sight of my brother than at that moment. He had climbed up the tree to get me when I told him I couldn't climb down by myself and had me cling to his back as he swung so easily back down to the ground. He held me while I cried in relief and waited for me to be done before we headed back so none of the others would see my tears.

I thought no one would ever find me, I had said as I clung to him in relief.

I will always come to find you, Ciran, no matter where you are, he had replied. *You're my brother, and that means I'll always be there for you.*

Now it was my turn to be there for Aeden. I would always come to find him as well, and I was not going to let anyone stop me, for the love of brothers was a strong thing indeed, perhaps the strongest bond that can be found, and no less so in our family. Nothing, not even the Goblin King, was going to stop me from getting to my brother.

Tierney came and sat beside me, bumping his shoulder against mine as he read my mood.

"That coffee's not going to drink itself," he said. "You still need the caffeine in your system to get some heat back in your blood."

I sighed but managed a smile, slinging my arm around his shoulders. "You've always been like another brother to me, Tierney. I thank you for that."

"Aw, Cir," he said in mock distaste, causing me to lose all the rest of my grief as I snorted a laugh, nearly choking on my coffee. "None of that sentimental tripe, please. You know I hate it."

But he quickly grabbed the back of my neck and crushed me in a sudden hug before leaning over to pour himself a cup of coffee. "But you know I think the same," he said seriously.

I sighed, suddenly very weary, and wished for nothing more than to lay down and sleep the rest of the day but I knew I didn't have that option. "What are we doing wrong, Tir? This whole mission has been a hash so far. We've done nothing but get ambushed, lost, nearly captured by Fae, and drowned. And we're only half way up, if that. Lorcan must know we're here by now since he's sending his Goblins after us—what chance do we have of finding the prisoners before he decides to either get rid of them, or use them against us?"

Tierney nodded across the camp at our own prisoner. "He's our answer to it all. A little bit of necessary roughness and he'll talk readily enough. He's already been through a lot, and he's mostly working on bravado right now, as I figure it. I don't think he's much of a veteran either. He can't be too much older than you or I."

I realized he was right, the Goblin was rather young, and looking at him now, all alone in the alcove, I saw a certain vulnerability about him that I hadn't before, or that he hadn't shown when he knew we were watching.

"I don't really want to have to torture someone," I said quietly.

"I don't think you'll have to," Tierney replied. "Just let Riordan growl at him, shove him around a bit, make it convincing enough, and he'll talk. The most he's likely to suffer is a bloody nose."

I still didn't like it. Yes, a prisoner was a good card to have, but he would be no use to us if I couldn't get information out of him, and if the only way to do that was brute force? Well, I didn't like that at all. But maybe Tierney was right; maybe it wouldn't take much to get him to talk.

I looked up as I felt a footstep behind me and turned to see Riordan standing there, his face a range of emotion from anxious, to angry to grieved. I offered him a kind smile, hoping to be able to keep him calm.

"How is he?" I asked.

"He's starting to get warmer," Riordan said and I saw Keevan curled up in several blankets by the fire. "If you would check him for injuries now? I know he won't like it, but it needs to be done."

"Of course," I said, standing up. I wavered a bit from exhaustion and Tierney clamped a hand on my elbow with a worried look but I shook him off.

"I'm fine," I assured him. "Just tired."

I took up the first aid kit and went over to Keevan again. He looked up at me balefully before casting a glance at Riordan that clearly said *you traitor.* I smiled as I settled down.

"Don't worry about it, Keevan, I won't take longer than I need. Sorry to have to take your blankets off again."

He suffered me to poke him for injuries, squirming as I checked his bruised ribs for cracks. I winced as I pulled his jumper up, seeing his collection of bruises. His fall had been more painful than mine, though it might have also been because he went farther down river.

His wrist was what had worried me the most, fearing it might be broken and it was only the icy water that had kept him from feeling the full pain before, but as I felt it and rotated it to check for broken bones, even if he did wince and growl at me, I was glad to find it was only a

sprain along with the bad bruises and simply bound it tight
to keep it from moving too much. His thick leather bracer
had probably gone a long way to save it from further
damage. I gave him one of my mother's mixtures for the
pain and to help him sleep and patted him gently on the
shoulder before I left him.

"You are one brave Finar," I said sincerely. "Not
many of us would have endured that for as long as you did.
I'll make sure Eamon hears of this. Because of you, we may
be able to get important information from our prisoner
regarding our families." He smiled slightly at that and
settled back into Riordan's arms.

"Glad to help," he mumbled, already somewhat woozy
from the medicine and I tucked the blankets tighter around
him before I left him to his brother's care as he dropped
off, snoring gently.

It was nearly evening and I went over to help Caitlin
cook. Supper was a quiet affair, for we all had our minds
elsewhere and Keevan was still thankfully caught in a
restful sleep. After we had finished, Riordan turned to me.

"Permission to interrogate the prisoner?" he asked, a
low growl in his voice that made it clear he was only asking
on principle.

"Riordan," I replied hesitantly. "I don't know if that's
such a good idea."

"Please, Ciran," he ground out, making me like the
situation even less. "I need to do this."

He stood up and I followed, gripping his arm tightly
before he could move off. I spoke quietly to him so the
others couldn't hear. "Riordan, I will not condone torture,
so don't get it into your head. If you need to knock him
around a bit, fine, but keep bruises to a minimum and
blood nonexistent. I'm not going to be marked as a torturer

of prisoners."

"I'll take the blame," he said grimly.

"No," I shook my head. "This is on my head, I'm the leader of this company. What happens under my watch is my fault whether I condone it or not. You do what you need, but you do it like a gentleman, understand?"

"That *beag nathair* nearly killed my brother, Ciran, what would you have done in my place?"

I closed my eyes, trying to find strength in my progressively weakening state of mind. "Please, Riordan, just do what you're told," I gritted out, not having anything else to say. He glowered at me a moment then sighed.

"Fine." He strode off to the Goblin and I cocked my head at Tierney to follow me. We went with him, and I winced slightly as he kicked the Goblin none-too-gently to get his attention, the prisoner having nodded off in our absence.

"Wake up, you filth," he snarled.

"Filth yourself, half blood!" the Goblin snarled and Riordan kicked him again.

"Smart comments aren't going to save your sorry hide. Give me one good reason why I shouldn't just drag you back to that waterfall and throw you off again."

The Goblin smiled slightly. "Because I have information you need."

I forced myself not to say anything when Riordan backhanded the Goblin across the face so hard he sprawled to one side, his arms jerking against the stake that held him down. He pulled himself up and I saw a dark spot of blood in the corner of his mouth. He looked defiant, but I could see the fear in his eyes, and I realized I would have felt much the same in his place. I was even frightened of Riordan right now and he was on my side.

"You threw my little brother off the waterfall," Riordan told him coldly, grabbing the Goblin's angular face and forcing him to look into his eyes. "If you think I'll show you mercy, you're dead wrong. It's far too late for that. I'll get the information out of you if it's the last thing I do. And I want you to remember something before you consider clamming up: you don't need arms or legs to answer my questions."

I wanted to close my eyes against the pounding in my head, but refrained. I couldn't let the Goblin see I was exasperated with my own man. That would only make the whole thing go flat. So I kept my steely countenance and decided that I would only step in if Riordan overstepped the boundaries a little too far. I was thankful he had left his weaponry back at the campsite, but then figured that he didn't need a weapon to cause damage, and knew he was also very aware of that fact.

Suddenly, Tierney leaned close to me. "There's something over there," he said quietly and I tore my gaze away from Riordan and the Goblin for a moment to take a cautious look, not letting on that I was actually looking. I caught sight of a pale face ducking behind a rock and leaned back over to Tierney, speaking quietly to him.

"It's a Goblin. Let's make like we're going back into camp and then go up and take him between us."

Tierney nodded and we casually left Riordan to it, making our way up behind where the Goblin was hiding. I knew that in only a matter of moments he would guess our game, but by then, he would be unable to find an escape rout that wouldn't land him in a compromising position.

I saw him beginning to panic up behind the rock and then he suddenly turned with the intent of bolting, but Tierney and I were there to stop him. He growled, putting up a fight and reached for an arrow in his quiver, but I leapt at him and brought him down. He struggled beneath me as I straddled his waist and grabbed his wrists as Tierney relieved him of his weapons.

"What do you want?" I asked him.

"My brother!" he snarled and I realized he was rather young, younger even than the other Goblin. That stopped me for a moment, an almost guilty feeling coming over me before I forced a hard expression back onto my face and shoved him onto his stomach as Tierney lashed his hands together behind him.

"Get up," I snarled, hauling the Goblin to his feet and keeping a tight grip on the back of his jacket as I shoved him down into the camp. I brought him over to the place Riordan was conducting the interrogation and threw the young Goblin to the ground. The other one broke his gaze from Riordan's angry face and looked in shock at his fellow.

"Gorlan!" he cried before Riordan backhanded him across the face.

"So you do speak?" he said calmly, in a way that was scarier than if he had yelled. "Why don't you try telling me where your king is then?"

"I told you I won't," he snarled and Riordan shoved him non-too-gently in the chest with his boot, sending the Goblin sprawling on his back. The younger one was trying to get onto his knees and he gasped as Riordan grabbed him and drew him up so that his feet weren't even touching the ground.

"And what about this little shrimp?" he asked as the Goblin struggled. "Maybe he'll be more forthcoming. I didn't think there were any more of you hiding up there."

"I don't think Goblins care about each other at all. It

will do little good to use one to get the other to talk," Tierney said, making sure the Goblins heard it.

The young one snarled but the older Goblin began to look worried. He cast Riordan a hate-filled glance. "Let him go."

"You're in no place to make any demands, *tá tú sceith láibe agus cad faoi carraigeacha*," Riordan growled. I forced the smile off my face. That might not have sounded like a real insult, but apparently to Goblins it was, for they looked very offended indeed. "Why should you care for one of your own? You have no blood ties, no humanity."

"You're wrong!" the Goblin shouted, anger making him forget himself and throw caution to the winds. "You know nothing of my race! Our king does what he does for us, for his *people*, so that we may know what it is to be equals with men," he gave a short laugh, "when we should by rights be above them, for this land once was ruled by us and the Fae, and it was man who came and drove us out to confined regions. And you Fianna and those like you are abominations, for you are half bloods! I will not let such scum stand there and tell me what to do, nor will I let you torture my brother to get me to speak!"

"Your brother?" Riordan asked calmly, indicating the young Goblin he still held upright and a look of horrified realization at what he had done crossed the older Goblin's face. "Well, my friend, if you recall correctly, you hurt *my* little brother earlier." He threw the young Goblin onto the ground and I felt the rage welling inside of him from several feet away. Riordan's face was twisting into a grotesque mask of anger and I took a step back myself even though I felt that I had to step in, had to stop the storm.

"*You* would not have shown him mercy!" Riordan

shouted, his voice echoing off the rocks and valleys. "And I shall show your brother no different!" I was about to shout at him but he suddenly clenched his fists and took a deep breath, turning around so that he could no longer see the goblins. "I will be back later, and you will give me what I want to know, and if you do not, then your brother will know pain."

He stormed off and I turned to Tierney. "Make sure they don't go anywhere," I said before I hurried after Riordan.

I caught up to him outside the camp, and grabbed him before he got back into the range of the others' hearing. He spun around, the rage still obvious in his eyes and I fought the instinctive urge to flinch back.

"Riordan, you're not really going to torture them," I told him firmly. It was not an inquiry.

"Don't stop me, Ciran," he growled and I knew he was trying to keep the anger at bay.

"I will," I replied firmly. "I will not let you do that. It is folly and it is cruel."

"Wake up, Mac Cool!" Riordan snarled at me. "They would not have shown mercy to any of us should we be in their place! That one would have killed Keevan if he had been able. Do you not think our kin in Lorcan's dungeons, *our* brothers, have been treated to anything but endless torment and humiliation? It would only be repaying the blood already spilled. They do not feel like we do, Ciran."

"I don't think that's true," I told him sincerely. "I think it would be a grave mistake to think that." I looked over to where the Goblins were staked out, their heads bent as close as their bonds permitted and the younger one looking up into his brother's eyes as if to seek reassurance. My stomach twisted and a pain entered my chest making me feel ill. Perhaps I was weak, needlessly compassionate, but I knew I could not watch them be tortured. I could not condone that.

"We can do this another way," I told him even as he shook his head at me. "Riordan, listen to me…"

"No!" he shouted, grabbing my shoulders and shaking me. My feet left the ground, but it was too late to go back now. "Keevan almost *died*! You'd feel the same if it was your little brother, wouldn't you?"

"I would!" I assured him, trying to calm him down. "But that is the Goblin's little brother too, and you can't possibly tell me you would feel nothing hearing him plead for you not to hurt his baby brother in front of him. What if it were Keevan? What if they tortured him in front of you and made him scream? Made him cry out for you to keep him from that pain, and you were forced to give up your country and your kin to stop it." It was horribly cruel of me to say that, and my chest ached so much I could hardly get the words out, but I needed to get his attention and I didn't know another way to do it. "You might give up anything his tormenter wanted for that, but it would still hurt you for the rest of your life that he had to suffer in the first place and was only saved because of your betrayal of everything else. Would you want to be put in that position?"

Riordan looked like he was going to calm down but the rage suddenly rekindled and he threw me on the ground, winding me, his fists clenching and I knew he was going to pummel me into the ground in another second, I was just bracing myself for it.

"You would dare liken my brother to such filth?" he shouted and I helplessly raised an arm to protect my face, when someone grabbed Riordan's arm and he spun around without thinking and decked them. I heard a grunt and when I sat up, I saw a sudden look of devastation erase all the anger on Riordan's features as he gazed down at Keevan who had been laid flat by his own hand.

"Keevan," he breathed and fell to his knees even as the redhead was hauling himself up. He only got halfway there before Riordan took him by the arms gently and reached out, his thumb brushing the split skin above Keevan's left cheekbone, mortified. "Oh Keevan, I'm so sorry, I didn't mean it."

Keevan thrust his hand away and staggered out of his brother's grasp, shoving him backward, anger plain on his face. "You're sorry, are you? Well, are you going to tell that to Ciran too? That's our leader, our *commander*, you bloody idiot! You can't throw him around like that! You can do that to me, you can hit me all you want, but hitting Ciran Mac Cool is mutiny and by rights he can put you to death or flog you or something for it. I don't even care either. You're *not* my big brother, I don't know what came over you, I hate you right now, how could you even consider...?" He broke off from his rambling and began to sob. I was on my feet by then and I reached out to put a hand on his shoulder as Riordan stood dumfounded, gazing at his little brother, Keevan's outburst the only thing that had worked through his rage-clouded mind.

Keevan shook, still weakened by his ordeals that day. He sank to the ground and I quickly took off my jacket to put around his shivering shoulders. Riordan crouched down cautiously in front of him. He reached out a hand and placed it gently on Keevan's shoulder.

"Keevan, please, what's wrong? Tell me?" he asked.

Keevan angrily scrubbed the sleeve of his jumper over his eyes and sniffed wetly. "You would kill anyone who dared look at me the wrong way, and I know that's because you're my big brother, and I'm okay with that. But keep it on the battlefield! You can't torture that Goblin. I know they're Goblins, I know they're the enemy, but that's still his little brother, and if you hurt him to make his brother talk, I'll never forgive you Riordan. That's bloody cruel and we—we don't do that. If we did, we'd be no better than they are."

"Then what are we going to do?" Riordan asked, seeming at a loss now that his rage had left him. "Keevan, we have to find our families; it's our orders directly from the High King himself!"

"He never said anything about torture, and if Eamon were here he would tell you the same!" Keevan cried.

I knew he was right and I turned to Riordan. "Eamon would not approve of this, but I do have a plan. It's still cruel, but it doesn't involve torture—at least not of the physical variety. Let's all get together now, and we'll discuss our next action."

I turned my back to leave them a few moments and before I left I saw Riordan draw Keevan up to his feet and enfold him in a hug that Keevan accepted grudgingly.

"I'm so sorry, I didn't think, I was angry, and remembered how scared I was when I thought I had lost you too," Riordan said as I walked away.

"You idiot," was all Keevan replied, but I knew it was in the highest affection possible coming from him.

I called Tierney and Deaglan over to the fire to join the meeting, positioning myself so that I could keep an eye on the Goblins and make sure they would not try to make a break for it.

"We've really gotten out of hand," I began with. "This mission has really done a number on us, and I think it's time to stand back and take another look at it. Find another approach. If I'm going to be honest, I think we've made a bloody hash of it so far." I glared around the fire, and everyone except Tierney—who knew I wasn't directing my anger at him—looked down with a sheepish expression. "I blame myself first and foremost, for that is where the blame is to lie—with the leader," I said, softening the blow a bit. "And I wish that I could go back and do it again." I took a deep breath and looked at them sincerely. "Going into this mission, I had no idea what I was doing. I don't pretend to even now, but I think that with all we've been through already, I have a much better idea of what will and will not work. I think the best thing we can do right now is to regroup and rethink a better plan. I say we go back to the safe house, spend a few days, heal, rest, get ourselves together again, and then go out with fresh heads to complete our mission. Who's in favor?"

"I say that's a good idea," Tierney said.

"Me too," Caitlin added, sounding almost relieved.

The other three nodded, but Deaglan raised a hand to broach another subject.

"And what of the prisoners?" he asked. "Are we going to use them for information? You're not planning on letting them go are you?"

"I am not," I replied sternly, casting a glance over at the prisoners again and taking a deep sigh, my stomach twisting at the thought of what I had planned. "I have an idea of how we can get the information we need. I'm not proud of it, but it's the only way. Now come, let's pack up and get back."

Chapter Fifteen
The Burden of Necessity

After all our running and getting turned around, I was surprised and extremely glad to find upon consulting the map, that we were only a few miles away from the place we had stashed the Rovers. Bad for the success of our mission as a whole, but good for our current position. I was just glad I had decided to drive up into the Faelands in the first place. If we had left them back at the safe house I don't even know whether we would have made it on foot. Thankfully, they seemed to be untampered with due to the iron charms I had left to ward off curious Faeries.

It was tricky getting the Goblins in, but I packed them in the trunk of one, blindfolded, and tied back to back, and set Riordan to sit in the back seat and keep an eye on them. They were quiet, stoic and cowed; I knew they feared what would happen, and I let them, even though it undeniably made me feel like a real villain and disgusted me because of that.

We were a sorry bunch to be sure. Everyone looked thrashed and I noticed it even more so when we stumbled

into the safe house. None of us felt clean enough to avail
ourselves of the furniture so we stood around looking lost.
Keevan had to sink into a kitchen chair for he was still
weak and his arm was hurting him. I helped Tierney take
the Goblins into the bunkroom and we tied them to one of
the bunks until we were ready to enact our plan.

"All right, first things first," I told the others.
"Showers, and then food. Keevan gets first dibs because
he's hurt, then Caitlin as our token female. The rest of you
can fight it out, I'll take last. Leave me some hot water." I
set about throwing something together for lunch. It wasn't
much and I wasn't in the mood to eat anyway. Tierney
helped me silently for a while, until he decided to broach
the subject I was dreading.

"I know you don't like it, but it's better than the other
option," he said quietly.

"I know," I replied shortly. "But I still think it's cruel.
I don't look forward to it."

"Nor do any of us," Tierney said. "But sometimes…
sometimes you have to play dirty when it's the only way.
And think, it will only be cruel until the end and then
hopefully everything will work out all right."

I closed my eyes and nodded but I knew this was one
of those things that I would hate myself for for the rest of
my life. But that was part of being a leader, and even more
so, simply part of being a man. I thought of what Aeden or
my father would do in the same situation, and decided I
was doing the right thing even if it went against every
feeling of what was right in my head. I felt a deep
melancholy in my heart as I longed to be able to talk to
Aeden about this, to just ask his advice, and speak to him
face to face. I could have called Daegal just to have
someone to talk to, but I hoped he never found out about

this, to be honest. And my father...well, it's not that I didn't want to ask his advice, I had just rarely done so when I had Aeden, and it would feel strange, and likely make me more nervous about the whole situation to seek out his advice now. No, I had to do this alone and hope for the best. Otherwise, how would I learn for the future?

"I just hope this works," I said to no one in particular.

I didn't shower after the others. We all ate a quick lunch and then Riordan and I went to fetch the prisoners. The two Goblins cast each other a fretful look before they steeled their gazes when we untied them and hauled them to their feet. The elder brother, we tied to one of the kitchen chairs, which we had brought into the bunkroom. The younger I held onto. Riordan took extra time in securing the ropes and then he bent down, hands on knees, and put his face right into the Goblin's.

"Are you ready to tell us what we need to know now?" he asked.

The Goblin took one glance at his younger brother who was trembling in my grip, but then cast his eyes down and hissed, "no."

"Fine then," I said and started to drag the younger Goblin into the bathroom off to one side. "It will be less messy in here." I held up a hand and Riordan tossed me a package of innocent tools, but the clink they made as I caught them sounded ominous and to frightened prisoners would surely conjure images of torture implements.

I shoved my charge ahead of me, and slammed the bathroom door behind us. He had sprawled into the bathtub and looked up at me with horrified eyes, no longer trying to put on false bravado now that he was certain of his painful demise. I took out a rag and stuffed it in his mouth, grabbing his chin and crouching low beside him so that I could speak in a whisper no one outside the room would be able to hear.

"Listen to me," I told him sternly and he looked at me with wide eyes as I rattled the bag and dumped it out to let the tools clink against the bathroom floor. "If you and your brother want to live, you will do exactly as I say, do you understand?"

He nodded, confused, but so obviously desperate that he would listen to anything I was about to say. I tried not to let that look cause me inner turmoil. "Your brother is going to answer our questions because he's going to hear you scream." The Goblin backed away from me, but I grabbed him again and he whimpered in fear. I looked him directly in the eyes.

"When I remove this gag, I want you to scream and don't stop screaming until I tell you to. I hope you're a good actor. Do you understand?"

He nodded frantically and I went to the door and opened it a crack, peeking out.

"Well?" I asked.

"He's not talking," Riordan said grimly.

I nodded slowly. "Maybe this will persuade him." I slammed the door shut, kicked the tools to make them clatter and then reached over and took the gag from the Goblin's mouth. "Scream," I hissed at him. And he did.

I had to cover my ears for his scream started slowly, but rose to something that seemed to paint pictures of unspeakable tortures that I wouldn't even have thought of inflicting on anything—human, Fae or otherwise. The guilt was mounting in my chest again, but I had to give the kid marks for being a good actor, even if it was born of desperation.

As his screams grew hoarse, I gave him the signal to

tone them down and he turned them into whimpers. I nodded approvingly, then quickly reached into my pocket and took out a package of fake blood (black for Goblin blood) I had made in the kitchen with die and corn syrup, and took off my jacket and breastplate, before liberally splashing it all over my arms and chest and even some on my face. I opened the door and peeked out to see Riordan smiling into the Goblin's face and the two of them looked over as I opened the door. I saw the pain and grief on the Goblin's face and made sure he saw the 'blood' on my hands. I nearly lost my nerve when I saw the utter fear and horror he expressed at the sight of me, but it would hopefully all be over soon.

"Well?" I forced myself to say nonchalantly.

"One more thing," Riordan said. "He's been singing like a bird." He turned back to the goblin. "How do you get into the palace?"

The Goblin hesitated, and I began to turn back into the room, when something like a sob escaped from his throat and he blurted it out. "It's a lever hidden behind a rock at the entrance. There's another back door, that can be accessed on the cliff face." He was utterly defeated but I felt no elation for our victory, only sickness. "There's a hidden staircase; you can only see it if you look at it from the right angle, but the door itself is never locked because it is hidden so well." He slumped in his bindings. "Is that all you need to know?" he asked in a hoarse voice. "Can I…" He gulped. "Can I see my brother?"

Riordan looked at me and nodded. I motioned to the Goblin. "Untie him."

Riordan untied the Goblin and I ducked back into the bathroom. The younger brother was still sitting in the bathtub, looking anxious. He flinched slightly as I reached over to haul him back up, but seemed incredulous when I untied him.

"What…" he began to say but I glared at him.

"You're still our prisoners. But you can hardly go anywhere either, so I think I'll allow you this small luxury." He looked up at me and met my eyes.

"You're not all bad, I suppose," he said grudgingly.

I ignored him, and grabbed his upper arm firmly as I took hold of the doorknob. "Just behave and no harm with come to you or your brother," I told him and opened the door.

The other Goblin Riordan had left locked by one hand to the bed. He sat slumped with his free hand over his face and I was sincerely glad when his younger brother called out to him to reveal he was still all right.

"Jarlath!" he called, pulling against me. I let him go, knowing he wasn't going any farther than his brother. The older Goblin's head shot up and looked in relieved joy at his younger brother who threw himself into his arms.

"Gorlan, I thought…" he glared over his brother's shoulder at me after checking him for injuries, pure hatred on his face.

"How could you do that?" he snarled. "That was cruel!"

"Crueler than actually torturing him?" I asked sternly, though his words cut to my heart in a way I could not reveal to him. "Be thankful your brother is unharmed. I do not even know if the same luxury has been afforded mine."

That shut him up. His face turned shocked then incredulous. He stared at me with an unreadable expression for a few seconds before he turned back to his brother and held him tightly. I had to take one of Gorlan's hands to chain him to the bed, but I didn't separate them either. I was done being cruel for the day, and I left them alone, locking the door behind me. They would be secure there; the room had no windows even if they could get unchained.

I slumped at the kitchen table and only then realized I was still covered in fake Goblin blood. I groaned and put my head in my hands. Caitlin silently wet a cloth in the sink and came over to me, forcing my face up and washing me like I was a bairn. I was experiencing too much inner turmoil to care.

"Your idea worked," she said gently.

"I hate myself for it, but it was the kindest thing to do," I said.

She smiled and washed some from my neck. "I think they'll remember it, and maybe someday they will thank you for it."

I wasn't so sure. She took a hand and wiped that too, then motioned to my shirt. "Let me have that and wash it out before it stains. Then you had best go have a shower."

"There's prisoners in there," I muttered as I pulled the shirt over my head, only managing to smear more fake blood on my face and in my hair. I cursed and Caitlin looked as if she were trying to hide a smile.

"Take a shower Ciran. You smell."

That actually forced a smile onto my lips and I nodded. "Fine then, if that's the way it is." I wasn't even worried by the fact I was standing bare-chested in the kitchen alone with the only female of our company. I must have been short a few marbles at the moment.

I went out to the main room and rummaged in my bag to find fresh clothes. "I'll be back in a minute, and Riordan will tell us everything we got for our troubles," I said as I left.

I unlocked the door to the bunkroom again and a wave of self-hatred washed through me as I saw the Goblin brothers straighten up in readiness for anything at my appearance. I shook my head, forcing a smile on my face. "No worries, just taking a shower," I told them and watched them visibly relax, supporting each other shoulder to shoulder. It was such a normal position for me to see and experience that I had a hard time even viewing them in that moment as anything but human, even if they were technically Fae.

The hot water restored some of my mental faculties and I was ready to discuss our plans for the near future by the time I finished. I dressed in a pair of old jeans and a grey and blue jumper my mum had made me and went out to find the others.

We were all weary; I saw for the first time, just how much so. Keevan was close to sleeping, curled up against Riordan on the couch, his brother with one arm wrapped securely around his thin shoulders. Caitlin curled on the other end of the couch with a book and Deaglan was leaning back in an armchair with his eyes closed. Tierney was the only one up but that was because he was building a fire. I took one of the other chairs and everyone looked up as I came in, even Keevan trying to make an effort to sit up and see what I had to say.

"Well, Riordan, tell us what we learned," I said without preamble.

He sat up straighter. "He said that the palace is hidden up by the Giant's Causeway, which is what we expected. You can't see it if you don't know where to look."

"Is it concealed with magic?" Deaglan asked.

I shook my head. "Goblins don't have possession of

glamor like the higher Court Faeries do. They are more craftsman like the dwarves of Scandinavia. They will conceal with sly tricks of the eye instead of magic."

Riordan nodded. "Apparently, there's a place that you can stand that is marked if you know where to look. When you stand there you will be able to see the entrance, and then it's only a matter of reaching behind the right stone to find the lever. There's also a back door, which is probably the one we'll use. According to our friend, it's down the cliff face above the ocean. It's a dangerous entrance, but it will prove to be a good one because being so inconvenient, it is not guarded. It will make a good exit too."

I nodded, thinking. "That will work. I'll have to get them to draw me a map so we can figure it out properly, but it sounds easy enough. As long as we don't run into Goblin patrols on the way."

"Which we will," Tierney said. "If they're as far south as the Border, then there can only be more of them up by their own stronghold."

"Did he say anything about what Lorcan was planning?" I asked.

"A lot of the normal clap trap," Riordan growled. "He wants Goblin rule and all that. It's not relevant, it's not going to make any difference. We just want our people back."

I wasn't so sure about his sentiments, but at the moment I was too tired to pursue it any further. I pulled myself from the chair with a weary sigh. "Good job everyone, we finally found something to go on. I'm going to call Eamon now and ask him what he would like us to do next. You've all earned a good rest, we'll make dinner soon and get an early night."

I went into the kitchen to make the call, and was

surprised to find I was followed in by Riordan who stood awkwardly with one hand on the counter.

"Did you need something?" I asked.

"I just wanted to apologize," he said quietly. "I acted like a yabo and that wasn't right. I shouldn't have gone off like that."

I smiled. "Hey, it's all right. I probably would have been no better if it were Fin or Daegal either. But I think we need to realize that the Goblins are just like us. They're just unfortunate enough to have a leader who's slightly on the crazy side. I think Jarlath was just trying his best to protect his little brother too."

"I know," Riordan said, shifting uncomfortably. "I feel really bad about it. I shouldn't allow my anger to get in the way; you'd think I'd know better than that."

I smiled kindly and reached forward to clap my hand on his broad shoulder. "Well, let's just be thankful that everything turned out okay this time, and everyone is all right, even our prisoners."

He smiled and nodded. "Thanks, Ciran. I'll let you get to your phone call."

He left and I quickly dialed Eamon's number. I waited a few rings before it was answered and Eamon's voice came over the phone.

"Ciran?"

"Yeah, it's me," I said.

"Did you find them? Are you there?" he asked and I could tell he was attempting to keep his voice calm though his anxiety was showing through.

"We ran into a little difficulty," I told him and explained about the mission so far and the Goblins we had in our custody.

"This is great!" he said enthusiastically, sounding

almost relieved.

"May I ask why, exactly?"

"The council has called in all the other kings to a meeting," Eamon said, sounding annoyed. "I tried to talk them out of it, but they said it was only appropriate that they did so, and I finally had to admit they were right. Sending men into enemy territory during a rocky peace is something that concerns everyone. But they're talking about the...*stupidity*, they call it, of the mission. Can you believe that? They wouldn't be saying the same thing if it were people from their garrisons who had been taken!" He was fuming and I couldn't blame him. I was too. For the most part, the kings and queen who were the lesser rulers of the different provinces, were good, honest Irish folk, but they resented Eamon his position, thinking he was too young and always tried to teach him 'lessons' by telling him he was wrong to do the things he did, even when everyone knew they were actually the right choices. He was like the favored child in a family where everyone was trying to mold his life so that he could make the most of it.

"Now that you have valid proof however, it will be much easier to sway the council," he continued. "Do you think one of the prisoners will speak out?"

"I believe I can convince them," I said, and hoped it was true. Maybe my 'kindness' had not settled in their stomachs any better than it had mine, but I supposed it was worth a shot, and I knew Eamon would make a good deal with them if they did.

"The meeting is tomorrow at three in the afternoon," Eamon told me. "Can you be there by then?"

"We should be," I replied.

"Let's hope this works this time," Eamon said grimly. "Because if we can't convince the council, well, we're going to have to think of another plan."

"We'll think about that if it comes to it," I said. "For now, let's just hope we'll have enough to convince them that this needs to be done."

"Yes," Eamon replied. "Now I'm afraid I've got to go, there are many preparations to make and Killian's champing at the bit. I'll see you tomorrow."

"You too," I replied before I hung up.

I didn't like how the council was involved in this. I knew they were going to make a stink, and thought it was more likely than not we would be spending the next night coming up with a contingency plan they would like even less.

I put it out of my mind for the moment, however, and went back into the other room.

"We have to be back in Tara by three tomorrow afternoon for a council meeting," I told everyone. "Until then, rest and I'll get something together for supper."

That night after supper I sank onto the couch in the living room with a huge sigh, exhausted. I propped my feet up on one end and folded one arm behind my head, closing my eyes. Deaglan and Caitlin were in the kitchen drinking tea. Tierney was in there with them making toast, and Riordan had made Keevan go to bed after he had fallen asleep in the chair by the fire, utterly exhausted after the last couple days' events. I suddenly remembered it had only been a day and a half ago that I had fallen off of a waterfall myself and, though I had no memory of it, had been resuscitated by Caitlin as well as kept warm by her and Tierney during the coldest parts of the night. I had never been so close to death before and I almost hated to admit it, but the idea kind of fascinated me in an unnerving, never-care-to-do-it-again sort of way. It was a rush, but I would probably never consider myself an actual daredevil. I had been trained too well for that.

My inner self was still smarting from what I had done to the Goblin brothers, Jarlath and Gorlan, though. I don't know why it kept bothering me so much; I had successfully found a way to get information out of them without hurting anyone, but there was still something about it that felt so off color. I supposed it had something to do with Jarlath's face when he thought his brother was dying behind closed doors and he could do nothing; could not be there to help him through it. I lowered my arm to cover my face, inhaling deeply as a thought flashed through my mind of hearing Daegal's screams when I could do nothing to stop them, and could not see what sort of pain he was in. The thought made me curl up on the couch and delve into even more self-hatred.

"Hey." I jerked around, seeing Caitlin standing beside the couch with two steaming cups in her hands. I smelled chocolate—dark, rich stuff—and instantly perked up a bit.

"Can I sit down?" she asked.

"Of course," I replied and sat up, scooting to one side as she sat down next to me, close enough that our shoulders brushed companionably. I would have thought nothing of it had it been Tierney or one of the lads, but with Caitlin, I felt a bit awkward against my will, realizing I really had to make a point to hang out with more girls on occasion. But I soon forgot it as she put one of the cups of cocoa into my hands, which warmed them, and I brought it to my face, inhaling the rich aroma as I waited for it to cool enough to drink. I sipped appreciatively, finding it dark indeed, but with hints of almond and a little bit of salt that brought out the flavor even more.

"This is good," I told her with a smile.

"Thanks, I made it myself," she said with a proud grin. "So at least I'm good for something womanly. Even if I can't heal."

I was unable to keep from smiling at the teasing twinkle in her eye. "You did save my life."

"No bandaging or sewing needed though."

"Well, for the record, I would much rather have you around should I need mouth-to-mouth again than one of the lads. That would be...awkward to say the least."

She laughed, punching me in the arm, and I approved of the fact there was no blush on her cheeks even if she was just very good at hiding it. "You'd all do what had to be done to save each other, no matter how awkward. I just did the same."

"So you're saying it was awkward?" I asked teasingly, pretending hurt.

"Not as much as this conversation," she retorted and that made me chuckle, shaking my head as I sipped my cocoa again. We were silent for a few moments, then she leaned back against the couch and turned to look at me.

"Don't beat yourself up about what you had to do today," she said gently, nudging my shoulder with hers. "You did the only thing we could, and in the end showed we were the better men. Jarlath and Gorlan will remember that, I think. It could go a long way to solving problems with the Goblins in the future."

"I hadn't thought of it that way," I said quietly then sighed again and leaned forward with my elbows resting on my knees, the cup still sandwiched between my hands. "I just...his face, when he thought I had tortured his little brother—I couldn't stand it. I don't want to see anyone feel that because I don't ever want to feel it. I don't really know what it truly made me feel…I just…I don't know. Just not good, that's all."

She placed a hand on one of my wrists and squeezed reassuringly, leaning forward to look into my face. "Ciran, you may doubt yourself, but you are a good leader—I can clearly see your high ancestry in you. You hold a natural authority that will make men years older than you follow and obey without question. But there's one thing that's keeping you back and that's that you don't believe in yourself. You keep second-guessing yourself because you feel inexperienced, you feel young, and sometimes I don't think you really believe you're worthy to lead. But if you can get past that and not worry about anything else, then you will be a *great* leader. It's instinctual to you. Eamon is the same way. You both have the confidence to succeed, but you never seem to put it to good use. Be more like Killian! He doesn't care what anyone thinks!"

I laughed at that, but took her words to heart. I turned to look her in the eye, her face closer than I thought. "If you believe in me, then perhaps I can indeed succeed in becoming a leader to make everyone proud. I vow that I will do the best in my ability to do that in the future. I have learned much already on this journey, and I look forward to learning more. I will work on my confidence though, I promise."

She smiled. "You had better. I want to see you succeed, Ciran. I believe you have a great future. You just need to seize it." She grimaced. "But we're getting a little too involved now, aren't we?"

I laughed and sipped some more cocoa. "Yeah, well, thank you for the advice. I will take it to heart." I reached out and squeezed her hand strongly. "And we'll find the prisoners and bring them home. That will be the first step."

Deaglan walked into the room then and smiled teasingly. "Aw, holding hands, how sweet."

"Oh shut up," I snarled at him and let go of Caitlin's hand as she got up, laughing, to head back into the kitchen.

The cocoa was drunk and I felt weary with everything finally catching up to me. We decided to call it a night and I went with the rest to the bunkroom. I had been reluctant at first to leave our prisoners in the same room we slept in, but then decided it was the best way to keep an eye on them, and so I lengthened their chain and let them have one of the bunks to sleep in instead. I had also made sure to give them some of the stew we'd made for supper. Jarlath at least seemed suspicious, but they must have been starving for they ate it all. Now they were huddled on the small bunk, Jarlath's free arm thrown protectively over his younger brother. On impulse, I put a blanket over them. Gorlan's eyes opened and he started slightly as he saw me, but I turned around and he settled again, pulling the blanket tighter around him and his brother.

I tumbled into the bunk on the other side of the room and pulled the blanket over myself, trying to get comfortable. My side was still hurting a bit but I knew it would be mostly fine by the next day since I hadn't broken anything. I drifted off, and thought I would sleep until morning but was woken sometime in the middle of the night by dreams I would rather not remember. I sat up, nearly hitting my head on the top bunk and tried to catch my breath. I shivered as the cold air hit my skin and I reached down to the floor to retrieve my jumper before swinging out of the bunk and heading into the kitchen to maybe make a cup of tea. I checked on the prisoners while I was up, but they at least were sleeping soundly.

As I walked out of the bunkroom, I was surprised to

see a light on and when I turned to the living room, I saw
Keevan sitting cross-legged on the couch, a ball of yarn in
his lap while he worked on crocheting something. He
stopped and looked up almost guiltily as I came in and then
sighed, lowering his creation.

"You caught me. Yeah, I crochet when I get anxious,
got a problem?" He smiled crookedly at the end, letting me
know he didn't care much whether I knew or not.

I smiled back and went to sit next to him. "No
problem. I just didn't expect it of you. But then, I've
started to realize I don't know a lot about any of you. But I
think I'm learning. I know you, Keevan, aren't really very
much like the young rip you usually play yourself up to
be."

He looked down at his lap, fiddling with his crochet
hook and twining the bright green yarn between his
fingers. "Yeah, well, sorry to disappoint you." I noticed
that he had not made an effort to fix his hair in its
customary untidy spiky mess it usually was in since he had
fallen into the river. With his red hair now flopping
around, some falling into his eyes, he looked even younger
than he was and far more vulnerable. I wondered if that
was why he usually wore his hair in such a style.

I knocked my knee against his. "Hey, are you all
right?"

He didn't look at me, but he took a long shuddering
sigh. "No, not really. I just..." he took a deep breath then
turned to look at me with unshed tears threatening to fall
from his eyes. "I guess I didn't really know what to expect
when I left home. I think...well, I thought it was just going
to be like on the movies, you know? That we would race
up there, against all odds, and storm the Goblin fortress
with glory and hacking swords and rescue everyone and go

home as heroes. But it's not really ever like that, is it? It's hard. There's suffering, pain, and...torture involved. Things don't work out right, and people aren't who they should be..." He took a shuddering breath and quickly scrubbed a forearm against his eyes. "I guess it's all my fault. I was too cocky when I left, I thought it would all go well. I know I'm the youngest one here, and I probably just feel the pressure of living up to everyone else. I don't want to be the weak link; I don't want to let everyone down."

"Keevan," I said as he fought back a sob. "You're a good lad, and a bloody fine warrior. I don't think you'll ever let us down."

"But what if I do?" he asked. "Who knows what will happen? I've never been in a really dangerous situation before, even I don't know how I'll act. This whole thing has turned every one of us into something we hate at one point. Even my own brother who's always so calm and collected..." A tear really did escape this time and I saw the raw fear on his face and knew that Riordan's outburst the night before had really taken its toll on him. Something he wouldn't even admit to his brother. I put a hand on his shoulder and squeezed.

"Riordan was only afraid. He was afraid he would lose you, and I can understand that because I'm a big brother too. He didn't mean to frighten you; that is the last thing he would have wanted, Keevan. You have to understand that he almost lost you and that scared him badly. But he had to be strong for you so he couldn't let that show, thus it came out in another way that might not have been right, but it was all he was capable of at the moment."

Keevan smiled somewhat. "That's why we need Pat. He was always the buffer. Riordan and I used to row all the time, but he was always the one to mediate."

"Tell me about your brother, I've never met him," I said.

He smiled sadly. "Pat's the sweet one — that's what my mother called him. He was the middle son and because of that he was always between Riordan and I, buffering when we fought and working all the time to keep us from doing it — usually in vain. Riordan and I...well, we got worse those first couple months after the patrol was taken, and I'm ashamed to say we drove our mother to tears on more than one occasion." He sighed. "So we began to try and mellow out and it actually worked. We realized that we both loved Pat and fighting each other wouldn't get us anywhere if we ever had hope to find him. We knew he wouldn't like that."

"He sounds like a good guy," I commented.

"He was — is," Keevan corrected firmly, grimacing for his slip. "My mother pretty much told us that if we didn't come back with him, she would never forgive us, and with my mother that is no idle threat."

"With your shield or on it," I commented with a small smile.

Keevan nodded, his own lips quirking up slightly. "Yeah, I guess so." He looked at me again. "She didn't want me to go, you know. Not at first. But I wouldn't let her talk me out of it. I wasn't going to let Riordan go alone. If Pat was going to be rescued, I wanted to be there when it happened. After my father died in that last battle, she's been almost too clingy, and I know that's a mother's job, but I needed more freedom, because the more people worry about me, the more I worry about myself because...because it makes me feel like I really am not capable of anything. I needed this, and she finally realized that so she let me go. Even if she was worried I might not come back. Like Da."

"You'll come back," I assured him. "I promise you that you will all get back home with your lost family members. I will see to it myself and if that doesn't happen, I will lose whatever faith in myself I have left."

"Don't ever do that," Keevan said seriously and I looked at him with a new light, realizing that this young man had many, many layers and I didn't know whether I would ever see them all. "You're a good leader, Ciran, and I would rather follow you into battle than anyone else."

I smiled, his words warming me. It seemed everyone thought I was a good leader. Well, that was all well and fine, but unfortunately, it didn't help me think the same.

"How is your arm?" I asked, changing the subject.

He shrugged and twisted his bandaged wrist slightly. "All right. Still a little painful, but nothing I can't live with." He looked at me meaningfully. "It's not this that keeps me up, if that's what you're wondering."

"I didn't think it was," I replied quietly, knowing well enough that physical pain was rarely as bad as anything mental.

"I am glad we'll get a couple more days to rest though," he admitted. "I actually think we need it. I was worried that I wouldn't be able to fight with this."

I nodded. "Well, I'm not going to say we won't be doing any fighting, but it will be of the verbal kind. The kind any true warrior hates the most. But you and the others probably won't have to worry about that so much. I'll be spokesman as the leader of the group."

"We've got your back just like on the field, brother," Keevan told me with a smile. I smiled back and made to stand up.

"How about I make us some hot chocolate and toast?"

I asked. "That should help us sleep."

He smiled and nodded wearily. "Yeah, that would be good."

I mixed some up and carried it back out to the living room, only to find that Keevan had dropped off against the side of the couch, snoring gently. I smiled slightly, glad he had finally gotten to sleep, and covered him with the afghan on the back of the couch. I quickly finished my snack and went back to my own bed, leaving Keevan peacefully where he was. This time when I lay down, I was very drowsy, and there was nothing that was going to keep me up. I drifted off into a mercifully dreamless sleep, not even bothering to worry about what would happen in the near future.

Chapter Sixteen
Back to the Beginning

Coming back to Tara felt almost like a defeat to me in many ways. I didn't want to have to do this, but we had prisoners in our custody and there was also the matter of us practically being summoned by the council. With as touchy as they already were on the subject of the lost patrol, I didn't think it would be a good idea to decide not to show up. So we packed up the two Goblins that morning and drove off to Tara, getting there around noon. Killian, always organized, had sent for all our dress gear and we donned it as we waited for Eamon to come meet us in the library. Our prisoners had been taken into custody and were awaiting the moment when they would speak with the council. As I waited in the study, gazing unseeingly over the shelves of books, I recalled the conversation that had passed between them and myself earlier.

"Why should we help you?" Jarlath had asked when I had told him we needed their report for the council. "We're going to be locked up either way."

"For a while maybe," I said truthfully. "But I can guarantee you that if we get our prisoners back, you and the others of your kin we have in our prisons will be released. It's only fair."

He still seemed to want to ignore me, but Gorlan gripped his shoulder. "Jarlath, I think they have dealt fairly with us so far. I believe they will again. Let us do this one thing. If it can get us our freedom, then it is a small price to pay. We have already given them all the information we could. Lorcan will already be mad at us."

"Perhaps it will indeed be safer in Tara's prison if our dear cousin finds out," Jarlath snorted and I frowned slightly. They were cousins of Lorcan? That might be interesting information to keep handy. "It's his fault with all his stupid grand ideas that got us into this mess anyway." He turned to glare at me, as if resentful I had heard their conversation. "Very well, we will help you, but you must give me your word that we will be set free if you find your prisoners again."

"Do you know?" I asked quietly, making sure none of the others overheard. "Do you know for certain that they are alive?"

Jarlath shrugged noncommittally. "Maybe you'll just have to find out for yourself."

Now back at Tara, awaiting the council, I found myself pondering that conversation again. I felt in my bones that Aeden wasn't dead, but a little proof wouldn't go amiss, and I could not speak for any of the other prisoners. Just because one survived didn't mean they all did.

The door to the study opened and in came Eamon and Killian, both dressed in their formal attire as we were. Our dress uniforms were mostly the same as Killian's Captaen of the Guard uniform but instead of a brass breastplate we wore copper like Eamon, though not nearly so embossed. We all wore green capes but Eamon's was longer and heavy with gold embroidery. Caitlin was the only one dressed differently, wearing the official Academy uniform: a long green dress with a brass breastplate and golden cape. She cut a rather fetching figure, looking in my mind something like the historical Queen Maeve. I suppose us fellows were rather dashing as well, Deaglan most of all, of course. I was a bit annoyed to see that the long days in the Faelands and a dislocated shoulder hadn't done anything to mar his handsome, playboy appearance.

Killian was tapping at his mobile, probably texting one of his men to get into position—or my sister, either was just as possible—but he put it away when Eamon came in and smiled tiredly at us as he stepped forward to clasp my forearm.

"Ciran, I'm glad to see you all back safe and sound."

"Aye," I replied. "Though I had hoped to have the lost ones come back with me."

"Well, unforeseen events happen," Eamon said with a smile, though I could hear the disappointment clear in his voice. "You will join me for lunch before the meeting, I hope? I've begged a private one so we will not have to listen to the prattle of the others before the meeting even begins." He rolled his eyes and Killian smiled broadly at his shoulder.

"If you all don't mind, I'm starving, and Eamon, I'm sure the poor weary travelers are as well, so if we can just..."

"Of course, my dear captain," Eamon said, mockingly rolling his eyes again. Killian ignored him and embraced his sister.

"Have they taken good care of you, dear baby sister?" he asked, kissing her on the cheek.

"Oh, on the contrary," Caitlin said with a smirk in my direction. "I've had to do all the caretaking. They're practically worthless, almost getting captured by Faeries, falling off waterfalls and nearly drowning. It was me who brought them all back safely."

"I'm sure it was," Killian grinned before he turned back to me. "Falling off waterfalls, eh? Well, I think you'll all have some stories to tell over lunch. You'll need something to sustain you. I'm afraid, gentlemen, that you go from battle with worthy opponents such as the Goblins to not so worthy ones such as old King Paunchias."

Eamon winced. "Don't call him that, please. Don't let that slip...again."

Killian leveled a finger at Eamon reprovingly. "Hey, we all know you were the one who nearly slipped up first. I just accidentally let it slip after reading your text."

We followed them, Tierney and I sharing an amused grin. While we ate, we told of our venture, leaving out the less than heroic parts. Those I would likely relate to Eamon later when we were alone to make my official report. There was much to tell and by the time we had finished it was nearly time for the meeting. I retired to one side of the room with Eamon, away from the others so we could talk.

"The prisoners you brought," Eamon said. "Will they speak in front of the council?"

"I think so," I replied with conviction. "We are not necessarily friendly, but I think we have an understanding of sorts."

Eamon nodded slowly, kicking the toe of his boot against the floor in thought. "I've been reading into Goblin history over the past couple days," he said. "Trying to understand our enemy more. I'll admit it makes me sympathize with them; they have not had an easy time of it by any means."

"I've come to see them in a different light myself," I said softly, remembering again, with that ever-present guilt the bond between Jarlath and Gorlan, which was just as strong as the one I shared with my brothers.

"They were always thought of as lesser Fae, because they were not able to use magic, nor were they as fair as the Sidhe of the Courts. They grew bitter and started trouble and were shunned from Fae society. The story goes that the Goblin King refused to pay the tithes to the Faery Courts as all Fae must, and that caused the Seelie and Unseelie both to join together and force them out into the Common Lands with the lesser Fae. Then when humans started to settle there, they were forced from that land and went back north to beg a place from the Faery Courts. They were allowed to stay only under the condition that they would stay in the far north and only build their palaces underground. And that set off the animosity that has gone on for years."

I listened solemnly to the story. I had learned a bit of it in school, but most of that was biased. I was surprised my mother hadn't told me the truth of it, for she was usually so adamant in the fact that the Fae were to be treated with respect. But then, she had lost her father in the second Goblin War and had treated so many in the last one, including Da, that I supposed even she might have become biased over time.

"What do you plan to do about this?" I asked him.

He shrugged helplessly. "I don't know. I like to think that if I could form a treaty with Lorcan that we could come to some agreement, but he is too proud for that, I fear. I hate to see anyone oppressed."

"Perhaps there is a way to win him over," I said. "But our first priority is to rescue our people."

"Most definitely," Eamon replied and looked past my shoulder as Killian strode over.

"It's nearly time to go, your majesty, don't want to be late and let them thumb their noses at us for that too."

Killian quickly liberated Eamon's mobile from his pocket with all the ease of a professional thief and fiddled with it.

"Don't forget to turn the volume off so we can text during the meeting," he said.

"Probably not the best idea this time, I don't think we'll be nearly as bored as usual," Eamon said, setting his phone on the table and neatly slid it further away as Killian reached for it. "I don't want to look like a rebellious teenager while I'm having a council meeting about the fate of my people. We've got to act like professionals once in a while, Killian. Keep our heads clear. It's going to be a blood bath in there."

"Not if I have anything to do with it," Killian said firmly. "I am your captain of the guard, and I have sworn to protect you, whether on battlefield or in conference room."

"I appreciate it even though I don't think that's actually in the oath," Eamon said. "I'll need a few good men at my back today."

"I only hope it's enough," Killian sighed. "Having the council together is hard as it is but with all the kings too…"

Eamon took the other man by the shoulders and shook him. "It'll be fine, you have to calm down."

Killian smiled weakly. "You might not be freaking out,

oh mighty king, but I am! I know exactly what's going to happen, and what will come of it! They're never going to agree to this again, not now, not even with the extra information. We'll end up having to do something ourselves and then..."

"Killian, get to your point," Eamon said, shaking him again.

"Ciran did a fine job by our standards, Eamon, but you know once they realize the entire mission failed they will never allow us to send another one."

"It didn't fail, Killie, we just didn't get as far as we thought and we had to turn back with the prisoners. They can't skin us for that," Caitlin said, trying to console her brother.

"You know *they* will not see it that way," Killian warned, turning back to Eamon. "They will not. And then we'll be forced to do something we're going to regret — "

"Killian," Eamon tried but Killian cut him off.

"I can't stand to see them sneer at you!" he snarled out viciously. "All the time they just sit there, and laugh behind their hands: 'oh look, it's the boy king and his cohort of untried warriors! Let's see how well we can humiliate him today'. And what's worse, Eamon, is that you *let them*. If you're not going to stick up for yourself, I will." He punched Eamon in the shoulder. "You're my brother for all intents and purposes, Ea! I practically raised you, after all!"

"We're the same age, Killie," Eamon said, trying to hide a smile.

"Beside the point!" Killian snapped and I could tell he really was angry. "I just can't take it anymore. You are a good king, Eamon. Your father would be bloody proud to see the man you have become. *I'm* bloody proud to have grown up beside you as your foster brother and to have fought with you, bled with and for you, and now be here at your side to help you keep these ungrateful people in line. They don't see that, they don't see the man you are. Have they forgotten so soon that young man, barely eighteen who charged an entire army of Goblins to lead his people after your father fell? They have forgotten it all, they only see some barely weaned whelp sitting on the throne; one they think they can manipulate to do what they want."

Eamon nodded, smiling gently. "Is it that young prince you lament their memory fading for or the brave young warrior who charged at his side?"

Killian slapped a hand against his heart. "You wound me, do you know that? I'm trying to have a serious conversation with you and all you do is mock my self important attitude that I only put on because if I didn't I would be a total wreck of anxiety with this job."

Eamon took his shoulders again. "You do realize how much I have always appreciated you being here by my side, defending me through thick and thin. You *are* my brother, Killie, and would make a better king than I."

"Don't say that!" Killian snarled at him. "That's exactly why they think they can walk all over you! Because you don't believe enough in yourself! Well, I'm done with it, and I'm not going to let it happen today of all days. If I hear one word against you, I swear I will stand on the table and give them — "

"Killian," Eamon admonished. "Please. I know what I'm doing. I will not let them make me back down, and if they want to hate me then so be it. I don't care what they say as long as we get our people back."

"But if they don't," Killian said in a pleading voice. "What then? What will they say when they find out you want to put the mission on again. They were reluctant enough in the first place, what about now?"

"They won't say a word."

We all turned to the door and I was shocked to see my father standing there, in his own dress uniform that I had not seen him wear in years. Oh how like a king he looked in it. His long hair braided in the style of ancient warriors, falling over his shoulders majestically and the sword he had inherited from his great-great-great grandfather, *Fuil-Amhránaí*, hung at his side—his right side now, but it still sat there, the most loyal companion a warrior could ever possess. Looking at my father there was no doubt that old lordly blood ran in my family's veins. Eamon stepped forward and bowed his head in a gesture that was far more respectful than a High King ever needed to show another person.

"*Tiarna* Mac Cool," he said. "I did not expect you to come."

My father bowed back. "I come foremost out of the duty I had to your father, *Airdrígh*. But that does not mean I have anything against serving his son. I am here at your back to try and sway the stupidity of the council as well as I can."

"Thank you," Eamon said sincerely and I thought there was a trace of a tear in the corner of his eye. "Your loyalty has never wavered, and I am honored to have you here."

My father nodded and turned back to the door. "It is time to go to the council now." He cast a glance at me and I nodded back to him.

Killian had his knuckles pressed to his mouth and as my father turned back out of the room, he leaned over to Eamon and whispered loud enough for all of us to hear, "If you don't aspire to do anything else, Eamon, I think you should really aim to be as majestic as Niall Mac Cool."

Eamon smiled even as he shook his head. "Let's get this over with."

We followed him to the throne room where I had the heavy feeling that the fate of our lost men weighed in the balance.

Chapter Seventeen
Unto the Breach

I had never been to a council meeting before, and found it very reminiscent of what I had always pictured when thinking of Arthur's Knights of the Round Table — an ancient British brotherhood that fought and went out questing. Many people might deny it, the English especially, but they stole the idea of their order from Na Fianna. Except that we were half Fae, and they were just normal men. Unlike us, the descendants of Arthur's noble knights were no more than university frat boys who would rather drink and gamble and 'fight' the occasional jousting match, than go out questing.

The council table was long and the other kings, the one queen and all their council representatives (three for each) were already sitting at the table, awaiting the arrival of the High King. I heard a ripple of conversation go around the room at the appearance of my father, and spotted my cousin Ceannt, who was a member of Eamon's council. Even he seemed surprised to see Da there, but my father ignored them all and took a seat at the right hand of

Eamon. Killian took his left and I sat at my father's side, the rest of my company seating themselves down the line at mine, Tierney closest as was his right by family. Everyone had risen when Eamon walked into the room and offered a loud *"Fada beo ar an rí"* and then took their seats again.

Eamon was silent for a moment, looking down the table at gathered people of import, and then he took a deep breath and began.

"Fellow rulers of Erin," he said, his voice echoing in the hall. "You all know why we are here today. There has been a matter of import on all of our minds for the past six months."

"On yours perhaps," muttered one of the kings, Proinsias of Connaught I recognized; a large man, looking far too much like a king and not enough like a warrior for being an Irish ruler. Life had been soft for him, it seemed, as could be attested by his rather large, rounded breastplate. His hair was also not what it once was, giving him an odd look with his kingly braids on each side of his face but a bald spot on the top of his head. I saw Killian tense at his comment, and Eamon cast him a quick look before he continued.

"Perhaps not on everyone's mind enough, however," he said in no uncertain terms. That shut everyone up, even Proinsias. I lowered my head to hide the smile that spread across my lips.

"Friends," Eamon continued, almost pleadingly, but still with the upper hand, I saw with admiration. "We have lost many good men in the Goblin Wars. There is not a family who has not suffered a loss of some kind—I too have not been exempt from that. There are some who might say that six men are obsolete—why save six when we have already lost so many? What are six more?"

Eamon's jaw tightened and I knew he was quoting things people had actually said in that very room and that made my blood boil. Several of the kings at the table had the grace to look down awkwardly and I knew they had been the fools to have said that at some point.

"Those six men, those few," Eamon continued. "Those are husbands, fathers, brothers and sons. Men who have risked their lives for their country so that their people might be safe in their homes. We owe them to bring them back. And when we finally find proof, actual proof of their survival, and find a man brave enough to go after them, why do we keep them from it? What is the possible meaning of that? If we can claim them, and bring them back home, we should be jumping at the chance!"

"Why lose more?" asked King Proinsias again, obviously one who had said things on the subject before and cared not that he had. "As High King, you should be protecting your people, not sending them off on fool's missions."

"It is not a fool's mission," Killian said, obviously trying to ease his anger. "You heard the evidence, the council allowed this mission to go, why do you draw back now?"

"Sending men into the Faelands is dangerous enough in times of peace!" Queen Niamh of Munster said. "We are certainly not at peace with the Goblins, and by tramping all over the land, we could make all sorts of enemies with the other Fair Folk! Can we risk all out war for six men?"

"Brave men deserve our recognition," Eamon said. "They deserve to believe that they will be rescued."

"And one of them is a prince," my father reminded. "Do you so easily forget that *Airdrígh* Eamon's own brother lies in those cells?"

"We do not forget that your own son lies there as well, Mac Cool," said King Proinsias meaningfully. That man just couldn't keep his mouth shut.

"And if it were yours, Proinsias?" my father asked coldly.

"A valid question," Killian said. "What if this patrol that had been taken consisted of your people? What would you do then? Would you still be so willing to let them rot? These are indeed men who belong to others familially, but they are also men of the High King, a crown prince and the Commander of Na Fianna himself, and as such, it is his duty to see they are returned safe to their hearth and loved ones if at all possible." He was raising his voice. "This young king who you scorn for his inexperience knows more about kingship and duty than all of you put together, obviously, if you do not understand his need to do everything he can."

"Killian," Eamon said quietly as Proinsias stood up, indignant anger reddening his jowly face.

"You obviously don't know what it means to be a king, boy. Not if you let your *Captaen* speak on your behalf and shame men far above his station. If he were mine, I would have him knocked to guardsman immediately!"

Killian looked like he was going to jump on the table as he threatened, but Eamon grabbed him and bent to whisper something. The two argued back and forth in hissed conversation, leaving an awkward silence in the room while Proinsias watched with satisfaction as if his point had been proven, but finally Eamon turned back from a fuming Killian and faced the council again.

"If you need more proof, I have witnesses who are here to testify. Ciran Mac Cool, please inform the council of our guests."

I felt slightly uncomfortable as all eyes shifted to me, but forced myself to stay calm. "On our mission we were able to take two Goblins prisoner, cousins of Lorcan himself, and they have agreed to offer proof of the prisoners' existence and exact directions to the palace of King Lorcan and how to get inside."

Killian beckoned a guard at the door and he opened it to reveal another guard who was leading Jarlath—who had chosen to act as spokesman—into the room. He was not cuffed, I had asked that he not be, knowing that he would do better if his dignity was not insulted, plus I knew he would not try anything with his brother still in our custody. Killian had been doubtful, but I had spoken for him myself so I hoped he would not prove me false. I stood now to go over to him, the guard stepping back several paces. Jarlath shifted awkwardly on his feet, and I suddenly didn't feel as nervous as I had, knowing that he, in the presence of all enemies, must be so much worse off.

"This is Jarlath, a cousin of the Royal Line of Faoicnoc," I said, introducing the prisoner. "Jarlath, will you explain to the council what you said to me?"

He swallowed hard and then without further ado, began to tell of the location of the palace and gave a detailed explanation of how to get in.

"And what of the prisoners?" Eamon asked. "Do they live?"

"They are still alive, my lord," Jarlath said, but was looking at me as he did so. "Your brother lives."

I felt a sudden sick knot in my stomach loosen, hoping that he really did speak the truth. I allowed him to go back to the custody of the guard then.

"Thank you, Jarlath," Eamon said. "You will be rewarded for you assistance."

He was led from the room, and I sat back down as Eamon appealed to the council again.

"Well, was that enough proof to give the mission a second attempt?" He asked.

There were murmurings around the room, many people shaking their heads. I felt a dark anticipation in my stomach and turned to look worriedly at Tierney who met my eyes uncertainly. I didn't think we could dare hope at that moment, as much as I wanted to. I only prayed this would not be the complete blood bath I feared.

Finally King Proinsias stood up, addressing the council. "There is simply too much of a risk. If you fail to retrieve the prisoners—and certainly you can't expect a Goblin's word to be true at all—then you will only succeed in starting another war, and we cannot afford the cost."

"That's why I'm not sending an army," Eamon said, angrily. "This is not some mass mission, we're not going up to retrieve them by force, they are to go as a clandestine unit and get the prisoners out in any way they can. Lorcan is not a fool; if the prisoners escape, he will not start a war just for spite, he will plan—make deals. If they get caught they will treat with him. If the prisoners are indeed still alive, then that is a testament to the fact that he thinks death is not a smart option. It could go a long way to recovering the peace with the Goblins."

"Are you so naïve as to believe that?" King Proinsias said unpleasantly. "Wake up, boy. One of these days, you're going to have to realize what it really means to be a king. It's a dirty business and requires many sacrifices you could never understand. No king has lived who has not spilled the blood of his own people as willingly as his enemies. It's time you realize that, boy."

Killian was about ready to fly out of his chair, but it

was my father who spoke. "That is *Airdrígh* Eamon, Proinsias. You do not call your High King 'boy' whether he is twenty-three, or thirteen. You need to show some respect."

"As do you, Mac Cool," Proinsias said in a voice that made me grit my teeth. No one spoke to my father like that. "You might be as close to the High King as family due to your ancestry, but that does not make you king. It does not make you higher ranking than me."

My father nearly smiled, but there was no humor there. "Look at you, Proinsias, demanding my obeisance. Your armor doesn't fit your girth, and even were you capable of fighting in your dotage, would you be at the head of your men, or cowering at the back? What scars do you hold from the old days? I little recall ever seeing you in need of medical attention, and I don't think it's because you're an exceptionally good warrior."

Proinsias fumed, his face reddening as he pointed a shaking finger at my father. "You are no more than a washed-up, one-armed lord, Mac Cool. How dare you speak to me as such?"

My hand was on my sword hilt, but suddenly, hands slapped down on the table and I jerked around to see Eamon standing up, leaning over the table to get as close as possible to Proinsias. "*Tiarna* Niall Mac Cool is a better man than you'll ever be. Never have I met a more noble man in all my life. He served my father on the battlefield, never leaving his side to the very end. He lost his own blood brother because he left his side to defend his king in his last moments." I turned to my father in shock. I had never heard that part of the story. He stared straight ahead, not meeting anyone's gaze, but I could see the pain behind his eyes and in his clenched jaw.

"Now he came to me today to stand by my side in *this* battle, even though he gave up his position on the council long ago, and for good reason," Eamon continued and glared around at everyone. "This table is filled with nothing but windbags. You might have commanded men in battle, do not think for one moment that I doubt your courage, but so have I. I have bled beside all of you as my father did. You may call me in-experienced, and I might be compared to you who are all at least twice my age, but I hope that above all, I am never a king who degrades any hero of Erin, whether he is a king or the scum of the earth. Because that is what makes you scum, even if you wear the finery and dare call yourself king." There was a snarl on his face and most of the council looked rather frightened, some even impressed. "And that is why I want my men back. Because they are heroes who sacrificed for their country. Some of them are veterans who bled with you in the War of the Red Hills, and others are young men who have not yet even had the chance to be tried in battle. Will you take that chance away from them? That chance to be a hero? To serve king and country, and even more importantly their brothers and sisters?"

Everyone was silent, not wanting to dare the young king after his passionate delivery, then Proinsias puffed himself up again, and my heart crashed after it had soared during Eamon's speech. I could see the heartless cur was un-swayed. "Heroes die every day. They are heroes because they are willing to give their lives for their country and their people. They will count it a sacrifice well spent and they will be remembered dearly for it. And their families should think the same. They should not shame their sacrifice by crying over them."

"And my brother?" Eamon shouted, pounding the

table again. "Oran is only sixteen! A boy who has not yet wielded a sword outside of training! He is a prince of the High Seat! My heir! If something were to happen to me, who would take my place?"

"And you are the High King, as Niall Mac Cool has been so kind as to remind me," Proinsias said nastily. "You should be spending your precious moments looking for a wife to give you a *proper* heir. Your brother is gone, and you need to face the facts. Do you really think that if he were actually still alive Lorcan wouldn't have sent a ransom demand yet? That Goblin your boy commander and his 'company' caught was lying to you. That's what they do. They're all dead, and Lorcan's only trying to lure you into a trap. It's time to turn back to your kingly duties and get married so you can produce a child as soon as possible. You never know when another war will crop up and leave you as dead as your father."

The whole council chamber was silent after that, just watching the two men standing on opposite ends of the table, glowering at each other. I could tell then that none of the others completely agreed with Proinsias and likely thought he was far out of his place in speaking so to the High King, but also knew that they would have to agree with him. Because that was just how politics worked. Killian looked beyond words, and Eamon...he was struggling. There were so many emotions fighting behind his face, and I knew if I were him, I wouldn't have even known where to start, would have exploded. But he somehow, with great will, forced those warring emotions down and then spoke in a dangerous, low voice.

"I will not bring a queen into this," he said. "When my heir is born, I want him to be born into an Ireland free of the horror of the Goblin Wars and the prejudice they have caused. I will not settle down and start a family until King Lorcan is dead or we can come to some lasting conclusion to our problem. And even if we didn't have need of a crown prince, I would cross deserts to get my brother back. I will not sacrifice the life of one I grew up with and love dearly for my nonexistent son."

"Be that as it may, we cannot sanction this mission. I'm sorry," Proinsias said, not sounding sorry at all.

"You are a fool, Proinsias," my father said, rising to his feet. "This young man, our High King, is a better ruler than any sitting at this table, myself included. He should put you all to shame, and if you don't feel shame at what he has said today, then none of you deserve to hold your positions. You are all parasites living off his mercy. If it were I, I would get rid of all of you. If that's your decision, then I want it well known I had no part in it, and if I can't sway you otherwise, then I will leave you to suffer the consequences. Eamon might be lenient enough to forget this, but I can assure you that I will not." And with that he left the hall, the door closing behind him.

The council was silent but Proinsias once again gathered himself. "Do not expect us to change our mind, *Airdrígh*. This argument is over. You will do yourself a favor to not think of it again."

"That's it then?" Eamon asked; far, far too calm.

"That is our decision," the man said, so obviously proud of himself it made me sick.

"Very well," Eamon said nonchalantly. "Thank you for coming and wasting your time here. Feel free to gorge yourself upon my hospitality until the morning."

And with that he turned and walked out, Killian on his heels and the rest of us not far behind. We walked down the hall, meeting up with my father and all the way

to the throne hall where we could speak in private. Eamon
waited only until the door was closed behind us before he
took his circlet from his head and slung it across the room
with such force it hit the opposite wall with a clank. He let
out an accompanying howl of rage.

"How can they do that? How did I let them defeat
me? I am such an idiot!" he cried, hands fisting his hair in
anguish. "I must be as naïve as they say if I can't even hold
rule over my own subjects."

"It was none of your fault, lad, you did your best, and
I daresay your speech won over everyone in that room, or
will by tomorrow," my father said in a kind voice, putting a
hand on Eamon's shoulder. "They might even decide they
were wrong. Don't mind Proinsias; that old windbag has
always been bad tempered."

"But have I really failed?" Eamon asked. "Did this
just prove that I am an incompetent ruler? Niall,
sometimes, I just don't know what I'm doing. I try so hard
to do what my father would have done, but sometimes I
just have no idea what to do, and I don't... I wish I could
talk to him. Sometimes I just don't feel like a king at all. I
really do feel too young."

"Eamon," my father said. "You are young, and you are
still learning, but you are never alone. Your councilors are
good men, and they will help you. You have Ceannt, and
he is as wise as his father. And I am always there if you
need advice." He sighed deeply and looked off as if far
away. "I never told you this, but when your father was
dying on the battlefield and I held him on my knee, he
asked me to please look after you. He was like a brother to
me, and serving him never felt a chore." He reached
behind him and pulled me forward so I was standing next
to Eamon. "If I am not wrong in my reckoning I think you

and Ciran share such a relationship, and I hope you keep that."

"You are a great king," I told him sincerely. "Every day, I thank the saints you are the one I answer to as opposed to any of the others."

Eamon smiled slightly and Killian came up to rest an arm around his shoulders.

"And you know you always have me, *dearthàir*," he said fondly, handing him back his circlet that he had retrieved. "I'll beat anyone who dares say anything against you. That's my job, after all. No one picks on my little brother."

"You're only one month older than me, Killian," Eamon said, smiling despite himself. "You couldn't even have held me when I was a baby."

"Still older," Killian said tapping his chest then turned serious again. "Don't you ever doubt yourself, Eamon. Only then will you actually start being a terrible king."

"Thanks, everyone," Eamon said, smiling genuinely now and reaching out to clasp my forearm. "I'm sorry for my outburst. He just made my blood boil."

"You speak for all of us," Tierney said. "He had no right to dismiss Oran as expendable."

"It was wickedly horrible of him," Caitlin said, coming over and giving Eamon a sisterly kiss on his cheek. "We'll show him one of these days. We'll hand his fat backside to him."

Killian tsked at his sister but the rest of us laughed.

"It doesn't get us any closer to starting the mission again though," Eamon said. "Whether I'm a fool or a great king."

"Well, as I see it we have two options," Killian said. "We either do nothing and let the council win, or we do it despite them."

"Or we wait to see if they change their mind," Eamon said. "I fear if we actually disobey them, it will only go poorly. But rest assured, I will not falter from that option if that is the only way. But as you say, Killian, I must have some sort of propriety."

"I've created a monster," the captain bemoaned sarcastically.

"You will decide what is right soon enough," my father told the king. "Think on it tonight. You will have a clear head in the morning."

"You're right," Eamon sighed in resignation. "Ciran, your company may have tonight to rest, and tomorrow morning, we can discuss what will go on. I want to see you here by eight-thirty sharp."

"We'll be there," I assured him and clasped his forearm again, bowing over it before I gathered my company and left. "You may all stay at our place."

Caitlin was suddenly beside me and I turned to her with surprise. "You're not staying with your brother?"

She smiled and winked. "Please, I've been camping out with you five for days, some female company will do me good. Besides, your mother will likely need some help with all the extra men in the house."

I smiled fondly at her and we piled into our vehicles, still using the Range Rovers since they had all our things in them.

We were a dejected, defeated bunch who came to my mother's welcoming embrace, and she did indeed embrace all of us. As I turned from her I found myself in Daegal's grip, his face buried in my shirt and I tousled his hair fondly. No one spoke of the mission over supper, and no one said anything at all about the council meeting. It was like it had never happened, and I was thankful for that. I was not ready to discuss anything and I really just wanted to go to bed. We sat around the fire in the living room for a while after supper as Maeve played old airs on the harp and Finbar took out his fiddle, but even though the fire was merry and the atmosphere was warm and I had a wolfhound lying across my feet, I felt little at ease. I should have had Aeden with me, and it was not right that I did not.

I retired early, wanting to get sleep since I was so weary, but lay unable to do so for a long time, just staring at the ceiling. Finally the door opened and feet padded over to me and a warm lump curled up against my side and without preamble, I began to tell Daegal all about it, perhaps the only one who hadn't been on the mission to ever know everything that happened. I even told him about Jarlath and Gorlan even though I hadn't wanted to before. But because I never knew what he might have seen in his dreams I didn't want anything to have frightened him because he didn't know the whole story behind his visions. He was silent throughout, and then finally looked up at me and asked, "What are you going to do now?"

"Same as we were going to do before," I told him. "Get them back. I promised, didn't I?"

He sighed deeply but we said nothing more for a long moment, then, "I dreamed of him again while you were gone," he said.

"Yeah?"

He nodded. "He was still a prisoner. But there was also fighting in the dream. I couldn't tell with who. It was on the Giant's Causeway." He suddenly looked up and met my eyes in the darkness, eerie because only the moonlight coming in the window shone off his pupils. "I'm afraid of what will happen when you go."

"Don't be," I pleaded with him, suddenly realizing how necessary it was that he was not afraid. "If you are afraid, I can't be strong. I can't think of you worried back here, waiting for me to come back. Just...keep the torch lit, and never lose hope." I smiled and ruffled his hair. "You're probably the only person who can do that. You have to keep strong for Mum. You're the strongest one of us all, Daegal. Don't ever lose that."

He smiled back and settled down again, hugging his stuffed dragon, and I wrapped a second blanket over him before I turned onto my side and felt his nose pressing against my shoulder blades. Comforted by his presence that helped to ground me to familiarity, I was finally able to drift off.

A buzzing woke me. I rolled over, disoriented with weariness, unable to place the sound. It was pitch black and my senses told me it was still the middle of the night so it couldn't be my alarm clock. Daegal moaned and poked his head out from the cozy nest of blankets he had made beside me.

"What is it?" he asked, rubbing his eyes.

I finally spotted my mobile sticking out the back pocket of my pants on the floor beside my bed. The face was lit up, and I realized the sound had been me receiving a text. I reached over and grabbed it, forcing my eyes to focus as I read it.

Open your kitchen door.

I frowned then saw it was from Killian.

"What the..." I groaned, hauling myself out of bed and dragging on my pants before brisking my hands against my bare arms in the sudden chill air outside my blankets.

"Where are you going?" Daegal asked, climbing off the bed with his blanket still wrapped around him.

"I don't know," I replied with a groan as we made our way silently down the stairs and into the kitchen. I unlatched the door and was greeted by two figures wearing hoodies with swords slung over their shoulders. As I stood gazing blankly, they pulled off the hoods and revealed themselves to be Eamon and Killian.

"Do I want to ask?" I said with a grimace.

"Sorry for the unconventional arrival," Eamon said. "We had to sneak out past the guards."

"Imagine the high king having to sneak out of his own palace," Killian said, shaking his head in disgust. "Past *my guards*. We did the rope out the window, the classic."

"He dropped me," Eamon added blandly.

"It wasn't pretty. Nor very majestic."

"But that was all we could do with five rulers telling me no," Eamon said. "I didn't want to make a scene but..."

"It's far too late for that, Your Majesty," Killian told him sarcastically.

"I'm sorry, but what are you doing here? Now?" I asked, still trying to piece it all together through my sleep muddled brain.

"Are you even awake?" Killian asked angrily, looking me up and down. "I suppose not. Well, to make a long story short, we had to escape from Tara Hall so no one would know we were gone until it was too late to stop us. Proinsias got everyone riled up at supper and it was pretty much like another council meeting, but with actual food being flung across the table—in my defense, it was mostly an accident, I put my hand down on the fork wrong...anyway. It was a mess, some people were insulted

by things other people said, Proinsias decided the entire
kingdom was being run poorly and would not allow
anyone else to reconsider anything said at the council so
they are all leaving first thing in the morning after passing
an official proclamation that the mission is not sanctioned,
and are going to force Eamon to sign it because how could
he refuse if the entire council was for it? So you see the
dilemma, and why we were forced to sneak out. Normally
we could have just walked out the front gate, but
unfortunately everyone saw fit to bring their own guards
along with them and they are *so helpful* to be keeping watch
with my men, thus giving them a break. I had O'Rourke
make a hole for us. We would have been here earlier, but
we had to come on foot. Eamon's darling is under lock and
key."

"No," I said, holding up a hand. "Why did *you* have to
escape in the first place? Where are we going?"

Killian gave Eamon a look that clearly implied *I can't
believe this idiot*, before he turned back to me. "We're going
to do a prison break in Lorcan's palace. What else could
we possibly be considering right now, a trip to the pub?"

"We're getting our family back whether the council
like it or not," Eamon added, less testy than Killian. "And
I'm coming with you. If Lorcan won't treat with anyone
else, he will at least have to listen to me on principle."

"I wasn't going to try talking him out of it," Killian
said. "So I decided joining him would be the best option.
Make sure nothing untoward happens. Besides, if we had
stayed, Eamon would have been pressured into signing the
proclamation, and if he had done that and then sent you
out, he would have been going against his own word and
that's not very kingly at all."

"So instead, I'm going rogue and am going to at least

make myself look heroic even if I come across as completely reckless and idiotic," he replied with a smile. "So rouse your company, Ciran Mac Cool."

"And get dressed," Killian added with a frown at my scant attire. "We leave in ten."

Daegal helped me wake the others quietly and then assisted me in putting on my breastplate like he had the last time I left. He handed me my jacket and I zipped it up before I leaned down to look him eye to eye, putting a hand on his shoulder.

"When you see me again, Daegal, I'm going to be bringing Aeden back home."

"Promise?" he asked in a whisper. "Promise that...that whatever happens, promise that you'll come back."

"We're brothers," I told him, shaking him slightly. "And that means that I will *always* come back to you." I handed him my mobile. "You keep this so you don't have to steal anyone else's. Tierney's number is on there where you can reach us. I promise to call you as soon as I've found him."

He nodded and then threw his arms around me and I held him tightly, both of us silent for a long moment. I reluctantly pushed him back, ruffling his hair. "I have to go. You'll have to tell Mum and Da what happened."

He nodded again. "Bring him back, Ciran."

"I will," I replied and then went to join my company and my king.

Part Three

The Gauntlet

Chapter Eighteen
On the Road Again

It felt good to be back on the road, and this time there was a specific road in mind, one that would lead us for better or worse to our destination. It was also rather exciting to have the High King himself along for the journey, dressed no differently than us and without his circlet. The only marks of his station he held at all were the two braids and the medallion with the royal seal under his breastplate. He wore leathers like the rest of us and to anyone who didn't know I think he would have looked like just another Fianna warrior, which was the idea. I respected him more so for that than if he had gone out with pomp and ceremony, as I knew Proinsias would have. But no, our *Airdrígh* had had to escape from his own hall after being dropped out a window by his captain of the guard. That was a man I could follow.

We decided to drive most of the way North and then abandon our vehicles to continue on foot to the Causeway and Lorcan's palace so as not to attract unwanted attention too soon. I ended up being in the Rover with Eamon,

Killian and Caitlin, Killian being self-instated driver while Eamon read the map and they argued back and forth while Caitlin and I shared amused looks in the backseat.

"Okay, you two, if you don't stop I'm going to take over the navigating," Caitlin finally said, after Killian nearly veered off the road grabbing for the map as Eamon held it away from him. "That's no way to speak to your king, after all. For heaven's sake, you sound like an old married couple!"

"Well, if His Royal Sense of Direction could actually tell which way is north on the map..."

"I know which way is north—we're *heading* north! See? And that is the coast of Scotland on the map right above the Causeway. *I* know exactly where we're going, it's you who's not driving in the proper direction!"

"You know I was always better at navigating than you. You were the one who always got lost in the woods when we went camping as kids."

"Well at least I could shoot a bow which you plainly told me was an English weapon and not fit for an Irish prince. You weren't so abusive of my talent when I got you supper when we were forced to stay out there all night, lost, were you?"

I looked to Caitlin, seeing her roll her eyes. "Are they always like this on road trips?"

"All the time," she groaned, leaning over the seat to grab the map from Eamon. "Listen, it's perfectly simple. You just stay on this road and head north! Look, no turnoffs! Stop the bickering already! You two are insufferable. And keep your eyes on the road, for heaven's sake!"

"I am keeping my eyes on the road," Killian said, ruining the insistent reply by turning around as he said it.

"And I know perfectly well how to drive, thank you very much, little sis —"

"Killian!" Caitlin cried an instant before Eamon shouted as well and Killian spun and slammed on the brakes, sending us all jerking forward painfully. I looked up to see what had elicited our stop and saw two figures standing in the road holding bows. My first thought was Goblins, but then I realized they did not have grayish complexions nor were they dressed in black leather. These were Fae.

"Who are they?" Caitlin asked, still catching her breath from the sudden stop. She was reaching for her sword hilt, but I reached out and grabbed her wrist.

"They're guardians of the Realm," I told her. "Come to ask us our way. You'll have to speak with them, Eamon."

He nodded and I turned around, holding up my hand to the others who had stopped behind us to tell them to wait.

Eamon put his hand on the door handle and took up his sword as he turned back to me. "Ciran, would you accompany me? It might help to have someone with a bit of the Fair Blood in them."

I nodded, not taking up my own sword. "Do you know the proper motions?"

He nodded. "I think I can manage." Killian didn't look so sure, but he didn't say anything either. Eamon and I got out of the Range Rover and stepped toward the two Fae guards standing in the road. They did not move forward, but they lowered their bows.

"State your name and business," one said, a dark haired male, with elegant features and strangely green eyes.

"*Airdrígh* Eamon O'Brian of the High Seat of Tara,

son of Raymond," Eamon said before motioning to me. "This is Ciran son of Niall of the ancient Lordly Line of Mac Cool; *Ceannasaí de* Na Fianna."

The Faeries nodded. The '*ceannasaí*', I'll admit, sounded a bit much without an 'acting' added to it, but it wasn't a lie either.

"What do you do here, *Airdrígh*?" the other asked, this one red-blond with dark amber eyes.

Eamon knelt on one knee—even though he was the High King of the people of Ireland, he was still required to show respect of the Fair Folk and the *Cinn A Tháinig Roimh.* "I come with a small company to retrieve six of my people who have fallen into the hands of King Lorcan," Eamon said humbly. "They are prisoners, one who is my younger brother, and I wish to see them safely home."

"Is this all you come to do?" asked the dark haired Faerie.

Eamon nodded. "It is."

"And you swear that you will not disturb our own people nor seek to make war with us?"

"I do not wish to fight anyone if I do not have to," Eamon said sincerely. "But I will not hesitate to make war with King Lorcan if he does not surrender my people."

"There is honor in your loyalty," the blond Faerie said. "But you must swear by your blood that you will only go to the Goblin Realm, retrieve your prisoners, and then go back home. Will you swear that?"

"I will," Eamon said and drew his sword. He nicked the base of his thumb and dripped the blood onto the elegant blade. "I swear with my own blood on the sword *Lucht Cuardaithe Fola* that I shall do as I have said or suffer the consequences of my actions."

He stood up and sheathed his sword and the Faeries

looked satisfied enough.

"We wish you luck on your journey, *Airdrígh* Eamon," said the dark-haired one. "The Goblins have long forsaken their ties to us and Lorcan grows stronger by the day. I fear the time will come when we are forced to put him in his place again."

"I will try and help you remedy that," Eamon said and we both bowed to the Faeries before turning away to head back to the Range Rover. The two Faeries stepped to the side of the road to let us pass and we were soon on our way again. This time Killian seemed to try harder to keep his eyes on the road, and he and Eamon didn't argue nearly as much about the direction. I think it was all becoming real to us now, what we were actually doing, and part of me was glad of that, while the other part wasn't quite ready for it.

We made good time in the Range Rovers and were approximately an hour and a half hiking distance from the Causeway—we had covered a good distance since three o'clock in the morning. Now the sun was just going down and we got our kit ready to make camp for the night.

I could almost pretend that we were just camping out and having a good time with the cooking, the laughter, and the joking that happened that night, but there was an underlying current of tension running through everyone like a taut string that held us all together. No one even mentioned it, not a word was spoken about our mission, because we didn't need to speak it. It was there, hanging over us with great anticipation of the dawn when we would have to push aside all pretending everything was a lark and get serious again. But tonight, we had the luxury of forgetting and we were going to do it even if we couldn't sleep a wink.

"Now I know why you wanted to bring Caitlin along, lads," Eamon said with a grin as he finished up his bowl of stew. "She's a brilliant cook. Even better than Killian."

"Hey now, who do you think taught her the finer arts?" Killian asked, but smiled fondly at his sister and wrapped his arm around her shoulders as she leaned against him.

"It's probably time we got to sleep," I said, crouching next to the fire and banking it for the night."

"Who's taking first watch?" Keevan asked, stretching and yawning.

"You should since you slept the entire way here," Riordan said, poking his brother's side while his arms were up and making him yelp and cover his ribs, only causing Riordan to go after his neck instead, grinning evilly as Keevan protested while we all laughed.

"I'll take first watch," Eamon said, setting his bowl aside and checking his sword.

"Unseemly!" Killian tsked, but he was already tucking himself into his bedroll, not seeming to be too upset about letting the High King take first watch.

"Are you sure?" Deaglan asked where he sat on his bedroll fletching arrows. "I can take it."

"No, sleep," Eamon insisted. "I'm not very tired at all."

I saw he was lying, it was plain in the unconscious slump of his shoulders and the dark shadows under his eyes that he was exhausted, but I also knew he wouldn't be able to sleep, and didn't want to bring it up in front of the others. I turned to them. "You heard him, get to bed. You can't disobey the High King."

They smiled and all went off to their respective bedrolls, lying down. I did the same, but with no real intention of sleeping. The night before I had been exhausted, now I was wired, and I knew I would not sleep a wink no matter how hard I tried. I lay with my arms folded under my head, staring up at the countless stars above. I just wanted this all to be over. I was tired of this anticipation that knotted in my gut, making me nauseous. I wanted to be able to go home and rest and know that everything was all right again, that everyone was home with their families and that we had won. I sighed and rolled over, thinking I would attempt to close my eyes, when I caught sight of Eamon, sitting on a rock to keep watch. But he was not watching the landscape, and his eyes were trained upward as mine had been moments before. I watched him for a few minutes, then I sat up decidedly, grabbing my coat and boots and walked silently over to him, standing at his shoulder without him knowing I was there.

"Want some company?" I asked quietly.

He gave a start, but he turned around to see me. "You should be asleep, Ciran."

I sat down next to him and gave him a meaningful look. He smiled tiredly and sighed, lowering his head to rub his eyes.

"How long has it been since you've slept?" I asked quietly.

He groaned. "Too long since I slept well." He turned to me. "I think it's the same for you."

"Let's put it this way," I said wryly. "The last time I got a good night's sleep, I was knocked unconscious falling down a waterfall and nearly frozen to death."

He chuckled but there was little humor in it, distracted. He looked down at his hands and I saw a glint there. Apart from the ring he always wore — his mother's —

the other item was Oran's braid cradled in the palm of one. My hand went unconsciously to the second medallion that was warm against my skin, and I felt the impression of it through my shirt.

"We'll find them," I told him, feeling like I had said it a thousand times to a thousand different people and still I had not made it happen. I feared that one day those words would go hollow.

He didn't say anything, just tucked the piece of beaded hair back into the pouch around his neck. "Can I tell you something, Ciran?" he asked finally.

"Of course," I replied.

"Sometimes I'm afraid I'm not strong enough. Not strong enough to be a leader, not strong enough to be a good king at all. The debacle at the meeting yesterday only proves it. How am I supposed to go to Lorcan, who is so confident in himself that he would start a war, and demand he release my men, when I cannot even believe I can do it?"

"Eamon," I said. "You've got to stop doubting yourself, man." I punched him in the shoulder like I would do to Tierney. "You're a good leader. Far, far better than I will ever be. I hashed my entire mission because I was inexperienced, and didn't take the time to really get to know my men, but now I think I know a little bit about leadership. It might not help, but I'll tell you anyway. First of all, it's okay to be wrong, and if you're a good man, and take it in stride, then no one is going to fault you on it. Everything is a learning experience, even things that you might not think are at the time. Trust your comrades, because when you're lost, they'll get you out of it. But even more than that, trust yourself. Never let the doubt find you, because if it does, then you really are defeated. Just

barrel onward, don't look back, and keep your head high."
I looked him straight in the eye. "Do not think of the
Eamon in the council meeting yesterday. Think of the
Eamon who led an entire army into a final charge and
ended a war. That's the Eamon who is going to go into that
palace tomorrow; not walking, but striding, because he is a
veteran, and he has killed countless Goblins and they'll
remember his name and the snarl on his lips when they
faced him. No more than a boy then—what horrible figure
will he be now?"

Eamon's lips turned up in a smile and I saw a little of
the light in his dark eyes that I knew from the old days.
"You think it will work?"

"Well, if worse comes to worse, just pretend to be
Killian," I told him. "Brimming with confidence and
cockiness."

He laughed lightly. "Thank you, Ciran. I think that
will help a bit. I'll try to be more confident. I just fear I
second-guess myself too much. I will try to be more bold in
the future."

"You just have to forget what everyone says about
you. They don't really know you or what you are capable
of."

"Nor do I, I fear."

I gave him a small smile. "Then I think it's about time
you found that out."

He grinned back and looked over his shoulder at the
others. Someone was snoring and I had a suspicion that it
was Killian.

"You should at least try to get some rest," he said.

I shrugged. "If you don't mind, I thought I would
share your watch with you."

He smiled and nodded. "Well then, I won't say no to

the company. Perhaps you can make some coffee then?"

"That would be even better," I said and got up to do so.

Chapter Nineteen
Chase

We ended up watching the entire night to let the others sleep. There was no point in wasting someone else if they could actually find the will to fall into slumber, and at dawn we made breakfast, and broke camp, packing everything we wouldn't need into the Range Rovers before we geared up, ready for our final trek.

Eamon pulled his sword belt over his shoulder and turned to the rest of us, making last adjustments to our weaponry.

"If everything goes well, this should be the last stretch of our mission. We will reach the Causeway and Lorcan's palace by the end of the day at the very latest, but it shouldn't take us that long. Once we get within a good distance of it, we will watch and keep an eye on any activity that might be going on there. Then we will head to the cliff face and go in the side entrance. Once there," he looked at us all seriously. "You will all go to rescue the prisoners, I alone will show myself, coming in the front, and beg audience with Lorcan. I will act as distraction so you can get the prisoners out. I would say you'll have no more than thirty minutes so make the best of it. I'll try to stall as long as I can."

"Are you sure this is wise, Eamon?" Killian asked, hesitation clouding his features. "I just think that someone else should go with you."

"Killian, if I don't go alone, peacefully, then I will not have a chance of talking to Lorcan and the entire mission will be a bust," Eamon said kindly, but with a sense of finality. "I need to speak with him king to king. Lorcan is not by any means a fool. He will probably think it's a trap anyway, that is why you must all act quickly. But we will have no chance at all if I do not go in there like a gentleman and a king to speak to him first. If we only use subterfuge, it will all be over and he is sure to wage war."

"But we're still using subterfuge," Tierney said. "How is it any different?"

Eamon smiled slightly. "We're using the kind Lorcan approves of. The kind he would use himself. And, if I am correct in my assumption of his character from what I know of him, he will respect us for it."

"We had better hope you're right, your majesty," Killian said wryly. "Because if not we're all going to get caught and thrown into the dungeons. And I don't know about you, but I don't think Proinsias will be in too much of a hurry about getting us back."

"Just stop worrying, Killian," Eamon told him with a smile, punching him in the shoulder. "It will all go fine. But we're wasting daylight, and that I will not allow, so come on, company, let's go!"

We struck off at the loping pace that we alternated with bouts of walking before we would start loping again. Na Fianna warriors could run at a steady pace all day, but we had three normal humans with us, so we tried to keep to their pace. They did quite a good job keeping up with us, considering.

We stopped in several spots to track, when one of us would catch sight of something out of place, or sense sign of Goblins being in the area. As we continued, I halted the company at one spot where I could clearly smell the earthy scent of goblins.

"What do you think?" Eamon asked, trusting to my sense of smell though he couldn't sense it the way we could.

"They just passed through, no more than twenty minutes ago," I said with surety, and that unnerved me.

"There will be patrols this close to their palace," Killian said. "It would only make sense after all."

"Ciran," Riordan called as he came jogging down a hill. "There are several motorbikes parked over in the lea. There's a road there. I think it leads directly to the Goblin palace."

"That sounds like a patrol," I said grimly, nodding to Killian. "How many?"

"Eight," Riordan said.

"We need to go," Eamon added, jerking his head. "Try and lie low. We'll hide in the leeside of the hills when we can. Stay in the valleys, whatever you do, don't skyline yourself."

"Oh, so you do know something about tracking," Killian said with a snarky glint in his eye.

"Another time, Killian!" Eamon said in exasperation as we hurried along, once again setting our pace to a jog.

We traveled for several minutes without incident and I figured that we were probably out of the danger zone by the time we passed the place where the Goblins had stowed their bikes. They would most likely be patrolling behind us, away from the direction of their place. The only thing we would have to worry about now was when they came back. But hopefully we would be inside the palace by then.

That was when Tierney's mobile rang randomly, and he cast a surprised look down at his jacket pocket. "Hey, what do you know? I didn't think we got reception out here. I don't know who would be calling me right now, though." He took up the phone, frowning. "It says it's you, Ciran, did you butt-dial me again?" Before I could reply he answered the call before turning to me. "It's Daegal."

I took the phone eagerly. "Daegal, did you…"

"Ciran, you have to listen to me. I'm scared that you're all in danger. You have to get away from wherever you are now."

"Daegal, slow down," I tried soothingly, but my brother was obviously frantic.

"No, you have to get out of there now or you'll be captured. Please."

"Ciran!" Riordan cried from his position standing farther up the hill. He was running down swiftly. "Goblin scouts!"

"Daegal," I said quietly, trying to keep my voice calm. "I have to go."

"Ciran, please, I…"

An arrow whizzed over the rise and buried itself into the ground at my feet. I ended the call, hating to cut Daegal off, but needing to focus on getting us out of this situation right now.

"We have to go! Now!" I cried to the others, waving for them to run along the valley we were caught in. We had to get out before we were trapped there. "We'll try and lose them."

We sprinted down the ravine. Keevan and Killian retreated backwards, taking up their shields to catch the arrows on, while Deaglan stood between them, firing back at the Goblins, several of his arrows finding satisfying marks. I raced forward to cover Eamon's back, Caitlin right at my side.

"There was a pass back this way," Tierney said, taking the lead with a running leap as he dodged another arrow with a roll. "If we hurry we might be able to lose them there."

I shook my head. "No, we won't lose them, not on their own ground. But we can split up, try to confuse them."

"Great idea," Killian said as he ran up next to me to grab Eamon by the shoulder. "You and I will switch clothes, that way they'll confuse me with you and go after me. Ciran can get you to safety."

Eamon laughed. "You'd never be able to pass for me even with a hood, Killian. We shall tempt fate as usual."

"No," Deaglan said, running up. "I can pass as you. We're both dark-haired and about the same height and build. It would be an honor, *Airdrígh*."

"There's no time to argue," I told Eamon. We had reached the small pass Tierney had mentioned, and I hauled the two of them into a small lee behind some rocks, helping Eamon out of his coat while Killian did the same for Deaglan. Eamon took his bow and quiver as well, spitting on his hands in an attempt to tame his wild curls. Deaglan smiled at his efforts as Killian mussed his perfect hair vigorously.

"It will have to do in a pinch," he said, buckling the last strap on Eamon's leather jacket.

"You look like a king," Eamon told the Finar with a grin as he handed him his sword. "Take good care of this sword, may she serve you well." Deaglan took it with a slight bow.

"Let's hope I don't fail you," he said humbly.

"I'll be more likely to fail myself," Eamon told him kindly, putting the hood of the sweatshirt he was wearing underneath over his head. "Hope you're good with a sword."

"Passable."

"No time," I said. "Keevan, you come with me and Eamon, the rest of you stay with Deaglan and Killian. It will look more convincing if more are protecting the 'king'."

They nodded and Tierney and I clasped forearms quickly in farewell. Caitlin looked like she wanted to say something to me, and I felt there was something I wanted to say to her too, but I couldn't think of it at that moment and she simply smiled and nodded before I could, running off with her brother and the others. I turned around and clapped Eamon and Keevan's shoulders. "Let's go."

We had stalled the Goblins for a moment, but as soon as we were out in the open again, they spotted us and started their hail of arrows once more. Keevan caught several on his shield before one grazed him across the upper arm. Eamon shot several Goblins with Deaglan's bow, surprising me at how accurate he was and on the run too. I hadn't even known he was good with a bow, it not necessarily being a kingly weapon. He grinned and winked at me as he caught a Goblin on the run.

"Not bad for a non-Fianna, eh?" he asked with a grin.

"Just keep it up," Keevan said frantically as he glanced around. "Ciran, more are coming, do you think they figured out our ruse already?"

"I don't know," I replied. "I was hoping to buy a bit more time."

"Over here," Eamon said, rushing in another direction, barely missing getting shot in the back as an arrow whizzed past him. He vaulted over a large stone and disappeared into a little hidden pocket. Keevan and I were right behind him as he shot off three more arrows with devastating results. For the moment, all the Goblins who had us in their sights were dead, but more were coming fast. We sank into our hiding place, Eamon catching his breath. Keevan and I weren't even breathing hard. Eamon looked over at us with an annoyed expression.

"I hate you Fianna," he said and we grinned, pressing ourselves farther into the shadows.

"Too much throne time, *Airdrígh*?" I couldn't help but quip.

"Is it too much to hope that they won't find us here?" Keevan asked, gripping the haft of his axe so tight, his knuckles were white. I slapped his side reassuringly.

"Don't worry, we'll make it out of here alive," I said. I was *nearly* positive of that. Though I wasn't so sure as to bet on the chance we would make it out of here without chains.

"Ciran," Eamon said quietly and I turned to look at him, his face in shadows, making it seem very serious. "I need you to know something."

"What is it?" I asked, frowning. "No offense, but this isn't really a good time for confessions."

"If this ends badly," Eamon said and stopped me before I could interrupt. "Just listen, Ciran, because law dictates someone must know, and for the record, Killian already does, but I thought I should tell you personally. *If* this ends badly and I don't return, and you are unable to recover the prisoners, namely Oran or Aeden, you are by right the next heir to the High Seat."

I looked at him blankly for a moment, unsure of whether I heard him properly. "Me?" I asked stupidly. "But surely my father...we aren't..."

"Your father declined the position long ago," Eamon said. "And unless you also decline it...your family is as close to the royal blood as we can get. And I would rather have a Mac Cool on the High Seat than any other."

"No, it is a great honor," I said, still flabbergasted. "It's just, I don't know if I really wanted to hear this right now."

"Shh!" Keevan hissed and Eamon gripped the bow, reaching back into the quiver and only finding one arrow. He cursed softly. I gripped my sword.

"Make it count," I muttered as we heard the Goblins coming closer. I knew they could smell us, and that we weren't going to be hidden for much longer. I realized I could also smell them now; their strange scent of moss and earth, mixed with the sharper tinge of fear and anticipation running through our veins. I could hear Keevan's heart pumping fast and watched him tense, ready for the fight that was coming.

"Let's meet them like warriors," Eamon said and we nodded. He raised the hood of the sweatshirt he was wearing under the jacket to hide his face.

The Goblins were almost upon us now. We all readied ourselves for the charge.

"One," Eamon started to count. "Two..."

The first Goblin showed himself and Eamon let out a roar as he leapt up, shooting point blank between the Goblin's eyes as Keevan and I rushed out at them, I slashing with my sword and Keevan screaming a meaningless war cry as he spun the axe with deadly accuracy.

We made short work of the first wave, but the Goblins kept coming and finally we were overwhelmed and over-powered. A Goblin in a military style coat and steel-toed boots, who I took to be a lieutenant or something, strode up as the Goblins were confiscating our weapons, forcing us to our knees and wrenching our arms behind our backs.

"What have we caught?" he asked, surveying us with an appraising look. "Three Fianna?"

The Goblin holding me on my knees yanked my coat off of my left shoulder to reveal my brotherhood knot tattoo. The one holding Keevan did the same.

"Why's that one trying to conceal his face?" the one holding me growled softly, nodding at Eamon.

The lieutenant strode slowly over to Eamon and I held my breath, though I tried not to give anything away. I didn't know why I bothered because I knew it would all be over in a moment. He grasped the hood partly concealing Eamon's face and yanked it down, revealing his two braids with beads sporting the royal design. Eamon smiled grimly up at him as the lieutenant smirked.

"Ah, so this one is King Eamon. Very good. That means we can forgo chasing the others."

"Is it wise to call the men off, sir?" another Goblin asked. "The companions might pose a problem."

The lieutenant looked bored. "Our numbers are far superior. Besides, by the time they figure out how to find the fortress, let alone infiltrate it, they won't have any reason to. And we've got more than enough leverage here to make them cooperate. Now bind them, and we will take them back to His Majesty before they try to get away." He turned to Eamon with a cold smile. "King Lorcan will be happy to have some royal company. Or at least some who might be worth the title."

Eamon's face darkened, but he wisely said nothing. I envied him that, for if it had been my brother the Goblin spoke of, I feared I would have taken his head off with my bare hands. It did sound promising for the fact that Oran and possibly the others were still alive as Jarlath said. For now.

Keevan struggled as they bound up our hands. "My brother will kill you all," he said. "He's a berserker and I know just how to make him snap."

The Goblin dealing with him backhanded him across the back of the head. "Shut up, you little demon sprite. After we're done with you, there won't be enough of you left for your brother to pick up in a thimble."

He jerked away valiantly but was only thrown on his face for it. Eamon and I didn't bother struggling. I wanted to tell Keevan to come quietly, but knew it would be no use.

"Let's go," the lieutenant said once we were all secure and they formed a circle around us, shoving us along. I glanced up briefly in the direction the others had gone and caught sight of them watching our capture discreetly from the opposite rise. I saw Caitlin first, but could not read her expression from where I was, though I saw defeat in the slump of her shoulders. Then I caught sight of Riordan, rushing forward, only to be hauled back by Killian and Tierney. I really hoped he wouldn't go berserk on them, but he seemed to calm quickly; at least, he wasn't throwing them off and running down the hill after us. I counted on them staying free so that they could help orchestrate our escape. Also, I still had Tierney's phone in my jacket pocket, and I would try and get a message to them if I got the chance...

"Move it," the Goblin leading me said, shoving me hard in the back and almost sending me to my knees. With this kind of treatment, we would be lucky to stay alive long enough to see Lorcan.

Chapter Twenty
Captives

The Goblin palace was truthfully amazing. I had never seen anything like it in my life and even though we were in dire straits, I had to admire it. There were lots of stories about their underground palaces, some thinking they would look more uncivil, more rocky and dark. I personally had always thought of it looking like Fingal's Cave off the coast of Scotland, but it seemed we were all wrong. It looked a bit like Tara Hall, but more ancient, and if it was falling down slightly, the rustic appearance only seemed to add more to its regality of character. Tara was splendid, but Lorcan's hall had something else entirely to say. It had something of the feel of the stone circles and Bru na Boinne. Ancient, mysterious and though nowhere near their original glory, they still commanded respect.

We were hauled into the huge hall with vaulted ceilings and a large skylight that let in the light of day, falling elegantly onto the throne at one end of the room on a built up dais. Lounging on the throne was Lorcan himself. He was tall, I could tell that even seeing him sitting down, and rail thin like most Goblins. In actuality, he was rather unassuming. He wore no kingly finery, being dressed in a plain silk shirt and black trousers underneath a long leather coat. His hair was ash blond and drawn back in a club to keep it away from his face. But it was not his appearance that told he held a position of power, no, it was all his presence, and that was obvious from the moment he raised his head to look at his lieutenant as we were shoved into the hall.

"Ah, Cronin, what have you brought me?"

"Several special guests, my lord," the lieutenant replied as we were pushed forward.

Lorcan stood, frowning over us. "Do my eyes deceive me or is that High King Eamon O'Brian standing there?"

"It is," Eamon replied himself.

Lorcan grinned. "Excellent! This shall go even better than expected. I have been thinking on the best way to get an audience with you, save making a trip to the Common Lands myself. Now you have given me that chance by coming here and saving me the trouble. Tell me, *Airdrígh*, what has brought you here to my humble dwelling?"

"I know you are no fool, Lorcan," Eamon said, his voice quiet, and I thought him very regal himself. "You have my brother and other warriors of mine. I came to see that you give them back to me."

"Ah, yes, the patrol I took," Lorcan nodded. "Very brave those men. Some more so than others. Some who have suffered greatly for their bravery." He looked at me here, and fear knotted my stomach. I tried to stay impassive but was unable to, especially when he started to walk toward me, his boots echoing on the stone floor. One hand took me by the chin and forced me to look into his pale blue eyes. "A Mac Cool, I see. The next younger brother, I would guess. Your brother was one of the brave ones." I glared at him, wanting to scream, wanting to demand to know whether Aeden really still lived as Jarlath had said, but I could say nothing. If I did, I feared it would all end horribly wrong.

"He lives," Lorcan added as an afterthought, nearly making me sink to my knees in relief. "For now. As do they all," he added, looking to Eamon. "Do not think I am some monster who kills willy-nilly; that would be a foolish assumption. It would not have gained me anything. No, why should I kill anyone unless it is necessary? They are worth more to me alive than dead. I cannot bargain with a corpse."

"Then where are they?" Keevan demanded, and I winced. I knew he wouldn't be able to stay silent for long, but I had hoped he would not start quite yet. "Where is my brother?!"

The Goblin holding him gave him a sharp jab to the kidneys and Keevan grunted, but didn't stop struggling. Lorcan looked at him with disgusted pity.

"Boys, Eamon? Is that all you brought with you? Warriors untried in battle?"

"They are not so much younger than you or I when the weight of the world was put on our shoulders," Eamon said quietly.

"Ah, but we were tried in blood and steel, Eamon. You must remember," Lorcan snarled in disgust.

"Our fathers destroyed each other, true," Eamon said. "But I wish peace, Lorcan. Let us learn from our fathers, and not make the same mistakes."

Lorcan laughed, a harsh, sardonic sound. "The only mistake my father made was not wiping out your kind completely. And *yours* tried to fix his mistake by killing *my* father."

"I don't want to make war," Eamon said again. "I don't want to lose more of my people, and I don't think you do either."

Lorcan was silent, his back turned to Eamon, his hands clasped tightly behind him. "No, I do not; no one wants to see their people slaughtered. But the ones who die for my cause will gladly give their blood so that we may stand in our rightful place once more." He spun around suddenly, a hard glint in his ice-cold eyes. "Why are you here, Eamon? Why have you come all this way without an army?"

"You know why I'm here, Lorcan. I came for my people. I just want them back. I don't want to fight you for them, but I will if I have to."

Lorcan gave a half smile. "Do you seriously expect me to believe you came all this way alone, just to rescue six prisoners with no ulterior motives?"

"I don't know how to make you believe that to be true," Eamon said firmly. "But we came only to claim two fathers and four sons and brothers. We want nothing more than that." He looked at Lorcan with a challenging glare. "What do you want, Lorcan? What will you take in exchange for their lives?"

The Goblin smiled again, but this time there was a harsh, determined light in his eyes. "It's far too early for me to reveal my plans to you, Eamon. Perhaps after supper when we can talk as kings together. You shall be my guest, and we will have some entertainment lined up." He turned to his lieutenant. "Cronin, please see that High King Eamon is put into one of my guest rooms. He will be made comfortable as befits his station, but the door will be locked and guarded. The others," he looked with contempt at Keevan and I. "They can go to the dungeons. Get them ready for tonight. They'll be the ones providing the entertainment."

"Lorcan," Eamon began to say but was hauled off at the same time we were and the guards made no point of being kind. We were shoved and buffeted and punched as we were pushed down into the dungeons and when we got to the anteroom where the guards sat, our guards searched us, taking our coats and armor and leaving us wearing only our thin undershirts. Keevan made quite a row as they searched him for weapons, and I was shocked myself with the fact that they kept pulling knives from his clothing. I had no idea he wore so many, but by the time we were done, there were five on the ground and then one Goblin slammed him up against the wall and much to Keevan's protest, pulled one out of the back of his trousers.

"Watch it, mate!" Keevan growled.

"Maybe you should think next time before you decide to stash sharp things in uncomfortable places," the Goblin retorted with a laugh.

After that, we were thrown into a small cell and the door was slammed. Keevan was at the bars, cursing, and the Goblin who locked the door, snarled at him and shoved him back. He sat down hard next to me and started to pull off his boot.

"Don't worry, they missed two," he said, pulling up his pant leg. "We can each have one, and when they come back we can—"

The door was thrown open again and the Goblin guard grinned triumphantly at Keevan before he tackled the young Finar onto his stomach, grabbing his flailing arms as he yanked up his pant legs and retrieved two more small throwing knives. He quickly turned Keevan over again and pressed one of the knives under his chin.

"Any more?" he growled.

"No!" Keevan snarled, jerking frantically to dislodge the Goblin. "Now get off me!"

The Goblin sniffed and slammed the hilt of the knife into Keevan's jaw, then got up, kicking him in the side before he locked the door again. I helped Keevan up as he cradled his jaw in his hand, growling incoherently in Irish. The Goblin smiled.

"You two should save some of that energy. King Lorcan wants you to fight for him tonight. If you do well, you might get some food."

"What do you mean fight for him?" Keevan asked but the Goblin just smiled and left us alone in the dark. Keevan growled and lunged forward, grabbing the bars and looking out. He kicked the door several times before I finally got up and hauled him back as he struggled, shouting obscenities in Irish, before he collapsed against me and I lowered him down to sit in the corner, crouching in front of him as I gripped his shoulders.

"Hey, listen to me," I said in as calm a voice as I could muster as he pressed his head against his knees. "We're going to get out of this and we're going to be fine. Killian will call in backup and we'll all be out of here within a day or so."

"I don't like being locked up," Keevan said in a muffled voice, and I gripped the back of his neck tightly.

"Yeah, I know, I don't either," I said and then sat down and pressed my shoulder against his for support. He finally looked up with a sigh and leaned his head back into the corner.

"What do you think they're going to do to us?" he whispered, and I once again saw the scared kid under the warrior façade.

"They said we're going to fight," I told him with a smile. "You're good at that."

He gave me a small crooked grin. "Yeah, I guess I am."

"Just think, Riordan will come for you soon, and he'll tear them up when he finds out they captured his little brother. Just don't lose your brass, Keevan, not yet. I know you've got a lot of it."

He smiled a little wider this time. "Well, as long as I can fight, I'll be able to keep it together."

"Good," I said. "Because I think we're going to need every bit of strength we have left."

Chapter Twenty-One
In the Halls of the Goblin King

Later that night, the door opened again and our guard came into the cell and chained our hands in front of us.

"Time to provide the entertainment for his majesty's supper," he said with a smile. "If you do a good job, you can have something to eat too."

"How kind," I muttered as we were jerked to our feet and taken from the cell, instantly surrounded by three more guards with swords at the ready. One shoved me in the back to get going.

"I hope you Fianna are as good as they say," he said. "Because if you aren't this night is going to be a big disappointment, for you most of all."

"Oh don't worry," I replied. "We'll be sure not to disappoint."

We were marched down a hall to a different room than the throne room we had been taken to upon our arrival. This one must have been the designated dining hall, but it was formed quite in the same fashion as the throne room, with the vaulted ceiling, and the stone pillars.

The floor here was not as polished and there was a circle marked in the area in front of the large dining table. I looked up as we were shoved forward to the long table, formed in the style of the old mead halls, with the king's table at the head and two others branching off for the lesser nobles. Around these, sat Lorcan's higher-ups, some with eerily beautiful, sharp-faced Goblin women beside them as well as children. That caught me a bit by surprise. One would not normally expect the dining hall of the notorious Goblin King to hold something so simple as families in it. Perhaps Lorcan did genuinely care for the welfare of his people, even if he didn't go about it in the right manner.

At the high table Lorcan sat, lounging in his chair. He was dressed in a high-collared velvet coat in black and wore a dark purple silk shirt underneath, looking rather dashing in his villainy like some classy baddie from a cliché adventure movie. Beside him to his right, sat Eamon, in the place of honor, who seemed to be dressed in some borrowed clothing—a white shirt and gold waistcoat under a black dress coat. I wondered vaguely if it was Lorcan's. I was glad to see he was not chained in any way, but then, where would he go? Lorcan knew he wasn't about to run away with his men and brother still prisoner, so he really had nothing to worry about. It made me sad to think that Lorcan did not think Eamon capable of formulating an escape, even if it was true, but then, if I was in his position, I would not be able to lift so much as a finger either. At least Lorcan had the common courtesy to treat Eamon as his station necessitated, even if I had the feeling there was some ulterior motive to his actions.

"Ah, *Airdrígh*, your two warriors have come to pay their respects," Lorcan said, setting his golden goblet down on the table and leaning forward to inspect us. I met Eamon's eyes, but said nothing.

"They shall offer a bit of entertainment for us," Lorcan said loudly enough that the entire room heard and there were several cheers. "I have long wanted to actually see the true prowess of Na Fianna—I've only had the pleasure of glimpsing them on the battlefield. I had my other prisoners entertain before, but they have grown wearisome and have lost most of their strength." My blood boiled at this and I had to clench my fists so as not to vocalize my feelings. "Hardly fit opponents for my finest men anymore. I am interested to see how you young warriors perform. What would you be willing to say, Eamon? Are they good? Worthy of my halls?"

"The very best," Eamon said proudly.

"My warriors are very fine as well," Lorcan said with a tolerant smile in Eamon's direction. "Their performance tonight will put any contest to rest." He stood and motioned with a hand to the side of the room. "May I present my own champions? Cronin and Fallogh!"

Two Goblins stepped up to the high table and bowed. One was the lieutenant we had been so fortunate as to meet earlier and the other was another one of the guards I recognized. Both had their hair tightly clubbed and were wearing only thin trousers so that I could clearly see the swirling tattoo patterns on their shoulders, and lower back right above the hips.

Our guards unchained our hands and Lorcan smiled at us, nodding.

"Well, are you going to salute your king and your host?"

We bowed slightly and Lorcan nodded.

"Very good; Fallogh, you're up first. I think you'll be a

fine match for the redheaded one."

The Goblin bowed again. "It will be a pleasure, *mo rí.*"

Keevan looked over to me and for the first time I saw confidence in his eyes.

"I got this, Ciran," he said with a wink and followed the Goblin over to the ring. I was led to one side of it to stand with Cronin, the two guards behind me. Another Goblin stood in the middle of the ring, holding up a dagger.

"The rules are simple," he said. "Anything goes; the object is to be the first one to draw blood—with the dagger." He held up the blade then leapt up onto one of the pillars and shinnied up it to deposit the dagger in a slot some twelve feet off the ground. "However, you have to get it first."

Keevan smiled and pulled off his undershirt, doing several stretches in anticipation. "Sounds fun."

Fallogh smiled. "We'll see how fun you find it when I'm smashing your pretty red head into the ground, half-blood."

"I'm glad Goblin blood is black," Keevan returned, years of verbally sparing with Riordan making him immune to threats or insults of any kind. "Goes classy with my hair."

Fallogh snorted and flexed his blade thin frame, rolling his neck. "I'm rather partial to red, myself."

The referee stepped out of the way, his hand in the air. "Ready?" At a nod of confirmation from the two fighters, he swung his hand down. "Fight!"

Fallogh wasted no time in launching himself at Keevan, but the redhead simply leaned back, one hand on the floor before he swung a leg up and delivered a kick to the Goblin's jaw. He leapt to his feet and threw another punch to the Goblin's face which the Goblin caught right before Keevan swung around and leapt up behind Fallogh and wrapped his legs around his waist, using the arm the Goblin still held to choke him. Fallogh was surprised by the sudden move, and was momentarily thrown off balance, but dropped to a crouch, and with a swift maneuver, extricated himself from Keevan's grip, tumbling the Fianna over his head and coming up in a low crouch.

Keevan sprung himself back onto his feet, and delivered a roundhouse kick to Fallogh's chest. Again, the Goblin caught the blow, but as before, Keevan was ready, and seemed to expect it. He used Fallogh's hands as a stirrup, and leapt up over his shoulder, rebounding off of a pillar and slamming into the Goblin's back, bringing him down hard. Fallogh didn't have time to get up before Keevan was straddling his back, putting him into a chokehold.

"Not bad for a half blood, eh?" he asked with a smirk.

Fallogh growled and gripped Keevan's wrist in a bone crushing hold. I realized with sympathy that it was the one he had hurt before, and winced as I heard Keevan cry out as he was forced to let go.

Fallogh threw him from his back and Keevan landed hard, the breath whooshing out of him. Fallogh stood over him with a grin before he turned and went after the dagger.

Keevan leapt up, still puffing, and tore after him, tackling him around the waist and bringing them both down. Fallogh flipped over and brought a foot between them, shoving it into Keevan's stomach and flinging him backward. Keevan hand-sprung backwards with the momentum and landed on his feet, before he swung at Fallogh with a wide throw while he went in with a sharp jab to the ribs with his other hand. The hit connected and Fallogh was momentarily winded, doubled over. Keevan took the advantage and delivered several more short jabs, and one vicious kick to the inside of the Goblin's right knee that sent him down with a yelp. Keevan then kicked him onto his back and raced for the pillar that held the dagger. He took a flying leap and swung his legs around it, using his bare feet for grip as he leapt up and caught the dagger before summersaulting backward and landing in a crouch at the base of the pillar.

Fallogh was hauling himself to his feet, limping slightly as he advanced on Keevan who was straightening up slowly, the knife in his hand, ready.

"Make your move," Keevan said, egging him on.

Fallogh waited, probably trying to force him to put down his guard but that was the first thing we were taught in training, and the practice Keevan had got in the field in the last few weeks had instilled the importance of that into him, so he was not about to take the bait. He only smiled and shrugged.

"Fine, if you won't do it," he said and lunged forward, not at Fallogh, but under his spread legs. The Goblin saw what he was doing not a split second too soon, and leapt out of the way before Keevan could slice him. Keevan rolled easily onto his feet again and this time Fallogh didn't bother hesitating, just went after him. Keevan kept the knife in a backhand grip, using the hilt as an added force to his injured wrist. Fallogh swung low and as Keevan went to catch the blow, the Goblin gripped his wrist at the same moment as he hooked a leg behind his knee and threw him onto the floor. Keevan fell hard, and he lost his grip on the dagger as he went down. He tried to roll over to grab it, but Fallogh grabbed his shoulder and slammed a fist into the side of his head. Keevan shook off the blow, trying to get the Goblin to release him, but another blow landed and I could see blood on his cheek.

Keevan kicked Fallogh back and flung himself toward the knife, but the Goblin dug his claws into Keevan's shoulders and drew him back, leaping over him and catching up the knife. Keevan was on his feet by then, wiping blood from under his nose as the Goblin smiled at him, holding the blade up tantalizingly.

"Not so good after all, are you, half-blood."

And just like that, he lunged, but the dagger never touched Keevan because he grabbed the Goblin's wrist and wrenched his arm behind him, forcing the dagger to slice through the skin of his back before he even knew what was happening.

Fallogh yelped at the sudden pain and clapped a hand behind him as Keevan stepped back, disbelief written on the Goblin's face as he tried to make sense of what had happened.

"Match over!" cried the Goblin acting as referee. There were cheers and laughs coming from the dinner guests and I glanced over to see a proud look from Eamon and a mildly amused one from Lorcan.

The referee took the dagger from Fallogh, and replaced it in the pillar. "Congratulations, Finar, you won that round. Let's see if your friend is as good as you."

I nodded to Keevan as he came off, nursing his injured wrist, but grinning through the blood on his face.

"That was fun, good luck," he said.

I tugged off my undershirt and nodded to him as I stepped into the circle, facing Cronin.

Cronin was rather broad for a Goblin, I was pretty sure he actually weighed more than I did, but I wouldn't know until I started fighting him. He was certainly not as willowy as Fallogh and most of the others, and I could clearly see the iron hard muscles that flexed beneath his pale skin. Apart from that, I could tell by the scars that covered his body that he was a veteran fighter, and his confidence showed that he was not afraid to take a few hits to win. I would have to be on the top of my game if I wanted to turn out as the victor.

The referee stood between us and held up his hand.

"You know the rules. Ready?"

We nodded in the affirmative.

"Fight!"

Unlike Fallogh, Cronin didn't just fling himself at me, and I hadn't expected him too. We advanced on each other slowly, ready, but testing the other, waiting to see who would make the first move. I kept my hands lose, my right foot forward for balance. I was not going to let him push me into the first move. I was going to wait patiently.

And then he moved so suddenly I almost missed it, and he nearly caught me with a flying kick. I swayed easily to one side and turned as he landed behind me and threw a punch that I caught on my forearm, flinging his arm to one side as I threw a punch of my own. He caught my hit too, and we traded several more blows, easily giving and deflecting as if our fight had been practiced. Neither of us was going all out yet, we were just trying to feel the other out.

He finally gripped my arm and made to throw me over his shoulder, but I leaned into the movement and landed in a crouch, sweeping a leg out that he just barely managed to leap over before I took him out. I rose slowly and caught the roundhouse he gave me and tried to tip him off balance by throwing his leg upward, but he just handsprung backwards and ran at me again instantly.

I ducked under one punch, then kicked. He caught my foot and I leapt forward, grabbing his shoulders, and wrapped my leg around the back of his knee before I jerked his foot from under him. He allowed himself to fall and I realized too late that he had maneuvered himself so that he could trap me when we fell, letting go of my foot and grabbing me in a chokehold, wrapping his legs around my waist so I couldn't move.

"Got you now," he growled in my ear.

I couldn't fight out of it, so I did the only thing I could and slammed my head back into his face. His grip loosened momentarily and I slid out of his hold and kicked him back, not wanting to waste any more time to leap for the dagger.

I was almost to the pillar before I heard him on my heels. I leapt onto the pillar, my hands and feet finding purchase, but he took a flying leap onto the other side and started to shinny upward. I grabbed at his foot, hauling him down as I slid upward, but them he kicked out at me, catching me in the ribs, and I lost my grip, falling backward and landing hard on the floor.

I groaned, seeing stars, and gasped for breath. I tried to take stock and see if anything was broken, but everything hurt so badly, I wasn't able to tell. A thud came to my left and I forced my eyes open to see Cronin standing there with the dagger in his hand, a satisfied smile on his face.

"Looks like I win."

But I wasn't done yet. I rolled over as quickly as I could, sweeping his legs from under him. He fell but held onto the dagger. I kicked out again and caught the hilt, and finally succeeded in driving it out of his hand. I leapt up and kicked him in the chest and he fell back against the pillar before he used it as leverage and ran a couple steps up it to fling himself at me. I used his momentum to grab him around the waist and toss him to the floor, winding him this time. He recovered way faster than I had and was already on his feet as I was just thinking of reaching for the dagger.

He swung a blow at my head and then gave me an uppercut to the ribs, driving me back against the pillar and winding me. I kicked at his chest and when he caught my foot, I put my hands against the pillar and shoved him backwards, putting him off balance as I brought my other foot up and kicked him hard in the chest. He fell backwards and I landed with my feet on either side of him, and leapt over him for the dagger. He was on me as soon as I picked it up, grabbing me from behind and swinging around as I tried to swipe at him, throwing me backward. I slammed into the pillar, winding myself again, and then he ran at me with a growl, reaching for the dagger, but I turned and leapt up onto the pillar and swung around it. He reached up to grab my leg, but I brought my feet up, putting the knife between my teeth and gripping the pillar in kind of a frog crouch. I felt like a treed bear, but I still had the knife, and I only had one shot to use it.

"Come down from there," Cronin snarled. "Are you afraid to fight me?"

I swung one leg around the pillar and then suddenly swung my entire body around, slamming both my feet into Cronin as I let go. He fell backward and then leapt at me as I stood there, but I simply bent out of his way and slashed him across the side as he passed.

He crouched, a hand to his side as the referee came into the ring again to stop the fight.

"The Finar wins again," he said, sounding a little put off by that fact. I grinned, breathing heavier than normal, and put a hand to my sore ribs. Lorcan was standing up at the table, and clapping slowly. All the other Goblins quieted.

"Very good, it seems you aren't completely hopeless boys after all. I apologize for insulting your men, Eamon. They are adequate warriors."

Eamon didn't say anything but he nodded slightly to us.

"As a reward, you'll get supper," Lorcan told us and snapped his fingers at a guard to come to the table. "Fix them a plate—real food, not scraps for our night's champions—and then put them back in their cells."

"Since we won, we should get a real room," Keevan said, licking blood from his split lip. Lorcan smiled thinly.

"Perhaps that can be negotiated next time. For now, good night, gentleman."

We were led back to the cell where we quickly tended each other's bruises—thankfully neither of us suffered anything too damaging, though I knew we would be sore the next morning—and then enjoyed a very nice supper.

We were both full by the time we lay down back to back on the meager mattress in one corner of the cell, trying to share what little body heat we had.

"I don't like this Lorcan much," Keevan was saying. "I don't trust him. There's just something about him—I can never tell whether he's saying what he means or is trying to hide something."

"I feel the same way about him," I admitted. "I'm worried, and I know Eamon must be too. I don't know what he has planned but we need to be ready for anything. And ready for any opportunity that arises that can lead to our escape. It's our duty to get Eamon out of here."

"I wonder what the others are planning," Keevan mused with a sigh. "I really miss my idiot brother, you know. I'd even let him go full granny on me without complaining."

I smiled. "Yeah, I know. We'll see them all again soon."

He mumbled something and then I realized he had fallen asleep. I sighed and tried to get comfortable, closing my eyes. But I lay awake a long time; all I could think about was what Lorcan might be planning and how it would affect us all.

Chapter Twenty-Two
Words

I had managed to fall into a light sleep finally when the door was hauled open and I felt Keevan jerk against my back. I sat up, rubbing my eyes blearily. "What do you want?" I asked.

"King Lorcan wished you to attend him," said the guard, reaching out and hauling me up before he chained my hands in front of me. Keevan made to get up too, but the guard shoved him back with a boot in the chest. "You stay."

I was led out of the prisons into the throne room, and in the hall outside, I could hear voices, one quite recognizable as Eamon's.

"I just want to know what you wish to accomplish, Lorcan," the high king was saying. "I promise that a treaty with me will give you everything you want, with more freedom. If you take it by force, you will only start another war, and we would both lose many good people because of it. I know that's not what you want."

We came into the room then and I was able to see

Lorcan and Eamon from where we stopped just inside the door. They were the only ones in the room besides Cronin who now sported several dark bruises, I saw with satisfaction. Lorcan lounged on his throne while Eamon stood at the base of the stairs leading up to the dais. The Goblin stood up slowly, walking down to meet Eamon.

"Do you think I'm really going to settle for some peace treaty, Eamon?" He shook his head with a humorless chuckle. "No. We already tried that, but your people can't keep a peace treaty."

"We can't?" Eamon asked indignantly. "Need I remind you that your people were the ones who attacked my patrol and broke the last one!"

"And you sent the patrol out in the first place, thus obviously showing the fact that you do not trust us."

"We always send out patrols," Eamon protested. "As do you. We don't go seeking one specific threat but any that could be there, human or Fae. But that day you were on our land, and we had every right to go and see if you actually meant us harm or not."

"Ah, and there is the thing," Lorcan said, stopping him. "That's the heart of it, Eamon. *Your* land, *our* land — what is that really? Ireland used to belong exclusively to the Fae — to *my* kind, not yours. Men came and pushed us all away up to the Faelands, saying we had no right to be on the lands that we had lived in for centuries."

"The Faery Courts pushed you out long before we did."

"True," Lorcan said. "But that only strengthens my resolve. You see, Eamon, it is time again for us to rise. We have always been the lesser of the Fair Royalty, hardly having what one can call a proper court at all; and it is our turn to go back to the grandeur we once had. We used to live in the south, did you know? Before we were driven to the north and forced to share the space that belonged to the Faery Courts. They did not like that one bit, which is why they drove us up here to the last reaches of the land. They can have their north back, but we want our own kingdom, and it's going to be yours."

"You cannot do this again," Eamon said, his voice very near pleading. "We have already lost so many. You have too; we cannot do this again to the families of those we rule. Surely, Lorcan, you must see that."

"My Goblins will gladly die for the cause," Lorcan said firmly. "As I know your men and Fianna will. But you're right; I don't want that if I can in any way avoid it. That is why I am willing to offer you a deal."

"And what kind of deal might that be?" Eamon asked tiredly.

Lorcan smiled and leaned over to speak into Eamon's ear. "Half your kingdom for your brother and the other prisoners, and no one has to die," he said quietly, but I heard him well enough.

"You know I can't do that," Eamon replied.

"Oh, but you can, Eamon, don't you see?" Lorcan said as if explaining something to a child. "You *have* to. Otherwise, there will be another war, and I will kill your brother and the others. Can you let that happen for your own pride?" He put an arm around Eamon's shoulders and the High King flinched away. "You see, I care too, Eamon, I really do. I don't want to see your people killed; I do not want to have their blood on my hands. Death does not interest me. If I killed everyone, who would I have left to rule over, after all? No, I really just want my people to have the same as everyone else. The Seelie and Unseelie have the forest courts, you have Tara Hall and the minor kings their kingdoms, but what do we have? Underground palaces that are fair enough, but what kind of life is that? In seclusion away from the world and scorned as lesser beings, used only as an idea to frighten children to bed with."

"I understand, Lorcan, I do," Eamon said empathetically. "I respect that you only want what's best for your people. But because of that you must also understand why I cannot do this."

"You don't have to decide right away, but I want you to think on it." He finally glanced over in our direction and motioned to Cronin. "We're done for now; see the *Airdrígh* back to his room."

Cronin left, shoving Eamon ahead of him and Lorcan beckoned for my guard to bring me over.

"Ciran Mac Cool," he greeted, smiling slightly as he strode over to me. "I wanted to congratulate you on your victory last night. It is not many who can boast that they have beaten my lieutenant in a fight. He's not very happy with you, I'm afraid."

"Is that all you wished to tell me?" I asked with a hint of malice, angry at how he had put Eamon in an impossible position. "Do I get any more winner's spoils for it?"

He smiled and there was amusement behind his pale eyes. "You do not like me much, do you, Mac Cool?"

"It's not necessarily customary for a captive to like his captor," I said.

"Perhaps that's not the only reason." Something flashed in Lorcan's hand and I realized suddenly it was a small, thin dagger, the kind usually used for skinning or filleting after a hunt. A shiver ran unbidden up my spine. "Why don't you just ask—I know you want to."

"Ask what?" I replied, though I knew well enough.

There was no way I was going to take his bait. It would only make him too happy.

Lorcan smiled and spun the knife again, this time catching it firmly in his palm and holding it up for me to see. "Come now, Ciran, you can't tell me you don't want to know about brother dearest."

My eyes flew up to meet his before I could stop them and he chuckled low in his throat, mocking. "I thought that would get your attention. He's brave, your brother. I've humored his bravery thus far, but it does get so tiring after endless sessions asking the same questions and getting no answers. Rest assured, I give him a few weeks to recover in between, let him think, but it's the same game each time. Refusals to cooperate, so sure he will not break. I wonder, Ciran, if you would be as brave." He stepped closer, the knife hovering in front of me. I stood my ground, not wanting to let him see my fear. He suddenly lurched forward, grabbing the back of my neck and thrusting the wicked point of the dagger up under my chin. I kept my eyes locked defiantly on his.

"You don't flinch," he said in approval. "I admire that, but what is bravery, after all? The rash acts of the foolish, for the most part. It almost always ends in death. Eventually, I will let your brother die too. I might even allow him a fine death for his courage, but that's how it *will* end eventually. However, now that I have you, I might finally be able to get him to talk. You see, the one thing our peoples have in common is familial loyalty. He might not speak when he thinks he's martyring himself for the sake of his comrades, but now that I have his brother for leverage? Well, that might finally loosen his tongue."

I wanted to say something, but I knew nothing I said would make any difference and it would only show how scared and angry I was so I kept my mouth shut. Lorcan smiled, seeming to approve of that, and finally let me go. A drop of blood slid down my throat from where his dagger had pricked me.

I don't know what would have happened next, but I never got the chance to find out for at that moment, there was the sound of running feet and Cronin came back into the room. Lorcan stepped away from me and turned to him as my guard came forward and put a firm hand around my arm.

"Yes, Cronin?" Lorcan asked his lieutenant.

"My lord, the scouts have intercepted a...visitor, it seems," the Goblin said, casting a swift glare at me before he turned back to his king.

"What kind of a visitor?" Lorcan asked.

"She said she came under truce, my lord," Cronin answered.

She? I had a funny feeling in my stomach. The only female I knew of in the near vicinity was Caitlin. What, by all the Fae, could they possibly be doing...?

"Show her in then," Lorcan said.

A few seconds later, a strange troop entered the hall, at the head was indeed Caitlin walking between two guards, but not detained, I was glad to see. Behind her, however, marched Riordan who was bound, gagged, and had several Goblins keeping an eye on him, swords at the ready. I caught Cait's eye just a second before she turned to Lorcan and gave her my *what are you thinking?* look, which she returned with another that said, *trust me.* I realized I had little choice but to do so.

"Well, you said you come under truce?" Lorcan asked her, impatient. "Who are you and what are you doing here?"

"Your majesty," Caitlin said, bowing to one knee before she stood again. "My name is Caitlin O'Hara. I came to offer you my services, and, as you can see, I brought you a gift of good grace. A Fianna warrior who is also a berserker." She motioned grandly to Riordan who glowered at her and yanked at his chains.

Lorcan smiled in a mocking sort of way. "Do you really think I'm going to fall for this half-baked escape attempt? Please, dear, show me a little more respect than that. I wouldn't even think your Eamon would fall for something so mundane."

"Exactly," Caitlin said. "So why would I use this as an escape attempt if I knew it would fail? The truth is, my lord, I came to help you because I'm sick and tired of being treated like a piece of meat. I thought perhaps you might aid me in return if I offered you my services."

"You realize I don't just let anyone in here, especially not someone who has recently been working with Na Fianna," Lorcan told her firmly, unimpressed.

"Na Fianna," Caitlin said with a sneer and a short laugh. "Those bloody womanizing idiots! I came on this journey to rescue my brother but all they think I'm good for is cooking and bandaging, among other humiliating things. If I hear 'give us a kiss, lass,' one more time I swear I'll kick someone's teeth in, among other things." I was shocked and impressed at her performance. I found myself feeling very glad her accusations weren't true.

Lorcan smiled slightly at that and she pretended offence. "You don't understand what I've been through. Nor could you. I thought I'd get back at the bloody eejits and trade this one for my brother who is the only reason I even stuck with them this long."

"You want to trade this man for your brother?"

Lorcan asked. "Is that why you came?"

"I came to do what I can," she replied. "I just want my brother back, but if you need me to prove to you that this isn't a trap I will do whatever needs to be done. I can tell you how to get into the prison at Tara. There are many of your own people there. Two cousins of yours as well, I believe. Jarlath and Gorlan? We caught them a while back. That one there," here she pointed at me, "he tortured Gorlan in front of his brother until he screamed and pleaded for him to stop, but still they wouldn't say anything. They would not give you up, your majesty. I'm sure your other kin in our prisons are the same."

I was surprised to see the look on Lorcan's face as Caitlin mentioned the two Goblin brothers. There was anger, maybe a little bit of surprise, as well as...worry? It was possible, I supposed. Perhaps Lorcan did really care about his people, even enough to show emotion at the thought of certain family members being tortured. Of course, it could also be because he was afraid Caitlin was lying about them not telling anything. He turned to me with an appraising look on his face and something else I couldn't read. I did my best to put on a serious expression to make it look like I really was capable of the feat, but I didn't know whether he bought it. It was hard to tell with the Goblin King.

"I will have to think it over, you understand," Lorcan told Caitlin. "You realize I cannot just give you your brother and let you walk out of here. That would be a rather senseless thing to do."

"Of course not, your majesty," she replied. "I wouldn't have expected you to. But I wish to prove that I only came here for him. Nothing else. I just want to go back home."

"And this man," Lorcan added, motioning to Riordan.

"Why should I want him?"

"He is a berserker, as I said, my lord. A danger to you and all your men. If you don't believe me, you can see plain enough the amulet of Thor he wears."

"And why does he come so quietly?" Lorcan asked with a smile, thinking he caught her. I caught my breath, hoping Caitlin would not falter now.

Instead of pausing to think like I probably would have done, a slow smile spread over her face even as Riordan turned to glare at her with so much hatred, I was very nearly convinced myself of the entire charade. "Let's just say I learned a thing or two while I had to treat their wounds. A little bit of certain herbs put into their tea can work wonders. Despite popular belief, there are ways to stop a berserker—as long as you get to him before he goes mad. I'd be happy to show you the concoction."

Lorcan smiled again, but this time there was genuine pleasure in it. "Careful, Miss O'Hara, I might actually end up liking you."

Caitlin smiled and bowed her head slightly. "So, my lord, will you at least consider my offer? I would have hated to come all this way just to be a pretty thing for the Fianna to look at."

"I will definitely consider giving you your brother if you indeed prove helpful to me," Lorcan said. "But you are right, I will need more than a few words from you to earn my loyalty. I will think on it, and let you know."

Caitlin bowed again. "Whenever you are ready, my lord."

"Good," Lorcan said, pleased. "I look forward to getting to know you better. I would be honored if you would be a guest at my table tonight. I have a most enthralling form of entertainment for the evening that I don't think you will want to miss."

"It would be my pleasure, my lord," she said, bowing again, and Lorcan motioned to one of the guards.

"Give her a room and have your wife find her something suitable to wear to supper this evening. The rest of you, put the berserker away, and make sure he is secure." He turned back to me. "We will continue our chat at a later date, Ciran. For now, rest up. You're going to have to work harder to impress tonight now that there is a lady present." He smiled and I was shoved back out of the room.

When I was back in the cell with Keevan he turned to me expectantly and I waited for the Goblin to lock the door behind him before I started talking.

"Don't get angry, Keevan, but I'm afraid Caitlin has just offered your brother to Lorcan for ransom."

Chapter Twenty-Three
Hidden Agendas

That night Keevan and I were once again fetched from our cell, a little sore from the night before, but thankfully none the worse for wear. I couldn't say the same thing for our opponents who sported bruises and, in Fallogh's case, a limp. I gave them a small smile and Keevan followed suit, blowing a kiss at them. He laughed as they scowled back.

I ignored them after that for Caitlin had just entered the room with Eamon and another Goblin guard behind them. Letting them walk free, but making sure they knew they were still under the watchful eye of Lorcan's people so that they wouldn't be tempted to try anything. She was wearing some sort of gothic-looking dark purple dress with a slim skirt that flared at the feet. She had piled her hair up onto her head and the only thing she was missing was black eyeliner. I decided I didn't like the look on her. She was not my Caitlin—the girl who wore green sweater dresses and practical boots. She looked like she was going to kill herself in the four-inch heels she was wearing. The Goblins had very strange styles, but I noticed she was dressed no differently than the other Goblin women sitting at the tables. She took her place on Lorcan's left while Eamon took up his seat from the previous night. I saw Caitlin looking over at us and she gave us a small smile. Lorcan leaned over to speak in her ear, all suave and smirking and I wanted her to slap the smile off his face. What a flirt! He was even worse than Deaglan. Caitlin smiled back at him, and then cast another glance at us, winking. I couldn't help but return a small smile.

Finally, the food was served and once the eating was underway, Lorcan stood up and everyone quieted down.

"My people," he said, "honored guests," he smiled at Caitlin, "may I present to you the champions of the ring?"

He waved a hand over to Keevan and me and the crowd applauded, much to the chagrin of Cronin and Fallogh who did not look pleased at all at their comrades' reaction. Keevan and I nodded slightly, grinning.

"It seems the Fianna have proven themselves far worthier than I gave them credit for," Lorcan said. "So tonight I am going to give them a chance to prove themselves even further. Cronin?"

The Goblin finally smiled and called into one of the anterooms off the hall, and six Goblins came out, stripped to the waist with wrapped hands, looking ready for a fight.

"Na Fianna are supposed to be unmatchable in battle," Lorcan continued, motioning to his men who cracked their knuckles, standing in the circle in anticipation. "Let's see how they do fighting a group of my finest warriors."

We shared a look and I sighed heavily, stripped out of my shirt and accepted the wraps our guard handed us.

"Looks like we're just going to have to bust a few heads, Keev," I said under my breath. "Are you ready?"

"I have two brothers and they don't train kindly," Keevan said surely, expertly wrapping up his own hands.

"Good," I said. "Because I think we're going to have to give all we have tonight."

He grinned, testing his wraps by punching his fist into the opposite hand. "I'm hungry enough to do it."

Our guard came up then with a chain linked with two manacles. I frowned and didn't get a chance to register what was going on, before my right hand had been attached to Keevan's left. The guard gave the five-foot chain between us a good yank and smirked.

"Just wanted to make things more interesting," he said before he left.

I looked to Keevan as the Goblins began to take up their places around us. I leaned in close and mumbled in his ear, "Are we finished?"

"Not by a long sight," he replied with a crooked grin.

"I hoped you'd say that," I replied and fell into a crouch. "Ready?"

"Born ready," he said and we braced ourselves for the first onslaught of Goblins.

The first Goblin to come at us just seemed to rush in with no apparent form or plan. He growled and I took a leap and kicked him in the chest, sending him skidding backwards on the marble floor at the same time Keevan took out another with a right hook. I was suddenly jerked nearly off my feet as Keevan turned to face another goblin, and had to readjust. This chain was not going to make matters easy.

"Keevan we've got to work together on this," I growled as he jerked me again and I in turn pulled him back a step to take down the first Goblin who was up on his feet again.

"I'm trying!" he growled back at me.

"Well, try harder!"

I was desperate to stop the next Goblin who came at me and yanked the chain up over his head and jerked it down behind his knees. Once Keevan saw what I was doing, he gave the chain a good yank from his end as well. The Goblin fell with a startled shout before the air was pushed from his lungs.

Keevan turned around and grinned suddenly. "Oh yeah, that's what I'm talking about."

"Got it now?" I asked with a smirk.

He nodded and we faced the other Goblins together this time, standing shoulder to shoulder and holding the chain between us. I punched one Goblin in the ribs and then Keevan leapt up and over his shoulder, pulling the chain taut so that we clotheslined him between us. He went down and didn't come back up. His comrades hauled him out of the circle and came at us with even more ferocity.

Keevan kicked one, then spun around and we stood back to back, locking arms so that when I spun him around for a second time, he was able to deliver an even harder kick to our opponent, sending the Goblin slamming back into one of the pillars. I set Keevan down and he went into a crouch and I slid low to one side, catching another Goblin in the legs. He fell to his knees where I kicked him in the jaw, knocking him unconscious.

Keevan and I grinned as he too was dragged from the ring and we knocked our wrapped fists together. I spun just in time to see another Goblin coming up behind us. I ducked one blow to my head, but missed the one to my stomach and doubled over where a knee connected with my face and I sat down hard, blood dripping from my nose. The Goblin grabbed the chain that was now slack and gave it a twist, bringing Keevan down next to me and wrapping it around his throat. Keevan grasped at the chain that was choking him and I couldn't get up or it would only make it worse, and I only had one good hand because my other was wrenched behind my back, practically strangling my comrade. The other two Goblins came up with evil grins on their faces as they saw how helpless I was. I growled as Keevan gasped behind me and beckoned them forward.

One kicked at me and I caught his foot, giving it a vicious twist and sending him backward with a howl. I hope I had torn his Achilles. The second one used a different approach, seeing how well it went with his comrade, and leveled a fist at me instead, but I deflected it and kicked him in the shin. He grunted and pulled back but I was getting more and more desperate as I felt Keevan slumping more heavily against my back, gagging, and the next time the Goblin came around, I grabbed his fist and kicked the inside of his knee, making a sickening pop as he collapsed with a yelp.

I then turned around and grabbed Keevan under the arms and drug him back and rolled him over me at the same moment I kicked out at the Goblin who held the chain, reaching up to grab his arm and then slamming my foot into his wrist with a crack. He howled and I stumbled back with Keevan supported in my arms. He was gasping for breath as I pulled the chain from around his neck, pulling him close and let him rest against my shoulder. I hoped he would recover in time and not prove to be a dead weight to me while I had to fight the rest.

More Goblins came to collect their fallen comrades and I saw with relief that we had somehow managed to defeat them all. I looked down at Keevan finally and saw some color returning to his face.

"You all right?" I asked him.

He nodded, still gasping and massaging his neck. "Yeah, I think so," he croaked.

I helped him to stand up and we turned back to the audience. Lorcan seemed rather quiet, watching us intently with something that might have been regret on his face. Eamon and Caitlin were watching with pent up breath and seemed relieved when we both stood up on our own feet. Finally the Goblin King smiled slightly and applauded.

"Very good. You continue to show your prowess. But maybe something a little different is in order. Something a little more akin to the battlefield." He motioned to Cronin who stepped forward and held out two long knives.

"Don't try anything," he growled at us as we took the weapons warily.

Two more Goblins came up to the mark, one with jet-black hair and the other with light blond like Lorcan's. They too held knives and I leaned closer to Keevan.

"You up for this?" I asked quietly.

"I'll do what I have to," he said. "But I'm afraid I'm much better at brawling than I am at knife fighting. Bet you wish you had Deaglan now."

"We're just going to have to make do."

The Goblins were advancing on us and we had no more time to discuss tactics. We both fell into a crouch and waited for them to attack.

They lunged forward at the same time, trying out several practice swipes before they switched places and attacked the other of us. I just got the knife up in time to block a blow, and I kicked out at the Goblin as I ducked another swipe. I was not practiced in knife fighting, but I knew the basics—enough to know I was making a hash of it already. Knife fighting wasn't about block and attack like sword fighting was. It was all about dodging until you could find an opening and then take it. Keevan was doing little better, I realized, as I cast a swift glance at him before I had to duck again and then give a quick hop backward to avoid a slash to my stomach. Keevan ducked and then swiped at his opponent but the Goblin kicked him down and he brought me with him. We scrambled up and both retreated until our backs hit a pillar. The two Goblins came after us and we ducked in opposite directions at the same time and ending up being yanked back by the other, nearly knocking our heads together. All the Goblins laughed and I growled as we picked ourselves up, before I had an idea.

"Keevan, grab my hand," I told him, reaching out.

"Oh, that's really manly, do you want to skip and play Ring-Around-the-Rosie too?" Keevan replied sarcastically, but I ignored him and gripped his hand that had the manacle around it.

"Trust me, this will be easier," I assured him. "Now, listen, don't fight me, but move with me, just like the back to back drills they teach in training."

He nodded and that was all the time we got before the Goblins came at us again. This time we both moved together and now that we were connected, I could feel Keevan tense before a move and vise versa so we always knew what the other was doing, and since we no longer had to worry about the chain flapping between us, we were able to move more swiftly.

I dodged another thrust, just barely, and earned a small graze on my ribs because of it. I then swiped at my opponent and nicked his ear just before he ducked all the way out of my reach. He came back with a vengeance and swiped hard, causing me to lean back, balancing on the balls of my feet.

"Change it up," I hissed to Keevan and he nodded. In another second we spun around and delivered hearty kicks to the other's opponent. It knocked them back several paces.

"Duck," Keevan commanded and I fell into a crouch as he let go of my hand and leapt over my shoulders to kick the Goblin and swipe him across the chest at the same time. A thin black line appeared where Keevan's knife had traced a path into his skin, but that was all the time I got to look as I felt the other Goblin coming up behind me and I stood up, blocking his downward strike with my forearm against his and then thrusting my own dagger forward. But before I could make contact, he slammed his head into mine and I staggered back, my already abused nose bleeding afresh. Blinded momentarily and seeing stars, I only felt a burning cut across my shoulder and upper arm as I fell back, but then suddenly I felt Keevan's hand in mine again, and I was spun around as I heard a loud grunt and the clatter of a knife on the floor. I looked around and saw that Keevan had kicked the Goblin right in the chest and he had lost his dagger on the way down. Keevan finished him off with a kick to the jaw and I spun around to see the other Goblin coming at me and I ducked and slashed him across the thigh, which was the only place I could reach with Keevan still holding onto me. The Goblin snarled but thrust his dagger forward, not at me, but past my shoulder toward Keevan. I grabbed the Goblin's wrist just as the blade entered Keevan's shoulder, causing my comrade to yelp in pain. I thrust the Goblin backwards and kicked him in his wounded leg, then walked over to step on his wrist that held the dagger.

"Are you finished now?" I asked him, grinding my foot threateningly against his wrist, bones shifting.

He winced and finally released his grip on the dagger. "Yes, I yield!"

I took my foot away and turned back to Keevan as he nursed his shoulder. He grinned at me and I punched him lightly in the arm, wiping blood from under my nose.

"And that's how it's done," I told him.

He laughed and punched me back.

Lorcan was standing up and motioning to Cronin who came and disarmed us, but also unlocked the chain from around our wrists. I started to unwrap my hands, wincing as I flexed my bruised knuckles.

"Again, you did well," Lorcan said. "I cannot help but admit it. I must congratulate Eamon on having such experienced warriors to surround him." He turned to Caitlin with a teasing smile. "Are you still unimpressed with these men, Lady Caitlin?"

She snorted, folding her arms across her chest. "Oh, I never said they couldn't fight, I just said they had no manners whatsoever."

He laughed lightly and nodded to Cronin and the other guards again. "Bring them back to their cell, and give them their supper, they have earned that *and* dessert for their performance tonight." The Goblins laughed lightly as their king smiled. "Give them water and rags to clean their wounds as well. I don't want them getting infected. Who would entertain us then?"

For some reason I didn't like all the attention and kindness. No, I had not expected Lorcan to be a barbarian, at least not in the common terminology, he was simply too suave for that, but I couldn't help but feel that we were to serve some other purpose and that was why he was being so extra careful that we met no doom. Apart from the fact we had been locked up and made to fight, we had been fed well—better than we had while Tierney and I were in training school, in fact—and our cell was not the traditional filthy, dripping dungeon one would expect. It wasn't entirely comfortable, but you didn't fear getting some nasty disease from it either, even with open wounds. My question was why Lorcan was having us fight? I know it was time honored tradition to hold fight rings and blood sports for entertainment—even the Fianna and the Guard went head to head in bare-knuckle championships on occasion and it was sometimes bloodier than these fights had been, but there was something more to it than that, I was sure of it. If I had learned nothing else about Lorcan, I did know that he did nothing without having a purpose. If he didn't, I doubt our prisoners would still be alive. Of course, we still didn't have proof of life, but I trusted him for some reason that they were. In a way, this not knowing what he was about, and this unnecessary caretaking scared me more than if he had put us on the rack and commanded every bone to be broken in our bodies. Was it maybe that he was trying to see what we were really capable of? Judging how much of a threat we would make on the battlefield? It seemed the most likely conclusion and that thought twisted uneasily in my stomach as we were put back into our cell.

Keevan and I cleaned each other's wounds and then heartily dug into the food we had been given before we lay down on the small mattress, sore and exhausted but at least with filled bellies.

"Do you think Caitlin's plan will work?" Keevan asked with a yawn.

I sighed heavily, my eyes closed and my arms crossed

over my chest to help store up body heat. "I hope so. I'm not seeing a better plan. But she's smart, and she's playing her part well. I think we have a really good chance of getting out of here. And when we do, hopefully Killian will have the Guard waiting for us. After that, we'll take it one step at a time."

"Do you think we'll have to end up fighting?" he asked quietly.

"You're good at that," I reminded him, turning slightly to look over my shoulder at him. "Don't worry."

He shrugged against my back. "Yeah, I guess. I've just never been in an actual battle before."

"Neither have I," I told him. "But you know something, Keevan? After all I've seen you do, there's no one apart from Tierney that I would rather have at my back during a fight. I'm bloody proud of my company, and everything we've accomplished and lived through. And I think that if we can pull off a pitched battle, then we can take on the world."

I couldn't see his face, but I knew he was smiling. "As long as you have faith in us, Ciran, that's good enough for me." And then he relaxed and soon I recognized his heavy breathing, indicating he was asleep. I settled more comfortably against his back and closed my eyes again, somehow managing to fall asleep myself, despite all the worries that clambered through my head, simply too exhausted to do otherwise.

Chapter Twenty-Four
A Friendly Chat

I sat up with a wince as the door to the cell was opened and Cronin came in this time, reaching down and unceremoniously hauling me to my feet.

"Get up," he barked curtly, and I got up, mostly because he was yanking me onto my feet and I didn't have much choice in the matter.

"Where are you taking him?" Keevan asked angrily and I caught the fear in his voice. He tried to follow but Cronin tersely kicked him back down.

"That's none of your business, runt. Now stay down." He hauled me out of the cell but instead of going down the hall to the throne room, we continued further into the dungeon. I had a moment's thought that perhaps he was taking me to see Aeden and the others, but then I realized that might not be such a good thing and began to hope I was wrong.

It turned out I was, I found with still a little disappointment, but that was soon replaced with a gnawing fear as I saw that the room I had been taken to seemed to be some sort of torture chamber; complete with chains, rack and nasty looking implements. And lots of old bloodstains.

I fought the urge to struggle, but instinct kicked in and I was not very cooperative as two other guards unlocked the manacles that were attached to a metal frame and Cronin yanked my shirt off before he forced me up against it. I got in one good kick before he punched me right in the solar plexus and drove all the wind from my lungs, leaving me gasping and hanging from the chains.

"Don't try anything funny, or this will only go worse for you," he said, then left the room. I gasped until I could breathe again and finally studied my dark surroundings as sudden realization came to me. This must have been where Aeden was tortured. A chill crawled over my back and belly at that thought and I wondered if I could indeed be as brave as he was.

I was pulled from my thoughts as I heard footsteps in the hallway outside and soon the door swung open to admit Lorcan himself, a wry smile on his lips.

"Ciran Mac Cool," he said formally. "I want you to know first of all, that I really don't enjoy this."

"Do you not," I replied sarcastically.

Lorcan sighed as he looked over the instruments on the table against the wall and I swallowed hard. "No, I don't. But it is necessary, and I do insist on doing all the...questioning myself. Despite what people like to tell you, torture does work, Ciran, it's proven. It's all about finding someone's breaking point. Most people break on the third day, the fifth if they are particularly strong; some might even go for a week or two." He turned to me, a thin knife like the one he'd held the day before in his hand, and I froze before he set it aside. "However I have been torturing your brother off and on for six months, and he has still refused to break, or utter more than a scream." He came over to me, his hand gripping my chin and I was forced to look into his ice blue eyes. "Will you be able to stand as much, Ciran? Will you be able to last months in torment, or will you break on the third day?"

I didn't answer him. There was no point in pretending bravery, for I wasn't feeling very brave at all and I feared my voice would waver. I honestly didn't know how much I would be able to withstand. I had never been tortured before, after all.

"Everyone has a breaking point, Ciran," Lorcan told me, his eyes still locked on mine. "And I believe you will be your brother's."

"No," I said. "I won't let you use me against him. Do what you want with me, but do not use me against my brother. Do not force him to give up his country for me. I would rather die than subject him to that."

Lorcan stepped away from me, shaking his head with a sigh, rolling his eyes slightly. "I swear, this family is so steeped in loyalty... I respect that, Ciran, I really do, but it's got to stop. You don't seem to see how it will be your downfall." He turned back around to look at the selection of destruction that sat against the wall. "So today, I will test your boundaries, see what you can take, and tomorrow, perhaps we will pay a visit to brother dearest. It might help him along to see you already a little battered. Lend a little to the imagination. Make him angry, not wanting to see his darling little brother in such pain again. The imagining is always the worst part — I'm sure you can attest. He will talk then, surely."

"Lorcan, I won't let you do this," I said firmly, though my voice shook a bit. No, I realized I wasn't afraid of the pain, I was afraid because I knew Aeden would talk for my sake and I couldn't let him do that. We had to get out of there now; I was losing time.

Lorcan turned around and was about to speak again when there was a tap on the door and it was opened by Cronin who looked rather annoyed.

"I'm sorry for interrupting you, my lord, but the lady says she wished to see you, and wouldn't let up about it."

"Actually, Cronin, that will work out fine, let her come." I looked to the door and saw Caitlin stride in, brushing against Cronin as he muttered under his breath and closed the door behind her. She cast a swift glance at me and, keeping in character — I hoped, anyway — she gave a satisfied smile at seeing me chained up.

"Lady Caitlin," Lorcan said in greeting. "Why was it that you wished to see me so urgently?"

"I apologize, King Lorcan, but I just wanted to know whether you had considered what you wished me to do for you. You said last night we would talk today."

"I did," Lorcan said. "Though you could have waited a few minutes for me to finish my business."

"With all respect, I have waited long enough," she said in no uncertain terms.

Lorcan simply smiled at her. "I can understand you are eager. It seems you're in luck, after all. I have just thought of a way for you to start on your path to earning my loyalty."

He turned back over to where I was still chained to the rack, motioning to me as if showing off a personal collection. "I was just about to see if I could get something from your companion, but I think it might be more interesting if you do the dirty work this once. Tell me," he said, taking up a long lash from the table of implements.

"Are you any good with a whip?"

"I think I can manage," she said, and the purely wicked gleam in her eyes actually made me more nervous than the thought of Lorcan holding it. She took the whip and strode right over to me. "I'm actually going to enjoy this." She stopped in front of me, putting a hand to her mouth before sneering. I glared back, helping her role along.

"You would betray us all?" I asked her, low, so that Lorcan could hear, but think he wasn't supposed to. "Just for a few offhand comments?" I winked.

She smiled, laughing derisively. "We'll see how you like it." She reached around my neck to grab me by the hair, yanking my head forward. "Don't clench your teeth," she hissed into my ear, this time so Lorcan couldn't hear at all.

"Don't what?" I started to enquire before I was forced to stop as she roughly pressed her mouth against mine. I understood her command as I felt her slide something hard and metal into my mouth before she pulled away and I quickly hid the object in my cheek. Lorcan was chuckling at the display and I put on an angry and humiliated look, though did not have to force the blushing.

"I do like her," the Goblin said as if to himself. "Begin when you wish, Miss O'Hara."

Caitlin was behind me and I got not a word of warning before she laid into me with the whip. I gasped despite myself, not having to fake one bit. Caitlin didn't play around, that was certain; probably something she had learned from Killian who rarely did things by halves either.

Each blow across my shoulders drove the breath from my lungs and several yelps from my throat. I lost count, but decided she administered about a dozen before Lorcan held up a hand to make her stop. I was glad he did, and wasn't sure whether for Caitlin's sake or my own. Probably mostly the latter. I had a feeling Caitlin wasn't going to be the one carrying scars from this altercation.

Lorcan came behind me to join Caitlin and inspect her damage. I was slumped in my manacles, breathing heavily to get my breath back. I arched my back and cried out as Lorcan prodded my wounds, digging his fingers into one of them just below my shoulder blade.

"Very good. I believe I'm quite on my way to being convinced," Lorcan said, sounding impressed.

"Thank you, my lord," Caitlin said, sounding unnervingly pleased with herself. I began hoping she was in actuality a very good actress and didn't really have some secret vendetta against me.

"I'll speak with you later about one last test you can do to prove yourself to me," Lorcan told her. "And if you perform as well as you did now, I will give you back your brother and let you go on your way."

She bowed slightly. "Again, thank you, my lord."

"Now, I just have to finish up here with Ciran, if you would like to go back to your room or get yourself some tea?" Lorcan said with a smile.

"Actually, I—"

Caitlin didn't get to finish, before the door opened and Cronin reappeared looking even more annoyed than before.

"Again, I'm sorry, my lord, for the interruptions, but your royal guest is asking for an audience and he's not going to take no for an answer."

Lorcan looked like he was going to refuse, but then he smiled slightly and nodded. "Very well, you can take him to my throne room to await me there," the Goblin King said. "I'll be there presently. Take Mac Cool back to his cell first."

Cronin moved over to me and reached a hand into his pocket, then frowned and reached into the other. I cast a quick glance at Caitlin and saw her smile and give a knowing wink. I fought the urge to return it.

"Is there a problem, Lieutenant?" Lorcan asked, turning at the door.

"Can't seem to find the key, my lord," Cronin growled.

Lorcan sighed impatiently. "Never mind then, just leave him. I'll come back when I'm finished with Eamon and continue our discussion." He turned back to me with a small smile. "Use the time to think about what we have discussed, Ciran."

Then they all left me and I saw the opportunity for what it was. I had a feeling Caitlin and Eamon had somehow managed to orchestrate this entire scenario and if I was to play my part, I was going to have to get loose. Now I just had to figure out how to do that.

I examined the frame I was chained to. It was mostly just a metal structure with a bar at the top where the manacles were attached. I took a deep breath and then shook my head.

"Well, I'll just have to go for it," I said to myself.

I was lucky they had not chained my ankles too; otherwise I might not have gotten out of there. I rose slightly, and then took a practice hop before jumping to grab onto the pole at the top. The chains from the manacles clanked, but I grinned, now hanging several inches above the ground. Now came the fun part.

I gripped the bar and pulled myself up like I was going to do a chin up then flipped my legs up and hooked my knees over the bar. The lash marks on my back protested the movement and I winced, but took a deep breath to focus myself. I moved the key from where I had been keeping it in my cheek and carefully maneuvered it into my teeth, praying I would not lose it. Once I got it into position, I reached to my right hand as well as I could, straining against the other manacle. I could just barely reach it with my mouth, but with deep concentration and many tries I finally got the key into the lock. Turning it proved extremely difficult, and I growled out several less than polite things before I finally got it undone and slipped my hand from the manacle. Giving a sigh of relief, I grabbed the key from the lock and quickly undid my other manacle before swinging to the ground. I only stopped long enough to grab my shirt from the floor and tugged it on with a wince over my lash marks before I sprinted out into the hall again to go find Keevan.

There was a guard in the hallway, and he looked up in surprise as he saw me barreling around the corner, but I quickly took him out with a swift right hook and drug him down the hall to where my and Keevan's cell was. I dropped my charge in front of the bars and unceremoniously rifled his pockets for the keys as Keevan scrambled over to press his face against the bars with a grin.

"Ciran! I guess Caitlin's plan worked then."

"I trust she told you?" I asked as I unlocked the door and with Keevan's help gagged the Goblin and shoved him into the cell and locked it. "She didn't get a chance to do more than slip me the key in a rather awkward manner."

Keevan grinned and reached under the pallet, producing our weapons that Caitlin must have somehow liberated from the armory and gotten to him. I took my sword with an instant sigh of relief. "We're to spring

Riordan, and head for the secret pathway. Eamon's going to ask for an audience with Lorcan—I assume he already did that? Caitlin is going to interrupt it, and you are going to go and wait in the wings in case anyone else needs help. Riordan and I will join you as soon as I get him out. When things start to go south, we'll create a distraction, grab Eamon and Caitlin and rush for the outside. Killian is waiting with a battalion of the guard. We're going to either let Lorcan surrender or, if he won't, we'll be ready to fight."

"Sounds good." I offered him the keys. He took them and we clasped forearms briefly.

"See you soon," I said before I rushed off down the hallway.

Chapter Twenty-Five
Escape Plan

I slowed down as I came closer to the throne room, and hung back in the shadows. Eamon was already there, speaking with Lorcan.

"Have you finally considered my offer?" the Goblin King asked. I edged forward a little more so that I could see what was transpiring.

"I have," Eamon replied, standing in front of the dais with Cronin and another Goblin behind him as if waiting to see whether he would try anything. "That's why I wanted to see you."

"I was rather busy, you know," Lorcan replied boredly. "I seem to be getting interrupted a lot today. I hope that doesn't continue. It might surprise you, but I do have things to see to, you know." He waved a hand dismissively. "But since we're both here, you may as well tell me what you wanted to. What is your decision?"

Eamon looked down and his shoulders heaved with a deep sigh. "I have decided that I cannot agree with your terms. I must do what is best for my people, and I feel I cannot betray them by letting who they believe to be the enemy into our own country."

Lorcan laughed, but there was no humor in it. "The enemy. Your people are prejudiced, and nothing else, *Airdrígh*. Have I not been most welcoming? Have I not treated you with respect?"

"You have," Eamon said with a nod. "I have no complaints about my stay, and I greatly regret my decision. I had hoped that we could have come to some understanding. But I am a king, and I must do what I know to be right."

"To condemn countless of your people to death with inevitable war?" Lorcan asked mockingly. "Tell me, Eamon, who is the real enemy then?"

"Does it have to be war, Lorcan?" Eamon asked quietly, looking up to meet the Goblin King's eyes. "We can end this here, you and I, and none of our people have to die. I will do what you wish. We can sign a peace treaty, or I can fight you in single combat, but please, neither of us really wants this to be the bloodbath it was before. There is no reason that has to happen."

Lorcan sighed, getting up from his throne. "Eamon, I honestly do regret this, but you have no understanding of how kingdoms are run. And I think you need to learn." He snapped his fingers and Cronin and the other Goblin grabbed Eamon roughly and forced his arms behind his back, lashing his hands together with thick cords. My heart lurched in my chest, ready for anything. What did Lorcan plan to do? I didn't think he would go so far as to kill Eamon, but the past few days had left me not entirely sure of his complete sanity.

"Lorcan, what are you doing?" Eamon cried. "This is no way to write a peace treaty!"

Lorcan ignored him and motioned to another guard standing on the other side of the hall that I could not see. "Go fetch the young prince, and bring Lady Caitlin as well."

I felt a deep fear settle in my stomach. This was not going to plan, I assumed. What if they found Caitlin in a com-promising position? What if they didn't find her at all? And what was Lorcan planning to do with Oran?

I held my breath, watching Eamon continue to struggle in his captors' grasp until Cronin slammed a fist into his stomach and he doubled over, coughing. I clenched my fists angrily.

"None of that, Cronin, he is still a king after all," Lorcan said blandly as he resumed his place on the throne.

A few seconds later, Caitlin was ushered in by a guard and she bowed slightly before Lorcan. She cast a glance at Eamon, but I couldn't see her expression.

"You wanted to see me again, my lord?" she asked.

He smiled at her. "Ah, yes, Caitlin, dear, I did. I have a perfect test for you to show your loyalty to me. If you pass this, I will allow you to tell me whatever information you have in regards to Na Fianna and Tara and then I shall give you your brother back."

"Anything you say I will do, my lord," she said with another bow, and the bad feeling in my stomach continued to gnaw at me but I would not let it manifest itself. Not yet. Not until I was entirely certain.

And then the other guards came back in, dragging Oran with them, bound and gagged and looking only half conscious. I caught my breath, watching the young prince with relief and horror at the same time. It was so good to actually see him, to know he was, in fact, alive, but his condition could have been better, and looking at him, I felt all my fear clench around my insides. If he could look this bad, then how awful would Aeden look? Aeden, who Lorcan had boasted about torturing for a good part of the six months he had been captive.

Oran looked like he hadn't eaten or slept well for weeks—he probably hadn't. He was so thin and had none of the liveliness he had always shown. And when he turned his head…there was a scar where an ear was missing.

"Oran!" Eamon cried, jerking against Cronin. Oran's head shot up as he heard his brother and his eyes opened and actually showed signs of life. He groaned past his gag and was slapped across the back of the head. Lorcan descended from his throne, and went over to him. He took up a fistful of Oran's hair, and I saw the longish uneven bit from what was left of the missing braid that I had found at the site of their capture. The Goblin King turned back around but he was not looking at Eamon as I thought he would. He was looking at Caitlin.

"What better way to prove your loyalty to me, Caitlin, than ridding Erin of the last heir of the High Seat?" he said.

"My lord?" Caitlin inquired as if she did not know what he had meant, but I knew that wasn't the case.

Lorcan smiled. "Come now, dear, I know you are not that dense." He walked over to her, taking a dagger from inside his coat and pressing it into her hand as he leaned close and practically whispered in her ear. "I want you to kill the prince."

"No!" Eamon shouted again and renewed his struggles. Cronin punched him again, but this time Lorcan didn't say anything against the action. I wondered whether I should step in, but Keevan and Riordan still weren't there, and I didn't know what was part of the plan and what wasn't. I just knew that if everything started to go really badly I would step in with or without the brothers Crimnal.

"I won't do that," Caitlin said firmly, refusing the dagger.

"Why not?" Lorcan asked, a nasty smile on his lips.

"Because that would be treason," she replied. "And I might have a grudge against Na Fianna, but that is still my king's brother and I cannot kill him. Besides, he's only a boy."

"As I thought," Lorcan said in satisfaction, casting the dagger aside so that it skittered over the marble floor. "Traitor. Take her away to the cells."

The Goblin guards stepped forward but Caitlin didn't give them a chance. She spun on her heel and tore off through another corridor as they shouted in surprise.

"Don't stand there, get her!" Lorcan cried. "Go after her, don't let her escape, for Mab's sake!" They went and he sighed, turning back to Eamon and the others, sweeping a hand over his hair and resting his hands on his hips as if he were exhausted.

"That's the problem with your people, Eamon. They are so predictable. So *loyal*. I know exactly what they are going to do because I can control them all just by holding one man. Or one prince." He smiled and motioned to the guards who still held Oran. Eamon jerked again as Cronin spun him around to face his brother.

"Your brother is weak," Lorcan said, and the guards threw Oran to the floor. He barely caught himself with his bound hands before he smashed his face against the marble. Eamon pulled at his bindings, growling under his breath. "He will not be able to withstand much torture. I think you should keep that in mind, Eamon. Your men have been protecting him thus far, but I need to find your breaking point, and as much as I hate to have to do this, to have to put you through the mental agony of seeing your brother in pain because of you, I will do it. For the sake of my people."

"Leave him be," Eamon said in a cold, dangerous voice.

"If you want me to leave him alone, you must beg me for it," Lorcan said with a contemptuous twist of his lip. He nodded to Cronin. "Bring him to me."

Cronin hauled Eamon forward, stopping him just out of reach of his brother. Oran looked up at him, his eyes large and pained above his gag. Lorcan stepped over him contemptuously to stand face to face with Eamon.

"You heard me, mighty *Airdrígh*. If you value your brother's life, beg."

"I did not mark you for such petty games, Lorcan," Eamon said coolly, meeting the Goblin's eyes. "I'm rather disappointed. I thought this would be so much more of a challenge."

"Oh, believe me, Eamon, the challenge has just begun. This is only the cream, so to speak; something for my amusement." Lorcan stepped backward and grabbed Oran by the back of his neck, jerking him onto his knees. "Do you not love your brother?"

"I would die for him," Eamon said steadfastly.

"Then surely you will suffer a little indignity for him," the Goblin King said. "Beg."

"This is just a childish game, Lorcan. You degrade yourself by asking it of me."

"You are no more than a boy," Lorcan sneered. "Childish games befit you."

"We are both kings and rulers who took over from our

fathers before our time," Eamon said. "There is more we have in common than I think you realize."

"I have nothing in common with you, you pathetic human," the Goblin spat contemptuously. "I might have had some respect for you when you first came here, but I've come to see you for who you really are. You are weak; you do not rule your people as you should, instead you foolishly risk your life for that of your whelp brother when you should be home, attempting to find a mate to give you a proper whelp for an heir."

"I will not value a nonexistent son's life above that of my living brother," Eamon said firmly, practically echoing the words he had said at the council. "And even if we both die today, you will find I am not without an heir."

I felt my chest tighten as he said that. I was not ready to see them die; I was not ready to be king. Just thinking it seemed wrong, unimaginable. I wondered where Keevan and Riordan were. If they didn't show up soon, I would have to intervene; there would be no other option. If I had to get rid of Lorcan myself, then I would...

"Just do what I ask or I will kill your brother. Seeing that I am serious might change your decision about making terms. We will talk of this other heir later."

"This is foolish," Eamon snapped, getting tired of the game. "It will prove nothing."

"Humor me," Lorcan said with a sadistic smile as he returned to his throne.

"Please," Eamon said quietly. "Please do not hurt my brother."

"On your knees!" Lorcan shouted, making me jump, as he stood up on the top of the steps to tower over Eamon, his voice echoing through the marble halls. Hatred spiked through me and I clenched my teeth. I could not watch my king suffer this indignity. I gripped my sword tight, whitening my knuckles.

Eamon dropped slowly to his knees. "Please."

"*Beg.*"

He didn't say anything. One of the Goblin guards walked over to Oran and shoved him onto his face, pressing a heavy boot into the back of his neck and putting a wickedly sharp knife against the back of his left ear. "He'll lose the other one, if you don't," he said to Eamon.

Eamon turned back to the Goblin King, anger and disgust fighting with fear in his features. "Please. I beg you."

"On your *face,*" Lorcan hissed. Oran cried out past his gag as a trail of blood trickled down his ear in warning.

I was not going to watch this. I knew what Eamon was going to do and I could not allow it. No matter how self-sacrificing he was, I was not going to watch my king humiliate himself in front of his enemy. I stepped out of the hallway.

"Stop," I said, my voice echoing around the marble hall. All eyes turned on me. Lorcan first showed angry surprise and then amusement.

"Well, you made short work of your imprisonment. I must remember to up security when I have the illustrious Fianna in my custody."

"You want to know who the other heir is?" I asked, unable to think of anything else to stall for time.

"Ciran," Eamon warned, but I wasn't going to listen. I spread my arms and bowed mockingly.

"You're looking at him."

Eamon closed his eyes and his guards hauled him to his feet again. Lorcan crossed the room toward me.

"So, the young Mac Cool has finally brought his

family to the High Seat. I'm actually surprised it hasn't happened before now," he said mockingly. I steeled myself as he circled me, stopping at my back. He leaned over until his mouth was almost touching my ear. "I was beginning to think you were more trouble than you were worth, but I'm having second thoughts. You might be useful yet. Join me, and I will assure you your place on the throne. Your family will be true royalty, and, having aligned yourself to me, you will no longer fear attacks from my people and we, in turn, can live without trouble from yours. Your people will love you for bringing them peace, and your reign will be prosperous."

"I don't want to be king," I told him firmly. "Nor shall I ever work with you. I just came to rescue the man I serve as king and friend."

"If you do not join me, you can die with him," Lorcan said nonchalantly. "You see? Say the word and I will rid you of him so you can take the throne in his place."

"I will not take a throne stained with the blood of one I view as a brother," I said firmly. "I've studied enough history to know *that* never goes well."

Lorcan gave a small disgusted chuckle, and whispered so that no one else would hear. "I'd almost admire you Mac Cools, if I wasn't so bloody exasperated with you. Do you know how long I have tried to cajole your brother into helping me with this plan? So long it makes me sick and yet I can't help but tip my hat to him for his stamina."

"What plan?" I asked.

"Oh, Ciran. I wish I had the time to discuss it now, but I don't. I need to have a grown-up discussion with your king." He turned around with a sigh, striding back to his throne and flicking a lazy hand at several other guards. "Take Ciran Mac Cool into custody again. I tire of him.

And make sure he's *secure* this time."

I readied myself for a fight; there was no way I was going to let them take me again without one, but we were all interrupted by the sound of shouting and boots pounding down the hallway I had been hiding in earlier. In another second, Keevan sped out, looking wild and hysterical.

"The beast!" he screamed as he ran. "The beast is loose! Run for your lives!"

Then he was out again, down the opposite hall. Lorcan shouted at his guards.

"By the bloody Fae, what is going on here?! Get him back here now! I will not have another Fianna escape my dungeon..."

He got no further because there was another figure running down the hallway, or more like tearing down it with the force of a tidal wave. A roar sounded out and the hair on the back of my neck rose as I realized what it was. While the Goblins stopped to watch in horror, I ran forward, shoving one guard to the floor and barreling into another who still held Eamon in a loose grip. Eamon and I fell to the floor as two other guards quickly hustled Oran out a side door and went to call for reinforcements.

"Oran!" Eamon cried out, but I was already hauling him to his feet and out of the room, just in time for Riordan to tear into the hall, throwing back the Goblins that had run to stop him with a swing of his twin blades.

"We'll get him back, Eamon, but we need to find the others first," I assured him, hauling him down the hallway. He stumbled and I realized his hands were still tied behind his back. I stopped a moment to cut them and then grabbed him by the arm as we doubled our pace, trying to find a way out, nearly barreling into Keevan and Caitlin who came around another corner.

"Well, it seems your plan worked, Cait," Eamon said with a tired smile as he clapped her on the shoulder.

"Is Riordan actually berserk at the moment?" I asked.

"Him?" Keevan replied. "Nah, you'll know when he really is, trust me. It's way scarier than that. But the Goblins won't know the difference."

Footsteps sounded down the hall and we all tensed and drew our weapons but it was only Riordan coming into sight, his twin blades, *Cuimhne* and *Tuairim* sheathed across his back once more.

"Come on!" he growled and pushed us forward.

"This way," Caitlin said, motioning down a hallway. "I got a chance to slip my escorts and explore a little bit the other day. I found the secret passage Jarlath told us about."

I shook my head, but could see the light ahead of us that indicated the exit. We burst out into the sunlight again and didn't even stop a moment to catch our breath before we continued on in the direction Caitlin was leading. I knew the Goblins wouldn't be far behind us and we needed to get to the rest of our comrades before then.

"What do we do?" I asked.

"We make a stand," Caitlin said. "Killian has called for reinforcements. They should be here before long. Lets just hope we can hold off Lorcan's army until they get here."

"What about the prisoners?" I asked. "Lorcan might kill them, or use them against us."

Keevan shook his head with a grin. "We closed off the dungeon and threw away the key. Even Lorcan can't get in now. There's only one key to the dungeons themselves."

"But Oran," Eamon protested. "He's not with the others, Lorcan still has him."

"We're not going to let anything happen to Oran," I assured him, gripping his shoulder. "I promise you that."

"Just a little further, we're camped right over the rise," Caitlin said, pointing as we rushed up a hill and I looked down on the Giant's Causeway below. Eamon seemed to see the direction I was looking and nodded.

"I suppose that's to be our battleground then," he said. "It will be tough, but, well, what am I saying, you're Fianna. You at least will do fine. Not sure about the rest of us."

I grinned as we slid most of the way down the other side of the rise and into the camp where Killian, Tierney and Deaglan were waiting for us. Tierney shouted in joy as he saw us and clasped me in a rough embrace, nearly picking me off my feet.

"You're all right, brother!" he said with a grin.

I winced slightly as his arms dug into the lash marks on my back, but couldn't help grinning back. "More or less. A little bruised and bloody, but I'll live."

Killian strode up with an angry expression as he confronted Eamon, his hands fisting at his sides.

"You!" he said, jabbing a finger into the High King's chest. "You let yourself go and get captured without me, when I wasn't there to protect you! How can you be such an idiot?!" He looked like he was going to deck him for a minute then lowered his fist again. "Propriety states that...oh, forget bloody propriety!" And he jerked Eamon into a tight hug, pounding his back before letting go and visibly trying to calm himself.

"Killian," Eamon said, gripping his shoulders. "You have a job to do. Prepare for war."

"Yes, your majesty," Killian said and nodded to Tierney and Deaglan who were already wearing their battle armor. "Get them the extra breastplates out of the Range Rover and help them suit up!" he said. He looked down the road as he did so, a worried expression on his face. "I really hope O'Rourke gets here in time."

"It will be fine," Eamon said. "If worse comes to worse, I will challenge Lorcan to single combat."

"And will he honor that?" Tierney asked as he was helping me on with my breastplate, cinching up the sides.

Eamon nodded slowly. "I think he will."

"He will," I added surely.

"It would be best that way," Eamon said quietly as Killian brought out his copper breastplate and settled it onto his shoulders.

"None of that," Killian snapped at him, smacking the back of his head with a bracer. "You know we'll all gladly fight and die here if we have to. We might very well last ten minutes tops."

Eamon smiled and looked around at us. "I wouldn't trade one of you for a thousand men," he said sincerely. "By the purity of our hearts, the strength of our limbs, and the action to match our words, we will win. No matter how few stand shoulder to shoulder."

We all stood silent, wondering if this was indeed to be the end. I wasn't about to allow that, I realized, because there was no way I was going to fail everyone back at home now who were waiting for their loved ones to be returned to them. I wasn't going to be a martyr for my cause; dying today wouldn't make a difference and if we all died, then Lorcan would kill our prisoners, and then it would all be in vain. No, we were going to live, because we had no choice, and I think Eamon knew that. However, that didn't mean I wasn't going to try and stop him from actually fighting in single combat. That was just my job, even though I knew it would be hopeless.

"Deaglan," Eamon said, nodding to the Finar. "Go up top and see what they're doing." Deaglan nodded, but Eamon stopped him as he passed him. "Thank you for the bow, by the way, and for trying to pretend to be me."

Deaglan gave him a winning smile. "Well, I obviously failed, so my apologies, sire."

Eamon grinned and punched him lightly in the shoulder. "No, you didn't fail. The Goblins were just too smart for us."

Deaglan hurried up as we prepared, checking over weapons, before he came jogging back down to us.

"They're outside the palace and look like they're massing to make search parties. What do we do now?"

"Colin will never get here in time," Caitlin said grimly, checking her sword.

"No," Killian replied with a resigned sigh as he carried Eamon's sword in its sheath over to the king. He looked up at Eamon as he buckled the sword around his waist. "Well, your majesty, what do you say we do?"

Eamon was silent, his hand finding the hilt of his sword. He drew it and held it up to his face, checking the edge before he flourished it and slid it back into the sheath.

"We fight," he said surely.

Chapter Twenty-Six
Fight

We stood on the ridge in clear view of the goblins. Several of them spotted us, and pointed, calling out to their lieutenants and readying themselves for battle. Finally Lorcan came forward to the front of his army and stood gazing up at Eamon. He too was dressed for battle, wearing a splendid breastplate of silver and a long black cloak that flapped in the wind, showing its purple underside.

"*Airdrígh* Eamon," he called up. "Were you so eager to be away from my hospitality? I'm offended!"

"I've had enough games, Lorcan," Eamon told him. "I want to settle this now, here. In front of our people."

I could see Lorcan's smile from there. "I mean no offense, Eamon, but it appears my men greatly outnumber yours."

"I'm aware of that," Eamon said. "But there are two kings here, two representatives of our kingdoms, and I don't think we need more than that, do we?"

"Are you asking for single combat?" Lorcan asked.

"You still have that romantic notion in your head?"

Eamon nodded once. "I think it is the best for both of us. I know you share my feelings on this matter. You have seen my men fight, and you know what they are capable of. Even with my inferior numbers, you know they would take many of your Goblins with them."

Lorcan was silent for a moment. Cronin was speaking to him, likely protesting that they get to the fighting, but Lorcan waved him off dismissively, making the large Goblin fume. He turned back to Eamon. "And the terms? What are the stakes for which we fight?"

"If I win, I want a peace treaty signed, and my prisoners returned," Eamon said firmly. "You will be left in peace to rule your people as is."

"And if I win?" Lorcan inquired.

"That's for you to decide," Eamon said firmly.

"Your kingdom will be mine," the Goblin said.

"And the prisoners?" Eamon asked.

"Returned; I am not a monster, Eamon, nor will I have need of them if you *give* your kingdom to me. I'll need someone to rule over, after all. It would do little good to kill my subjects."

"I accept," Eamon said and began to descend the hill. Killian caught him by the arm.

"Are you making a mistake?" he hissed.

"No," Eamon said firmly. "Because this time I will not take losing as an option." He grinned suddenly. "Besides, this is just one-on-one combat. Not nearly as hard as dealing politics in the conference chamber."

Killian gripped a handful of Eamon's cloak. "Whatever you do, don't get killed. Or I will never forgive you. If I lose two brothers today…"

Eamon gripped the back of his neck and smiled. "Hey,

mo dearthair. I'm not going to let that happen."

"You had better not," Killian replied dangerously.

"No, you see," Eamon replied wryly, "I can't." And then he turned and walked down the hill. Killian shook his head and muttered something under his breath but we all followed him. I caught up with Eamon at the bottom, right on the Causeway, and watched the Goblins massed about thirty meters in front of us. I leaned close so that only Eamon would hear me.

"Let me fight as your champion," I said.

"No, Ciran."

"Just thought I'd try," I replied with a smile as I took his cloak from him, folding it over one arm. I let him draw his sword and then took the belt from him as well so the scabbard didn't knock against his leg during the fight.

"If this ends badly, Ciran," Eamon whispered. "Don't let him take my kingdom."

"I won't," I promised and then stepped back as I saw Lorcan readying himself on the other end of the stretch. He cast his cloak off with a flourish and drew a long thin blade with the make of a scimitar.

"Try to catch your sword on the inside curve of his blade," I told Eamon. "The outside will slip if you're not careful."

He nodded with a small smile. "Thank you." Then he seemed to consider something. "Ciran, don't let them try anything stupid."

"I may not be able to give you my word on that one," I said seriously. "But I know you can trust them to do the right thing. Always."

Eamon looked like he was going to say something else, but Lorcan was striding forward and I gave him a pat on the back. "Go win this," I said.

Eamon nodded and started forward to stop about a meter in front of Lorcan. The Goblin smiled and they both nodded to each other.

"So it comes to this," Lorcan said. "Fighting man-to-man just like our fathers."

"Yes," Eamon admitted. "I only hope that we can end the war this time."

"That all depends on you," Lorcan said. "But I assure you that I am a man of my word."

"As am I," Eamon replied.

"You have an eager audience," Lorcan said with a small smile, nodding behind him. I looked past the fighters and saw Cronin holding Oran at the front of the Goblin army. The prince was gagged but watching wide-eyed as his older brother readied to fight. I wasn't sure whether I could trust Lorcan not to kill him if things started to go badly for him. I nudged Tierney slightly, nodding, and he nodded back. If Cronin tried anything we would be over there in a minute whether it was against the rules of combat or not.

Eamon and Lorcan took places, facing each other and readied themselves, their swords held loosely in their hands. They saluted each other with a flourish, and stepped back into a crouch. My concern was that we had never seen Lorcan fight, and I didn't know what he was capable of. Yes, Eamon had seen him in that last battle, but that had been several years ago, and I knew how hard Eamon trained since so as not to duplicate the scars he gained in that battle. If I had learned anything from the fights we had, it was that Goblins were good warriors, swift and dangerous—they didn't play around, and Eamon didn't have Fae blood like I did to give him any extra advantage. I had a feeling just from the way Lorcan carried himself—almost like a dancer but sturdier, more dangerous —that he was a master of the art, and he held the sword in his hand as if it were an extension of him.

But one thing I also knew was that Eamon would not lose. Because, as he had said, he couldn't.

I only hoped that would be enough.

Then Eamon leapt forward with a shout, bringing his sword down in an arc toward Lorcan's head. The Goblin parried, his thin, curved blade sliding easily away from Eamon's shorter broadsword. Eamon did what I had suggested though, and kept to the inside curve of the blade. It would still be hard to get any purchase on it because of its shape, but not quite so bad there. Our swords usually looked so elegant but I was shocked to see how clumsy they appeared against the Goblin blade.

Lorcan allowed Eamon to test his defenses, letting him strike somewhat tentative blows to get into the feel of Lorcan's style, before he did the same. I leaned toward Killian.

"He's doing good by easing in. They seem pretty evenly matched, but neither are going full out yet."

Killian nodded, his eyes never leaving the two, his hand white knuckled on his sword hilt. "Let's just hope he keeps on top or at least even. I'm just afraid Lorcan won't show his full prowess until he has Eamon in a position where he's confident he'll win."

I didn't comment, but I feared the same outcome. If I had learned anything in the last few days it was that Lorcan was a sly manipulator and couldn't be trusted. I leaned over and spoke more quietly to the captain. "If they make a move toward Oran, Tir and I will go get him. Just make sure Eamon is all right, okay? We'll take care of anything else."

"Thanks, Ciran," Killian said, a tight smile on his lips. "Ah, first blood!"

Eamon had scored a nick on Lorcan's wrist. Nothing hampering, but still, a good sign that he could actually get through the Goblin King's defenses. Lorcan stepped back and smiled, bringing the cut to his lips and sucking on it with a wince. "Well, the honor of first blood goes to you, *Airdrígh*; we'll see if your luck holds out through the rest of the duel."

They met again, and this time with a more enthusiastic clash of steel, blades flying and glinting in the sunlight. Eamon was doing an impressive job of keeping grounded on the uneven landscape—a battlefield constructed of basalt pillars at all different heights was not necessarily ideal. I kept waiting for one of them to trip, but thankfully, it didn't occur—at least not yet.

Lorcan hopped lightly from pillar to pillar, dancing around Eamon, but our high king was not a heavy stepper either, being tall and thin, and having a certain grace about him that made me sometimes wonder whether he did in fact have Fae blood somewhere along the line.

And then he suddenly miss-stepped, and instead of catching Lorcan's blade on the inside, he caught it on the outside along the curve, and the Goblin disengaged fluidly, slashing the blade across Eamon's upper arm as he did so. Red instantly covered Eamon's sleeve and he stepped back, clasping a hand to the wound that even from where I stood, I could tell was bleeding badly.

Lorcan advanced on him again, leaving little time for recovery, and attacked without remorse. Eamon stood his ground, deflecting the blows and striking hard himself, but I could tell the wound, being on his sword arm and likely deep, was taking a toll on his movements and strength. I could see how tense Killian was beside me, watching.

Eamon struck out desperately at Lorcan, a snarl on his lips. The Goblin grabbed his arm and, already overstepping in what is oftentimes, regrettably, a fencer's mistake (which is why broadsword combat should never be taught with foils) he was thrown off guard and as Lorcan tossed him aside, he sliced low at Eamon's midriff.

Thankfully, the breastplate took the brunt of the blow, but Eamon's hip had been opened up, and blood dripped down his leg onto the ground.

Killian cursed under his breath, and I put a hand on his shoulder as a caution for him not to rush out there. He shook me off, and gritted his teeth. Eamon staggered, but rallied his strength, and lurched forward, forgetting propriety and head-butting Lorcan, slashing his sword at the Goblin as he stumbled backwards. The blade sliced across Lorcan's thigh and I saw a spatter of black drops land on the ground.

Lorcan gained his feet all too quickly and threw a barrage of harsh blows at Eamon, who was fighting through the pain of his wounds, unable to hold his stance properly and unable to put the weight he needed behind his sword. Eamon still managed to keep up, which impressed me a lot. I had never had the opportunity to see him fight outside of training, and realized for the first time that he was a dedicated and stable fighter.

Then something caught my eye across the field. Oran was struggling in Cronin's grasp and finally stomped on the Goblin's foot. Cronin cursed and gave the prince a vicious cut with the knife he had been holding to his throat, cutting into the flesh between his neck and shoulder. Oran cried out in surprise past the gag and Eamon, hearing his little brother in pain, couldn't help looking over to see what was wrong.

It was all the distraction Lorcan needed.

I saw the catastrophe a moment too late as Eamon backed up and stumbled over a raised pillar. Lorcan took the moment to kick him in the chest and sent him sprawling, his sword clattering a few feet out of reach. He lunged for it, but Lorcan kicked him back again, setting his boot into Eamon's chest and putting his sword point to his throat.

Killian growled and started forward but Tierney and I grabbed him and held him back. On the other side of the field, I saw Oran being restrained by Cronin as he tried to go to his brother's aid, getting punched and thrown to the ground for his troubles. But I didn't have time to worry about him. I had to concentrate on keeping Killian still.

Eamon looked up at Lorcan with a wry expression. "Kill me if you will," he said. "But I still expect you to keep your end of the bargain. And know that if I do die today by your hand, you will get nothing but resistance from my men."

Lorcan smiled. "Oh, I'm aware of that, which is why I'm not going to kill you. I just want to make you bleed a little. Humiliate you in front of your men." He lowered the sword from Eamon's throat to right under his collarbone and pressed, causing the man to tense. I had already seen enough of this. Without even drawing my sword, I ran forward before the others could stop me and kicked Lorcan's blade aside, standing over my king.

"Ah, the younger Mac Cool," Lorcan said with obvious pleasure. "It seems you really are as foolish and brave as your brother. This might actually work out for the better. Your king seems to value you quite a bit. Maybe I should make an example of you so that the others will know what happens when they try to get in the way of my only wanting what's best for my people." He grabbed me by the throat, and I stared him down as I felt his blade press into my side, up under my breastplate. He smiled unpleasantly. "Shall we?"

Another sword crossed his, pressing into his own side. Lorcan looked down and then up again and I smiled as I felt the familiar shoulder pressed against mine.

"You'll have to get through me first," Tierney said.

"And me," Keevan added, his axe appearing threateningly close to Lorcan's neck.

"And me," Caitlin added, her sword held ready.

"And me," Riordan growled, his twin blades held across his chest.

"And me," came Deaglan's voice from behind me, along with the creak of his bow being drawn back.

Killian had helped Eamon up, and retrieved his sword, standing firmly at his shoulder in case he fell down. Eamon put his blade against Lorcan's throat, a smile on his lips.

"Surrender, Lorcan. I think you're finished," he said.

"Unless you enjoy the prospect of getting run through with various weaponry at the same time," Killian added, pressing the Goblin's sword away from me, and shrugged. "Which may be your thing, I won't judge."

"And if I don't?" Lorcan sneered.

"Why, then we'll fight you," Killian said, giving him his *are you an idiot* look. Lorcan only smirked.

"Pardon me for being rude, but it appears you have forgotten to bring an army with you."

"No he didn't." We all turned at the voice to see Colin O'Rourke, Killian's first lieutenant, come striding up with his sword slung nonchalantly over his shoulder and a lazy smile on his lips, his bright red hair glinting in the sunlight. "We were only a little late."

"Something you'll answer for later, I assure you," Killian hissed at him.

Colin's grin broadened. "Unforeseen traffic incident. Nothing we couldn't handle."

The rest of the Guard and several more Fianna warriors were forming ranks behind us. We all took our place in the front rank around Eamon who was limping slightly from the wound to his hip, but I knew he wasn't about to stop and rest. Lorcan's Goblins came forward to form behind him as well and the two kings eyed each other across the space in between. My sword was out, held loosely against my thigh.

"There's still time to reconsider," Eamon said.

Lorcan gave him a small, tight smile. "I'm afraid it's far too late for that, Eamon."

And with that the Goblins started forward with a concentrated yell and Eamon raised his sword, shouting, "*D'Éirinn! Le haghaidh ár dearbháireacha!*" and ran forward to meet them, the rest of us only a pace behind.

The clash was immense and exhilarating. I had never felt anything like it. It was not like a skirmish, but so much bigger and not nearly as glorious as it looks on the movies. It was messy, tight, hardly any room to swing your sword, and the noise was deafening, but I was able to pick out sounds and found that if I just engaged and concentrated on one enemy at a time, I was able to fight, to defend, and to kill all the more easily.

In a moment, I felt a familiar back against mine, and didn't have to look to know it was Tierney. Our shoulders were just barely touching so that it was like a thin hair wire that connected our movements so we would be able to know exactly what the other was doing without actually being able to see them. It was a gift of a Fianna warrior, the extra sensory bond between us and our Fianna brothers, and Tierney and I had trained like this for years, waiting for this moment when we would put it to use in battle, and we knew the other as well as we did ourselves.

Every time I got a lull, I cast about the field, looking for Eamon, looking for my comrades. Eamon seemed to be holding up, though he was continuously surrounded and he was still losing blood from his wounds; but he had Killian at his back and I knew the Captaen would not let anything happen to him. Eamon would be looking for Lorcan but the king seemed to be elsewhere, battering the Guard's defenses who were trying to form a wedge to get through the Goblin line and scatter them.

I caught sight of Caitlin another time, after I drove my sword through a Goblin's shoulder and sent him for a long recovery. She was fighting back to back with Deaglan, and I was a little envious of how good they looked together. Her with her smallsword flashing about and Deaglan with his double short blades wreaking havoc in the Goblin ranks, his bow set aside in favor of the knives for close fighting. I then caught a movement off to my left and had to turn in time to block a blow from Cronin who came at me out of nowhere, a snarl on his face. He knocked me back and I fell against Tierney before I regained my footing.

"Now you'll see what I'm really capable of, you little half-blood!" the Goblin snarled and swung a deadly looking scimitar at me. "This isn't some dinner theater performance. This is the real thing!" I stepped up to meet him, leaving Tierney to fend for himself for a moment while I saw to my enemy.

I didn't bother wasting breath. I just attacked, and Cronin caught my sword with his and easily slid his blade away to lunge at me. He had been good at bare-knuckle combat, but he was much better with a sword in his hand, and for a moment, locked in combat, I feared that I wouldn't be able to beat him. The rocky terrain didn't help either. Every few steps I would either have to step up or step down on the pillars and none of them were big enough for more than one and a half feet so it was awkward, and dangerous, for one wrong step could end the entire fight for either of us. I was lucky to have my Fianna instincts and began to wonder how the Guard was holding up. I had a feeling the Goblins trained on the Causeway all the time, and were likely experts. Cronin didn't seem to let it bother him too much.

I swung heavily at him as he leapt up onto one pillar and nearly gave him a gash on the thigh, but he was out of the way too quickly and kicked, catching me in the chest. I flew back, winded, but kept ahold of my sword and brought it up as he leapt at me again, landing with one foot on either side of me, his sword coming down.

We were locked in a battle of wills; he pushing down as hard as he could, and I refusing to give him the upper hand even though he was forcing both our blades closer and closer to my throat. I ground my teeth, grunting in exertion.

"Give up, little Finar," Cronin snarled, pressing harder, now practically sitting on my hips, his knees digging into my ribs. "I'm stronger than you."

The next event was almost comical. One minute, I was grinding my teeth, just trying to keep the blade from my throat, and the next a huge shape barreled over me and took Cronin with it. I sat up, leaping easily to my feet and saw Riordan holding the Goblin off the ground as Cronin struggled and tried kicking out at the berserker. Riordan threw him onto the ground and bellowed at him to pick up his sword. Cronin did, and charged the Finar in what really was a brave effort, but Riordan spent no time and simply ran him through with a cold easiness that, I will admit, rather frightened me. Cronin slid to the ground and before I could think or act, a contingent of Goblins surrounded Riordan, shouting their vengeance. He spun around with his twin blades, but even then he was no match for all of the Goblins who continued to press into him to avenge their lieutenant. I ran with the intention of helping him, but a scream of rage stopped me, and I turned to see Keevan, a furious streak of red and black come stampeding up with his axe raised. He actually cast his shield aside, throwing it so that it took out a Goblin as if he had been poleaxed. When he crashed into the ones who had assaulted his brother, several literally flew back from the ferocity of his axe swing. Soon he and Riordan were back to back and once I got over my shock, I ran to them as I saw more Goblins converging.

But then Riordan caught my eye. "Run," he growled at me, and something in his look made me obey. I had a feeling I wasn't going to have to worry about those two, even when I saw them practically covered in Goblins.

"Ciran!" Tierney finally ran up to me, splattered in some Goblin blood. "Eamon!"

I ran over to him and together we forced our way through to where Eamon and Killian were being beset by a final effort from the Goblins. Colin was in there with them now, and Tierney and I forced our way through the press to him.

"Fine day for a fight, isn't it?" the lieutenant asked

with a wild laugh as he ran a Goblin through and shoved him off his blade with his foot. He was covered in black blood and it gave him a wild look.

"Couldn't be better," I replied jokingly, and he laughed again, giving a Celtic scream and charging forward.

Tierney went to stand behind Eamon and Killian, but I was beset by three more Goblins that I needed to defeat before I could get to them. A sudden thought struck me as I wondered what had happened to Oran when we had joined in battle? He was likely kept back with a couple guards. I only hoped he was all right.

After I dispatched the last Goblin, there was a sudden lull, and I looked around, bending with my hands against my knees to catch my breath for a moment. There were several small scraps going on still, but for the most part, we seemed to have contained the Goblins well enough. I turned around to see Eamon had sunk to his knees, breathing heavily; Killian crouched with a hand on his shoulder, speaking to him while Colin stood above them, his sword held ready. Killian tore off the skirt of his tunic and began to bind Eamon's arm that was soaked in blood from his wound and I could tell the fight was taking a toll on him. And then I had another thought, looking frantically around the battlefield with a frown. Where was Lorcan?

I started toward Eamon to ask if he knew what had become of him, when a shout stopped me in my tracks.

"*Airdrígh!*"

I looked up to see Lorcan standing on a group of particularly high pillars off to one side, but what made me catch my breath was the fact that he had Oran in his grasp, a dagger point pressing into the soft place under his chin.

"I have your brother, Eamon. Surrender now and I will spare him."

"Oran!" Eamon cried, hauling himself to his feet with the intention of rushing over, only to be dragged back by Killian.

I was far enough away so that Lorcan's attention was not on me and I was going to use that to my advantage. I sheathed my sword and instead drew a dagger from the back of my belt. I crept forward, around to one side so I could get behind him. Tierney caught my eye and we shared a look before he turned back to watch Lorcan, careful not to draw attention to me. I hoped I was covered in enough Goblin blood for Lorcan to ignore my scent long enough to get close to him. I climbed silently up the rocks to the group of raised pillars he was standing on. I would only have one shot at this. I knew I had to make it count.

"Last chance, Eamon. What is your decision?" he asked mockingly.

I was right behind him. I had to move quickly before I was spotted. I raised my dagger.

"My lord!" one of the Goblins cried out and I made my move, leaping up and grabbing the hand Lorcan held the dagger in at the same moment I drove my own blade up under his breastplate. I apologized with a wince as I kicked Oran away from him. The prince fell hard, but he was free. Lorcan screamed in shock and pain and spun around to strike out at me but I disarmed him and kicked him to one side, close to the cliff edge. We were right on top of the highest part of the Causeway where it was the longest drop down to the rocks and ocean below, and I was trying to maneuver him over it. I could hear shouting as we struggled, my knife still stuck in him. He growled and scratched at me with his claws, trying to gain purchase on the rocks as I forced him ever closer to the edge of the cliff, but suddenly, one of his feet caught on an uneven spot and he fell backwards over the edge. I let him go, thinking I had finished it, but was suddenly yanked forward, realizing too late he had managed to grab onto my belt, taking me with him.

I clutched the top of the cliff at the last minute, fingers and palms tearing on the rocks as I fought for purchase, but I was over, slamming against the cliff face as I fought to hold on with the tips of my fingers. Lorcan's hand was smashed against the rock as I slammed against it and he fell. The loss of his weight made my plight slightly better, but I was in a bad place. I looked down and saw his body splash into the sea below, likely smashing against the rocks. I swallowed hard. I had managed to finish him, but I feared that I would share his fate.

I tried to find a foothold to no avail. My hands were bleeding, torn up against the rocks, making them slick and even harder to hold on with and the more I moved the worse it got. I cried out, but just as I was slipping the few final inches to my doom, Deaglan of all people was at the top of the hill on his stomach, grabbing my wrists just as I lost my grip. Tierney fell beside him in another instant and grabbed the shoulder strap of my breastplate, helping Deaglan to haul me up. We all fell in a heap, breathing heavily; my face was pressed into Tierney's shoulder and I just rested a moment, enjoying the fact that I was still alive and that I had gotten rid of our enemy, effectively ending the battle. Tierney slapped a hand into the center of my back.

"That was good work, Cir," he said breathlessly. "But don't fall off any more cliffs, all right? It's starting to become a bad habit."

I sat up finally, glancing down at my torn up hands with a wince. I looked over to Deaglan who was crouching nearby, a smile quirking up the sides of his mouth.

"Well, have I proved my loyalty yet?" he asked.

My exhaustion dissolved into a grin and I gripped his forearm, jerking him into a weary embrace. "You have, *deartháir*, you have that."

He and Tierney helped me up and I looked over to see Eamon making his way to Oran finally, the rest of the Fianna and Killian's guardsmen rounding up the remaining Goblins into a group of prisoners. Eamon fell to his knees beside his brother, cutting his bindings and helping him to sit up, seeming at a loss for a moment what to do. He put his hands on either side of Oran's face, just looking him in the eyes for a moment as if making sure he was really there.

"Oran," he said quietly, gently brushing away the hair on the right side of his face where the ear was missing. He then yanked him to his chest and crushed him in a fierce embrace, which Oran returned with all the strength he could muster, burying his face in his brother's neck and shaking with silent sobs. I left them to their reunion in peace and went to see my other comrades.

I had not seen Keevan and Riordan since the latter had been surrounded and his brother had flown into a frenzy and Riordan told me to run in no uncertain terms. I was worried about what had happened to them. I broke into a run when I saw Keevan lying on his back amidst a pile of Goblins, and Riordan crouching over him, a hand on his chest.

"Riordan!" I shouted, skidding to a halt, and crouching down on Keevan's other side, looking worriedly at his pale face. "Is he all right?"

Before Riordan could answer, Keevan let out a long groan and stirred, reaching up to put a limp hand over the one Riordan had pressed against his chest. His eyes fluttered open and he looked up with a frown.

"What happened?" he asked. "Did I pass out?"

Riordan suddenly laughed and pressed a hand against his brother's cheek. "You saved me, little brother. I was nearly dead, and you came out of nowhere and took out at least twelve Goblins single-handedly. I've never seen the like! You are a natural berserker, Keevan. No training needed."

I looked at them with surprise. "Is that even possible?" I asked.

"It's rare, especially outside of Scandinavia, but it is possible," Riordan said. "There's no other explanation for what he did. That wasn't normal." He helped Keevan to sit up and the younger groaned, putting a hand to a cut on his leg.

"I'm feeling rather light-headed," he said. "Why am I so hungry?"

Riordan laughed. "Don't worry, we'll get you something to eat soon."

Keevan suddenly threw his arms around his brother's neck, surprising him as tears fell down his cheeks.

"I just couldn't watch them kill you! I had to do something. *No one* hurts my brother and that's that."

Riordan smiled gently at him and held him tightly. "You know that's the truth. Let's not tell Mum about this for a long while though, all right?" Keevan nodded and I grinned, clapping them both on the shoulders, before I let them be, deciding that any small wounds would be taken care of later.

Caitlin met me next and I smiled tiredly at her as she

returned the look. There was a cut on her shoulder and a bruise on her forehead but she looked all right otherwise. "Well, I guess we succeeded," I said, not knowing what else to say.

She laughed, and I pulled a handkerchief out of my pocket to tie around her wound. "I don't think it will need stitches," I assured her. "It looks fine to me."

"Your hands look awful," she said sympathetically and I was once again made aware of my bleeding palms. I really looked at them for the first time, and saw them still seeping, almost all the skin torn off. I scrunched up my face. "I wish you hadn't mentioned it."

She smiled and ripped bits from her already torn tunic and began bandaging my hands gently. "How's that?" she asked once she had finished. "Am I getting any better at this?"

I smiled and fondly tugged a lock of her hair. "I may be able to make a healer of you yet."

She shuddered slightly at the thought. "I've decided I much prefer the sight of Goblin blood." She sobered and looked up to meet my eyes with a slightly sheepish expression. "I wanted to apologize for the beating I gave you. I hope you're not mad at me for that. I just went for it and realized too late I had done so with a little bit more gusto than was required."

I smiled at her and shook my head. "Don't worry about it. It wasn't pleasant, no, but I know you had to do it, and do it well, otherwise Lorcan would have known you were faking. Besides, I'm sure if I haven't already done something to deserve it, I will eventually."

Her face softened and she smiled with a mischievous glint in her eye. "Oh, so you think I'll let you get away with it the next time you do something to make me mad? I don't know how I feel about that one."

I laughed and turned to Killian who was coming over with a mock serious look on his face. "Stand a little closer, I dare you," he said and Caitlin made a face at him.

"Thank you for calling in our cavalry," I told him sincerely and we clasped forearms as well as I could with my clumsy, bandaged hands. "I know I can always trust you in a pinch."

"Well," Killian shrugged modestly, though I could tell he was hiding a grin. "It's my duty after all as Captaen to the High King's guard." He looked around. "Speaking of his majesty, he has wounds that need to be tended to. I have to go find a healer." He turned and I decided to follow him back over to Eamon, hoping he'd had enough time to reunite with Oran.

He still had his little brother held close to him when we got back and I had a feeling it would be a few days before he would stray too far from his side.

"I tried so hard to be strong like you, Eamon," Oran said with a hitching sigh and I could see his face wet from newly shed tears. "I fear I failed."

"Never," Eamon told him gently. "No one can be brave all the time, and I have a feeling you were very brave. I won't let you say any differently." I was about to move on and leave them once more, but Eamon saw me and caught my eye over Oran's shoulder, smiling through eyes that were brighter than usual.

"Go release the others," he said quietly. "Let everyone else reunite with their family."

I nodded and was about to turn before Eamon continued.

"You did well, Ciran. I thank you for saving my brother's life. You are every inch a Finar warrior and I am bloody proud to call you friend."

"As am I," I said and turned to Tierney and Deaglan who lingered a few paces away. "Let's go rescue our people," I told them.

Chapter Twenty-Seven
A Rescue

The trip to the dungeons was actually the most painful part of the journey. Everyone was filled with equal dread and anticipation. I actually knew Aeden was still alive, or he had been when I had spoken with Lorcan, but for him to know I was there, that he was being rescued, to be able to embrace him again and take him home, that was what I needed more than anything.

Caitlin still had the key she and Keevan had taken from the guards when they had locked up the dungeons and I opened the door to the lower floor, breathing a sigh of relief to see that it had not been tampered with. We descended once again into the dungeons and I shuddered even at the thought of my short stay there.

"Shout out prisoners!" I called out, "It's Na Fianna. The Goblins are defeated!"

There was a chorus of ragged cheers, and we all pounded down the hallway to a large cell and my hands trembled as I fit the key into the lock but almost lost it. Riordan gently moved me to one side and then kicked the door in without ceremony. He and Keevan were the first into the cell and in an instant their brother, Padraig was hauled out between them, looking much the worse for wear, but grinning as the three brothers shed tears of joy. Padraig had both hands on either side of Keevan's face and set his forehead against his while Riordan held them both in a fierce bear hug.

"You two haven't killed each other," was all Padraig said. "I'm so impressed!" Then they all collapsed against the wall in a heap, heads close together.

Flagan was the next one out, trying to make his own way, but falling and being caught neatly by Caitlin and Killian both. They held him so tightly he couldn't breathe, and Caitlin wept in his neck and kissed him over and over as Killian too shed tears into the top of his brother's head as they all held each other without the intent of letting go.

Tierney was already in the cell and pulling his father to his feet, but Breandan only got halfway there before Tierney's arms were around him, unable to help himself another minute.

"Da!" he choked out as they both sunk to the floor again and Breandan wrapped his thin arms around his son.

"My lad," he said fondly, kissing his forehead.

I looked around at the last prisoner who was making his own way up to his feet and I spun around to see Deaglan standing in the doorway awkwardly, his bow still clutched in his hand and a bit of a lost expression on his face. I slid past him, grabbing his arm and leaning close to hiss in his ear. "What are you waiting for? Go greet your father."

Still he hesitated. "We had a bad fight before he left. He wasn't very proud of me."

I hit him in the shoulder hard and meant to hurt him.

He flinched. "Well, I'd say he has the right to bloody well be proud now." I shoved him forward and he walked a few paces to his father who was slumped against the corner, trying to get his bearings. Darragh Mac Dairmuid looked up expectantly.

"Deaglan," he said.

"*Athair*," Deaglan replied respectfully, bowing his head.

Then Darragh smiled and held out his arms. Deaglan seemed surprised, still hesitant, then he dropped his bow and lunged the last pace to his father's arms and held him tightly.

"I'm so sorry for what I said before..." he began. "You were right, you were always right —" but his father shushed him.

"No. That's all in the past. Let us not speak any more of it. I'm proud of you, lad. I always knew deep down you were a good man."

I was so caught up in the happiness of watching everyone else reunite that I forgot about my own reunion for a moment. It was Tierney who reminded me of it. He was helping his father to his feet, both of them with tears unashamedly running down their faces and I went to help him, clasping Breandan's hand firmly in mine with a relieved smile.

"Ciran," Tierney said, looking around as he wiped his face on his arm, only managing to smear some Goblin blood into the tears on his cheeks. "Where's Aeden?"

Breandan put his hand on my shoulder and squeezed. "He's been kept in another cell. Lorcan paid him special attention. He wasn't kept with us for long." He gripped my shoulder hard as I turned to leave and looked me straight in the eye. "Your brother, Ciran, he was the bravest of us all, I am both shamed and proud to say. He fought daily, and allowed himself to be tortured without ever giving in, just for us, for all of us, and for Oran most of all. He has taken after your father surely enough, and I think you are of that blood as well." He then put a hand on my cheek and pushed me away. "Go to him, Ciran. Let him know it is finally over."

I could only nod, for my throat was quickly constricting. Unknown to the others who were simply catching up with their family members, I took the keys I had dropped on the ground and walked further down the hall. I did not call out this time, for all I had to do was close my eyes, and feel where Aeden was. I knew it when I got to his door, and I put the key into the lock and heard the loud *clunk* as the tumblers turned. The door popped ajar slightly and with one hesitant breath, I pushed it open, afraid of what exactly I would find on the other side.

And then there he was. My brother.

It had been a normal day. I had been training with Tierney that morning, and was on my way home to have lunch. Tir was with me, and we joked the whole time. And over lunch Daegal had said something that was really funny, I couldn't remember what afterward, but I had nearly snorted lemonade through my nose and Tierney had to pound me on the back though he couldn't stop laughing either and that only made me laugh harder.

But that had all changed when the doorbell rang and my mother went to answer it, shaking her head fondly at our antics. It was Daegal who stopped laughing first and disappeared down the hall, a grave expression on his face as he went to find my mother. Tierney and I sobered up in confusion and followed him, finding my mother talking to Eamon of all people, standing in the doorway, looking distressed and fighting through some strong emotion just to keep everything together. I felt instantly ill and I turned to my mother, seeing her expression of horror and knew. I instantly knew.

Eamon turned to me and I saw tears unshed in his eyes. Daegal's arms were already wrapped around my waist and his face was pressed into my back.

"Eamon?" I asked in a whisper.

"Ciran," he replied, but didn't finish for my father had come to the door from his forge, wanting to see what was going on.

"Airdrigh," he said. "What is this?"

"Oh, Niall," my mother had chocked out. "It's Aeden."

"My son?" Da whispered, the calm before the storm. He turned and grabbed Eamon by the front of his jacket and dragged him close to his face. "Where is my son?"

"Niall, the whole patrol was taken by Goblins," Eamon said wretchedly. "We don't know anything. Only that they were taken back to the palace. I'm sorry, I'm so sorry. They took my brother too. All the others...by the Fae, I don't..."

Tierney had gasped at that and I reached out to grip his shoulder even as my heart shattered. His father had been on that patrol. My brother. Eamon's brother. Da let Eamon go and stalked back outside. Eamon turned to my mother and took her hands in his.

"If they still live, I will get them back, I swear it," he said to her, tears falling down his cheeks.

Mum had nodded and put a gentle hand on Eamon's cheek but said nothing. None of us could say anything.

And now six months later, six long months, we had done it. I had found my brother.

He was slumped, seeming to be unconscious, in an awkward position with his wrists and shoulders bearing all his weight. Whatever had made me hesitate before was gone when I saw him, for I ran forward and knelt by his side, my hand trembling as I tried to work the manacles from his wrists, having to try several times to get the key into the hole. Aeden, my brother, at long last—and alive, more or less. But not unscathed, not nearly so. His back, what I could see of it, was a field of lashes, and the rest of his exposed arms, face and torso were covered in cuts, burns and bruises—there was not a clear patch of skin. There was a large, dark patch on his left side that I knew meant at least two cracked ribs if not more, and several horrible weeping wounds on the back of his neck and under his ribs where it looked like he had been flayed in patches. I choked back a sob, and fought the urge to throw up.

I finally got one shackle done and he slumped heavily against the wall with a thud. I wanted to scream seeing him like this; my strong brother reduced to skin and bones, unable even to move he was so weak. But he had cared for me many times in my youth; I supposed it was my turn now.

I put my arm under his so he wouldn't fall over when I undid the last manacle. He stirred slightly, moaning now, and I spoke gently to him in the old tongue to comfort him.

His arm dropped limply to his side as I unlocked the chain and he slumped against me as I finally gathered him into my arms as tenderly as a bairn and cradled his head against my shoulder, leaning back against the wall.

"You're all right now," I told him, trying to keep from crying for some stupid reason. I don't know why, maybe so I could show him I was strong too after all he had been through, but it was bloody hard when I had lost him for so long and to find him in this condition. He had been brave indeed, and he had paid for it. The badges of his bravery were scored into his flesh.

His eyelids fluttered, and a small smile, a ghost of the one I knew so well, flicked across his lips.

"Ciran," he whispered.

"I'm here, brother," I told him. "I knew I'd find you one day. I never gave up hope, nor did Daegal. He knew all along." I was babbling. I didn't know what to say, only that if I stopped talking I feared I would finally crack.

"Good lad," he whispered, grimacing in pain. I ran my fingers through his shorn hair—Lorcan had viciously chopped off his warrior braid too as a mark of shame and I soothed that longer, ragged bit among the chopped auburn waves that now stuck up at odd angles, some parts matted with blood. I began to realize I would probably never know the true amount of humiliation and pain Aeden had suffered. But nor could I allow myself to think of it. My rage would not comfort my brother, and Lorcan was gone, his cruel reign at an end.

"It's all right now, I'll take you home," I told him gently. "Mum will care for you."

"Home," he whispered and reached for the hand I had put on his knee, not knowing where else to put it for fear of hurting him somehow. He wrapped his fingers around mine and squeezed weakly. "I never...I never thought I'd see home again..." he tried before he finally collapsed, and his frail body shook with thick sobs. I had never seen Aeden cry before and it pierced my heart so that I could no longer hold in my own pain and relief. Part of me argued that I needed to be the strong one, but I already had been, and it wasn't going to happen another minute. I wrapped my arms around him as gently as possible and pressed my forehead against his before letting my own tears come, and even though the others had been open enough about their reunion, I was glad that there was no one there to witness our private moment of weakness, for Aeden's sake more so than mine. He had been a hero, and he deserved to weep in private and I was not going to stop him.

I had only cried for Aeden once after he went missing. I never knew why, only that I rarely cried when I was lost in a moment of real, true sadness; I just always seemed to hurt too much to cry. Like crying would be a relief but I never seemed able to manage it. Maybe later, I realized it was actually because I had never truly believed that Aeden was dead. Losing him hurt, it hurt a lot, but a part of me still had a flame of hope.

But the one time I did break down was one day when I had been foolish enough to go into Aeden's room. I hadn't done so for a month after his disappearance. I couldn't. There were too many memories there and I knew it would break me, but I was missing him so much that day, I can't remember exactly why, but I think my father's growing despair had something to do with it, and I went there against my better judgment.

But when I had reached the door, I'd found it ajar and my mother sitting on the bed, crying into one of Aeden's shirts. The scene broke me and I didn't say anything, only sitting next to my mother and putting my arms around her as the tears started to flow down my own face. We just held each other and cried for a long time and neither of us ever went into the room again after that.

I don't know how long we sat there but Aeden finally seemed to run out of tears and I gently dabbed them from his bruised and bloody cheeks. He smiled and brought a hand up to put on my neck.

"You are such a hero, little brother," he said fondly, tugging my braid in an almost regretful fashion. "Thank you for never giving up. I was prepared to die, I was ready, Ciran—don't ever let anyone tell you that you are not when you think your time comes, but it's always nice to know you don't have to leave after all."

I shook my head, sniffing wetly. "No more, please. I can't cry anymore." He laughed thickly then gasped, a hand fluttering over his side as his breath hitched. I pulled him more upright and he finally got his breath back. I reached under my breastplate and fished out the second medallion that I had kept for him, for this very moment. I drew it out and reached down to press it into his hand. His fingers curled around it and a smile found its way to his lips.

"I thought I had lost this," he said.

"You did," I told him. "I just found it for you." I shifted and started to get to my feet.

"Come on," I said determinedly. "We need to get you back home and there's a long drive ahead of us."

He nodded and tried a pitiful attempt at getting up, but I stopped him firmly, laughing almost incredulously.

"Aeden, what are you doing?" I asked, shaking my head. "No." Before he could protest, I had wrapped one of his arms around my neck and picked him up, shocked at how light he was, for though Fianna were strong, I should not have been able to lift him so easily. He moaned in protest, but must really have been weak, because he didn't make a huge fuss.

I carried him down the corridor to meet the others. Everyone looked up as I came in with my brother and they stood as one, even the wounded, in respect for what he had been through to protect them. I shook my head.

"Let's get out of here. Let's bring our people home."

Those words seemed to be what everyone needed to hear and we all trooped out of the dungeons and the palace together, helping our lost ones outside. Aeden smiled even as he squinted. "The sun," he whispered against my shoulder. I couldn't say that I shared his enthusiasm for it. The light of day only made him look a thousand times worse than he had in the dim light of the dungeon.

Eamon was waiting when we came out, Oran still close to his side, as he was patched up by one of the Guards' medics. He looked up as we came out.

"Everyone is returned, Mac Cool?" he asked me formally.

"Everyone is returned, *do Maórgacht*," I replied more tiredly than I had meant to but seeming unable to help it. "The quest has been successful."

I set Aeden down against a rock and one of the guards brought me over a first aid kit and some blankets, and a sweatshirt for Aeden to wear. I did a cursory cleaning of his wounds after making sure to dose him up on pain medication, not wanting him to look quite so horrible when I brought him home. It did improve his appearance a bit, but it was still going to take many days and my mother's skills to bring him back to even looking human again, let alone like a Fianna warrior.

I bandaged his ribs tightly to keep them safe during the trip back and then helped him into the sweatshirt before wrapping him in a blanket. He smiled up at me as I helped him up again, this time, letting him have a bit more dignity to walk for himself.

A Range Rover was parked close by for transport back, and Colin strode up, proclaiming that he was to drive us. He helped me get Aeden into the back seat and I followed, sitting sideways on the seat and leaning Aeden up against my chest so he could breathe easily.

"Are you ready?" Colin asked once we had gotten situated.

I looked out to make sure the rest of my men and their families were being seen to as well and then I finally nodded, exhausted. "Yes, I'm ready."

He climbed behind the wheel but before he could start the vehicle, Caitlin slid into the passenger's seat and turned around to offer me a smile. I looked at her with a frown.

"What are you doing here? Why aren't you with Flagan?" I asked.

She still smiled. "I'm letting Killian have him on the way back since I'll be doing the majority of his nursing while he sees to things with Eamon about the new truce and such." She laughed. "Good thing I got a lot of practice nursing on this trip. I'll need it. Though I may have to ask your mother's advice as well."

"I'm sure she'd be happy to oblige," I told her.

She turned to the front as Colin started up the vehicle but then suddenly turned back to me again and slid something from her pocket. "You may want this," she told me.

I reached out and took her mobile from her hand, smiling in gratitude. I flipped it open and dialed my own number. It rang only once before it was picked up, and I could feel Daegal's anxious demeanor on the other end.

"Ciran," he breathed, not asking the question we both knew was on his lips.

"I've got him," I said simply, and Aeden's eyes opened and looked up at me. He reached up for the phone and I held it to his ear.

"Daegal," he said, his voice weak, but it was there and that was all that mattered. "I'm coming home, *beag amháin*. I'm coming home."

He waited a few seconds before he ended the call, but no words were spoken after that. We were all too overcome with emotion to say anything. And indeed, there was nothing else that needed to be said.

Part Four

The Heroes

Chapter Twenty-Eight
The Return

The whole way back, I happily let Colin drive while I sat in the back seat of the Range Rover with Aeden, listening to the lieutenant hum along with whatever was on the radio. I wouldn't let my brother go and I didn't think I would be able to release his grip on my hand anyway, so I wrapped him in the blanket, sitting sideways on the backseat. As he rested with his back against my chest, I made sure to position his head right under my chin so that I could feel his breath on my neck. I just needed that simple assurance of life before I could let myself relax.

I dozed off at one point, exhausted, realizing I had hardly slept at all for at least three days, and with Aeden and the others rescued now, I had nothing to worry about. Nothing to keep me up. Yes, Aeden might need some repairing, but he was alive, and he was strong enough to get through. Of that I was certain.

Someone shook my shoulder slightly to get me to wake up and I started from sleep, still running with flashpoint adrenaline from sleeping out under the stars for so long. Aeden groaned in protest at my movement and I soothed my hand through his hair to settle him and looked up to see Caitlin turned around, having shaken me.

"We're almost back to your place," she said with a smile. "I thought you might want to wake up."

I smiled back at her and nodded in thanks. "Yes, thank you."

I reluctantly nudged Aeden into wakefulness and he too jerked with a gasp, fear lighting his eyes before he settled, seeing only me there.

"We're almost back," I told him gently. He still gripped my hand and only renewed the hold on it, a small smile flickering over his lips.

"Home," he whispered.

We passed Tara Hall and lost several of the vehicles from our cavalcade there. That was Eamon and Killian with Flagan and Oran in their company, but all the others I had offered to come to my place as I knew my mother would wish. Tierney had called his mother to meet them there.

The drive up to the manor was the homecoming I had wished for so long. It was true that Aeden could not run out to meet the rest of our family, but he was here with me and I would be his legs. I had brought him home just as I had promised, and that made me feel wonderful, better than I had ever felt before in my life. I had my big brother back, and I was bringing him home to everyone else.

The Range Rover was parked and the others came up behind it. People poured out of the house, Tierney's mother and sisters, Deaglan's family, and another woman with red hair who I suspected was Riordan and Keevan's mum. She was the first one to us, and I watched her reunite with the lads, holding Pat and Keevan to her while

Riordan wrapped his arms around them all. Deaglan's mother and sister met him and his father as well, another family put back together again. I watched fondly while I slid out of the car and began to help Aeden out with Caitlin's help.

Tierney left his father with his mother, sisters, and Seamus and came over to me, giving Aeden a hand as he was dragged from the back of the car and settled unsteadily onto his feet, breathing heavily from the exertion but grinning past his battered face.

"At long last," he said as Tierney and Caitlin let him go, leaving him to my care. He turned to me. "Help me to them, Ciran," he said in a whisper.

I had my arm around his waist to steady him, trying to be as gentle as possible; he demanded I let him walk on his own feet, though he gladly leaned against my shoulder.

We didn't even make it to the door before it was opened and my mother, sister, brothers and wolfhounds raced out to throw their arms around us — and slobber on us in the case of the dogs — particularly Aeden. Mum was weeping already, and checking him for inevitable hurts but he gently pushed her to one side with a kiss and turned his full attention to Daegal as I put my arms around my mother and she squeezed my hand firmly, too overcome for words.

Daegal had been shoved aside, pushed against me in the press, fighting to get his arms around his brother who I knew he felt more possessive of than he thought anyone else capable of. Aeden reached out and grabbed his shoulder tightly, smiling down at him. It was still not the smile that we knew but it was getting better.

"Come here, little brother," he said gently, and Daegal threw his arms around Aeden, causing him to wince, but he never let go, and pulled the boy's head to his chest. Daegal's shoulders shook with contained sobs. My mother saw Aeden's exhaustion and put her arm gently around him. "Come, I will see to you."

"Not yet."

We all turned to see my father standing behind us, having come up unnoticed.

"Will you not greet your sire first, boy?" he asked.

Aeden looked taken aback for a moment at the formality in Da's voice, but then I saw the unspeakable joy in Da's eyes and knew he was on the verge of breaking. Aeden left the support of my mother and I, and walked to meet Da on his own. He wavered slightly, but never fell, for Da stepped forward and caught him more gently than I thought him capable of, and pulled my brother's frail form to his broad chest, burying his face in the shorn hair on top of Aeden's head. Aeden collapsed completely then, seeming to allow himself to finally give in to the exhaustion and everything within the comfort of our father's arms. Da didn't say anything, he just held him and wept, his one good hand pressing Aeden's head to his shoulder. He then picked him up bodily and carried him inside, my mum and the rest of my family following. My mother called to the others to bring their families inside as well and everyone began to move in that direction, helping their lost heroes on their way. Happiness and relief flooding off of them.

For some reason I couldn't follow them yet. I needed a moment to gather myself without them; to let them have Aeden for a while since I'd had him all the way back. I did not want a hero's welcome. My job was finished, and I was happy. If I never got any recognition I wouldn't care a whit now that I had my brother back with me. That was all I had ever wanted.

Tierney and Caitlin seemed to want the same thing, for they lingered with me, coming to stand on either side of me now, he putting an arm over my shoulder and she gripping my hand tightly. We just stood there in companionable silence, smiling, knowing in our hearts that we had succeeded and that this was all over.

When I did finally go inside the house, Tierney and I taking leave of Caitlin as she drove back to Tara Hall with Colin to be with her brothers, the house was in an uproar but a happy one. My mother had offered accommodation for all of the lost patrol and their families so she could tend them and they would not have to travel back to their places of residence, which, in the Crimnals' case would have been far to the south. Tierney and I shared a look, smiling, relief and weariness emanating. I reached out to grip his shoulder tightly and we clasped hands, mine still bandaged heavily.

"I can't believe it's over," I said with a slight laugh, shaking my head.

He grinned wider. "I know. There were several moments I really thought...ah, but that's hardly important. We did it, and everyone is safe." He turned as he heard his sister Meghan's voice down the hall. "I think I'm going to go be with my family now," he said and drew me into a rough embrace. "See you later, sword brother."

I decided to do the same and so I headed down the hall to the room beside my mother's herbarium where I knew she had put Aeden. I pushed the door open almost timidly, and slipped inside, seeing the happy scene that awaited me. Aeden was lying on the bed with his head in my mother's lap. She had seen to his wounds and he was bandaged and salved and likely dosed with something as well—he had a somewhat dreamy appearance, though that might have been the relief. Daegal was sitting on the side of the bed, holding one of his hands tightly and Sean, Finbar and Maeve were sitting on the other side. My father stood at the foot of the bed, his arms crossed over his chest, but with a look of utter happiness on his face. He was smiling again. I had not seen him smile since before Aeden had been taken. No one noticed I had come in, until Aeden looked up and saw me, holding out his free hand to beckon me closer.

"Come in, little brother," he said with a smile. "My rescuer."

I went and sat behind Daegal, tucking an arm around his neck and resting a hand on Aeden's knee. "Daegal was the one who guided me to you. He deserves the real credit."

"He does deserve credit," my father said, coming up behind me. "But Ciran is the hero. And I'm not going to bloody let him deny it." I suddenly found myself in his grasp, turned around to face him. "I hope you forgive me all I said to you, Ciran. I should never have doubted." He reached out to stroke Aeden's bruised face gently, his expression pained and joyful both. "I hope you never lose that courage, Ciran. You keep it close, and you wear it proudly. Never let anyone tell you differently. And never let anyone wrong you as I have."

"Oh, Da," I whispered, unable to say it any louder.

And then he grabbed me and pulled me into his arms, crushing me to him. "Thank you for bringing my son back to me."

And then I pulled Daegal into the embrace as well, and in another second we were all sitting around Aeden on the bed, our arms around each other, crying and laughing in turn. I might have had a long life ahead of me, but I don't think there will ever be a moment I will cherish as much as that one. Aeden's homecoming was everything it should have been, and I knew that we could now all rest in peace. Everything seemed to be in order.

If only I had not been wrong.

When we finally extricated ourselves and left Aeden to his drugged slumber, my mother went to the kitchen to whip up a large pot of soup for the visitors and the wounded. I offered to help, but she forced me away to clean up and rest, but not until she had seen to my hands that had been torn by the cliff top. Even with the blood cleaned off, they looked pretty nasty, and I thought ruefully that using a sword would be a challenge for a while, and hoped dearly that I would not have to do so.

I left to take a shower, feeling relieved to change into an old pair of jeans with holes in the knees and a jumper, not having noticed how much my body ached from the punishment I had endured on the journey. As I dried myself off, I took stock of all the new scars I had accumulated. Most had been from the fighting in Lorcan's halls and then there were the lash marks on my back that I was too weary to tell my mother about, and bruises everywhere. Nothing was bad enough to need bandaging, but all together it really took a lot out of me and made me long for the days of rest that I was promised now that the mission was over.

I left my room and almost ran into Finbar who was standing in the hall, his back against the wall, waiting for me, a self-conscious expression on his face.

"Hey, Fin," I smiled at him.

His expression crumpled and he rushed forward to

throw his arms around me. I returned the embrace, somewhat surprised.

"Hey, what's up?" I asked gently.

He sniffed and pulled back, scrubbing a hand over his face. "I just wanted to apologize again for what I said before...when I was angry. I knew you'd bring him back if you could. And just...thank you, Ciran. Thank you for your faith, for not giving up. Thank you for bringing him back. Da's right, you're a real hero."

I smiled and ruffled his hair. "I just did my duty, Fin. I'm glad I was able to bring him back to us. But Fin, I'm glad to know that I have someone around who can take good care of the family when Aeden and I are away. I know you're very capable of it, and it makes me feel better. You're a hero too."

Fin smiled at that, and ducked his head. I slung my arm around his shoulders and pulled him toward the stairs. "Come on, let's go get something to eat. I'm starving."

We went back downstairs and saw most of the visitors at the table eating my mum's hearty sausage soup with fresh soda bread. I sat down between Tierney and Keevan and smiled at them.

"How did you fare?" I asked the redhead.

"Well, since I went berserk, I didn't really feel everything to begin with," Keevan said ruefully. "Now, I'm kind of in a lot of pain. Your mum gave me something and saw to my wounds though so they feel better now." I noticed a marked change in him. Yes, he was exhausted, but he was calmer, more mature. This mission had been more than just a mission to all of us. If there was anything in us that was still clinging to boyhood before, it was gone now, and we were men and warriors. I think we all realized this and it felt good. I felt good.

"You know this isn't the last time we'll work together," Keevan said with a grin. "I think we all have adopted you as a leader. If you want us, we'll take you."

I was touched by his offhanded way of putting it. I smiled. "I would be honored. We'll have to see how things go. But for now, I think it's best we just rest for a few days."

Keevan snorted, but he was grinning. We all finished our supper and it wasn't really late, but afterward we all went off to bed. I was nearly asleep on my feet by then, but I stopped by Aeden's room one more time, needing just that last little reassurance that he was there and that he was all right.

He was sleeping peacefully, and I didn't want to wake him, but I bent to touch my forehead against his briefly before I tucked the covers tighter around him and left the room, nearly bumping into my father on my way out.

Da smiled and caught my shoulder to steady me. "Easy there, lad, you should be in bed."

"That's where I'm heading. I just…needed to see him one last time."

"I know." He rubbed his thumb over a bruise on my cheek before bending and kissing me on the forehead. "But you need to rest. I'll watch over him. Don't worry."

I nearly fell down and slept right there, but I somehow managed to the couch in the solar—with all the guests, I'd had to give up my bed, but I didn't mind. I could have slept on a rock right then. I pulled a blanket off the back of the couch and stripped my sweater off, not bothering to change out of my jeans. My eyes were closed as soon as I stretched out and I was asleep in only a matter of seconds, finally feeling like I could rest, now that everything was back to normal again.

Chapter Twenty-Nine
A Lesson in Poor Judgment

It should never have happened. But the fact was that I had been so exhausted, we all had been, that we slept so heavily, thinking it was all done, that our enemies were dead or quelled, and there was nothing to fear. There were more Fianna warriors in the house than usual, and *someone* should have known something was wrong, but even great warriors make mistakes and we were certainly no exception. Therefore, I woke to sounds of a great upheaval coming from down the hall.

I leapt off the couch and ran down the hall, grabbing my sword from where I had left it against the wall earlier. I was still bare chested, but hardly cared at that moment, not having time to put on my breastplate. Adrenaline pumped through my veins in the sudden fright, pushing some of my drowsiness away as I nearly fell on my way around the corner to the downstairs guestroom. But I made it without incident and barreled into Aeden's room where the noise was coming from. The first thing I saw was that the door in the room that opened onto the veranda was hanging open, letting in the cold night air. I knew Da had been with him, and as I ran into the room, I nearly tripped over him, lying in front of the doorway, wounded, unconscious or dead, I couldn't tell.

"Da!" I screamed, caught off guard, falling to my knees beside him, seeing blood matting the back of his head.

"Ciran, watch out!"

I spun around, raising my sword just in time to ward off a blow that swung down to split my head in two. I cried out in shock at the figure who materialized in front of me from the shadows behind the door, Aeden held in an arm lock in front of him. It was Lorcan.

"Surprised?" the Goblin asked mockingly. He limped, and there was blood dripping from him where I had wounded him earlier, badly bandaged, but he was alive and he was in my house, here to hurt my family.

I growled my hatred at him, swinging my sword to take his head off, but he blocked my blow almost carelessly, holding Aeden in front of him like a shield.

"Careful, Ciran," he admonished mockingly. "You don't want to hurt brother dearest." He laughed.

"Don't worry about me, Cir, take him out," Aeden said, but Lorcan tightened his grip around his neck and choked him, causing him to claw at the Goblin's arm in an attempt to loosen the hold.

I swung a vicious blow to Lorcan's legs and as he leapt out of the way, Aeden somehow managed to struggle from his grasp and gripped Lorcan's sword arm, trying to wrench the weapon from his grasp. But he was still too weak from his poor treatment and the Goblin kicked him contemptuously, slamming him against the wall, so that he fell into a heap with Da who still seemed to be unconscious. Aeden hauled himself up with a groan and cradled Da in his arms as he watched me and Lorcan with desperate eyes. I barely got my sword up again to block the blows the Goblin rained down on me. I was being pressed back against the wall. He swiped viciously, cutting into my arm. It was all shadows in the room and I knew Goblins could see much better in the dark than I could. I grit my teeth and kicked out at him, but he caught the kick against his shin and twisted his leg around mine, trapping it. He grabbed my sword arm to immobilize it at the same time as he pressed his sword to my chest.

"I'm not going to make the same mistake as last time," Lorcan said. "I knew I should have killed you when I had the chance. But I'm not going to do that now. That would be too easy a fate for you, Mac Cool."

I was leaning backwards in an awkward position and I simply shifted my weight, letting myself fall and taking him with me and kicking my feet into his stomach, sending him with a yelp of pain over my head. I wriggled free as soon as he hit the floor and retreated to stand in front of Aeden and my father.

"Ciran," Aeden said weakly, unable to get his feet under him.

"Stay there," I told him as Lorcan hauled himself up to came back at me with renewed fury.

"No one takes me for a fool," he snarled. "You and Eamon ruined me just like his father ruined mine, and I will not stand for it. I will not be defeated so easily, so you will pay for it with your brother's life, and when I'm done with him, I'll make an example of your whole family in front of your beloved High King. But you," he chuckled darkly and it was then I saw how crazed he was. No longer the cold calculating tyrant I had seen before. He was now driven by nothing but revenge and bloodlust. "You, Ciran, I shall keep alive to watch their demise, as I have watched the demise of my kin. And you shall serve me to the end of your days so that I can make sure you remember."

I blocked a blow, but was driven to my knees with the power of it, forcing myself not to let his words distract me. I had not realized just how powerful Lorcan was until this moment; even wounded and after all the events of the last few days, and I was exhausted and not in full health. To make matters worse, my hands were bleeding again from where I had torn the skin from them hanging over the cliff face, and I could feel them slipping on my sword hilt. I had to finish this fight before I lost it.

But I was finished with a well-aimed blow. Lorcan saw my distress, it had been his design, and aimed a blow toward the tip of my sword. The torque tore the hilt from my slippery grasp before I knew what was happening and he followed it up instantly with a blow that sliced me across the stomach. I fell backward, gasping in pain and slumped against the wall, curled around my wound.

"Ciran!" Aeden cried, trying to get his feet under him to make it to my sword. I saw my father stirring, but quickly turned my attention back to Lorcan who was pressing his sword under my chin, raising my head.

"It's over, Ciran. You're not worth my trouble. Admit defeat and I might make a quick end to you after all."

I winced as I groped for my sword or anything I could use as a weapon, my hand finding only stone floor. Aeden struggled to get to my weapon for me, but I knew he wouldn't find it in time. Lorcan shook his head.

"You Fianna are really pitiful," he said in disgust. "I wonder that you have any Fae blood at all." He raised his sword for the final blow and I readied myself to die. "Oh, that I had a worthy enemy."

A desperate cry sounded out, and a figure streaked through the door with a flash of steel and Lorcan arched his back with a cry of pain as a blade drove between his shoulder blades before being pulled out and, in a flashing arc, swept his head from his shoulders.

The Goblin's body slumped to the floor and with shock, I realized the figure standing behind it was Daegal, breathing so heavily it sounded like sobbing, as he held his sword, black with Goblin blood, still in a fighting crouch.

"Dae," I whispered, unable to move.

His eyes met mine, and the façade wore off. He dropped the blade with a clatter and threw himself into my arms, sobbing against my chest. Aeden crawled over to us and wrapped an arm around his shoulders.

"You saved us all, Daegal," he said gently. "You are a true Mac Cool and a true Finar."

"Lads," my father gasped out, hauling himself over to us and folding us all into his arms. I rested between him and Aeden for a moment, exhausted, hurt, and just enjoying the comfort, the smell of forge fire and steel that always clung to my father's clothes. It made me sleepy. I realized with a sudden fear that I was slipping away and pulled myself out of the dark blanket encircling me, back into a jangling world of pain. I clutched at Da's tunic as if to anchor myself to the world. Da's arm stiffened around me and his hand pressed against mine where I held it over my wound.

"Ciran," he said. "Hold on. Daegal, go get your mother. Now."

He extricated himself from the embrace, his eyes wide with horror, and my father and Aeden held me between them, pressing a blanket to my wound. Aeden put a hand on my cheek, leaning over me as I continued to fight the blackness, finding it only got harder and harder.

"Ciran, you'll make it, just hang on," he said. "Don't leave me now."

I tried to tell him I wasn't going anywhere, but I couldn't keep my eyes open and I wasn't entirely certain I was going to be able to keep that promise. My strength was slipping away with my blood that wouldn't stop flowing and I didn't want to fight it anymore.

"Ciran!" my father commanded. "Open your eyes!"

"Ciran!" Aeden added, his hand behind my head, raising it and shaking me. "Come on, little brother, don't do this!"

But that was all I could take, and I surrendered to the blackness that came for me, too tired to resist it another minute.

Chapter Thirty
Waking

Waking didn't feel quite real somehow. The world felt slow and peaceful, and something in that didn't seem right to me for it had been so hectic when I had fallen asleep for some reason, and this just wasn't how I expected to wake. I felt I was walking through a fog in the moorlands, one so thick it dulled all my senses. But finally I was able to drag my eyes open and saw a streak of morning sunlight falling onto my face, warming me. I could barely move, and finally realized it was because there was a heavy quilt laid over me. I moved my hand slowly up to the top of the blanket and began to pull it down so I could swing my legs over the side of the bed, but only got so far as to almost turn on my side before pain sparked across my belly, and made me stop.

I moved a hand down to my middle and found a thick bandage. Memories fought for attention in my clouded brain, but I could not quite grab the right one. I groaned instead, and then was startled by a voice right next to me.

"Finally awake?"

I turned to the other side of the bed that I had failed to look at and saw Aeden sitting up against the headboard with Daegal wrapped tightly in a blanket and resting against his chest. I finally remembered what had happened and saw that I was in the invalid room. I shifted but Aeden put a hand on my shoulder, to keep me still.

"Best not," he said kindly, but there was exhaustion and worry in his eyes too. "I will personally kill you myself if you open that wound again. Though I probably wouldn't get the chance. Mum had a time of it getting you closed up. You lost so much blood, Ciran." He stopped and the smile slipped from his lips. "If you weren't Fianna you would be dead."

I didn't know what to say to that. Instead I looked at my brothers, taking them in. I noticed that Aeden looked a bit better than the last time I had seen him. "How long have I been unconscious?"

"Three days," Aeden said accusingly, as if I could have helped it. "You had a fever until early this morning. Mum stayed with you for the worst of it, everyone took turns, but Daegal would never leave you—and I, of course, had little choice with my own hurts. I don't think Dae really slept from that time until now. He finally fell into an exhausted stupor after your fever broke." He stroked the boy's hair absently, pulling him closer in a protective manner that was so familiar to me it made me happy and comforted to see it. "I think he was afraid that if he slept he would dream," Aeden said quietly. "He did not want to see what we all feared."

"He killed Lorcan," I said, remembering it suddenly; the fantastic scene when I thought the Goblin would kill me and he didn't because my little brother had been there to protect me.

Aeden nodded. "Aye. Our little brother is a warrior and a bloody fine one to do what all of us could not." He laughed and Daegal stirred in his arms, blinking his eyes tiredly, until he saw mine open and then he gasped and slid out of Aeden's embrace over to me. He was about to throw himself at me, but then stopped, obviously afraid to do me harm. Instead, he knelt at my shoulder and smiled down at me.

"Ciran! You're okay!" was all he said.

I extricated a hand and reached up to clasp his shoulder. "Because of you."

He shook his head. "No, I just..."

"You killed Lorcan."

He nodded slowly and I couldn't quite read his expression. "I did what I had to. I..." he hesitated. "I dreamed that you were in trouble, so I came to rescue you. I couldn't let him take you away now that we were all back together again."

I tugged his hair fondly. "You are a fine warrior, Daegal. Bloody fine," I told him, echoing Aeden's words. "I will always trust you at my back and anyone with half a mind will do the same."

He smiled, then buried his face in my shoulder, sighing deeply. "I'm so glad you're okay." He mumbled and I shifted my arm to wrap around him.

"I am," I assured him. "So you should probably rest. I heard you haven't done a lot of that lately..."

But he was already snoring gently and I looked up at Aeden with a smile. He grinned back and ruffled my hair like he used to when I was only Daegal's age. "You too, little brother. Mum will be angry if we keep you up."

I wasn't entirely ready to protest, being exhausted myself, and when Aeden slid over against Daegal's back, and put his arm over him to place a hand protectively on my chest, I felt safer than I ever would and allowed myself to slip off again, to let my body heal.

The next time I woke, it was from the sound of the door opening and I opened my eyes tiredly to see my mother poking her head in. I smiled at her, and I saw her give me a relieved smile and a small sigh in return, hurrying into the room and closing the door behind her.

"Ciran," she whispered and bent to stroke my head, kissing me gently. I took her hand, but she slipped it free with a fond squeeze an instant later to see to my wounds.

"How do you feel?" she asked.

"About as well as is to be expected," I told her. "I'm fine as long as I don't try to move too much."

She tucked me in tightly again after checking my bandages and turned to Daegal and Aeden, both of whom still had some hold on me. She smiled and replaced Aeden's hand on my chest after she tucked me in and my brother opened his eyes and smiled up at Mum.

"It's all right now, Mum," he whispered. "We're all back and in one piece. Mostly anyway."

"Oh my boys," she sighed with love and weariness in the same breath and placed a fond hand on my and Aeden's heads while she bent over to kiss Daegal on the cheek. "I'm glad he's finally sleeping," she whispered.

"I told you he would," Aeden said.

"You too," she scolded and Aeden smiled gently but made no move to shift his position. I was glad, for I didn't want them to leave. I reached up and put my hand over his so he wouldn't be able to. My mother seemed to see that the three of us weren't quite ready to relinquish each other yet and she simply tucked Aeden and Daegal in as well.

"I'll be back with some broth later and we'll try you on that," she told me. "Until then, get some more rest."

"All right," I replied, not willing to protest now, even though I knew within a couple days it would grow wearing. Hopefully though, I would be up and about soon.

"Eamon will be by tomorrow probably," she told me. "He wanted to see you when you woke." She smiled. "It seems the other kings are quite shamed for what they said before."

I smiled at that. "Good for them. How is everyone else?"

"All the other prisoners are recovering. Most of them are still staying here. All your comrades have been helping watch over you too," she said. "Even Deaglan, much to your father's surprise." She laughed lightly and I smiled. "As for Caitlin, I think I will make something of a healer out of her yet." There was a twinkle in her eye that made my face feel a little heated. Aeden wiggled his fingers against my collarbone teasingly before I crushed them in a pitiful grip. I sighed and my mother kissed me again before she left.

"You'll get your strength back, *mo stór*. Do not fret about it."

I smiled, my eyes already closing and Mum plumped my pillows one last time before turning around and heading back out the door.

"Caitlin likes you," Aeden murmured into Daegal's hair and I opened my eyes to glare at him half-heartedly to see him fluttering his eyelashes teasingly at me.

"Remind me again why I missed you so much, big brother," I replied.

He shrugged. "Just thought I'd let you know because I figured you're too obtuse to see it. I've been gone for six months after all. Who knows what kind of bad habits you've formed when I haven't been there to correct them. Thinking only of me and not at all of the numerous pretty colleens around for the taking…"

"Just shut up," I moaned, throwing his hand off of me and wincing as the sudden movement pulled at my wound. He smiled and tugged my braid gently before resettling his hand over my heart.

"Hey, little brother, I missed you," he said for the first time and I turned to see the relief and happiness in his eyes as he rested his cheek on the top of Daegal's head. I leaned over so I could put my forehead against his and closed my eyes again with a deep sigh.

"I missed you too," I whispered shakily and he knocked my forehead gently before he pulled back and allowed me to fall asleep again. It felt good to know that I could actually rest with no thoughts of bad fortune, or lost family to worry about.

Chapter Thirty-One
A Chat With the King

The next morning I woke after having slept through the entire night and sat up on the bed with Aeden's help as I grudgingly allowed my mother to feed me oatmeal.

"I can probably manage it, Mum," I grumbled, annoyed by Aeden's silent laughing that I could feel from resting up against his chest, unable to sit up by myself.

"Hey, little brother, I had to deal with it too, it's only fair," he said.

"Both of you need to complain less and just let me look after you!" my mother scolded gently. "You're still very weak, Ciran, and I want you to save your strength for when Eamon visits you later."

"Yes, because eating porridge is so obviously an Olympic event," I replied blandly.

My mother made a face that was not very amused and finished feeding me. "At least I know you're feeling well enough for sarcasm." She shook her head and I thought I saw tears in her eyes as she reached out and put a hand on Aeden's face. "I forgot how horrible you two could be when you were together. It's been so long…"

"Hush, Mum," Aeden said gently, taking her hand and kissing it. "I told you, we're all okay now. Stop it. We can be much more horrible for you, I promise." He turned to me. "And you shirking your sarcastic duty as a Mac Cool while I was gone, shame on you! Who would Killian have to contend with?"

The door opened and my father came in, smiling as he saw Aeden and me sitting on the bed while my mother attempted to feed me another spoonful. I looked up and felt such a relief flow through me at seeing that smile. It had been so long since I had seen it last and I very nearly got teary myself, but…well, there wasn't time for that.

"Your sons are being unbearable," my mother said as she stood up.

"Perhaps he has only had enough of your gruel, woman," Da replied with a wink in our direction that made me grin.

Mum sighed in exasperation and shook her head, then kissed Da's cheek and left with the unwanted porridge. "See if you can talk some sense into them."

"Oh, I'll give it a go." Da stepped into the room and bent to kiss me on the forehead, stroking my mussed hair back fondly. "Stop grieving your mother," he told me sternly.

"I will, Da," I replied with a grin, rolling my eyes as he put the back of his hand against my cheek to check for fever. "Da, I'm fine; you're as bad as Mum."

"I know," he replied, pulling his hand back. "I just came to tell you that Eamon called and he's coming to see you. So you had best clean up a bit to receive your king. At least get a clean shirt on."

"Don't worry, Da, I'll make him presentable," Aeden

said, slipping from behind me and going over to a chair where a stack of clothes were situated. I noticed there was still a limp in his step, though from what injury, I wasn't sure. I hadn't seen all of them and I hoped it wasn't permanent.

Da went back to work and I was left to the not so kind ministrations of my older brother who combed my hair roughly and shoved a jumper over my head. He sat on the side of the bed to scrutinize me when he had finished and frowned thoughtfully.

"Not perfect, but as well as can be expected in your condition." I made a face at him. He smiled. "Don't worry, it will only be a month until you can get out of bed."

"You're not serious," I said. "I am Fianna you know."

"Hmm, I don't know, you might be adopted."

I groaned and leaned my head forward to rest against his side when there was a knock at the door. I sat up with a wince and the door opened, revealing my mother, smiling.

"Eamon's here," she replied and opened the door wider, admitting the High King. Aeden stood and headed toward the door to the veranda.

"I'll leave you two for a moment," he said with a smile. "I don't think I have much reason to be in on this conversation since all I did was sit around in a dungeon for six months." He closed the door behind him and, for the first time, I felt awkward in the presence of Eamon, even if he was without his circlet and wearing an old leather jacket and jeans, not to mention limping slightly from his own injury. He smiled at me and pulled up the chair sitting by my bed, which he sat on backwards, resting his arms against the back of it.

"How are you feeling?" he asked.

"I've been better," I told him wryly. "Can't say I've

actually been worse either. How about you?"

Eamon chuckled. "Between your mother and Killian it would seem I was dying on my feet, but I'm well enough. Admittedly a bit sore, though." I smiled in agreement as he continued. "I heard about Daegal's part in the fight. That is one brave lad. I am going to honor him for his bravery at the council meeting Friday."

I smiled proudly. "He's the only one who deserves it out of all of us."

Eamon shook his head, an amused smile on his lips. "You know that's not true."

"Of course my company must be rewarded," I told him, feeling a heat wash over my face, uncomfortable with the praise I knew was coming whether I liked it or not.

"You and your brother are infuriating, do you know that?" Eamon asked. "On one hand I have Killian who will willingly take the credit for everything, and then I have you and Aeden who it's like pulling teeth to get to accept even the simplest thank you. Like it or not, you are a *hero* Ciran, and you're going to have to deal with it because the entire country thinks the same."

"My company is who should get the praise," I said. "They had to put up with my mistakes, and they still got through it. I made so many of them."

"And you're saying I haven't?" Eamon asked with raised eyebrows. "Ciran, men are only as strong as their leader. He is the one who keeps them all together. I think I've finally learned that, and I hope that you have too, or you soon will. I know you hate taking credit, I appreciate that, but you've got to stand there and receive the honors you deserve, you and your brothers and your company. Will you do that for me? For the people of Ireland?"

"Of course, Eamon, just don't expect me to *like* it," I

told him with a smirk.

He grinned. "Don't worry, I'm only using you to rub it all in Proinsias' fat face. You do realize this is a once in a lifetime opportunity to pull something over on him, right?"

"Well, if you put it that way," I laughed, then winced as it pulled at my stitches. Eamon sobered.

"You saved my brother's life, Ciran. I'll never be able to thank you enough for that."

"It was nothing."

"No it wasn't," Eamon said firmly. "And you know it."

I didn't know what to reply to that. There wasn't anything I could say. I felt almost guilty saying it was nothing because that seemed to put less importance on Oran's life, even though I was sure Eamon knew I hadn't meant it like that. He was right, I was just going to have to swallow my pride and take the praise.

"How is Oran?" I asked to break the silence that had fallen between us.

"He's alright," Eamon replied. "We're all going to need time to recover fully from this, but he is glad to be home, and he can't stop talking about the brave brothers Mac Cool who came to his rescue countless times when he felt it was himself who should have suffered for the sake of his people. You and Aeden are the true heroes bringing everyone back. I can't say enough of how good it feels to know all my lost men have been returned to their families, safe and sound, as my brother has been returned to me. I feared so many times that someone would be left in grief but, mostly because of you and your company, Ciran, no one had to suffer such. Of that I firmly believe."

"And to me that's reward enough."

"Aye," Eamon sighed with a longsuffering smile. "I only wish politics saw it that way. Things are so convoluted now. But we have to 'please the peasants' as Killian loves to tell me."

I laughed genuinely this time even though it hurt. "All right then, let us 'please the peasants'. Friday you said? I'll see if Mum will let me out of bed. I would hate to have to go to the council wheeled in like a granny."

"Oh, I don't know, it would be much more impressive. Get you more sympathy, and think of the lasses you would have fawning over you. The brave wounded warrior. They can't get enough of that. You could have them all in the palm of your hand and have the pick of the crop, even before Deaglan."

I smirked. "Not the one I'd like to have; she's too sensible for that."

Eamon gave me a knowing look that soon turned into a slow smile, one dark eyebrow raised. "Oh, is that so? Hmm, well I think I might have something to share with my Captaen an Garda."

"Oh no you don't!" I warned. "It is *not* official. At least wait until I actually ask her out to dinner or something. Or until my wounds heal enough to defend myself."

Eamon laughed and tapped the side of his nose. "All right, your secret is safe with me." He stood up. "I really need to get back. There's a lot of things going on this week. I've actually appealed to the Goblin court and they are sending in a contingent to sign a new peace treaty. It seems that they will appoint a new leader, and he is more than willing to comply—again thanks to you."

"Me?" I asked, this time at a loss. "I really don't know what I did this time."

Eamon smiled. "Lorcan had no heir but his closest kin is Jarlath, the Goblin you captured. He told me that he wished to avoid what happened again and have peace—

real peace this time — between our peoples. He said that the nobility of you and your company even when it wasn't necessary made him realize that he didn't wish to fight us and make us or his people suffer as we did before. He was very happy to know that all of you made it back alive, if not unscathed, and with the prisoners to boot. We've been having many long discussions about it."

I smiled, feeling actual pride for this unknown accomplishment. I never would have guessed it.

"They will announce it formally on Friday, and the contingent of Goblins will be here by Monday to finish the deal with the proper documentation."

"I'm glad this all worked out," I said sincerely.

"So am I," Eamon said, reaching out to clap a hand on my shoulder. "Heal up, and get lots of rest. I'll see you Friday."

He left the room and I lay back, feeling rather tired, but happy. A month ago, I could never have pictured any of this happening but here I was making a national hero out of myself without doing anything but what I thought was right. I shook my head as I settled more comfortably into the bed and closed my eyes. Life was all rather funny at times, but at least it was never boring. I only wondered how many ridiculous adventures the future would bring.

Chapter Thirty-Two
Things Gone Unsaid

Only several days later, it was time to head to Tara for the official meeting about the mission. This time, however, I found myself almost more nervous than before. Before I had gone geared for battle, now it was for acclamation. I didn't do well with praise, never had, never would. But at least this thing mattered enough to me that I would be gracious in accepting it, even if I was embarrassed at the same time. Besides, getting the chance to rub our success in the council's face would be worth it. That is if I could simply manage to get myself dressed.

I winced as I stood in front of my armor stand, just trying to tie an extra bandage around my middle so the armor wouldn't rub my stitches. I shouldn't have been up by rights, but my mum had let me out of bed only for this and then I would likely have to go straight back. I wasn't complaining about my new freedom, but I had to admit I was still pretty sore and tired. I was just tying off the bandage when there was a sharp knock on the door and Aeden poked his head in.

"Hey," he said with a smile as he came into the room all the way. "Thought you might need some help."

"Thanks," I said gratefully. He was already dressed in his formal wear, his breastplate newly shined and the cloak ironed and swinging finely from his broad shoulders. And his sword—it was not his own, not *Glacadóir-Croí*, but Da's, the sword of our ancestors. I pointed to it with a smile and he grinned back.

"Da gave it to me," he said proudly. "Said it was time she was passed on. To a real warrior, he said." His expression turned sad. "I don't know that I am a warrior worthy of such a sword. I feel I didn't do much of anything but get tortured and scream."

"Please don't joke," I said sharply, not meaning to sound so harsh, but there was something in his tone that did not sit well with me, like he was making light of it and I was not going to let him do that. He had told me what Lorcan had actually been trying to do to him and the other prisoners. First, he had tried to get information out of them, but when he found them tight-lipped, he had thought up a new plan, the one he had hinted to me, but that I had never gotten the chance to hear. Something to put the prisoners to better use. He apparently had been trying to break Aeden to force him over to his side. He wanted to have turncoats serving him to help break down the structure of the Common Lands and who better to start with than the *Ceannasaí* of Na Fianna, the very man responsible for the safety of the people of Ireland? Oran had related the same story, saying he had been the original target, but Aeden had manipulated Lorcan into paying attention to him instead. So the Goblin King had set about to break my brother to make him one of his own to aid in the conquering of the kingdoms, and planned instead to use Oran as a valuable hostage when he had his new tools ready for battle.

"He was sure I would break, but he was wrong," Aeden had told me grimly after he had recounted it all to me. *"He promised us all freedom, immunity for our families and power when his plan succeeded. But none of us would take it. I don't know what he would have done if you had not come to rescue us when you had. Lorcan was getting weary of our defiance."*

I tugged my undershirt on viciously as I recalled that conversation—too viciously, I winced and Aeden came over and put a hand on my shoulder, turning me to face him.

"Ciran, I'm not joking, it's just…" he shrugged, "What am I going to do? What *can* I say? What happened happened, it's in the past now. Yes, there are still scars, but, that's life, and we live lives that are dangerous, and sometimes very life threatening but if we let that weigh on us, we would never get out of bed in the morning, so what can we do but let the past be past and push through to the next day?"

"Is that really healthy? Denying it all?" I asked suddenly, looking at the copious scars on his bare arms, some on his face and so many others covering the rest of his body under the armor he wore—one particularly deep scar on his thigh he had gotten in the attack that hadn't been treated properly and now gave him a slight limp that he would have for the rest of his life. His hair was still shorn, though he had gathered a tiny bit into a braid behind his left ear and I could see the scars on his neck disappearing under his collar. It had not escaped my notice that the brotherhood knot tattoo of Na Fianna on his left shoulder had been slashed through viciously so that it was hardly recognizable for what it was. The wounds might have healed for the most part, but the scars would always be there, both physical and mental, and I would never be able to not think of my brother chained in that cell, broken and bleeding without a hope of being rescued. Lorcan had been sure he hadn't broken Aeden, but I saw differently. My brother was broken sure enough, just not in the way the former Goblin King had wanted him to be. Only in the way that mattered.

"Don't look at me like that, Ciran," he said softly, but I could see the pain in his eyes as I tore mine away from his scars and met his own.

"I can't help it," I said sadly.

"Well, try," he said, not unkindly, but firmly enough that I knew he wasn't joking. "Because when you do, it almost makes me regret what I did and I can't do that." He took both my shoulders in his hands and shook me gently. "Yes, Ciran, it hurts, and, yeah, I have nightmares that I'm still there, that I am being tortured and my comrades are killed before my eyes. I wake up screaming, you know. I haven't told anyone, because it wouldn't make any difference. It's there, and I've got to live with it now. But you know what? I kept Oran safe while I was there, I kept the others safe, and people want to call me a hero, but I was really just a coward, and you know why? Because I couldn't stand to hear their screams, or the thought of the possibility of coming home without them. So you can't take that away from me with your own regret, okay *mo deartháir*? If you really want to help me, can you do that? Can *you* forget?"

I nodded, but felt weary and sad, like there was a huge weight upon my shoulders. Aeden bent to look into my lowered face and frowned worriedly.

"We haven't talked since we got back, you know. We

still have a little time," he said in suggestion, raising his eyebrows.

And just like that I knew what the weight on my shoulders was and I sank onto the edge of my bed and Aeden was there beside me and we sat shoulder to shoulder as I told him everything that had happened since he went missing, all through the mission, and like with Daegal, I did not leave a thing out, even added more for Aeden's benefit because I knew he would understand. He listened the entire time without saying anything and when I finally finished, he just smiled and reached out to put a hand on the back of my neck.

"It looks like my little brother grew up while I was gone," he said proudly with a hint of sadness.

"Sometimes I wonder," I said wryly but he only smiled broader.

"You know what?" he said. "You've hugged me plenty of times since you found me, but I haven't really hugged my little brother once, and you look like you need one." He held his arms out invitingly, like when I was little, and I was about to give him some sort of snarky comment, when I realized in a sad way how right he was, and I flung myself against his chest like I hadn't done for years and buried my face in the crook of his neck, ignoring the copper breastplate my cheek was resting against. He squeezed me against him, one hand carding through my hair before he pulled back and butted his forehead against mine.

"How's that?" he asked with a smile, and it was finally his old smile again—maybe a little older, a little more world-weary, but it was still Aeden's smile and that made me feel all the darkness that had been in me previously— that I didn't even know I had—fly away like a banshee's cry on the wind.

"Much better," I said truthfully as he stood up and dragged me with him.

"Just fixing my family one person at a time," He grinned, but it was almost sad.

"We should be the ones fixing you," I said. "I feel horrible."

He shook his head. "Don't worry about it. I need an occupation."

"Well, it helped, if that's any consolation."

"Good, because we need to leave," he said and I suddenly balked as I looked at the clock and saw the time. He helped me into my armor and then we rushed down the stairs to the others who were all waiting and out the door. Even Daegal was wearing a Fianna dress uniform — provided by Killian for the occasion — and I smiled proudly at him and slung my arm over his shoulders as I drew him over to the car. I would drive him and Aeden while everyone else went in the Rover. Daegal clambered into the backseat and Aeden settled into the passenger seat with a cautious glance toward me.

"I do hope your driving has improved since the last time you drove me around," he said.

I grinned at him. "Sorry, probably not." And stomped on the gas and sped out of the driveway while Daegal whooped and Aeden held on for dear life.

"Where is my Lotus anyway?" Aeden asked suspiciously.

"In the extra barn," I told him with a wink. "Don't worry, we didn't get rid of it. Though Tierney and I would occasionally take her for an outing just to keep her running smoothly."

"Didn't even wait until my corpse cooled," Aeden said,

and I winced slightly, still not over the fact that I almost lost him, but smiled for his benefit.

We made it to Tara Hall, unsurprisingly before my parents, and I saw Tierney and his family getting out ahead of us. He waved and we strode over to him. I clasped his forearm as he grinned.

"Good to see you up and about," he said.

"Same to your father," I said, smiling a greeting at Breandan who was coming over to greet us as well. He took Aeden and me by the shoulders and smiled down at Daegal who stood between us.

"Ciran, Aeden and Daegal, the heroes of the hour," he said. "It does my heart good to see such fine sons given to my dear friend."

I smiled. "It does me good to know I am worthy of such a father," I replied.

"Speak of the devil," Breandan said with a grin and strode off to my family's car that had just pulled up, yelling out some kind of insult to my father who returned it heartily. Tierney turned to his mother and sisters and bid them to follow him.

"Come on, let's go. We have to get Ciran to his finest hour." I made a face at him but he graciously ignored me.

As soon as we stepped into Tara Hall, we were set upon by Killian who separated us from our families with a neatness that was to be admired.

"Lady Brenna, please go with my lieutenant, O'Rourke, and he will find a place for you in the hall among all the fat politicians who have no right to be there." I saw Colin masking a grin as he helped Tierney's family off down the hall as Killian shoved us into a side passage.

"Go there, Eamon's waiting and he'll tell you what to do."

We hurried, not wanting to get on Killian's bad side on a day like this, and found the rest of our company, the prisoners, and Eamon himself, standing proudly in his full dress uniform and looking very kingly indeed; well on his way to being almost as majestic as my da. At his shoulder was Oran, decked out as a prince of the High Seat and while he still looked a little thin and pale, he was smiling and the grin only widened when he looked over and saw us.

"Ciran! It's good to see you, how are you feeling?"

"I'm fine, Oran, how are you?" I asked, clasping his forearm with a nod.

"Attention Mac Cool's company, your leader is here, let's all give him a hand and embarrass him!" Tierney called out and to my chagrin, all my men lined up and gave me a hand, soon joined by everyone else in the room. I smiled but felt a flush on my cheeks as Tierney yanked on my braid with a wicked grin.

"Yes, yes, thank you; you know this is practically treason while the King and prince are standing here, don't you?"

"Oh, yes, and we wouldn't want to have to execute you all before you win your acclamations," Eamon said with a grin and finally stepped over to my brothers and me, greeting us each in turn.

Tierney's father was the last one in the door, followed by Killian and two others who were somewhat a surprise to me, but a good one.

"Ciran Mac Cool," one called as I turned to greet the two Goblins, glad of the chance to do so in friendship and without the chains.

"Jarlath, Gorlan, I'm glad to see you," I said genuinely, as I clasped forearms with them. They were both smiling, and I took in their fresh appearance, dressed in silver breastplates and deep blue cloaks with silver trim. I motioned to the ensemble. "This is good, I like it. Not nearly as dour as your cousin's wardrobe."

Jarlath grinned. "Oh, don't worry, there will be plenty of changes being made once I get back to the palace. Your smiths and tailors helped us with these." He turned around and saw Aeden standing protectively at my side and gave him a respectful nod, holding out a tentative hand.

"Your brother is a fine warrior, as you are," he said. "You should be proud of him."

"I am," Aeden said fondly and finally took Jarlath's proffered hand. "As should you be of your brother from what I have heard."

Gorlan grinned and Jarlath put an arm around his shoulders. "He'll be my councilor and my captain of the guard. I think we will be able to keep office civilly and peacefully."

"I believe you will," Eamon said, striding up. "Now, Killian's motioning for us to get a move on, so we had better do so. I believe everyone is waiting. Let's go."

He pulled Oran with him and the rest of us followed, to an antechamber off the throne room where Killian halted us.

"Wait until Eamon calls you," he said.

Aeden suddenly looked around and frowned, turning to me. "Where's Daegal?"

I looked around too, but didn't see him anywhere.

"What's wrong?" Caitlin whispered.

"I can't find Daegal," I told her.

"I'll go look for him," Aeden said.

"No," I replied. "I'll do it. If I'm not back before

Eamon calls us, send someone to get me."

Before he could protest I was walking back down the corridor and before long, I found Daegal sitting beside a suit of armor, underneath a wall hanging, his knees pulled up to his chest and his face pressed into them. I sighed and lowered myself gingerly down next to him, bumping his shoulder with mine.

"Hey, what's wrong?" I asked him.

He took a shuddering breath and finally raised his head to look at me, his face streaked with several tears.

"I don't...want to go out there," he said. "I—I don't like it."

"Why?" I asked. "I don't like it either, you know I hate it, but we're doing it for Eamon, because that's what people want to see. They want to see the people responsible for stopping the Goblin wars. Everyone has lost someone to them, and it's a big deal now that they're over for good. I know it's stupid, but that's how people are. They just want a chance to thank us for it and then we can all forget it tomorrow. And you, you were the one who really ended it all together when you killed Lorcan."

Daegal's face crumpled and he buried his face in his knees again. "That's the problem. I killed him. I don't think anyone should get an award for killing someone. No matter how bad he was. I just did it to save you and Aeden and Da, I don't want credit for it!"

"Oh, Dae," I said gently, reaching out and pulling him against my chest. I felt instantly guilty. In all that had happened, I had only viewed my little brother as the hero of the hour, but I forgot the fact, as I sometimes did, that he was only eleven years old and he was only just training with his sword, and certainly hadn't been in or even seen a real battle. I had foolishly thought he was all right, we all had, and now we were the only ones to blame while my brother suffered through it silently like he always did.

"Daegal," I said, pushing him away from me so I could look at him. "Listen. I want you to tell me what was going through your head when you killed Lorcan."

He took a shuddering breath. "I—I thought he was going to kill you. I knew he was, and I couldn't let that happen. I—I saw it in my dream and I only hoped I wasn't going to be too late."

I brushed away the new tears and smiled at him. "There, see? That is what drives every warrior. The need to protect his brother in arms; whether they are his blood brother or otherwise. Every time Tierney and I go out on a mission, we are always prepared to take a life for the other. It's a hard thing, and it's certainly the hardest part of being a warrior, especially when you find out that your enemy is just as human as you are." I smiled slightly at him in encouragement. "But sometimes there are people who are very cruel, and who need to be taken down. And Lorcan was like that. If you had not stopped him that night, he would have started a new war, you can be sure of it, and thousands of lives would have been lost instead of just one. It's hard, Daegal, I know it's hard, but you have to think about the lesser of the evils sometimes. And remember that protecting your brothers on the field of battle always comes first. Do you understand?"

He nodded and I pulled him against my chest again, hugging him tightly. "We've all been through a lot, Dae. We're still picking up the pieces. But today is a new day, and many good things will happen before the sun sets, and we just need to figure out how to wake up and keep going, and forget the past, or learn to live with it. I am bloody proud of you, brother, and I owe you my life, and that is something I'm not going to let you forget." I pulled him back and saw he was smiling, rubbing the tears from his face. "Are you ready to go and receive your prize now?"

He nodded and stood to help me up onto my feet as I winced, my wound protesting. I turned around as I heard someone walking down the hall and saw it was Aeden.

"Everything okay?" he asked, a worried expression on his face.

I smiled. "Yeah, Everything's fine."

"Good, because Eamon's called us. We have to go."

We hurried back down the hall to receive the future that awaited us.

Chapter Thirty-Three
Honored

"And it is with great honor that I am able to present to you today, the company of Ciran Mac Cool, the brave warriors who were responsible for rescuing the lost patrol, and ending the tyrannical reign of King Lorcan. And on top of that, they have brought back my brother, the official heir to my kingdom until the time I have a son of my own." There was a hearty applause as Eamon smiled over in our direction and I forced a smile on my face for the crowd. I'll admit it was easier when I saw Proinsias' face looking like he had sucked on a lemon. I might have even winked at him cheekily.

"But we must not also forget the wounded heroes we lost who are now returned to us," Eamon said and the former prisoners filed out, looking far better than they had when we rescued them. Eamon gestured to my brother. "Most of all, the award of bravery goes to Aeden Mac Cool *Ceannasaí de Na Fianna* who through his bravery that he himself would call stubbornness, the others, and most importantly my brother, were kept from the worst of it."

He turned to glare out at the gathered people. "If any man does not honor this warrior and belittles his sacrifice, you should know that you will never be so wrong." Aeden ducked his head as there was a respectful applause and I saw my mother wiping away a tear before she quickly covered it with a proud smile. Eamon turned back to Killian who gave Daegal a nudge out with the rest of us.

"But there is also a third Mac Cool brother who has distinguished himself on the field. May I present Daegal Mac Cool, Vanquisher of King Lorcan."

There was a mass applause from everyone as Daegal stepped out and looked back at Aeden and me as we gave him encouraging smiles before he went to stand in front of Eamon.

"Thus the first medal shall go to him," Eamon stated. "A token to show that these are my finest warriors, the finest men and woman in the country, and they above all deserve to bear the mark of the High Seat of Tara." He turned to Oran who held a tray of medals and took one to put over Daegal's head, then turned to do the same to me and the rest of us. I looked down at it, a simple golden medallion on a green ribbon that bore the arms of the High Seat on them. I looked proudly upon my comrades and gave them a silent nod. I could have said any number of poetic words, but that seemed like all that was needed. And indeed, after we had been through so much together, words were not necessary.

After Eamon had handed out the medals, he turned back to the crowd that was still applauding our heroic doings.

"I would like to offer Ciran the honor of officially recognizing his company as the Company of Ciran Mac Cool, which is how this brave group should now legally be known to everyone in the kingdom."

This time I really did feel pride swell in me. It was one of the greatest honors of a warrior to have a company actually nationally recognized. That was only reserved for those who had done great deeds and I suppose we had. It meant that, while attached to Na Fianna, we also acted as our own group and would have to be officially recognized as such in all the kingdoms—even by Proinsias. I looked upon my comrades, my company, with pride and they smiled back at me with a deep respect that I would cherish, and loyalty I knew I could count on whenever we went into battle again. I turned from them to look at my father and saw the smile on his face and had never felt so light and proud in all my life.

"But we are not only here today to celebrate our mighty warriors," Eamon continued. "We are also here to form a bond that we hope will last for centuries. And so I am glad to welcome to my court today, Prince Jarlath, heir to the Goblin Throne of the new Royal Line of Clochslébhe."

Jarlath and Gorlan stepped out and stood by Eamon. There was applause from the gathered people but it was still somewhat wary. I knew it would be a while yet before they truthfully believed that the Goblins meant us no harm. But I had utter faith in Jarlath and I hoped that the feeling would be widespread after a few more years of peace.

Eamon motioned them over to a table standing off to one side where there was a document waiting. He bent and signed it with a flourish then waited while a scribe poured wax onto it and he pressed his signet ring into the blob of wax. Jarlath did the same, and Eamon turned to the gathered kings and queen to one side of the hall.

"I ask that you all sign this in good faith," he said. "It

is not compulsory, but there is little reason to refuse, as I hope you see."

Queen Niamh was the first to step forward to sign and stamped her seal with a flourish. "Well, I for one am happy to have peace again, and I do pray that it will be a lasting one." She turned back to her fellow rulers with a glare. "Well, come on then, you louts, sign the bloody document!"

That got them all off their tails, even Proinsias who didn't look particularly happy about it, but then, he never looked happy about anything. Once everyone had finished, Eamon turned to clasp hands with Jarlath over the document.

"May our people fight no longer," he said.

"And our peace last till end of time," the Goblin added and this time the applause was more sure.

Eamon turned back to everyone. "Now that all the business has been settled, we shall celebrate in the way of our ancestors."

And that got the loudest cheer yet. I turned back to my companions and grinned.

"Well? To the feast!"

The going away feast at our house had been grand, but this was ten times as huge and raucous and loud, and it was so joyous, for we had everything back together this time, everyone back with us, sitting at our sides and laughing at the same jokes. I looked over fondly to see my and Tierney's fathers laughing uproariously with their own shield brothers, acting just like us, the younger set, and perhaps more rowdy to boot. Padraig was sitting between Riordan and Keevan and trying to keep them from flinging food at each other, but finally gave up and simply joined in.

Deaglan was, quite surprisingly, not attempting to flirt with any of the copious girls looking around the table at us warriors with sly grins and cheery winks, but was sitting with his parents and his sister, his father's arm casually around his shoulders and a contented smile on his face. He caught my eye as I looked over at him and raised his glass. I raised mine back and turned to see Killian, Flagan and Caitlin, all arguing happily with each other. Maeve sat next to Killian, holding his hand in hers and grinning happily at the chaos. Eamon and Oran were sitting at the head of the table, chatting happily with Jarlath and Gorlan who were sitting next to them and the sight made me happier than anything else.

I had Tierney on one side and Aeden on the other and I was happy to stuff myself and drink perhaps a little too much until I couldn't take another bite or drop. Tierney, groaning as he rubbed his full stomach, turned to me finally with a grin.

"Well, it seems I'm bound to you now, brother, for better or worse. Your own company! Very impressive!"

I grinned back at him. "Yes, you're mine now, so no mercenary work for you. It would be against the law, I'm afraid."

He wrinkled his nose at me and nibbled a piece of bread. "I think we need something to show that we are all part of Ciran's Company. Maybe a group tattoo, or a torc? You should think on that."

"I will," I said. "Maybe Riordan and Keevan can make us funny hats."

Tierney nodded sarcastically. "Yeah, that will be great. All our enemies will die laughing before we even get to draw our blades."

"And the ones who survive will have to suffer the

wrath of the berserk brothers who don't like their knitting talents belittled."

"It's crochet! I crochet, not knit!" Keevan yelled across the table and almost the entire room burst into laughter at his loud outburst. Padraig patted him kindly on the shoulder.

"Good going brother, you just let out your dark secret," he said as Keevan reddened as bright as his hair and looked like he wanted to duck under the table, especially after his mother leaned over to kiss his cheek.

I laughed and raised my glass to clash against Tierney's. "To my company. The biggest band of misfits Ireland ever saw."

I was feeling a sudden need to process the happenings of the day so I excused myself to a knowing look from Aeden and strode out to the balcony off the dining hall.

The sound faded a bit as I stepped out into the fresh air and leaned against the railing, breathing deeply and smiling to myself. I was content now. Everything had been taken care of, all the problems, even the ones I wasn't sure even existed, had been solved, and I could finally, at long last, take a real rest for the first time in six months.

I heard a footstep behind me and turned to see Caitlin standing there, smiling, and looking incredibly beautiful in her green gown sans breastplate, the new golden medallion resting against her chest.

"Are you all right?" she asked me.

"I'm perfectly fine; more so, in fact," I told her sincerely. "Just trying to process it all. Not really having much luck. Tomorrow maybe."

She came over to me and leaned against the railing at my side, our shoulders touching. "It's been a long few weeks," she said. "I never would have thought we would do so much; have so much happen to us. And look at us now, Ireland's greatest heroes. Before long they'll be writing songs about us."

I laughed and she looked up at me with a mischievous smile. We were silent for a moment as I looked into her green eyes, and then I suddenly reached out and put a hand over hers.

"Caitlin, I was wondering if, maybe now that it's all over, you might like to go out to dinner sometime. Just you and me."

She smiled wider. "I think I'd like that, Ciran. Just come get me when you feel like it."

I grinned and we both turned our attention to the landscape. She finally turned back to me with a sly look. "Oh, I thought it might be nice if I did this for real finally." And before I knew what she was doing she had leaned forward and pressed her lips briefly against mine before pulling back, a twinkle in her eye.

"It is rather nice when I actually get the chance to enjoy it," I told her and leaned forward to kiss her myself for a lot longer, when someone cleared their throat behind us, and I turned to see Tierney standing there with a smirk on his face.

"Sorry to interrupt, but they're about to start the dancing, and I figured you two love birds might like to get in on it. And out of Killian's line of sight. If your wound will permit that is, oh noble leader mine." He grinned. "I won't tell the Captaen what I saw, if I can have the honor of at least one dance."

"I'd be obliged," I replied with a matching smirk as I bowed courteously. "I'll put you on my card." And then I strode past him with Caitlin on my arm, laughing.

"I hate you," Tierney said as he followed us back inside.

I grinned back and took a deep sigh of contentment. Yes, things were definitely brighter now, and I only hoped they would get brighter still.

Chapter Thirty-Four
Dispersing the Shadows

That night I jerked awake, bolt upright in bed, my chest heaving and sweat sticking my shirt to me and soaking the bandages that still bound my middle. I ran a shaky hand through my hair and tried to dispel the images still fresh in my mind. It took me a few moments to remind myself that Aeden was just down the hall, not being tortured in Lorcan's dungeon; not needing my help. I took a deep breath and peeled off my shirt, shrugging into a new one as I slipped out of my room silently and walked across the hall. I hesitated at the door. I didn't want to wake him, I knew it was stupid and childish, but I just needed to see him. To make sure he was still there.

I pushed the door open as quietly as I could and slipped inside, heaving an involuntary relieved sigh as I saw my older brother sleeping on his bed and breathing deeply. He groaned suddenly and jerked in his sleep, his jaw clenched. I stepped over to the bed to rearrange his blanket but he seemed to sense my presence and lurched awake with a muffled cry, shrinking away from me.

"Aeden?" I inquired, shocked by his reaction.

He relaxed, almost slumping back onto the bed as he heard my voice. He sat up and rubbed his eyes as I took a seat on the side of his bed.

"Ciran, what are you doing here? It's been a long time since you came to me with your nightmares." He attempted a chuckle but it stuck in his throat.

I swallowed hard. "I wish it were just the childhood nightmares of monsters that brought me here."

He looked up at me and a sad expression washed over his face. "Ciran, you know it's all right. I'm here, and I'm not leaving." He sighed again and slumped forward, his elbows resting on his knees. "It's going to take a while to get over this fully. I know. You know. That's just the way it is. You can't expect everything to just go away. The mental scars last long after the physical ones fade."

I nodded slowly and leaned forward, my head resting against his side. He put one hand on my shoulder and tousled my hair with the other. "There's no shame in it," I whispered to him, thinking it odd that I was the one who had come to him for comfort but was actually the one who ended up giving it. His hand faltered, but he didn't stop entirely. "There's no shame in being afraid and admitting it. It makes us stronger in the end."

I couldn't see his face, but I could sense the tight-lipped smile he was giving me. Pretending everything was okay when we both knew it wasn't. "We'll just have to get each other through it," I told him. "And I *will* get you through it, brother. I will. I promise you."

"When did you become the big brother, Cir?" he asked gently, shaking my shoulder.

I sat up and looked at him. "When you were the one who needed rescuing and I was the one who vowed to come find you."

He smiled, tears in his eyes and then grabbed my shirt and clutched me to his chest, burying his face in my shoulder. I held him just as tightly, feeling him shake, how frail his body still was, and knowing that I had been wrong. It wasn't over yet, but we would be damned before we let it beat us and we would get through it together or not at all.

The door opened again, and we didn't even look up when a pair of smaller arms joined the embrace and simply gathered our little brother into this private moment of weakness that would never leave this room and that we needed before we could move on and confront our ghosts head on to disperse the last of the shadows that still lingered.

Finally Aeden pulled away, and offered a teary smile, kissing Daegal on the head. "Okay, that's enough of that. Now I know we're not going to sleep for the rest of the night, so Ciran, go pick a movie and Daegal, get the carton of ice cream and three spoons."

We hurried off, laughing as we gathered our items and spent the rest of the night watching movies and just enjoying each other's company and the simple fact that we *could*.

I can only imagine the sight it afforded our mum the next morning when she came to check on us who had only gone to sleep a few hours previously, cramped on Aeden's bed with the laptop and an empty ice cream carton. Thinking of it, I imagined her fond smile and a small shake of her head before she closed the door and let us sleep. Whether or not all the shadows had run away that night, the three of us felt stronger for the fact that together, we would never let them beat us. For we were Mac Cools, and

we dined with kings and warriors, and nothing was going
to bring us down easily.

Epilogue

Niall Mac Cool stood at the window, a fond smile playing over his lips as he watched Aeden, Ciran and Daegal sparring together. Every time he saw them together, new relief and joy sparked in his heart, and he felt that despite a few scars that would always be there, things had not changed from the time before the patrol had been captured and he thought he had lost Aeden forever. During that horrific time, there was nothing he wouldn't have done to see just this again, and he wanted to weep with joy and thanks that he was able to witness it.

It was undeniable that there were brothers and then there were brothers. It was true that it might not have been healthy by normal parenting standards to encourage the exclusive trio, but he knew that they shared a bond that went beyond that of blood. Theirs was a bond that ran deep, as if they were triplets, inseparable, and he knew that any attempt at separating them would go poorly. Even Aoife had expressed concern to him in the past, afraid there were separate loyalties between them and their other siblings, but Niall had brushed off her concerns, unable to explain to her why. Only that he knew, because he had been the same with his brother.

Nollaig had been his world, his little brother, and losing him had hurt too much for words. It had hurt far more than losing his sword hand, both physically and mentally. His hand was not all he had lost that day. He felt as if he had lost part of his soul. No, he could not have borne seeing Ciran and Daegal suffer that. And he hoped they and Aeden would never have to.

There was a quiet step behind him and a hand slid into his as Aoife came to watch with him, a fond smile on her lips.

"We did well with them, didn't we," she said.

He smiled and bent to kiss her on the side of the head. "Yes, we did."

"Will they be all right?" she asked after a while, a little worry finding its way into her voice.

"They will," Niall replied. "They have each other."

She squeezed his hand tighter and they both smiled as they watched Aeden and Ciran tackle their younger brother on the ground, tickling him until he dropped his sword, shouting protests before he succumbed to helpless giggles.

"They'll be perfectly fine now," he added and pulled his wife away from the window as the three brothers continued their sparring. The shadows had gone now, and life could go on, and despite the horrors of the past, the Mac Cools would forge a new future and build it on the bonds of family loyalty and love. Niall knew that there was nothing that could break them now.

The End

Extras and Pronunciation Guide

Names and Pronunciations

The Mac Cools

Niall (Ny-all)
Aoife (Eva)

Aeden (Traditional spelling of "Aiden")
Maeve (Mayv)
Ciran (Keer-an)
Finbar (phonetic)
Daegal (Day-gal)
Sean

Nollaig (Nole-ag) (desceased)
Ceannt (Gaelic spelling of "Kent")

Fionn (Fin)
Oisin (O-shen)

The Royal Family (O'Brians)

Raymond (deceased)
Maolisa (mail-issa) (deceased)

Eamon (A-mon)
Oran (phonetic)

The Mac Mornas

Breandan (Brendan)
Brenna (phonetic)

Meghan (Gaelic spelling of "Megan")
Tierney (Teer-nee)
Aednet (Ey-nit)
Cara (phonetic)

Seamus (Sham-us)

The Mac Dairmuids

Darragh (Dare-ah)
Cliona (Clee-ona)

Deaglan (Gaelic spelling of "Declan")
Deirdre (Deer-dra)

The Crimnals

Alroy (deceased)
Iona (I-oh-na)

Riordan (Reer-dan)
Paidraig (Paw-rag)
Keevan (phonetic)

The O'Haras

Killian (phonetic)
Flagan (phonetic)
Caitlin (alternate spelling of Katelyn)

Lesser Kings and Queen

Proinsias of Connaught (Prawn-she-as)
Niamh of Munster (Nee-am)
Cahal of Ulster (phonetic)
Dillon of Leinster (phonetic)
Tomas of Mide (phonetic)

Goblins

Lorcan Faoicnoc (Lore-kan Fowk-knock)
Jarlath Clochslébhe (phonetic- Clock-shlee-va)
Gorlan (phonetic)

Cronin (Kron-in)
Fallogh (Fawl-low)

Sword Names

Cuimhne — Memory
Fuil-Amhránaí — Bloodsinger
Glacadóir Croi — Lifetaker
Lucht Cuardauthe Fola — Blood Seeker
Tuairim — Thought

Irish Dictionary

Airdrígh — High King
Athair — Father
Beag — little
Beag amháin — little one
Beag nathair — little snake
Beart de réir ár mbriathar — Actions to match our thoughts
Captaen an garda — Captain of the Guard
Ceannasaí — Commander
Cinn A Tháinig Roimh — Ones that Came Before
Dearthair — brother
Deirfiúr — sister
Deirfiúr leanbh — baby sister
d'Éirinn! Le haghaidh ár deartháireacha! — For Ireland, For our brothers!
Do Mhórgacht — Your Majesty
Fada beo ar an rí — long live the king
I cairdeas — in friendship
Laochra — warriors
Laoch ha hÉireann — Warrior of Ireland
Máthair — mother
Mo Chara — my friend
Mo dearthair leanbh — my baby brother
Mo fuaime — my son
Mo Stor — my darling
Mo thighearna Mac Cool, iarraim cead isteach... — My Lord Mac Cool, I request admittance into your house. I come as a friend and apologize for the sake of my ancestors and the wrongs they performed in the past.
Nathair — snake
Tá tú sceith láibe agus cad faoi carraigeacha — You spawn of filth and what lies under rocks
Tiarna — lord

A Look Into the World

The world of *Blood Ties* is a cross between the times we live in now (post 2000) and what Ireland would have been like in the pre-medieval days of the High Kings of Ireland, indeed the time period that the original tales of Na Fianna came about and were set in. I wanted to take modern technology and comforts and introduce to them the society of ancient Ireland—one of great warriors, noble kings, and of course, a small dose of magic. Even with just the historical texts, the Celtic peoples have always seemed slightly fantastical to me, and it's mostly their folklore that does it. A world of Faeries and mythology that has always fascinated me, and I've wanted to write about it for a long time, but thought it would be interesting to take a modern spin on things.

So the Ireland of *Blood Ties* as well as the rest of the world functions pretty much like ours. They have fast cars, computers, and television shows—and of course modern plumbing. The one thing they don't have is firearms. I liked the idea of keeping the traditional weapons because it adds a more fantasy element and proves that true warriors do not need firepower to come out on top of a fight. Pretty much anything we have, they do too.

The society they live in mirrors a medieval one, so there are certain ideals that come through. First and foremost, I think some of you will probably ask why there are no female Fianna. Simply because there weren't originally. But are girls still warriors in this society? Obviously. As Caitlin says, there is a whole school dedicated to female warriors. Ireland has produced many amazing female warriors and I wanted to pay homage to that, but will there ever be actual female Fianna? No.

On the subject of schools and normal society, yes, they do have normal grade schools that children attend. Candidates for Na Fianna on the other hand, like Ciran and his friends, did their grade school until they were thirteen and then went to the Fianna training academy where they would be put through the traditional tests of a Fianna warrior. Though, they still had their maths and other lessons on the side.

History and Other Races

History

Figuring out the history of this world was one of the trickier parts of writing this alternate universe, and for the most part you're just going to have to take it at face value. Obviously, because my Ireland is still functioning as it did in the ancient times, and is obviously not a democracy, things are already different right off the bat. I also mentioned things like the Nepoleonic War and the World Wars, so yes, things did still mostly happen, just maybe not the same way people expect. Plus, my Ireland has had its own wars to deal with, namely the Goblin Wars that have been going on for centuries. Other historical people are mentioned as well, like Brian Boru who was a High King of Ireland back in the Dark Ages. Eamon is related to him as well, being an O'Brian (where the name originates). While not the same line of kings that ruled when Fionn Mac Cool of legend was head of Na Fianna, it ties it back into the actual history of Ireland. As for how everything fits into the history we all learned in school, I think it's best if you decide that for yourself.

Ireland and the Faelands

My Ireland is split up into the five kingdoms of ancient Ireland with a king or queen leading them acting more as lords as they still answer to the High King, which is

Eamon. These kingdoms are Ulster, Munster, Connacht, Leinster, and Mide, and then the Capital City of Tara where the Hall Eamon rules from sits on the legendary Hill of Tara, overlooking my fictional Tara Village. While the kingdoms have the same names, however, they do not have the same geography. My Ireland is separated into the Faelands and the Common Lands. The Faelands are the upper third of Ireland while the Common Lands take up the rest, the five Kingdoms filling that space to the Southern Coast to the Borderlands up against the Faelands. The Faelands likewise are home to three Fae Courts: the Goblin Court up in the far north residing in their underground palaces, the Seelie Court of the Light Fae in the East (the allies of the humans) and the Unseelie Court of the Dark Fae in the West. Between the three Courts is the free land where all other Fae creatures reside, at least those who are not living among the humans in the Common Lands.

England and Scotland

England, like Ireland in this story, is also a High Kingship with multiple lesser kings in the old kingdoms, very much like it was in the days of Arthurian legend, in fact, the High King is a descendant of Arthur himself. Apart from that, yes there is a London and chip shops, and double decker buses, and everything you have come to expect from English culture as a whole, much like in the Ireland of this story. There was a mention of the Arthurian knights, how they attend a university in Camelot where they learn knightly duties, but are more like glorified jocks and frat boys and Ciran wasn't really lying—however, that is a story for another time.

Scotland is mentioned in this series as being wild and a dangerous place to be, with Fae living among the humans and oftentimes killing them. They don't have a king so much as lairds of the different provinces, which are usually well run despite the common feuds that crop up on occasion. You may very well get to see later on what this Scotland is really like.

Scandinavia and The Rest of the World

It's mentioned in this story that Riordan went to Norway to an academy where he learned to be a berserker, so I'll talk a little about the Scandinavian culture in this book. In the same vein as my Ireland, they are a culture based heavily in the folklore of the actual countries, which means, trolls and dwarves and modern Vikings—though ones more like the Fianna warriors and not ones who typically go raiding. Berserkers are trained to control their abilities, and wear a Thor's hammer pendant to show their rank — and they do have to be licensed.

As for the rest of the world, take your guess. Each culture would be partly modern, partly ancient and contain elements of their folklore and mythology. Use your imaginations! I only wish I had time to explore them all.

The Lore

Not only is the Ireland of *Blood Ties* steeped in the ancient traditions of Ireland and the folklore of the country, it's also based off of the legends of Fionn Mac Cool and Na Fianna. When I set out to write this book, I found this harder than I thought. There are so many versions of the Fianna Cycle that even branch out into more 'children's stories' that have no correlation to the cycle in my mind, like one where Fionn Mac Cool is actually the giant who built the Causeway. Thus, I decided to stick with one source apart from the basic cycle and that was mostly Rosemary Sutcliff's retelling of the legends. I highly suggest you read it because is it well written, and is an enjoyable collection of tales, and a very nice retelling of the old stories that I only really touched on in this book.

Apart from the tales of Na Fianna, there is a lot of Fae lore that went into this book too (more of which you will see later in the series.) I wanted to incorporate traditional Faery lore into a modern, and really everyday setting. One big inspiration for me really was the song "Faeries Stole My Keys" by Emerald Rose—that was really the feel I wanted for this story. Making Faeries seem like a normal fixture of everyday life. There are brownies who clean your house and if you don't give them cream or honey they may get angry and turn into a boggart, and decide to tie your hair to the bedposts. Or you may have pixies in the garden, and you should always check the swimming holes in the summer before the kiddies have fun because there might be a kelpie or nixie there up to no good. As for the Faery Courts I wanted them to be more like the traditional Fae, stately, warriors, and sometimes, in the case of the Unseelie very dangerous and conniving. These are the Faeries from the old stories like Tam Lin and Spencer's *Faery Queen* the ones Tolkien based his elves off of. In this book the Seelie or the Light or Summer Court are allies of the human kingdoms of the Common Lands, but the Unseelie and the Goblins are not.

I think writing this book I had the most fun coming up with how to make goblins different. Obviously, they have a sort of tainted reputation as ugly slimy creatures who live in caves and do harm to people. But I wanted to portray them as more human and up with the other Fae Courts, though not attached to either, and while they do have grey skin, and pointed ears, they still look human and can be just as attractive as elves, thank you very much! I didn't want them to be monsters but just like everyone else. They're considered Lesser Fae by the other Courts because they have no magic properties. They cannot use glamour, though they are brilliant architects as is seen by their palaces. I hope everyone enjoyed this hopefully new take on goblins as well.

Sausage and Lentil Soup

Ingredients:

2 cups beef stock plus two cups water (lentils take up a lot of water so you'll need extra)
1lb ground sausage meat (I used original Jimmy Dean's. Alternatively, you can use ground beef)
1 cup uncooked lentils
3 to 4 potatoes
Half a head of cabbage
1 cup frozen corn
1 Tbs dehydrated onions (or fresh if you prefer)
1 tsp basil and time
1/2 tsp curry powder
1/4 tsp ground red pepper
Black pepper to taste

Instructions:

Cook sausage meat until browned add dehydrated onions while cooking. Add oil if needed. Once meat is cooked, pour in beef stock and another cup and a half of water then add spices. Once everything is stirred up, pour in lentils. Cooking instructions for the lentils should be on the bag, but usually takes about 20 minutes to cook fully.

While cooking, dice potatoes and cut the cabbage. You can also add carrots and/or peas if you wish. You may need to add more water to the broth when the lentils are cooking, that's up to you whether you want a thicker or thinner soup. Add potatoes and corn after about fifteen minutes, then continue to cook the soup for another fifteen at a low boil, or until the lentils and potatoes are soft. Add the cabbage at the end so it doesn't get overcooked.

Serve with Irish soda bread and cheese. Serves about 8

Lady Mac Cool's Apple Muffins

Muffin Batter

3/4 cup milk
1 egg
1/4 cup applesauce
1/4 cup sour cream
2 cups floor
1/3 cup brown sugar
3 teaspoons baking powder
1/2 teaspoon salt
1 1/2 teaspoon cinnamon
1/2 teaspoon nutmeg
1 medium/large apple (Macintosh work best)

(For Crumble)
Mix brown sugar, cinnamon (to your specifications of how much crumble you want) and add a tablespoon of flour. Add nuts if desired.

Mix milk, egg, applesauce, and sour cream together in mixer. Sift together dry ingredients (flour, sugar, salt, cinnamon, nutmeg, and baking powder) and then pour it into the milk mixture and mix thoroughly.

Apple Mixture

In another bowl, shred the apple (peeled) and add two tablespoons of butter or margarine, 1/8 cup of brown sugar and 1/2 teaspoon cinnamon. Heat in microwave until butter melts (30-60 seconds) and set aside.

Grease muffin pan, pour half the batter into the bottom of the cups, then spoon the apple mixture onto the batter. Take remaining batter and pour it on top of apple mixture. Add crumble and bake at 400 degrees for 12-15 minutes.

Acknowledgements

As usual, there are many people to thank for the making of a book. First as always, my mum, always my first beta reader. On the subject of beta readers, thanks to Abigail, Karen, and Amanda for being my first "test group" for the start of a new series—thanks for your input, ladies! Thanks is also due to the bands who soundtracked this novel, a combination of mostly Runrig, Flogging Molly, Gaelic Storm, and Emerald Rose. And a special thanks to the lads from the *original* *Top Gear*, Clarkson, May, and Hammond without whom, I never would have known how to execute a J-turn and what the merits of traction control were. They may not approve of all the cars my lads drive, but at least now I know what they are capable of. And thanks to anyone who took the time to read this book, I hope you enjoyed it and continue the journey of Ciran and his friends in later volumes.

Turn the page for a sneak peak of

An Earthly King

Book Two of The Modern Tales of Na Fianna

Coming soon!

Chapter One
In the Library
Eamon

Tara Hall

Finally, a moment of peace! I'm going to be honest, it's not all about the fact that I'm only twenty-three and the weight of Ireland rests on my shoulders. It's that sometimes, I just really need a break from the simple bustle of castle life to clear my head so I'll be able to think properly later. Normally, I might have found my relief out in the lists with my bow and a few targets, but the castle grounds were crawling with Killian's men at the moment, making preparation for the insanity that was about to break loose, and so I couldn't risk going out there and accidently shooting a cadet or servant. Even though—if I say so myself—I am a crack shot, they were like a mass of ants bent on their duty as if it was the last important role in their lives and I could never be certain one wouldn't end up in my sights. Completely on accident, of course.

Instead I chose to find refuge in my library. I remembered my father had always done the like. I had many a fond memory from when I was a boy of curling up at his feet, or on his lap when I was still small enough, beside the roaring fire and having him read me the old tales and histories of Ireland. It had fascinated me as a boy learning of my ancestor, Brian Boru, and Fionn Mac Cool and his Fianna and the great warrior Cuchulainn and all the battles they fought and the enemies they defeated. I loved the library now because I felt closer to my father here, as if his ghost haunted the shelves—and it's all quite possible it did, though he never showed himself to me. In any case, I could pick up his favorite books and sit in his tired leather chair more befitting a scholar than a king, and take a much-needed rest from the stress of my position.

Sometimes Oran would join me and I would read to him as my father did to me or we would read silently to ourselves and just enjoy each other's company. Lately, after the trauma of his capture and then rescue six months ago, we were both in need of the simple comforts we had always known before and when I was sleepless, as I was often for one reason or other, I would find solace in the library and if Oran's nightmares plagued him, he would come to me and sit by my chair and rest his head against my knee and I would read to him until he fell asleep. I was glad to find those nights were becoming fewer and fewer as the months passed and healing of a physical and mental nature ensued. But there were still those small reminders that would always be there. Like how he wore his hair long now to cover the scar where his left ear had been. I had never spoken of it to him, but I think he knew how much it bothered me, a constant reminder of the cruelty he had suffered at the hands of the Goblins, and so he had made that small gesture, I think, mostly for my sake.

But now I had a whole new problem to worry about: my impending doom. And by doom, I mean matrimony.

I knew I wasn't going to be able to escape it forever, and letting it go this long had been pushing it as far as the council was concerned, and after everything that had happened when I went behind their backs, literally escaping from my own castle to go rescue my own men, I had agreed—under some duress—to appease them in this matter at least. By their own admission, it was the very least I could do. I found it continuously amazing that even as High King I was constantly treated like I was a teenage delinquent—not actually my words but Killian's, though I agreed with him all the same.

I had secretly hoped when I was crowned that by the time the issue came around I would have secured a lass for myself and wouldn't have to go through the whole process of finding a 'proper' one. But when the patrol and Oran along with it had been taken, nearly a year ago now, any romantic notions had been put on the backburner as I worked just to find my brother, and keep the kingdoms from falling into turmoil again. If life never threw out unexpected events, I would still be simply crown prince and would have had leisure to choose a bride and woo her properly. But after my father had been killed in battle in the last Goblin War, I'd had to step up to the plate, and not only attempt to rule a kingdom and five other kings and queen who could never agree on anything, but also command Na Fianna and look after my younger brother and train him in the position I had just left.

I daresay I never would have been able to do it without the fatherly guidance of Niall Mac Cool and the everlasting friendship and brotherhood I shared with

Killian O'Hara my Captaen na Guarda. Without them I don't think I ever would have been able to get through everything and not have cried myself to sleep every night with the weight I had to bear on a daily basis.

But there was a flip side to everything. Killian wasn't only a spectacular Captain of the Guard, he was also a more than adequate steward and he liked to make that fact known every chance he got. I knew I was blown as soon as I heard his purposeful gait coming down the hall and braced myself only a second before the door flew open, emitting a rather harried looking Killian. I suppose I would look like that too, if I had to keep me in line. I was, after all, a delinquent at best.

"What are you doing in here?" he demanded as if he didn't already know. Killian and I had an unspoken agreement that he would not disturb me in the library unless it was absolutely necessary. Well, it's not saying he never did, but if he knew I really needed to be alone he would leave me so, and saints preserve the poor idiot who tried to disturb me then. But if it wasn't a matter of sanity, he would barge in without a by your leave.

"You're needed for inspection, your majesty!" he continued, coming forward and grabbing my dark green cloak off the back of my chair. "We need everything to come together by tomorrow when the guests start to arrive!"

"I thought you were handling this, Killian?" I told him with a small smirk, making no move to budge from my seat.

"Yeah, well, I'm bloody sick of it, so you have to suffer too," Killian stated and threw the cloak at my face. "Misery wants company and all that. They'll never stop picking until you go out there and say everything is fine. It won't take long, I promise."

I smothered a grimace and stood up, swinging the cloak over my shoulders and putting on a longsuffering attitude. "Fine, but if I'm going to be stuck in society from tomorrow until the wedding festivities then I'm going to need a little downtime."

"Of course, I know exactly what my majesty needs," Killian snarked mockingly. "You'll get your bubble bath and smelling salts, princess, but not until we *go*." He ushered me out of the room in a very distrustful manner and we met Oran along the way, also coaxed into his dress uniform, and he grinned at me as I gave him a roll of my eyes.

"Eventually, you're going to have to be the one doing these inspections for me, little brother. If you're going to be the steward, I will expect you to have them done before anyone even thinks of asking me to conduct them."

He made a face. "Well, I've got to have someone to show me how to do it."

"Oh it's not hard, you just look and say yes," I told him with a grin. "And if you want to cause a real panic, try saying that you want to make changes. That always gets them going."

Killian turned on me with a deadly glare in his eye, his finger right under my nose. "No changes. I swear, Eamon, if you delay this, I'll not get to sleep at all tonight!"

I took him by the shoulders and pushed him to the side, patting him reassuringly. "Don't worry, my dear captaen, I wouldn't dream of it. I'll need you on your top game to protect me from all the females that will be flooding the place."

"Quite right. You know, I think we should just find one for Oran while they're all here, save the fuss later."

"Oh no, I am not attaching myself to one of them, I've seen the guest list," Oran said with a laugh.

"Comforting," I said and pinched his nose before I had to put on a dignified face as we left the Hall and entered the courtyard where all the tents and tables had been set up for the tea that would occur tomorrow afternoon when all the guests had arrived, where I would be obliged to 'mingle' with the ladies and get to know them. It would be a bloodbath.

Colin O'Rourke, Killian's loud, redheaded lieutenant was busy briefing his guards when he saw us and grinned, giving a salute to Killian and a quick bow to Oran and me.

"Your Majesty, I assure you that everything is set up and ready. The men have been briefed on all protocol concerning you and our prettier guests." He winked.

"Thank you," I said and spotted Aeden Mac Cool back in position once again as the commander of Na Fianna who answered only to me. He caught my gaze and strode over to stand beside Colin.

"King Eamon," he said respectfully for the sake of the servants, even though we were old friends. "The Fianna will be at your service tomorrow as usual. And we have coordinated with Killian's guards as well, so there should be no problems."

Over the past few months with all the new Fianna rising in the ranks and new Guard cadets likewise coming out of the Academy, there had been some friendly competition between the two factions, which had led on more than one occasion to bloody knuckles and broken noses. It was nothing new, of course, for there had always been a rivalry between the Guards and Fianna, but it had caused problems on several occasions recently. Problems that wouldn't be welcome with everything else that needed to be seen to.

"I'm sure the boys will behave," Colin said. "If not, they know to take it out back."

"And where are Ciran and his company?" I asked, looking around for Aeden's younger brother.

Aeden smiled wryly. "I believe Ciran took them to drink your health, your majesty."

I smiled. "Very well then, I'll see you later tonight at the briefing. I need to go see how things are in the kitchen right now." Taste testing.

We made our way back into the Hall to the most dangerous part of the establishment, but before I could continue my inspection, a guard came hurrying up to us and bowed slightly to me before he turned to report to Killian.

"Sir, I'm sorry to interrupt, but there's been a bit of a rumble at Lanagan's."

"A rumble?" Killian asked, raising an eyebrow. "What kind of a rumble?"

"A bit of a disagreement between the Guards and Na Fianna," he said.

"Who?" Killian asked sternly.

"Sean Casey and Ciran Mac Cool's lot," the guard said. "They've all been brought into the throne room to await your judgment."

Killian sighed and turned to me with a longsuffering look. "I'll fetch Aeden. It looks like the kitchens are just going to have to wait."

About the Author

Hazel West lives in Purgatory, er, Florida, with her books and her hedgehog Horatio. When she's not writing, she's reading other people's books, studying folklore, or binge-watching something on Netflix — drinking coffee is also a given.

If you liked this book, she asks that you please take the time to write a review for it on Goodreads or Amazon or wherever else you wish to write a review.

If you're into social media, you can also follow Hazel all these places:

Blog: http://hazelwest.blogspot.com

Writing blog: http://talesfromamodernbard.blogspot.com

Twitter: @artfulscribbler

Goodreads: Under Hazel B. West

Pintrest: http://www.pinterest.com/artfulscribbler/
(If you wish to see the boards for all my novels)